1

OFF THE RECORD 2

AT THE MOVIES

A CHARITY ANTHOLOGY

Published By Guilty Conscience Publishing

Off The Record 2 – At The Movies – A Charity Anthology

Edited by Luca Veste and Paul D. Brazill

Cover Designed By Steven Miscandlon
http://www.stevenmiscandlonbookdesign.co.uk/

All enquiries, please email
guiltyconsciencesubmissions@gmail.com

Praise for Off The Record

'Hitmen, cons, winos, bag snatchers, killers and psychos, the wronged, the vengeful and the damned, all darken the pages off this superior crime anthology. Off The Record is seriously cool.' - Howard Linskey

'Buy this NOW! It's a great collection of stories from a great selection of writers. And it's for charity.' Paul Johnston

From well known authors to virtual unknowns, the depth of talent on display in this anthology is staggering. If there's been a better crime fiction anthology published this year, I don't know about it. – Ben Cheetham

Top work, a good range of styles, mind-rattling stories with a great mix. It turned me on to a lot of writers I hadn't heard about before. Excellent anthology! – Liam Sweeny

This is another excellent collection of short crime fiction by an assortment of current writers. It's of uniform high quality. I was glad to see some authors I'm already familiar with standing next to ones I've just discovered. There's a lot to look forward to from all of them. – Timothy Mayers at www.z7hq.com

The past year seems to have been a bonanza for short story collections, and editor Luca Veste proves that last is certainly not least with his collection Off the Record. – Elizabeth A White

The Charities

Off The Record 2 is for the benefit of two charities who deal exclusively with Children's Literacy. All proceeds from sales will go directly to them.

They are…

In the UK, National Literacy Trust. More information available at their website...

http://www.literacytrust.org.uk/

In the US, Children's Literacy Initiative. More Information available at their website...

http://www.cliontheweb.org/

Two very worthy charities, who help children read every day. Please visit and help in any way you can.

CAST LIST

5

6

Introduction
by
Chris Ewan

In 2011, I did something that made me very happy: I purchased a copy of 'Off The Record'. Why did it make my heart sing so? Well, a couple of reasons. One, I got to read a whole bunch of fantastic new short stories collected together under a neat unifying theme (I mean, stories inspired by song titles – brilliant!). And two, I had the satisfaction of knowing that all proceeds from the anthology were going to some wonderful Children's Literacy charities.

Zip forwards in time and now you, dear reader – yes, you! – must be feeling pretty cock-a-hoop. Go ahead and crack a smile. Why not? You deserve it. After all, what you have in your hands or on your screen right now is a massive win-win. Seriously. Off The Record 2 features stories from some of my absolute favourite contemporary writers. These are supremely skilled authors at the top of their game. And they're sharing the bill with some truly exciting emerging talent. It's an intoxicating blend, all mixed around the ingenious concept of short fiction inspired by classic movies. We all know Vertigo, Get Carter, Don't Look Now and The Life of Brian – but trust me, we don't know them like this!

But there's more, of course. By reading this collection, you're helping others to start reading, too. Remember how it felt when you first gained access to the wonderful world of books? When all of a sudden you could read anything, everything, you cared to? I do. I have Taunton Library to thank for some of the best moments of my childhood because I accessed nearly all my reading there. Adventure stories, crime stories, classic novels – the books that made me dream of one day writing books myself. That library and those books unlocked my future. And by buying this collection of stories, you're unlocking futures, too. You're enabling the National Literacy Trust in the UK and the Children's Literacy Initiative in the US to do just a little more of the great work they already carry out. So give yourself a pat on the back – hell, make it two – and then relax and get on with the fun part: start reading.

Chris Ewan — author of Safe House and the Good Thief's Guides novels. www.chrisewan.com

Night of the Day of the Dawn of the Son of the Bride of the Return of the Revenge of the Terror of the Attack of the Evil, Mutant, Hellbound, Flesh-Eating Sub-humanoid Zombified Living Dead
Part 2 - in Shocking 2-D

A Short Story with a long title

By Will Carver

Copyright © Will Carver 2012

It's simple.

Take one end of the celluloid from the film supply, wind it around the loop, thread it through the feed, another loop, a shock absorber, the optical sound reader and into the take-up. It will wrap itself around a giant spool, ready for the next showing.

Then look through the tiny rectangle of glass as innocent people take their seats below, their arms full of overpriced confectionary and over-sugared liquid.

Now count them.

Keep that number in your head.

Don't tell anybody else.

That is how many will die.

Today, shows one and two have both been empty. No patrons. Not many people go to the cinema on a Thursday morning to watch a horror movie.

So Harry hasn't had to flick the switch that turns on the projector bulb. He hasn't had to kill anyone. He hasn't had to stand and watch and do nothing as the automation kicks into gear and the tables turn and whir. And he doesn't have to pretend.

Through that small window the projector lens points at, he spots three people sit down, each with a large bag of popcorn and a drink the size of a bucket.

They're too close to the screen.

That's a mistake.

They'll never get out.

With the forefinger of his left hand trailing behind him, resting against the black flip-switch, trembling, sweat washing away at his fingerprints, he stutters. He can't start the film. He can't keep killing.

'Just do it,' Johnny sighs, sitting behind Harry, perched at the station used for splicing the film reels together when they arrive from the studio courier.

Harry says nothing. He's trying not to listen to Johnny any more. Johnny doesn't care who dies. Johnny is bored. Johnny doesn't want to go back.

Harry waits. Poised.

Nobody else has entered the theatre in the last five minutes. He's only two minutes late in dimming the lights and starting the picture. *There's only three of them.* Students. They didn't even pay full price to get in. *Would anyone really notice if they went missing?* Would anyone miss three truant scholars?

The one on the right with the long, straight hair and black T-shirt inscribed with the album cover and tour dates of a 1980s soft rock outfit looks at his watch and mouths something to the other two.

Leave.

Just get up and leave so I don't have to do this.

The young man walks out of the theatre, leaving his friends behind.

Two. Only two. Nobody would notice two.

Two is nothing.

It's the same as nothing.

Harry looks over his shoulder and grins at Johnny, who is rocking back on a chair, reading the work schedule pinned to the wall above the splicer. He rolls his eyes. His clothes look more dated than the bands on the students' T-shirts. But that's how they dressed in 1968.

Suddenly, a crackle followed by his name.

'Harry. Are you there?' A soft female voice dances out of the walkie-talkie. 'Some guy says his film should have started a couple of minutes ago. You know the one.'

It's one of the ushers. Tilly. The cute one. The petite one. With the lisp. The one who makes speech impediments sound sexy.

Thound thekthy.

Harry unclips his own radio from his belt, pushes down the button and informs her that it is starting up now. All the ushers on the ticket gates have this equipment, and every manager hears every conversation they have. So he knows, at this very moment, Brownall

11

will be trudging her thunderous calves up the stairs to release her misery and discontent in his direction. As he fumbles around trying to regain composure.

'I told you. You should have just turned it on.' Johnny breaths out, resigned.

'Shut the fuck up, Johnny. I don't want to kill these people.'

'They're not really dying,' he responds, elongating the word *really* as though it's merely a technicality.

This is the key to eternal life.

The long-haired student returns, seemingly triumphant in his deluded quest to take down the corporation from the inside, and Harry dims the lights in the theatre to signify the start of the film. And the end of their monotonous lives, laborious studies, plunging them into the tedious monochrome of death.

Harry turns around to a smiling Johnny.

'How many this time?'

'Three. I'm about to kill three more.'

The door to the projection room swings open suddenly and the man who calls himself Johnny hides.

'Do you need help, Harry?' the bitch says patronisingly.

'I'm sorry?'

'Can you not handle all the screens by yourself? Do we really need another person in here?'

There's already too many.

'No. I'm sorry.' He tries to pacify her with apology.

'Always with this fucking film. Get it sorted. It's not brain surgery.'

'OK, Maria. The film is on now. It was two minutes late. I cut the advertisements. It won't happen again.' He reels off the sentences like a stream of consciousness, each one delivered with an equal level of malaise.

'It better not. And it's Ms Brownall.'

Johnny rolls his eyes from behind the wall.

'Oh, and I need you to do the double shift.'

Classic Brownall. Comes in here shouting her fat mouth off then expects a favour.

She's saying, *You'll have to kill more, Harry.*

'We still can't get hold of Neil. He's disappeared off the face of the Earth. Doesn't look like he'll be in tonight, either.'

'Yeah. Fine. I'll do it,' he agrees, speaking with his eyes closed, knowing exactly where Neil is. Recalling the night he went into theatre eight to see what was wrong with the picture, why the image was *out of rack*. He soon found out. And now he is stuck.

Three more will join Neil shortly.

At the point where the light from the projector hits the screen.

Their lives reduced to a flat, black and white image.

That nobody is coming to see.

Brownall turns on her heel without uttering a word of farewell, a semblance of gratitude. I let out an exaggerated exhalation to mark her departure.

When I turn around, Johnny is peering through the glass at the screen below. The three students shovel popcorn into their mouths as the black and white footage of a car winding around a country lane shoots out from the screen and onto the retina of my next three victims.

'Here they come,' he says excitedly, metaphorically rubbing his hands together.

The car snakes around the roads, eventually stopping in the graveyard. The blonde woman sits in the passenger seat while the driver, who should be the man that's standing next to me now wearing a tweed jacket and glasses, his dirty-blond hair parted neatly to the right, is not the man standing next to me in a tweed jacket and glasses, his dirty-blond hair parted neatly to the right. He is no longer the uncredited actor from the opening sequence of this iconic movie. He escaped. Just stepped out. And he has been replaced.

'It's Neil.' Johnny's eyes are as wide as his grin.

13

On the screen, next to the woman, in the driver's seat of a car that has parked inside a cemetery, is the missing projectionist Neil.

And the woman on the passenger seat doesn't seem to realise.

She thinks he is her brother.

She calls him *Johnny*.

* * *

It's simple.

Take some flowers to a deceased relative's grave to mark the anniversary of their death. Casually stroll past the slow-moving man, leaving your sister a few paces behind to be attacked by this figure who happens to not only be the living dead but also evil, a mutant, bound for hell and a flesh-eating sub-humanoid zombie.

Now go through this five times each day.

Six on a Friday and Saturday when the cinema has a late-night showing.

Realise that this is your fate for all of eternity.

Then leave.

Step out of the repetition and exit the black-and-white world of the screen. Stop being an unknown actor, a character from a movie, and become an unknown person in the real world. Escape. Move away from the hell of a celluloid illusion into the three-dimensional reality of life on the other side of the projection. Kill whoever is watching. Murder your audience.

Now wait for the lights to come up at the end. Watch as the dead body disintegrates into a billion pixels. Know that it is not gone. That it will rematerialise in the space you left behind in the film. It has found a new home.

Tell yourself that you are now free.

Try to convince yourself that this is somehow better.

The three students are dead.

It is show four.

14

Thirty-eight tickets have been sold.

And Johnny still won't go back.

'Please stop this, Johnny. I can't kill thirty-eight people. It's not like those three students or the two underaged girls or the drunken double-date. It's nearly fucking forty lives. Innocent lives, Johnny. Don't let me kill again,' I plead, knowing deep down that I'll flip the switch.

'I'm not going back to that routine, Harry. It's worse than death for me. They'll find it exciting, I promise you. They'll want to stay. I felt the same way initially.'

'How is this better? Sitting in the dark all day, watching me run around to twelve different projectors, threading film, turning on bulbs, selling duplicate promotional posters to desperate film-fan ushers?'

Harry finishes lacing up the blockbuster movie on the theatre-five projector. He won't have time to run across to the east wing and up the stairs to get this sell-out movie going on schedule unless he does this now. It starts ten minutes after the zombie film in theatre eight, but he knows that will begin late. Again.

There are more to kill.

Sometimes, it's faster for Harry to detour through the lobby rather than negotiate the back-room labyrinth of the projection corridors. He sneaks into the back of theatre eight to peruse the soon-to-be dead audience.

The noise is high and the air full of rustling wrappers, slurping, incompatible voices and intrigue. Before the feature begins, the paying customers are treated to a slide-show of facts and quiz questions.

What is the longest film title of all time?

Did you know that the carpet design in Sid's hallway in *Toy Story* is the same design as the hallway carpet in *The Shining*?

Scramble: What True Malta (Actor)

Harry listens as the crowd attempts to decode the anagram.

'Is there an actor called Matthew Latura?' one idiot asks her boyfriend.

15

Of course not, you dolt. It's Walter Matthau.
Maybe some of these people do deserve to die.

Harry exits the screen, paces across the lobby, up the stairs, into the projection booth, disregarding the skulking and clearly bored Johnny, and hits the button that dims the lights and starts the film trailers rolling.

'This is the last fucking time I kill for you. Make a decision. Get back where you belong and do your job or go back and change it, make a new story for yourself, rewrite the ending. Just get out of here. I am the only one who is supposed to be trapped in this room.'

This is my shitty life.
Get your own.

He spins on his left foot and exits without a hint of adieu, leaving no opportunity for the man known as Johnny to respond.

Then he's back downstairs as the hoards of moviegoers are let in to their special-effects-driven blockbuster, each of them passing theatre eight and hearing the screams of thirty-eight people about to meet their deaths and mistaking them for shrieks of fear at the film's brutal storyline.

They look up at the red lights on the sign that says *Night of the Day of the Dawn of the Son . . .*

They say, *I've never heard of it.*

The credits roll and the lights come up in theatre eight.

The seats are empty.

All is dust and ash.

* * *

It's simple.

They tell you to wear the white gloves but you soon realise that lacerations are a part of the job and that you have a better feel for things with your bare hands. You wind the film on until you feel the cut, the tape, the point at which you spliced the reels together. Then

16

you take your scissors and make a clean line down the centre and pack away the opening sequence into its case.

   You repeat this several times until you reach a roll of film small enough to hold in one hand. These are the adverts for fizzy drinks and cars you can't afford. These are the trailers for the films you wanted to see or avoid or wish you'd have made. You can put that into the cupboard ready to attach to the next film that arrives. You are recycling.

   Now look down at the locked spool cases.

   Count them.

   There are three sections of film.

   And nearly eighty people dead. Trapped.

Harry unfolds his wallet and pulls out two notes. He slaps the money into Johnny's open hand and closes it for him tightly, forming a fist and clamping it as he gives his instructions.

   'Buy yourself a ticket and some food, or a coffee. Walk around the lobby. See these real people. See that they are no better than your zombies, your parasites. Then sit in the theatre and watch the film from the other side. See how things have changed, how the cast has grown with each victim. Then tell me you don't want a part of that. Tell me that you don't want to be Johnny again.' Harry entices the man who calls himself Johnny to watch the movie he has always been a part of until a few days ago. He baits him with the prospect of greener grass.

   It's always greyer.

   'Take the money, have your experience, and go home. You need to go home, Johnny.'

   This is my home.

   This is my head.

This new world is brighter than it was in '68. The monochrome confines have transformed into green and yellow fluorescence encircling a confectionary list; it has developed into the red bulbs of a cashier's desk and neon surrounds of film posters. Johnny has to squint. He sweats in the warmth of his tweed and removes his glasses for a moment to rub at his eyes. His perfectly straight parting glistens under the plethora of hot bulbs.

When your fantasy becomes reality, one understands that all truths lie within *the pit*. All existence is in *shade*.

The man once known as Johnny feels more comfortable in the impending gloaming of theatre eight. He is the only patron. This is a private viewing. The lights are low. The anagram says *Mash Tonk*, but he has no idea who Tom Hanks is.

He doesn't belong here.

Harry gazes down at the solitary figure sat in the very middle seat of an empty cinema and he knows his loneliness, he understands that sense of absence and extinction. Because he is the same. Only, he has learned to accept it.

Harry knows who he is. What he is. Why all of these people have died at his hand. He knows what it is to take life. But Johnny is not alive. He is light and imagination. He cannot be killed. Only returned.

So, this time, when he flips that black switch down, his thumb is dry and tremble-free and decided. He is not here to kill for anybody else. This is for himself.

The darkness descends below and Harry remains next to the thrum of the ever-rotating cogs of the projector. The car zigzags through the hills as it always does, it makes that final turn through the gates of the burial ground just as it has hundreds of times before and it stops, cutting to a medium shot of two people, a man and a woman, in the front of a car, just as it did in the last show when thirty-eight people were drained of colour.

The woman in the passenger seat calls the other man *Johnny*.

The man in the centre seat, on the wrong side of the screen, is infused with a sadness.

18

'Miss Brownall, could you come to screen eight, please? A customer is requesting the manager immediately.'

Action on the screen ceases and the two characters from the opening sequence look out in silence, into the nearly empty theatre, at the real Johnny. They step out of the car and are joined by three dead students and thirty-eight recent cinema patrons, four of whom think that Matthew Latura is a famous actor. They crowd together on the screen and stare out at the one who caused all of this. They want him back.

The two girls who were three years too young to watch this film want him back.

The double-daters want him back.

The Evil, Mutant, Hellbound, Flesh-Eating Sub-humanoid Zombified Living Dead want him back.

He is climbing up to the screen as Brownall enters.

'Excuse me, sir. What on Earth do you think you are doing?' She speaks in her usual condescending tone as her hefty calf muscles propel her to the front row. Harry spectates in hope.

This is my kill.

The last show.

And then she's with thirty-eight other people who don't know what the fuck is going on and it's ninety minutes later and all is black and she doesn't exist if the film isn't playing.

Harry brings the lights up in theatre eight. He packs the final piece of the film into its container and takes it to the front of the building where a courier loads it into the back of a truck for safe distribution.

The film is gone. The victims transported elsewhere. His manager reduced to hearsay and legend.

Then Harry is packing the tarnished white gloves from the projection booth into his bag and swiping a card with his name and staff number printed on the front through a machine to clock himself out. As though nothing important happened today.

About the Author – Will Carver is the author of two novels in the Detective January David series 'Girl 4' and 'The Two'. The third book in the series, which at the moment is untitled, will be released in 2013. More information can be found at www.willcarver.net and he can be found on Twitter @will_carver

9 songs
by
Steve Mosby

1.

I can't fall asleep to silence anymore.

When I go to bed, I set my laptop's music library to shuffle, then pass out with one of my eight thousand songs playing in the background. And despite the size of my collection, I always wake up with the exact same song playing.

How is this possible, you ask?

I'll tell you.

The first thing I do every morning is crawl out of bed and cross the room to the flimsy desk with the laptop on it. I have a cheap studio flat; it's all I can afford. The room smells of the cheap green carpet, which is fuzzy and rough, and the air itches with dust. In summer, the heat is unbearable. But it's mine.

The first task every day is to check the downloads. All eight thousand songs in my library are stored in a folder that the peer-to-peer software I run has access to. Many people have this software. You type in the title of a song and the program searches the online folders of other users until it finds a match, which can then be copied and downloaded.

The screen informs me that there were thirty-eight completed downloads last night. That's the number of people who searched for one of the songs in my library, then copied it successfully over the Internet. The software's anonymous, but it's possible to send a message to the person you downloaded from, and vice versa. I click on the drop down menus until I reach my inbox, where a number of messages are waiting for me. I scan them without hope, which turns out to be the right thing to do.

What the fuck bro??!

Yeah thanx for that

Blocked!

FUCK YOU TROLL FUCK YOU FUCK YOU

Twelve messages in total, all of them similarly vitriolic. There are sexually-detailed threats to my bodily integrity, and pointed questions about my parentage. Twenty-six people didn't bother to reply, but that doesn't mean they were happy with the file they got; it just means they didn't care enough to abuse me. It would be depressing, except that I experience much the same thing every day.

I sit down and, as best I can with my ruined hand, start typing.

That's the second thing I do every day: add to my music library. I copy a file at random and paste it several times into the same folder, then patiently rename each one as something different. Scanning the charts helps. I choose whatever songs are inexplicably popular right now and title my duplicate files the same. Thank you the music industry, which provides a constant churn of material, each song barely distinguishable from the last. A production line of inauthentic emotion that, for some reason, people want.

I never run out of titles.

The whole time, the music player continues shuffling the songs in my library. Aside from a one second break between tracks, the soft music is unbroken. The same piece of music, of course, because every single file is identical. It's the only one of Sasha's compositions I ever managed to record.

Nobody wants to hear it.

I live in hope that one day I'll get a message that says *thank you* or *wow, that's beautiful*, but it never happens. This is the truth of it: people don't want to know. It's hard to get people to care about the things that matter to you.

2.

Sasha was my second love. My first was the guitar.

Standard guitar tuning for the six strings is EADGBE. If you strum those strings open, it doesn't form a chord. The sound is ugly. It's *almost* there, but the notes don't fit together. You need to use the fingers of your left hand to fret a few of the strings and bring the notes into the same key. If you hold down a couple of strings at the second fret, for example, a strum gets you EBEGBE instead. Those notes align: you get E minor.

I can't manage that one.

My left hand has only an index finger and a thumb; the other fingers are stumps. I can play the simplest chord with that one finger: E minor 7. EBDGBE. That's about it. Appropriately enough, it's the loneliest chord I know.

My first love, then. And it used to be a very good relationship indeed. That all changed when my friend Mark asked me to help demolish his front wall.

There was only the two of us, and I was skeptical, but Mark is very *let's-just-do-this* and *we-can-do-this* and difficult to resist. He smashed most of it to pieces with a sledgehammer, the two of us snorting dust and leaping back from the falling debris like children at the edge of the sea. The majority of the pieces were easy to move to the skip, but there was a large one left: a hefty chunk of cement and stone. We thought we could do it – got ourselves in position; got ourselves ready – but Mark lifted before I was ready, and the thing tilted and pinned my hand against the pavement.

I remember the air going out of me, and that the pain was secondary to the panic. *You must move now*, my nerves told me desperately. *This is far more serious than being in pain. You are damaged.* For a moment, I couldn't do anything at all, but then the rock toppled and the rough texture ground what was left of my fingers against the tarmac. Every bone was crushed, the digits mangled beyond repair. There wasn't a lot of blood, but I sat down on the pavement – slumped there, really – my whole arm throbbing emptily, and then lay down backwards through a wall that wasn't there anymore.

First love over.

We staggered on, of course, the guitar and me. For example, here are some things you can do. You can use your single finger to pin down one string and pick that and a few of the strings around it, gradually summoning the ghost of a chord. You can also tune the instrument more specifically, so that just strumming plays a chord. One finger barring down the neck can then play all the major chords.

I tried all this.

Relationships often end abruptly, but you don't always realise it at the time. And like many a lover in denial, I attempted to make it work long past the point when I should have walked away. The more I tuned and altered the guitar, the more I realised I was limiting the instrument to fit me. It just didn't work. Love, you see? Whether it's a person or something else, you can't change the things you love to make them fit you. Eventually, you have to let go of them.

It was different when I was with Sasha. Briefly, I came alive again. Since she left, though, there's no point in playing. Sometimes I pick the guitar up and try, but it always feels incomplete. It's a mockery, really, of how it used to be.

I don't pick it up very much anymore.

3.

Carpe Diem is my hangout and place of work, more or less in that order of priority.

It's a pub on a busy street, halfway between the city centre and the university, and pulls its evening crowds mostly from the latter. Inside, it's old-fashioned: dusty stone floors and cracked red leather booths. There's a small wooden stage at one end, and the walls are covered with photos from the gigs we hold on weekends. You'd know some of the names, but they're mixed in rather than pride of place. Mark puts all the small local bands up regardless. *They're all good*, he says. *It's just that some of them get lucky as well.*

We're running through tonight now. Mark's behind the bar. I'm perched on a stool, civilian-side.

"First up's Hairstreak," he says.

24

"Hairstreak?"

"The name? Yeah, I know. Hipster fucks."

He shakes his head. Leaning on the bar, his shirt sleeves are rolled up to reveal beefy forearms. Physically, he looks like a wrestler – or maybe a roadie: big and burly, with long brown hair and a fairly mad beard. Even though he's the same age as me – twenty-nine – we couldn't look more different.

"Female lead singer, anyway," he says. "She's very strong, so you won't need to up that much in the mix."

"Right."

And so it goes on.

I do most of the work with the bands – helping to set up equipment, sorting lighting and sound – and help out with the bar when it gets busy. For that, Mark pays me a small wage that tops up my meagre disability, along with unlimited beer.

To be honest, most of the time I'm just sat on my seat at the far end of the bar doing very little, but Mark doesn't mind. There are two reasons for that. The first is that he's my best friend. The second is that he feels, and is probably correct to do so, that he owes me. While we waited for the ambulance after his wall destroyed my hand, he was sobbing and telling me over and over again how sorry he was. Time after time, he said it. I remember thinking: *it's* my *hand, you big fucking lump. Please stop crying.*

Anyway. There are three bands on tonight. Hairstreak, Clown Around Town and The Ceilings. It's two pounds in at the door, with a "who have you come to see" tick-sheet so Mark can gauge who's popular and move them up the bill next time: refer them to other bars, and so on. In our own small way, we endeavour to swirl the local bands upwards, giving them the support they need but won't notice. Why do we do it? Well, partly for the money, of course. But there's not much of that. It's also for the music, and our respect for the people determined enough to make it. Basically, we do it for the love. If you play in our bar and make it big, you don't have to remember us. We're proud of you anyway.

For tonight, the arrangements look straightforward.

"And Rachel's coming by later," Mark says.

I don't reply.

"You remember I told you about her?"

"Vaguely."

He met this Rachel in a club when he was chatting up her mate. Mark's a gregarious force of nature. He'll go out and meet hundreds of people, and many of them stream in here in the weeks that follow. He's kept in touch with Rachel, and has said a few times that he thinks she'd be perfect for me. He does this a lot, like a cat bringing its owner a present. Despite the fact that I technically work for him, the damage to my hand has created this weird emotional power differential between us.

"You remember that I told her all about you?"

"Yes."

"So don't get too drunk this evening. That's an order."

I immediately resolve to get as drunk as humanly possible, and I inform him of this fact.

"Oh, just give it a chance." He leans away. "That's all. It doesn't have to be amazing. You know? It doesn't have to be anything. But sooner or later … you've got to get out there."

I nod.

"You've got to come back to life."

I nod again.

He moves away. Sasha is pretty much a taboo topic between us, but she's often there anyway: the shape of her revealed in the spaces. Mark never liked her. Actually, that's not fair. He *liked* her well enough, but he was my best friend and he sensed that I would fall in love with her, desperately and helplessly, and that she would end up breaking my heart. He was right about that, although he would never know how.

And he wouldn't believe it if he did.

You've got to come back to life.

So here it is.

Drum roll.

Building chord – major, of course.

I turn my head and look at the empty stage.

4.

Sasha was the first act on that night. She took the stage nervously, tensely.

A healthy crowd was already spread over the stone floor. The audience was full of young men in hoodies with hard-gelled hair and earlobes stuffed with polished black discs, and young women in striped leggings and blue jean hot-pants. Checking the door sheet later, it turned out that none of them were there for Sasha. Even Mark wasn't sure how she had found her way onto the bill. He couldn't remember booking her.

"Okay," she said into the mic. "Be gentle with me."

There was the standard smattering of applause. She was attractive: long black hair and a pale, pretty face; dressed in jeans and a black jumper. She was also endearingly vulnerable, but with a wry half-smile that said she knew how nervous she looked, and that it was okay.

Sasha had brought a stereo with her, which I'd hooked up at the front of the stage. The CD had backing tracks for her vocals. She started it playing, then closed her eyes as the first delicate notes unfolded through the bar, the tension visibly lifting from her. Her whole body seemed to *sigh*, almost, like an alcoholic feeling that first blissful mouthful melting into her system.

And then she began to sing.

I don't know to describe her material. The backing tracks were mournful and sad, laments of some kind, but they followed patterns and structures that collapsed as you caught them. Back in the day, I used to be able to play most songs after one listen; even now, I could still dissect them. That was impossible here. I could barely even disentangle instruments and timings. Notes would surface, riffs repeat, but although each piece was coherent and complete, the music was too alive to be analysed.

And then there was her voice.

27

It soared over the underlying music, occasionally dipping into the soundscape below, intertwining with the melodies there, then emerging bright again, shaking droplets of song away as it leapt. There were no recognisable lyrics, only hints of language: half-delivered words that dissolved before meaning could coalesce. And yet somehow there *was* meaning. It emerged in the gaps, emotion formed from the abstracts…

No. I can't describe it.

All I can say is that I had never heard anything like it before. I don't expect to again.

As Sasha performed, a light seemed to grow around her, like a soft white aura. I couldn't stop looking at her, and my eyes kept moving imperceptibly, leaving ghost edges around her like an aura. That was how I explained it to myself at the time anyway.

It was only as her set was drawing to a close that I glanced at the rest of the bar – and the spell was broken immediately. The audience was distracted, not captivated. Some people had drifted away to the pool room at the back; most that remained had turned away and were talking amongst themselves. The ones still watching were doing so patiently, patting their pints politely by way of applause, obviously waiting for her to finish.

I couldn't believe they couldn't *hear* it.

When Sasha's voice finally fell away, her eyes were closed. The music swirled slowly down and disappeared. I saw her eyes tighten slightly as it did. The tension seemed to return to her body. In fact, just for a moment, she appeared to be in pain.

Then she took a deep breath, opened her eyes and smiled. "Thank you."

The audience responded with reluctant applause, claps passed back through the bar like a tossed ball nobody wanted to catch. But my heart was thudding in my chest. Sasha picked up the player, giving me an awkward smile as she left the stage. Clapping's not something I do well anymore, so I smiled back and mouthed *wow* at her. Her smile broadened – and then suddenly turned shy again as she disappeared past me.

I had to talk to her.

The next band had already advanced on the stage, unspooling cables and clicking open guitar cases, but there would be a few minutes before they were ready. I slipped out from behind the controls, determined to find Sasha before she left.

The musician in me wanted to hear that backing music again – wanted to tease out its secrets and figure out how it had been done. But the truth is, I hadn't been a proper musician for a while by then, and really I just wanted to talk to her.

5.

"Mark says you used to be a musician?"

I nod.

The evening is done now, and we've ejected the last of the punters out of the doors of Carpe Diem. It was one of those nights where most people had come for the second band and left afterwards, meaning The Ceilings ended up playing to the walls. They didn't seem to mind. Mark thanked them, gave them their cut of the door takings, and waved them goodbye. Now, he's sweeping up around the corner, whistling to himself, leaving me to talk to Rachel over a lock-in beer in one of the booths by the door.

I say, "Guitarist, really. My parents got me one when I was five, and that was it." I click my fingers. "I was in love as soon as I got hold of it. It felt right. It made sense."

"Typical boy." She smiles. "I can imagine you striking rock poses in front of the mirror."

She has a nice smile, to be honest; it's relaxed, and it takes the piss out of you the way old friends do. In fact – full disclosure here – she's all-round nice: slim and attractive, with brown tumbledown hair that hangs in rough curls over her shoulders. She's wearing an open velvet jacket with a web of several flimsy tops overlapping underneath, revealing a red birthmark at her collarbone. Black trousers. A tattoo of musical notes runs from the back of her wrist and disappears under the sleeve of her jacket.

29

"I'm guessing you're a musician too?" I take a sip from my pint then nod at her hand. "From the ink, I mean."

She shrugs off her jacket unselfconsciously, revealing a bare arm and the wiriness of her frame, as well as the full extent of the tattoo. The notes circle around her arm all the way up to her shoulder.

"Trying to be." She ponders the ink, as though there's something puzzling about it now.

I say, "If you're trying to be then you are."

"Yeah, but you know how it is. You have all these ideas. And then life…"

"Gets in the way?"

"Exactly. Don't get me wrong, music's still the most important thing. Still what I want to do – *all* I want. Not sure my life always agrees though."

I smile. "Well, I'd like to hear you some time."

"I've got a CD somewhere."

She starts to rummage in her bag, and I think *she has a CD on her*. The musician's equivalent of bringing a condom on a first date. I do want to hear it, but I can't help being reminded of Sasha. She never did let me listen to the background music she'd brought to the bar that first night. It was only when I listened to it anyway that I understood why.

Mark arrives with a fresh pair of drinks for Rachel and me, and one for him, then slides into the booth on my side. I shuffle up to make space. On the other side of the table, Rachel matches me, edging over to stay facing me, sliding the CD over.

"How are you guys doing?"

"Good, thanks."

"We were just talking about music," Rachel says. "About Sean's guitar poses."

"Oh yeah, he was always … actually, no. I won't joke. This guy." Mark claps me on my shoulder. This is because he is horrifically drunk. "This guy right here, he was one of the best guitarists I've ever seen. Seriously. The first time I saw him play live, when we are at Uni, I was blown away. It was like watching … Clapton. Not that I ever have. But you know: magic. An epiphany. I thought *that's my mate up there*. I had no idea before then that he could do that."

Rachel raises an eyebrow at me. "You were in a band?"

Mark slaps the table. "In a band? In a band? Well, yes, he was in a band. But he *was* the band. Do you know what I mean? When he was on stage, you didn't watch anyone else. They might as well not have been there. He was a fucking … maestro."

"Wow."

Rachel sounds genuinely impressed, her eyes glittering as she looks at me. I smile awkwardly. Like I said, my first love. It was a good relationship. It really was.

Mark then runs through a list of my musical achievements – grade eight at thirteen; national competition winner at fifteen; reducing him to tears one night when I was improvising in a flat we eventually shared; etc; you get the picture – and I feel embarrassed. Not for me, so much, but for Mark. He's blundering into a trap, and I'm sure he knows that because he often does this. On the surface, he's trying to help by bigging me up, but these conversations always lead to the same place: what happened, and how it was his fault. Perhaps it's a subconscious act of penance on his behalf, but I've never really wanted him to feel bad.

Rachel says, "So do you still perform?"

"Not anymore."

"How come?"

As always at this point, Mark falls silent. He's almost hunched over his pint, like a drunk who's regaled strangers with a story of how much he loves someone, and has only just remembered that he lost them long ago.

And I don't want him to feel bad.

But it is what it is.

"I can't."

I hold up my ruined hand. Rachel looks shocked, but I smile, and actually I mean the smile. *Life gets in the way*. Sooner or later you accept that. You adjust.

I put my hand down and take a drink.

31

"Can't," I say. "That's all."

6.

"I can't ever have children."

Sasha said it to me when we were lying in bed together one morning. We were both naked. I was propped on one elbow, facing her; she was lying on her back, one arm thrown back so as to rest her head on her forearm. I was staring at her face. She was staring at the ceiling, or through it.

I said, "Okay."

"No, I can. But I won't, is what I mean." She closed her eyes and sighed, then opened them again. "I have a condition. It's genetic and it's very rare. It's not the kind of thing you would want to pass on."

"Okay."

The bedclothes were tangled around our shins: kicked away for comfort in the night. It was still early, but my top floor flat catches the sun in summer; it was already simmering. We'd left the window open through the night, and from beyond the curtains behind our heads I could smell the fresh air. You could only ever hear the traffic below slightly – a constant, gentle rush. Although small and central, my flat can be sunlit and peaceful if you catch it right.

I said, "What condition?"

"It's difficult to describe. It's a degenerative condition. Parts of my body fail, if I let them. And it's hard not to. It's a struggle."

"I don't understand."

"No." She smiled gently. "You will though, eventually. If we stay together."

"If?"

"Well, that's up to you." Finally, she turned her head to look at me. "That's what I mean. This has been the best three months of my life, Sean."

"Mine too."

And it had. I'd always been someone who fell too quickly, so I'd been careful this time. Even though I hadn't told her yet, I knew that I was in love with Sasha.

She said, "Which means it's only fair for you to know. So you can decide whether you want to stay involved with me."

Was she breaking up with me? I still didn't understand. It was obvious she'd been thinking about this conversation for some time, and so it had the feeling of a confession: one she'd been putting off. But it had come out of the blue to me. I couldn't keep up.

A condition.

Degenerative.

I can't ever have children.

"Of course I still want to be involved with you." I sat up. "*Of course.* What are you talking about?"

She said, "I'm dying."

***

I'm dying.

Of course, I didn't understand that at first either. Or rather, I refused to accept it. Partly it was because, no matter how hard I pressed her for the details over the months that followed, she refused to explain.

"What is this condition?"

"It's so rare it doesn't have a name."

"That can't be right."

"It doesn't. I've seen specialists, and none of them have ever encountered it before. It's unique to me."

Parts of my body fail, if I let them.

"Can't it be treated?"

"No. It can be ... slowed down, I suppose. But it's degenerative. I can't get back the ground I lose. I can only lose ground at a slower rate, depending on what I do. How I treat myself."

"All right."

I pictured tiny boxes of pills, a different one to be taken every hour. Ones that made her feel sick and made life difficult and uncomfortable. Exercise, of course. Perhaps a strict special diet. *A struggle*. It was impossible to imagine a condition without a name that couldn't be treated in those conventional ways, but she never seemed to do any of them, and when I brought up the subject of treatment she would only shake her head.

"But – "

"There aren't any buts, Sean."

It was final on that first day, and it was always final afterwards. Sasha was perfectly resigned.

"No buts," she said. "I've lived with this for a long time, and I've come to terms with it. I'm telling you because it's only fair for you to know. So that you can walk away now if you want to. Maybe you should."

"I'm not going to walk away."

I meant it. Back then, I didn't understand what staying with Sasha would involve and what it would mean for both us. She did. That's why, in the end, because of how much she loved me, she had to leave me.

7.

Here's a snapshot. A memory.

Sasha and I are in my room. I am sitting on the bed, playing my guitar, which I have tuned to D Major. She is cross-legged on the floor in front of me, singing gently. There are no lyrics, no words at all, but together we are producing music that feels coherent and whole and meaningful. Whenever I open my eyes, hers are closed; I imagine the same is true in reverse. For a while, we are both totally lost. All that exists is what we are together.

But then I realise that something is wrong with her voice.

It's not that she's out of key, or that her vocal is weak, or that the overall sound doesn't work. It's something I've never encountered it before, so it takes me a few moments to work out what it is.

34

Sasha is singing more than one note at once.

She is singing in chords.

Which is impossible. The voice is a single string; it cannot be plucked simultaneously on multiple frets. And yet that is what she is doing.

I stop playing, stunned, and watch her.

Still lost in her music for a second, Sasha continues singing, and I have time to confirm what I'm hearing before she realises my guitar has gone silent and stops. The notes seem to die one by one, making their existence even more obvious.

We stare at each other for a moment.

"Sasha – "

"Did you like it?" There's an eagerness to the way she says it, as though that's the only thing she wants to know or talk about.

"Yes. Of course I did."

She smiles at me. There's happiness there, but so much else besides. It's impossible to interpret. There are as many emotions in that expression as there were musical notes in her voice a minute ago.

I didn't realise it at the time, but this was close to the end. It was just before I lost her.

8.

I found her again, obviously. By then, I had to.

At first, after she left me, I gave her a degree of space. Physically, at least. There were numerous texts and phone calls: long conversations in which I pleaded with her to come back to me and reassured her that I could deal with her condition. I told her that I loved her, and that whatever happened I wanted to be with her. There were emails where we each set our positions out at painful length.

I still have them, of course. Sometimes I read them back, and what strikes me most is that when I said I wanted to be with her, what I really meant was *needed*. It would be unfair to say I wasn't thinking about her, but it was more about me. My second love had brought my first love back to me. So the main reason I pursued her – and it shames me now, to think I was so selfish – is that I needed her.

In the end, after she stopped replying to my messages, I traced her address online and went round to her flat.

When she opened the door, I was shocked by her appearance. It had been less than a week since I'd last seen her, but the face peering out through the gap was so pale and hollowed out that I hardly recognised her. Her condition had deteriorated. One arm, holding the door, was so emaciated that I could have encircled it with my finger and thumb.

We looked at each other for a few moments.

"Are you sure you want this?" she said.

"Yes."

At the time – when she opened the door and let me in – I was arrogant enough to think she was concerned about me: what it would take out of me to watch her suffering.

Are you sure want this?

Afterwards, I understood how wrong I was.

And yet, at the same time, how right.

***

Sasha died five days later, and I stayed with her until the end. But I'll come to that.

In the period between, I looked after her as best I could. Her flat was dirty and uncared-for, so I tidied and cleaned. When she had trouble walking, I helped her move around. If I suggested calling a doctor, she refused outright. *When it happens*, she told me, *you won't be blamed. Don't worry.* In all other respects, she seemed grateful to have me there.

Sometimes, I'd notice her grimacing, as though her condition was very painful for her. Other times, we played music together and it was a relief to see the peace and tranquillity on her face. Her eyes closed; her face relaxed, Sasha produced those impossible chords, and

I complemented them as best I could. Together, we still created something complete.

She was happy in those moments, I think, and so was I.

***

One day, Sasha went to lie down for a rest, and I was left alone in her ramshackle front room. I found myself searching through it, although I don't know what I was looking for. Some insight into her condition, perhaps – or some clue as to what else I could do. What I discovered, buried beneath a pile of jumpers in the bottom of a cupboard, was the stereo she had brought to Carpe Diem on that first night.

The backing music. I remembered how it had affected me, but after the first few refusals I'd given up asking to hear it again. Now, I plucked the stereo carefully from the cupboard, wincing as the cable unspooled and the plug rattled against the wood. It was a transgression, I knew, like flicking through a diary. But I wanted to hear it. I plugged the stereo in and checked inside. The disc there was labelled with the date of her gig at Carpe Diem.

I turned the volume down and pressed play.

And…

There was no sound at all.

At first, I thought it must be an error. I turned the volume up as high as it would go, but heard nothing. And yet the red LCD display showed the track numbers slowly ticking upwards. The disc wasn't blank. Sasha had recorded nine songs of silence.

That had been her backing music on the night.

I put the stereo away again, then went and stood in the doorway to the bedroom, leaning on the frame and watching her sleep. The covers rose and fell, conducted by her breathing. With each awkward out-breath, I heard the faintest trace of melody.

***

"Do you know what I'd like?" Sasha said that evening.

37

"What?"

She smiled at me, but the pain she was suffering was obvious. Lying in bed, her body was skeletal and still, and her face was damp with sweat.

"I'd like us to play together. I think that ... right now, that would be nice."

"Sasha – "

"And I'd like to record it." She smiled brightly at that. "So the world has something to remember me by. So that you do."

"All right."

I gathered the necessary equipment together, connecting it all up by her bedside. Then I brought my guitar through, perched on the end of the bed, and we began to play, as we had so many times before. It was very beautiful indeed. When I looked at her, she seemed as happy as she ever had; it was obvious that the music eased her. I was beginning to accept the truth, but it was only afterwards, looking back, that I really understood. She was happy because she was making me happy.

It's difficult to describe.

It's a degenerative condition

"I love you," she said.

As she spoke to me, the strange thing was not that she managed to continue singing. The strange thing was that it didn't surprise me at all.

Parts of my body fail, if I let them.

"I love you too."

I stopped playing and took her hand: hers, thin and weak; mine, broken and useless. I held it for a moment, staring at the peaceful expression on her face. Music continued to fill the room, louder and more complicated than before. The sun streamed through the bedroom blinds, even though it was dark outside and raining. The bedroom was aglow.

And it's hard not to. It's a struggle.

Sasha gave a gasp of relief, her body arching slightly, and I looked down just in time to see her hand as it disappeared from mine, dissolving into song.

9.

It's late when I get back home, but I'm not quite ready for bed yet; the walk back in the cold has sobered me up a little. I toss my coat and bag onto the bed, get myself another beer from the kitchen, then sit down at my laptop.

Rachel's CD. Before I left Carpe Diem, Mark had insisted that I listen to it fairly. He was very drunk and very adamant. *You've got to come back to life*. So I slide it into the drive and wait for my music software to load. Nine songs. As it begins playing, I automatically set the program to save the tracks onto the hard disk.

What is it like?

It's okay, actually. Just her and a guitar, but her voice has a certain character to it that manages to differentiate the music from all the other girls with guitars out there. The songs follow conventional structures, but the lyrics are only superficially simple. She plays well, which is to say that she doesn't play perfectly: the music has personality.

I like it. That's all I can say right now, but it's more than possible it will grow on me.

It's something.

***

The last thing I do every night is check the downloads.

There have been several while I've been out, and there's a handful of messages waiting for me. I scan them: they're all the same. These people came looking for the bland, the conventional, and got Sasha's recording instead. They don't understand, these people. They don't appreciate the wonderful thing they're hearing and what it means. But then, it's hard to get people to care about the things that matter to you.

I shut the messages down, and look at the music player instead. Everything stored in there, whatever the filename, is that last recording of Sasha. Not of her music, but literally *her.*

Except Rachel's tracks are there now too.

A part of me thinks I should delete them, but I don't. Let's give them a shot, shall we? They stand an insignificant chance of turning up on shuffle, but it's not impossible. It's not.

Eventually, I press [play], flick off the lights and lie down in bed. I don't fall asleep right away, so there's opportunity for Sasha to play over and over again in the room. It's likely she will still be playing when I wake up, and that she always will be.

I close my eyes.

We'll see.

About the Author - Steve Mosby is the author of seven psychological thrillers, including The 50/50 Killer, Cry For Help, Still Bleeding and Black Flowers. His latest novel is Dark Room. In 2012 he won the CWA Dagger in the Library award for his body of work, and was also shortlisted for the Theakstons Crime Novel of the Year award. He lives in Leeds with his wife and son. His website is www.theleftroom.co.uk

The Postman Always Rings Twice
by
Claire McGowan

The body lay on the kitchen floor, legs curled up, eyes dull and stopped. The removal man prodded it with one large boot. 'Crawl in anywhere out of the cold, they will. Then they get trapped and die and you're smellin' it all year.'

Mary shut her eyes slightly. She was no good at death; could barely cook raw meat. 'Could you move it, please? I can't...'

The man gave her a look she recognised, a silly-little-girl look, and picked the dead rat up in his gloved hand, chucked it out the back door. The door led to a bit of uninspiring yard, a plastic chair with rain pooled in the seat, unused paving slabs leaning against the wall. There were no flowers or grass, only a churned-up patch of soil, but all the same Mary was ridiculously pleased to have an outside. Hardly anyone she knew had a garden. So it didn't matter that the flat hadn't been cleaned at all since the last tenant. It didn't matter about the dirt, the dead rat, the faint cheesy smell round the rooms. It was a place she could go and shut the door and not have to breathe the same air as Michael.

She'd barely believed it when she saw the ad on the housing website – cheap, no references needed. Quick rental to quiet female tenant. Over email the landlord had explained the last girl left him in the lurch- could Mary move in soon? Too right she could. By that stage she'd have lived in a tent. He'd left the key under the mat and she'd put cash in his bank account. They'd never even met. She was surprised he hadn't asked for a deposit, though, after the last girl did a flit. Some people were far too trusting.

It was true; the girl had really left a mess. Supermarket herbs died along the windowsill, and in the fridge there was even food rotting away. What was weird was how many things she'd left, shoes under the bed, a kittens calendar on the wall, drawers full of hairbands and pens and odds. Her post was still arriving too, clattering onto the dusty doormat and making Mary jump as she paid off the removal man. He couldn't resist one last bit of advice. 'Get that door blocked up, love. If you see one rat, you can bet your bloody breakfast there's more. Tell your bloke to do it.'

'I don't have a bloke,' said Mary frostily. 'Anyway I can do it myself.'

The door slammed. Mary bent to lift the post, breathing a deep sigh of relief at the aloneness, the quiet. MISS ROSIE HART. A Boden catalogue, a credit card bill, a copy of Vogue, which was a bonus. She'd read that later, once she'd cleaned up and scoured away all trace of the untidy Rosie.

It took hours. There were even clothes in the washing machine, unbelievably, damp and stinking. Mary used bleach and rubber gloves and the hoover and washed all the clothes again (some of them were very nice) and when it was done, glowing with effort and a pleasing sense that she was tidier than the other girl, she felt better than she had since the day six weeks ago when she'd finally cracked and said, Michael, this isn't working, is it. Remember when she'd thought being single was the worst possible thing? Well no, it was being single and having to live with your ex, since you'd stupidly bought a flat together, as though love and money and the housing market would always last. Her a freelance designer, him unemployed since his firm downsized, home was like being locked together in a cell that got smaller every day.

She curled up in her sleeping bag- she couldn't bring herself to take any of their bedclothes with her, not the ones they'd shared. New sheets for a new start. She listened to the strange new silence of the flat, a faint rush of traffic from the main road. Was that a noise? It sounded like scrabbling. Mary got up in her pyjamas and padded through to the kitchen, feeling grit under her bare feet. She'd have to brush up. The garden was empty, lit toxic orange by the street light. There was nothing.

On the bedside table was a nearly full bottle of nail varnish – Chanel, bright red. She fell asleep wondering what kind of girl would go away and leave Chanel nail varnish. One who was used to having things, probably.

Saturday. A chance to finish up, make it hers. A trip to the supermarket, new duvet, some scented candles, food for the now-clean fridge. She even bought daffodils, a cheery yellow that made it impossible to feel down. While cramming them into a water glass, she saw a swarm of movement in the fractured bit of soil outside, a thick coiled tail – rat! She banged the window until it scurried off. How disgusting! She'd been planning to take her coffee outside to the postage-stamp of sun that made it over the rooftops, but that put her off.

Around two, when she was relaxing back with the other girl's Vogue, the phone rang, making her jump. Michael couldn't have, could he – no, of course, it would still be connected in Rosie's name. She remembered it could take two weeks to change something like that, and Rosie didn't seem the type to have bothered.

'Hello?'

'Rosie?' A woman's voice.

'I'm sorry, she moved out.' Silence. 'I'm sorry, did you – she's not here anymore, I said. I took over her lease.'

'Who are you?'

'Er- Mary.' She shouldn't have said her name, probably, but she didn't know what else to do.

'Yes, but who are you? How do you know Rosie?'

'I don't. I just leased the flat, because she moved out in a hurry. She left the place very untidy, too.'

The woman on the other end caught her breath. 'I can call the police, you know.'

'Well I'm sure you can. But why?'

'They'll find out what happened to her. You can't hide it forever.'

'Look, I—'

The phone was banged down. Mary stood holding her end, bemused. Well! Were all Rosie's friends as weird as her? The phone was in a retro style, the kind people paid a fortune for in those little boutiquey shops where a greetings card cost £5. Mary tugged it out of the wall and shut it into a drawer, trailing wires. No one else would be calling now. She turned back to the sofa, where the shiny magazine lay, all skin and hair and smiles. Suddenly she didn't want it, didn't want anything that belonged to the other girl. She took it to the yard and slammed it into the green recycling bin. Another scurry of movement caught her eye – God! Another rat! It was scrabbling in the soil near the back wall. Panicking, Mary lifted an empty can of beans from the bin and threw. The rat scrammed and she dived back inside, heart hammering.

It could be sorted. It could all be sorted. Cut off the phone, call an exterminator, contact the post office, throw out all Rosie's things, and then it would be her flat, somewhere she was safe and could shut the door and just be. She made a list on the edge of an envelope and then found herself just sitting for an hour, brooding over Michael and the weird phone call and how much she had to do, change addresses and tell everyone they'd broken up and ring banks and offices and the tax people. That was the thing. It was so easy in your head to change your life, but then you did it and you realised all the paperwork involved. Maybe they made it hard on purpose, so people stayed in their jobs and homes and relationships, scared to get out. Well, she wasn't scared. It could all be sorted.

Mary had her head under the sink when the doorbell rang. It was amazing how many layers of life a person could put down. All those things you owned and didn't know it – washing tablets, dusters, bin bags, knives and forks, a packet of kitchen ties. Rosie had left a frightening amount behind. When the bell went Mary sat up, banging her head. She peeled off her pink rubber gloves and cautiously went into the hallway. No one knew she was there, did they? The postman came earlier, so who could it be? Not the Jehovah's Witnesses, she hoped.

The frosted glass was dark. Blocked out by the body of the man who was peering through it. 'Rosie!'

Mary dithered. There was no peephole or security chain – her landlord was so naïve!- so she called through the glass. 'Rosie isn't here, she moved out!'

The man began to rattle the door. 'Open the door, Rose, for God's sake! I'm sorry, OK! I didn't mean it!'

Didn't mean what? Mary backed away. 'Look, I don't know who you are, but Rosie isn't here. She moved out, OK? She left.'

'Open the bloody door!'

'NO!' Mary surprised herself by shouting back. 'It's my flat now, and you can't come in. Just go away! Leave me alone!'

For a second the man's features were flattened against the glass, and she could almost make out his face, distorted and terrible. A small scream escaped her. Then he was gone.

Christ. Christ! What was up with this Rosie girl? Had she really just walked out of her life, not told anyone? The woman on the phone had sounded like her mother. And that man, had he been her boyfriend? What had he done to be so sorry for? Not knowing what to do, Mary took out her mobile and dialled the number she had for the landlord, scribbled on a scrap of newspaper. It rang and rang, eventually going to a generic voicemail. When she spoke she realised she was close to crying. 'Hello? It's Mary here, Mary from the flat. Erm…things have been a bit weird. A man came to the door- he scared me. I think he wanted the girl who used to live here – Rosie? Anyway….could you call me, please? It's Mary.'

She hung up, feeling the silence of the house all around her, tugging on her clothes like little hands. She had to get rid of everything Rosie had owned. That was the only way.

There was a lot. In the bathroom cabinets, odd ends of toiletries and the bath mat and a sliver of soap in a dish. In the bedroom, clothes stuffed into high cupboards and deep under the bed, a few books still in the case and a pile of magazines by the desk, a bedside lamp with a purple shade. It was all good stuff – Rosie was into fashion, clearly – but it had to go. It looked as if she'd packed half her things, then given up and left. Maybe she'd run from the man at the door? Mary shuddered. She wasn't going to think about that.

45

The kitchen was the worst, food in the cupboards still and utensils and tea towels in every drawer. Mary swept it all into bin bags and went out the back. She piled the bags round the bin, and as she stood up something caught her eye – not another rat – no! A man was climbing over the back wall. Tall and bulky in a black leather jacket, he had slicked-back dark hair and was struggling with the crumbling bricks in slippery city shoes.

Mary didn't stop to think. She ran back inside, slamming the door and fumbling with the lock. The man raced across the bit of soil, planting his shoes deep into the dirt, and threw himself against the glass. This time she could see him clearly, his cold dark eyes and sharp nose.

'I've called the police!' she lied, shouting. 'Go away, just go away!'

'Look, I want to see Rosie.' On the other side, she could see his chest rise and fall. His voice came muffled through the glass. 'Who are you – where is she?'

'She's not here, I told you! I live here now – you have to go! You're trespassing!' Mary looked round wildly. Where had she set her phone after ringing the landlord? Oh God. She dashed back into the living room, hunting round the surfaces. From the kitchen came the sounds of slamming – he was trying to break in. Oh God, Oh God, where was her phone?

Another sound – a key in a lock. She spun round to see another man coming in the front door. Pale, pudgy, any age between thirty and fifty. 'Mary?' he said, in a voice thick with phlegm. 'I got your message.'

'Oh thank God, thank God – the man's here! He's in the back! Please, you have to help me!'

The landlord licked his tongue over dry lips. He wore cream combat trousers, a green jumper with food crusting on the front. 'He's here?'

'Yes! Please, stop him! We have to ring the police, but my phone, I can't find it, I don't know what to do!'

Then it was too late. There was a splintering noise, muffled cursing, and the man in black burst into the room. 'What the fuck have you done with her?' He was speaking to the landlord.

'She left,' the landlord said, licking his lips again. 'She just left.'

'You're a fucking liar.' Then the man lunged for the landlord. Mary shrieked and dived, spotting her phone on the cushion of the sofa. As the men grappled, she scooped it up and ran past to the kitchen, out into the yard. Scrabbling over the soil, she tried to dial 999 with shaking hands. She tripped, stumbled down, and caught her foot on something in the ground. Oh God. Oh God. Mary looked to see what had her ankle. The soil was disturbed from the man's climb over the wall, and there in the middle of it, there was a flash of something white, like a swollen grub brought to the light. Ignoring the smashes and shouts from inside, she dug it out with her bare hands, the soil cold and clinging. Within five seconds she could see the red nail polish that still flaked from the dead stiff fingers.

Then Mary was up, running back into the flat, everything tilting and whirling. The man had the landlord round his plump neck and was squeezing. 'It's her!' she shouted. 'It's Rosie, she's in the ground, she's dead! He's killed her!'

Both men looked round, the man in black relaxing his hold on the landlord's neck for just a shocked second. Then a flash of something in the landlord's hands - a blade. A long carving knife produced from his combat trousers, rust-red stains on the steel. 'Look out!' Mary shouted, and the man in black swung, and his fist connected with the landlord's face. The landlord stumbled back, the knife skittering across the floor towards Mary's soil-stained feet – she jumped as the blade slid to a halt.

Panting, the man in black looked round at her. 'You really shouldn't let strangers into your house,' he said.

Mary slumped down, curling her knees into her chest, a thin wail leaking from her. As she listened to the heavy breathing of the man in black, the bubbling bloody wheeze of the fallen landlord, and her own scratching sobs, she found herself wondering what Michael was doing.

About the Author - Claire McGowan grew up in Northern Ireland and now lives in Kent. Her first novel 'The Fall' was published in 2012 and 'The Lost' will be out in April 2013. She is also the Director of the Crime Writers' Association. This is the first crime short story she's ever written...

The Time Machine
by
David Jackson

I was ten years old when the man selling time arrived on our doorstep.

My heart sank when I opened the door. I was hoping for Jake Davies, eager to show me the latest addition to his collection of insects, even though most of them were either dead or disabled. Or maybe for Craig Boscombe, bringing me dubious tales of what his dad was getting up to in the secret service. Even Katie Wescott would have done at a pinch, despite her woeful lack of football-related knowledge.

But no. All I got was a dull-looking man in a flasher's mac. The beige coat looked far too big for the man's scrawny frame. Belted tightly at the waist, it gave him the shape of an egg-timer. His dark hair was heavily oiled and slicked back. His eyebrows looked as though they had been drawn on; sharply arched, they lent him an expression of continual surprise. In his right hand he carried a battered black case – the type that a doctor might possess. The overall impression was of a spiv trying to offload black-market goods.

Apparently uninterested in me, the man craned his neck to peer into the gloom of our hallway.

'Is your dad in?' he asked.

I shrugged. 'Dunno.'

At this, he deigned to lower his gaze. 'You don't know whether your own father is at home?'

'No.'

'And why, may I ask, is that?'

'He doesn't live here.'

The man straightened up. 'Oh. And your mother?'

'Yes, she lives here.'

'Could I speak to her?'

'No. She's not in. And if she was in, she'd tell you to sod off.'

The man's arrowhead eyebrows did a little dance, and a hint of a smile crossed his lips. For some reason he seemed to find me amusing.

'So you're here alone?'

'I didn't say that. We've got a dog. A massive dog. His name's, erm, Gnasher. One word from me and he'll bite your head off.'

We didn't have a dog, but my mother had told me never to answer the door when I was alone in the house. The imaginary canine was my insurance policy against cold-calling child abductors and door-to-door serial killers.

'I'm starting to get the impression I'm not very welcome here,' the man said. 'May I ask the reason for all this hostility?'

'You're a salesman. And my mum says all sales people are the scum of the earth. Well, actually she says a lot more than that, but I'm not supposed to repeat it.'

'What makes you think I'm a salesman?'

I looked him up and down. 'The way you dress, the way you put on a fake smile, and the fact you carry a big bag that nobody would carry unless they were paid to. Oh, and the way you take ages to get to the point about why you're here.'

The man's eyebrows did another jig. 'You're very astute.'

'Up yours,' I said, and went to close the door.

'No,' he said hastily. 'That was a compliment. I was trying to say how I impressed I was at the way you just summed me up like that. Sherlock Holmes couldn't have done it better.'

I wavered. I'd always liked the thought of being a great detective. This weird guy had just bought himself a chunk of my nicer nature.

'Okay,' I said, 'but whatever it is you're selling, we don't need none.'

'You mean you don't need any.'

I gave him a pitying look. 'If you keep agreeing with people like that, you'll never sell a thing.'

50

He shrugged and nodded, obviously impressed by my wise advice. 'I'll bear that in mind. Now how about if I tell you what I've got here...'

He made a move to open his bag, and I waved my hand at him. 'Don't bother. We've already got everything we need.'

He paused. 'Everything?'

I nodded vigorously. 'Everything.' I didn't see any merit in telling him that I didn't own a football signed by the England squad, but I thought it unlikely he had one of those in his scarred old bag.

The man stroked his chin, as if weighing up the scale of my challenge.

'What about time?' he asked.

This didn't make any sense to me, and I was certain that few would have coped better in my shoes.

'What?'

'Time. Have you got time?'

'Time to do what?'

He jabbed his index finger into the air. 'Precisely!'

I was beginning to suspect that my earlier decision to close the door in his face was the right one. This guy was a freak. And yet something about him held my attention.

'Mister, what are you selling?'

'I told you. Time.'

He stood motionless, as though daring me to figure it out. And then I got it. Or at least that's what I thought.

'Oh! You mean clocks and watches and stuff. We've already got them. Lots of them. I've even got a waterproof watch, only it's at the bottom of our fish-tank at the moment.'

The salesman wagged a finger at me. 'No, no. You misunderstand. I mean I sell things that can save you time. Like this...' He opened his case and dipped a hand in, and this time I didn't try to stop him. I wasn't impressed with what he brought out, though.

'It's a toothbrush,' I said.

'Not just any toothbrush,' he countered. 'This one dispenses its own toothpaste. Think how quickly you'll be able to brush your teeth with—'

'Got one,' I said.

It was a lie, but that was my game plan. I was going to claim ownership of whatever he produced, and eventually he'd have to admit defeat. Thinking back, I suppose it wasn't much of a game, but it seemed entertaining enough at the time.

The man's cheery smile faded a little, but he tried again. He pulled out a device that looked like a miniature whisk.

'What about this? It ties shoelaces with a simple flick of a switch.'

I have to admit I was intrigued. I dearly wanted to seen it in action. But I stuck to my guns.

'Got one.'

The man nodded thoughtfully. I got the impression he was determined not to be beaten by a kid. The match was well and truly on. He tried again and again, device after labour-saving device, and each time I merely repeated my simple mantra: Got one.

But the man wasn't beaten yet.

'Tell you what,' he said. 'I don't make this offer to everyone, but it's clear to me that you're an intelligent young man. Suppose I told you that you could really buy time.'

Now we were getting into loony-tunes territory again.

'How do you mean?' I asked, the suspicion evident in my voice.

'Let me explain. You watch television, right? Well, what does the hero do when he gets into trouble?'

Before I could concoct a suitably imaginative scenario, the salesman continued: 'He tries to buy time, right? He tries to stall, to put things off until he can escape. That's what I mean by buying time.'

'Ookaaay,' I drawled, still uncertain as to where this conversation was leading.

'Now, what I'm offering you is the chance to buy time from me.'

52

'How?'

'By using one of these…' Again, he reached into his bag. My eyes grew wide as I wondered what mystical machine he might have in there, and the disappointment hit me hard when he revealed his hand-held electronic device.

'Big deal,' I said with derision. 'A calculator! I know it can save me time when I'm doing maths, but I can save more time by making Michael Pemberley do it for me.'

The man's grin took on clown-like proportions. 'Ah, but this isn't a calculator. It just looks a bit like one. This is far more interesting.'

I held my enthusiasm in check. If he were about to tell me this was a combined music player and TV remote control, I was going to snatch it off him and stamp on it.

'What is it then?' I asked.

He didn't tell me immediately. With the air of a comic spy, he looked up the street and down the street before leaning towards me and whispering:

'It's a time machine.'

I stared at him for a few seconds, waiting for the eruption of laughter over his practical joke. When it didn't come, I said, 'I've got to go now,' and I went to close the door.

His reaction was unexpected. I thought he might jam his foot in the doorway, or blurt out some sales spiel in a desperate attempt to rescue his pitch. Instead, his voice remained calm and level.

'Then you'll miss the opportunity of a lifetime,' he said.

I hesitated again. I had to admit, he was good at keeping me dangling on the end of his line. Slowly, I pulled the door open, but just to ensure he got the message that he hadn't yet won me over, I put on my best sceptical face.

'That's not a time machine,' I said.

He nodded. 'Yes. It really is.'

'Crap! I've seen that film called The Time Machine, and at school we read the book. It's by some guy called H Gee Whiz.'

'H Gee Whiz, eh?'

'Yeah. And in the film the time machine is huge, with a seat and dials and everything.' I pointed to his box of tricks. 'That little thing couldn't take me to the toilet, never mind the future.'

The salesman seemed unperturbed by my inescapable logic. 'Ah, but not all time machines work in the same way. This one is more like a computer. You tell me how much time you want to buy, you give me the money, and then I program the device to get you the time. It's as simple as that.'

'What do you mean, it gives me time? I don't need any more time. I've got lots of time to do whatever I want.'

'Everybody needs more time. It's just that not everybody realises time can be bought like a tin of beans from a supermarket.'

I still didn't understand what he was offering, and I told him so.

'All right,' he said. 'Let's work with an example. Tell me, do you have to be in bed by a certain time tonight?'

'Yes,' I said dejectedly. 'As soon as my mum gets home, which is nine-thirty on the dot. It's a real bummer because the best programmes are always on at that time.'

'Well, now. That is what I call a prime example of needing to buy more time. How much money do you have?'

I investigated the pockets of my jeans and discovered a packet of chewing gum, an elastic band, three football cards, a ball of fluff, and a single twenty-pence coin.

'Is that all?' the salesman asked. 'Okay. I'll tell you what I'm going to do. For that amount of money you can buy fifteen more minutes of your favourite programme. That's a special introductory offer because I like you so much. How does it sound?'

I wasn't about to be turned by his flattery. I may have been young, but I wasn't stupid.

'It sounds like a con. My mother is always on time. Always. If she says she'll be in at half nine, then that's when she'll get here.'

The man rubbed his chin again as he mulled this over. 'You drive a hard bargain, son, but I don't like to walk away without a sale.

I'm prepared to give you a money-back guarantee. I'll come back next week, and if you're not satisfied, I'll return your coin. Is it a deal?'

I studied him for a moment. Then I looked down at the coin, shining brightly in the palm of my hand. It wasn't exactly a fortune I'd be risking. Truth be told, I'd forgotten I even had the coin in my pocket.

I raised my eyes. 'Deal,' I said.

I handed over the coin, and then we shook hands to forge the contract. The man typed a few buttons on his little device, then slipped it back into his bag.

'Wait,' I said. 'Is that it?'

'That's it. See you next week.' And then he walked away, whistling merrily.

As I watched him disappear down the street, I felt the urge to chase after him. I wanted to tell him I'd changed my mind. What I'd just done was absurd. It wasn't the money – that was a paltry amount – but the fact that I felt cheated. Of course he wasn't going to come back next week. Why would he? He'd realised he wasn't going to make a sale, and so he'd made the best of a bad situation.

As I trudged back into the house, my sullenness grew. I thought I was more streetwise. I thought nobody could put one over on me. But that snake had just done exactly that. What an idiot I was!

At nine o'clock I switched on the television to watch the cop show I wanted to see. My mum had told me I wasn't allowed to watch it because of the bad language and violence, so I always had to turn it off as soon as she came home. Normally I'd be glued to it until then, but this time I was distracted. My mind kept pulling me back to the encounter with the salesman, punishing me for my foolishness.

When the clock chimed the half-hour, I picked up the television remote control, my thumb touching the off-button in readiness. My ears pricked up for the sound of the doorbell, or a key in the lock.

Nothing.

I checked the clock on the wall. Yes, half-past nine. I continued to stare at it, transfixed as its hand nudged into the next minute. This was impossible. My mother was to lateness what Genghis Khan was to social etiquette.

Fifteen minutes, the man had said. Fifteen minutes more of television. But sod the television. Was this real? Had the salesman actually delivered on his promise?

I got up from the sofa and walked over to the wall-clock. I stood right in front of it. The noise of the television became a meaningless drone, and then faded away from my consciousness. I ignored everything in the room except the steady ticking of the clock and the barely perceptible drift of its minute-hand. As the hand edged nearer and nearer to the horizontal, my mouth grew dry. I could feel my pulse pounding. It was happening, right in front of my eyes. I had actually bought time!

Nine-forty-five. I stood on tip-toe to confirm that the minute-hand was precisely aligned with the nine. I awaited the chime.

When the doorbell rang, my heart nearly shot out of my chest. I ran to the front door, my head filled with wonderment and excitement. The salesman hadn't duped me after all. I had altered time, and I was desperate to let someone know it.

But when I saw my mother, and she came bustling in like she always does, words failed me. What could I say to her? How could I possibly explain what had just happened?

'Hello, darling,' she said. 'Sorry I'm late, but Mrs Plackett had one of her funny turns, and I had to hold her ankles up to get the blood back into her head... What's the matter with you? You look like someone's just dropped an ice cube down your trousers.'

***

The following week seemed like a lifetime. Far from buying time, I wanted to compress it. I was desperate for that salesman to return, and I took every opportunity to go outside, ostensibly to play, but really to spot him at somebody else's door. It worried me that there was no sign of him anywhere. Surely I couldn't be his only customer? There must have been people out there who had a need for toothbrushes and lace-tying machines. And time. Didn't everyone want more time?

Or was he out of my life forever? Had he disappeared, as mysteriously as he first came to our door, taking his magic with him? No, I couldn't believe that. He had promised me he would return, just as he had promised me he would sell me time. I had every faith he would come back.

And I was right.

He turned up again, precisely a week after his initial visit. He looked the same, carried the same bag, and acted as though everything in the world was normal.

'Hello, young man,' he said. 'How are—'

'It worked,' I interrupted.

'What did?'

'Your time machine. It really works, doesn't it?'

He flashed me his familiar grin, and his eyebrows did their familiar dance. I was starting to like this curious salesman.

'Well, of course it works. Do I look like the kind of man who would try to swindle his customers? Like I told you—'

'I want to buy some more.'

His reaction was not what I expected. I thought he would do what sales people always do. I thought he would be whipping out contracts and getting me to sign on the dotted line before I changed my mind. I thought he would be rubbing his hands together in glee at the prospect of another sales coup. But no. His smile drooped and his previously excitable eyebrows came together as if to debate the seriousness of this turn of events.

'Well, now,' said the man. 'Let's not be hasty here. Time is a very precious commodity, you know. Last week's offer was a special introductory one, if you recall. I don't usually just give the stuff away like that.'

I held out my hand to show him what I had managed to scrape together. 'I've got six pounds and five pence.'

He looked down at the pile of coins in my palm.

'Hmm. Not a huge amount, is it?'

I could feel my disappointment building. He was going to say no. He was going to say it wasn't worth his while to keep doing me favours, and then he would say goodbye and leave. I just knew it.

'It's all I have,' I told him. 'My pocket money's in there, plus all the savings from my piggy-bank, plus the twenty-five pence that Michael Pemberley gave me for being his bodyguard.'

The man looked into my pleading eyes. 'All you have, huh?'

'Yes,' I said, and I could tell he knew it to be true.

'Well, that's different.'

Something inside me lifted. 'It is?'

'It certainly is. I could count on one finger all the times anyone has ever offered me all the money they possessed. Generosity is measured not by how much you give, but by how much you have left after you give. Offering me a hundred pounds isn't so great if you're a millionaire, is it? But a financial sacrifice like yours... well, that's different.'

'You mean... You mean you will sell me some time?'

'Sure, if that's what you want. You have to be careful, of course. Time can be a dangerous thing. Some people just don't know how to make the best use of time. Then there are the hidden costs – the human costs...'

But I'd stopped listening. I was too excited. 'Let me tell you what I want to buy,' I said.

The man watched me for a moment. I think there was something else he wanted to say to me, but he didn't. Instead, he reached into his bag, and there it was again: the time machine.

'Fire away,' he said.

***

As I said before, my encounters with the salesman happened when I was ten years old.

That was twelve years ago.

58

Since then, time has robbed me of many things. My friends have all grown up and moved on. My mother has turned grey and flabby. Even my cat has gone senile.

And me? Well, they think I'm a freak, a medical miracle. Peter Pan, they call me – the boy who didn't want to grow old.

You see, I enjoyed being a kid. It was fun. And like most kids, I didn't see the attraction in becoming an adult, with all the responsibilities and seriousness it entails. So I asked the salesman if I could buy some time before my next birthday. The only problem was, I didn't specify how much time I wanted.

I spend much of that extra time at my window now, praying for the return of that salesman. And when I'm not hoping, I'm wondering.

I'm wondering just how much time you can buy with all the money you have in the world.

About the Author - David Jackson is the author of a series of crime thrillers featuring NYPD detective Callum Doyle. His debut novel, 'Pariah', was Highly Commended in the Crime Writers' Association Debut Dagger Awards. The sequel, called 'The Helper' is available now, with the third book in the series hitting the shelves in January 2013. Further details about David and his writing can be found at his website www.davidjacksonbooks.com, and you can find him on Twitter as @Author_Dave.

Goodfellas
by
Luca Veste

I don't remember all that far back.

    I remember that feeling . The one you get in the pit of your stomach, nauseated butterflies fluttering back and forth. It arrives again, like bumping into an old school friend you half recall, and the half you do remember isn't good times. Third time this week, and we've only been here four days. It's not a nervous feeling, the normal butterflies you get when you're slightly anxious. Nor the flip-flop sensation you get when you're excited to see someone you love. It's more a sense of something wrong. Something was coming. A bad thing , just around the corner, normally with a baseball bat ready to smash your little brains in. A vodka bottle held too loosely, smashing against the wall next to an eleven year olds head.

    For me, that bad thing had already happened.

    It followed me everywhere, even here, I can feel it coming. Close my eyes, allow the darkness sweep over me and BOOM, I'm there. In that room. Senses on fire.

    TOUCH – Bare feet sticking to the floor.

    SMELL – Burning. Copper.

    TASTE – Tinned spaghetti hoops, rising up my throat.

    SOUND – Crying. I think it's coming from me.

    SIGHT – Red.

    It never leaves you. Every counsellor they'd made me see had told me the same thing. *Give it time, the pain will ease. You'll move past it. You're strong.*

    Bollocks. Wrong, wrong, wrong. They were all fucking wrong. It was still there. As clear as the fucking cloudless sky that was suffocating the boat I'd been forced onto. Forced is too strong a word. Coerced.

    I've never been on a boat.

Not even the ferry?

No. And don't sing the song…HAHA!...Stop it. We're in disguise remember? We're not being the token scousers abroad. You wouldn't even let me wear trackies on the plane.

The room.

The man.

The blood.

It should be left miles away. I should be able to lock it up all in a box and put it away in a safe place.

If you board a plane at Manchester, it takes four hours to fly here. Sometimes more, sometimes less. Depends on different conditions.

No smoking for two hours before the plane takes off. Have to go through security. Take your shoes off. Go through the doorway which BEEPS if you've got something metal on you. Take off your belt. Put your keys and phone in a tray. Go through again. BEEP. Three sets of eyes staring at you. They've been through already with no problem. You're holding them up from searching the duty-free shops. A more menacing pair of eyes comes toward you, holding a black paddle kind of thing. Makes me stand in a star-shape, arms outstretched, legs far apart. Sweeps the thing over me, pausing at my head.

It's me. It's you. It's all of us.

Metal plate in my skull.

A nod, and I'm allowed to put my shoes back on. Spend forty quid on 200 smokes, and hope they last the week. Let the kids choose their own magazines for the plane. Spend twenty five quid on breakfast.

I was eight when I knew my Dad was different. Mum, she was quiet. Always there. Dad didn't work. The odd job here and there. Cash in hand, couple of days, thank you very much. Rest of the time, he'd sit in his chair, television on. Mum sitting in the back room, reading mostly. Trashy romance novels, with strange looking covers. Impossibly coloured men with open shirts, long hair blowing in an unseen wind.

They barely shared a word in front of us. I never saw them have an actual conversation which lasted more than three sentence exchanges.

I heard them later, at night.

He never drank during the day. Had to give him that. Seven on the dot, first can would appear. Three or four of those, and then onto the vodka. Of course, I didn't know that at that age. I just called it 'angry juice'.

Fragmented memories, pushing through the tangibility of here, now, this place. I'm on a boat. It's smaller than I was expecting when we booked the trip, carries forty passengers at a push. There are seats which run along the sides, under cover in the middle, and a small open deck at the back of the boat. The stern? I should have asked.

Now have we all got our pirate hats on?

Kids entertainment team. Four happy SMILEY faces. Plastered, fixed. Everything is GREAT. Nothing bad can happen here.

Mum saved her smiles for me. That's what Peter said. Late one night, when the noise had got too much and I'd snuck into his room wanting solace. Comfort. Something. Anything. I'd asked him why Mum never smiled at Dad. He told me she had to save them all for me. Because I was special. I was her special little boy. He wouldn't tell me if he was her special little boy as well.

I don't remember anything but half-formed blurs before the age of eight. A smell can assail me, enter my nasal cavity, and transport me twenty five years back, aged six, eating opal fruits with Becky the girl who lived two doors down.

Then my head is filled with images of later.

One memory leads to the worst memory.

Be careful sitting there Lily. Don't want you falling off.

She's fine Andy. Stop worrying. Relax.

Mum started writing her own stories. It was our little secret. I was home from school, a cold or something, and she shared her secret with me. Dad was on one of his temporary jobs, working on a building site or something. He'd come home later, a musty working smell emanating from him. Mum was sat at the table in the back room. I realised later it was supposed to be a dining room, where families came together and ate meals, talked about their day. Normal stuff. We ate off our laps in front of the television.

I asked what she was doing. She smiled and shook her head. *Keeping busy.* I spied one of the pages. Line after line, filled with words. I didn't read them.

I'd found them again a few weeks ago.

When I was sixteen, and my foster parents couldn't handle me any longer, I was sent away with a black bin bag full of clothes that hadn't fit me in years, and a cardboard box full of photos and papers. I got rid of the clothes. Sold the named stuff and threw out the rest. I kept that box though.

Right kids, are you ready to walk the plank?

They're not seriously suggesting the kids can jump off here are they.
Amy, are you listening to this? They're talking about the kids jumping into the sea.

They have life jackets. And no, they won't let them jump off you tool.
Look at that scenery. It's gorgeous here.

I can count the memories I have before the age of eleven on two hands. I don't need any extra. My wife doesn't understand that. She'll talk about things that happened throughout her childhood, and I just nod and smile. Constantly wondering why I can't remember anything.

I wonder if Peter would remember better.

I remember that night clearly.

It had started weeks before. Dad had found out Mum was writing stories. Peter told me one night. He'd overheard them talking in the backyard. Mum was smoking, something she rarely did. Dad followed her out there, so Peter put his ear to the back door. Told me Dad wasn't happy about something he'd read in one of them.

You can get to Kos in four hours. Sometimes a little less, or a little longer. It's a Greek island, closer to Turkey than Athens. If you get a hotel at a certain point on the coast, you can see Bodrum from your balcony. Face the other way, and there's a beautiful mountain range.

Last night, my wife and I sat on the balcony facing the mountains. Crickets chirruped in the open field in front of us, as various flying insects buzzed and flapped around a solitary streetlight. The kids were asleep in the other room. It's more an apartment than a hotel room. Five star resort. Cost us a fortune, but worth it for the view and the all inclusive.

A flash of lightning lit up the sky in front of us. I'd dropped my cigarette in surprise.

Did you see that? A proper fork of lightning.

Yeah. It's not even raining.

Must be somewhere. That's amazing.

Have you not seen one before?

No. Just the normal flash.

We'd sat with our backs to the wall. Listened as the SHOUTING swirled around the air of downstairs like a pollutant, ready to assault us as it made its way upstairs and underneath the closed door. Couldn't hear everything note of the conversation, every sentence or syllable. Just YOU the FUCKING odd BITCH word. I'd asked Peter if he thought they'd ever stop. He put his arm around me, drew my head onto his shoulder and said nothing.

You're still not here. Not with us.

I'm trying. I really am.

I thought it'd do us some good. Coming away. You're becoming more and more distant Andrew. I can't keep going like this. It's like you're not here. Have you thought of going back to Dr. Woodland?

It wasn't helping. I'm just…I don't know what I need.

We never went on many holidays really as kids. One or two, here and there. A friend of the family might have a caravan in Anglesey and let you stay for a few days in August. First time I went abroad, I was ten and it was on the ferry to Ireland to see some twice-removed aunt or cousin or something. Dad made a big deal of going over there, to the old country. Spent most of the time watching Dad drink and laugh at jokes I didn't understand. Mum sat quietly. She asked Dad if they could go exploring, SEE things, DO things, a

PROPER FAMILY holiday. He told her to shut up and enjoy the craic.

Ten months later and everyone was quiet.

Last night I told her. I'd never told her much of anything about my past. She knew the man she married. The man I am now. The man who was slowly falling apart. She knew I saw a counsellor from time to time about losing my parents. She never asked for details.

What is it?

I need to tell you something.

What? If you tell me you've been cheating, I'll cut your dick off.

No! Nothing like that. I need to tell you what happened to me. Why I don't have parents any more.

I was eleven. Just turned. For my birthday, I'd got a Shoot annual and the promise of a Liverpool match ticket when the new season kicked off. Mum sneaked me a new book when Dad was out getting more drink. He didn't like me reading. READING is for POOFS. Brian Jacques. She'd given me the first two in his Redwall series a couple of months earlier, and I'd read them in bed by fading summertime light. I'd unwrapped the new one. Mattimeo, the third in the series. I thanked her by giving her a tight squeeze. I'd been almost up to her chin. I'd have outgrown her within months. She looked at me and told me I should always read. To get lost in the words. The characters, the story. It's a different world. One that only exists in your imagination.

She was dead thirty hours later.

I blink away the thought of reading about a young mouse called Matthias. Look around me, try to drink in the surroundings. Clear blue water, blazing sunshine. My wife. My kids. I smile. Fixed. Rictus. I want to do more. Be more. But it doesn't work. Never has. Any semblance of normality, of genuine happiness, and I'm instantly back there.

It doesn't go away.

Are you going to jump in?

I don't know. I've never swam in the sea before.

Really?

We were always told the Mersey was dirty. Not to go in that water, because you could catch something.

Depends where you went. Some nice beaches on the Wirral side. Anyway, we're not on the Mersey now are we?

I guess not.

We'll take turns.

After it happened, I was looked after by a policeman with a dark beard and kind eyes. He asked questions, seeming to believe the story I told.

I left bits out. Mainly about being so scared, instead of acting like Peter, and trying to save Mum, I hid under the bed covers and tried to block my ears. I was too embarrassed about that.

On the plane, I'm a ball of nervous energy. Every few minutes asking Amy about another noise, or shift in position.

She thought I just didn't like to fly. She was wrong. I wasn't scared of crashing and dying a terrible death. I was scared of surviving. Of being alone.

It happened like this.

I'd snuck into Peter's room as normal. He was more tense than usual. I think he knew there was something different this time. He was four years older than me. Wanted to play right wing for Liverpool FC.

He tried to save Mum whilst I hid.

The noise was louder than usual. Dad's voice reverberating around the house. He'd been saying things since he'd got home at around tea time. About SOMEONE not knowing HER place. Peter went out to play footy with some mates. Asked me to go with him, but I went upstairs instead. Read some more. I could hear Dad getting louder and louder.

I didn't go back downstairs. When Peter came back home, he came straight up to his room, slamming the door. I pulled back the cover on my bed, and tiptoed to his room. He was pacing up and down, his fists clenched.

'He's hitting her Andy.'

I didn't understand.

66

'He's got to be stopped.'

Who? Why was Peter so angry? I didn't get it. Mum and Dad were just arguing. I didn't understand who was getting hit.

We heard banging coming up the stairs. Mum screaming. GET OUT OF MY FUCKING HOUSE.

I'd never heard mum swear before. Dad swore every other word, but mum never did.

I backed away, sat on Peter's bed as mum and dad's bedroom door slammed. BANG. I could her Dad running up behind her, roaring.

I blocked my ears as Peter left the room. Muffled words, screaming.

Then, quiet.

I waited. Five minutes, half an hour, six months. I wasn't sure. Mum and Dad's bedroom door was off its hinges, resting against the dark brown dresser which was in the room as you walked in.

Mum was on the bed, not moving.

Peter, on the floor, his face masked by red. Not moving.

They're both not moving. Not breathing. Which is understandable, given the amount of RED in the room. You need that to stay in you.

Dad stood smoking, looking out the window, breathing heavily, holding onto a half bottle of vodka, alternating between taking a drag on each. He turned as I walked in, his eyes never leaving me.

'You have to help me now Andrew. You have to be good, understand?'

I didn't say anything. Couldn't.

'You listening fella? You've got to be good. We need to sort this out.'

I was shaking, I could feel tears brimming behind painful eyes as I drank in the scene before me. I couldn't take my eyes off SMASH.

I looked up to see him minus his bottle of vodka. It lay beside me on the floor. I turned, saw moisture on the wall dripping down where the bottle had smashed near my head. Broken pieces of glass at my feet.

HE walked over to where my Mum lay.

My eyes moved between him and the broken bottle. On his exposed neck.

If I'd have helped Peter, maybe this wouldn't have happened. That was all I was thinking.

I SHOULD HAVE HELPED. I SHOULD HAVE HELPED. I SHOULD HAVE HELPED.

The police arrived some time later. Next door neighbour must have rang them. Took their time of course.

They found me still clutching the broken bottle in my fist. Blood stained my hand. Dad slumped over on the floor, one hand over his neck.

'I should have helped Peter save mum.'

When I was twenty four, I got into a fight outside a nightclub. Someone slammed my head against the concrete pavement so hard, it left an indelible mark, and a metal plate, on me. Amy was a nurse at the hospital as I recovered. That's how we met. Last night, she held me for hours after I'd told her what had happened to the eleven year old version of me. Now, I watch as she swims off the side of the boat. The kids don't want to go in. AT ALL DADDY.

I watch as she pulls herself up the ladder and back onto the boat. Smiling.

It's great in there. You should definitely do it.

I have my doubts, but I acquiesce. I can't jump off the plank like Amy did though. I lower myself down, expecting this to be the moment I died as I sunk to the bottom. My swimming skills not being what they ever had been.

SCOUSER DROWNS – 'HE JUST SUNK LIKE A STONE' SAYS WITNESS DRESSED AS A PIRATE.

I let go of the ladder and enter the sea. You have to keep moving, but it's surprising how buoyant you are. I wave at Amy and the kids who are looking over the side of the boat. Lily is taking pictures with her Peppa Pig camera. I lie back and float away.

The impossibly blue sky overhead stops being suffocating. Becomes beautiful. The warmth of the sun counteracts the coolness of the sea water. I smile. I think of my wife. The way she talks, how passionate she gets about things. Talking for hours about space and Brian Cox.

I think about my kids. How every day, something new is learned and appreciated. How everything for them is a new experience and is loved.

They say there are five stages of grief.

DENIAL – I refused to accept they were gone. Used to ask my foster parents when my Mum and Peter where going to come and get me.

ANGER – I used to walk around the streets, just waiting for someone to look at me wrong.

BARGAINING – I would pray. Tell that supposed benevolent power in the sky of all things I would do if they just came back.

DEPRESSION – Doctor Woodland would tell you all about that stage.

ACCEPTANCE…

I think this is what happiness is.

I let go and just drift. Smiling.

You never forget. You just learn to live with it.

About the Author – Luca Veste is a writer of Italian and Scouse heritage, currently living on the wrong side of the River Mersey. He was the editor of the first Off The Record anthology and co-edited True Brit Grit with Paul D. Brazill. He has stories published in Radgepacket 6, The Lost Children Anthology and online at Thrillers, Killers and Chillers. He is currently a mature student, studying Psychology and Criminology at the University of Liverpool. He has recently completed his first novel, a psychological thriller set in Liverpool. He can be found at www.lucaveste.com

How the West Was Won
by
Matt Hilton

'So it's as simple as that is it?'

'Yeah. Bring me two thousand by this time tomorrow and I'll forget about Trisha and you can both go back to your sad little lives together.'

'Where am I going to get two grand?'

'Not my problem. You can walk away, but then Trisha works for me until she pays off her debt.'

'You can't do that?'

'Who says?'

Alan Richmond glanced away from the old man seated before him. His gaze fell on a big guy standing in the shadows, whose eyes were as flat and menacing as a straight razor. He was the old man's eldest son, Iain McCoubrey. He was also his father's bodyguard, and Alan knew what to expect from the tough guy if he even raised his voice to old Tonner. There were other McCoubrey brothers lurking within earshot, not to mention a couple of tag alongs – cousins, or half cousins or whatever.

'I don't want any trouble with you or your family, Tony,' Richmond said. 'But there's no way I can lay my hands on two grand. Not by tomorrow evening.'

'Like I said,' said Tony "Tonner" McCoubrey, 'it's not my problem, it yours. You shouldn't have let your girlfriend borrow more than she could pay back.'

'She only borrowed five hundred,' Richmond pointed out.

'At a four hundred per cent return. She knew the deal before she signed for it.' Tonner was losing patience. He wasn't a man predisposed to explaining himself over and over. 'And now you know the deal, Richmond. Two grand in my hand tomorrow or Trisha goes to work for me. Got it?'

Richmond didn't answer. There was nothing left to say.

Tonner ignored him. He picked up his cup of tea. It was in a china cup decorated with small blue flowers, far too delicate for his scarred old hands. He sipped at the tea. Then glanced up. Richmond hadn't moved. 'Go on. Fuck off, there's a good lad.'

'Let me work off the debt for her,' Richmond said.

'There's nothing I want from you, except the money.'

'I could run *errands* for you.'

'That's not the kind of work I'm talking about for Trisha,' Tonner said. He allowed a smile to creep onto his florid face. 'See, I'm thinking of getting myself a woman for a few days, and as tight as your arse is, I think I'd still prefer screwing a good looking young lass.'

Richmond bit down on his retort, but his anger showed in the tensing of his face and shoulders. Big Iain took a step forward. His hands were larger and carried more scars than his father's.

Tonner made a dismissive motion with his left hand. 'Go on, Richmond. Fuck off. My tea's getting cold.'

'You heard my father,' Iain said, his voice like a bass fiddle. 'Move it.'

Richmond moved. Iain fell in behind him, one hand shoving him in the small of the back. They went through into a narrow corridor that ran alongside the bar that the McCoubrey family owned and used as the headquarters of their criminal empire. Richmond could smell piss coming through the vent in the bathroom door. From a door to the bar drifted voices, the clinking of glasses, and the strains of jukebox music. Some old time Country and Western song: Hank Williams-old. Richmond moved for the bar door, but Iain clutched at his shoulder.

'You're not going in there, Richmond.'

'I fancied a pint,' Richmond said.

'You need to save your pennies if you intend buying Trisha back.' Iain shoved him towards a fire exit door.

Richmond found himself in an alley next to the pub. Iain had followed him outside. One of the other brothers, Davey McCoubrey, had ghosted them along the corridor and stood with the door propped

71

open. He wasn't as big as Iain but his reputation was every bit as scary. He looked on with the same nonchalance as Iain had in the back room. Richmond could sense the air of menace wafting from him.

'Piece of advice for you, Richmond,' Iain said. 'Don't fuck my dad around. He doesn't like it when people don't make an effort to pay off their debt.'

'It's not right, Iain, and you know it.'

The bruiser lifted one eyebrow. 'By whose say so? Deal with my dad and you go by his rules.'

'Trisha was desperate. Does your dad know why she needed the money so quickly?'

'Does it really matter?'

'Her little lad, Michael, had to go all the way to London to see a specialist doctor, and she needed train fare and stuff. The little one has cerebral palsy for Christ's sake!'

'Nice to know he's got such a dedicated mother,' Iain said. 'My dad did right by her. Now it's her turn to pay him back. Or you can if you care so much about a little cripple that isn't even yours.'

'Don't call him a cripple, Iain. That's uncalled for.'

'It's what he is, ain't it?' The thug could tell that Richmond was steeling himself. Where he'd allowed Tonner to threaten Trisha with rape, he wasn't going to stand by and hear anything said about an innocent little kid with health problems. 'Wind your neck in, Richmond. It's not like he's your kid.'

'He's as good as. I've looked after him for the last two years.'

'So look after him now. Go find that money and get his mother back to him. Best thing for everybody.' Iain nodded at Davey and the brother opened the door a little wider. Iain looked back at Richmond before he went back inside. 'I don't have to remind you not to call the law, right?'

'What are they going to do anyway?'

'Exactly. But you know what'll happen if they do come sniffing around?'

'Not going to happen.'

'Good.' Iain closed the door, dismissing Richmond.

He stood in the alley, angry, confused, feeling absolutely useless. He pulled out his cigarettes and sparked up, not yet ready to show his face on the street. Not while his eyes were red-rimmed and he was sniffing down snot.

He was having crazy thoughts.

He was so desperate he was considering committing an armed robbery or something. Maybe doing the bookies or the post office on the estate. But he knew it wasn't in him to rob anyone. Despite having a string of petty crimes behind him he had standards, and they didn't include crimes against the person. The chances of getting away with a robbery were too slim to contemplate anyhow. What would happen to Trisha and little Mikey if he were banged up? Chances were that Tonner would never let Trisha off the hook and she'd be forced into prostitution along with all the others who'd made the mistake of accepting his offer of a payday loan. Shit, most girls who needed Tonner's kind of financial assistance didn't have such a thing as a steady job, let alone a frigging pay day!

He threw away the stub of his cigarette, hardly conscious of having smoked it down to the filter, then immediately lit another. He'd only two fags left in his packet and would need to buy more. But Iain McCoubrey's words came back loud and clear: *save your pennies if you intend buying Trisha back*. The six or seven pounds it would take to purchase a fresh pack wouldn't break the bank. Hell, he didn't have a bank account. Where was *he* going to find two thousand pounds?

Nowhere. That was the simple answer.

He walked out onto the street with no clear idea of where to go or what to do. Familiar faces passed him by, some nodding or calling in greeting but Richmond was too caught up in his concerns to reply. With no real sense of forward volition he found himself standing outside Patel's Convenience Shop about twenty minutes later. His cigarette packet was empty.

Feeling in his pockets for change, he scraped up enough coins for a ten pack, with change for a Mars Bar to take home to Mikey. The little one liked his chocolate – even though most of it ended up smeared over his wheelchair or down his chin. For the first time in days, Richmond smiled at an image in his mind. He had to do right by Mikey, not by feeding his chocolate addiction, but by bringing home his mother.

Entering the shop, he ignored the stands crammed to overflowing with tinned goods and packets, and walked directly to the counter. Mr Patel must have been having an hour or so off, because a young white girl was holding the fort. Momentarily Richmond wondered how much cash was in Patel's till. If he chose to take it, some skinny little girl with arms like twigs wouldn't be able to stop him. The thought sent a shiver through him. No way was he going to frighten the girl, let alone harm her.

'Ten Bensons,' he said, laying out coins on a stack of newspapers the kid had been folding. 'And give me one of those scratch cards, please.'

The girl handed over his cigarettes then tore a scratch card off a strip.

'Good luck,' she intoned.

'Thanks. I need it.'

Richmond wondered if she was old enough to buy a scratch card, let alone sell him one. He'd gone for broke when pointing out which card he wanted. There were a number of them, each depicting higher winnings and he'd gone for gold and a hefty million pounds jackpot. If he won, would he get paid out if the ticket had been sold unlawfully? Fuck it, if his luck was in, he'd bung Mister Patel a grand or two to say it was him serving at the till. He'd probably give the girl a grand to keep her mouth shut too.

He had a couple of pennies left over from his purchases, and he dropped one of them in a charity box. Maybe the fickle God of chance would pay his good-natured deed back in kind. He waited until he was outside before bending to the card and scraping off the golden seals with the edge of the penny.

His heart jumped a little when he saw what he'd won.

He went back inside. Handed the girl the ticket.

'I won,' he said.

'So you did,' the girl said, actually looking pleased for him. She opened the till and took out a pound coin and handed it over. 'Unless you'd like to try your luck again?'

'Nah, lightning never strikes twice for me,' Richmond said. 'Give me a Mars Bar, will you. One of those double ones.'

He took the chocolate bar, and dropped the twenty-odd pence change into the charity box. Outside again he lit up a fresh cigarette, and continued back to his place. His mother had stepped in to watch Mikey while he was out. Trisha was doing a stint behind the bar at Tonner McCoubrey's place, probably unaware that when the doors of the pub were locked tonight, she'd still be on the other side of them. He'd planned on tipping her the wink before Iain had guided him outside via the fire exit, and now she was stuck there at Tonner's mercy.

'No fucking way,' Richmond promised.

He'd laid all on winning at the lottery, and Lady Luck had smiled on him in a very small way, but also she'd reminded him of a favourite phrase. *Fortune favours the bold, Richmond*, he reminded himself. Time you showed a little spine.

The men of the McCoubrey clan were known as hard bastards. No denying it. But like many legends and reputations theirs was only as strong as the rumours that gave them power. To be honest, Richmond doubted that half of what he'd heard about Tonner and his wild sons were true. More likely a length had been added to each story and their record of brutality wasn't quite as terrifying as what everyone had been led to believe.

He returned home to Mikey and handed over the Mars Bar. The boy couldn't speak well, but his warbling voice, sparkling eyes and grasping hands told Richmond of the boy's gratitude. Richmond felt a similar flip of his heart to the pleasure of winning back his stake on the scratch card.

His mother was standing in the kitchen, arms crossed, a cigarette sending a thin plume of yellowish smoke between her breasts, up over her left collarbone to mingle in her permed hair.

'Where have you been?' she asked. 'You know I needed to get off. I wanted back home before Emmerdale starts.'

'You've got Sky plus haven't you, Mam? Why don't you put your favourite programmes on planner?'

'Y'know I don't understand all that new fangled stuff.'

Richmond had heard the same complaint dozens of times. He'd also explained how to do a series link and to record and then play back all her favourites dozens of times. But his mother never paid attention to him. 'Waste of money having it. Don't know why you didn't just stick to Freeview.'

'It was your father who wanted all that diggie stuff. For the sport. I never watch it. Just me soaps.'

Richmond's father had died sixteen months ago.

'So get it cancelled.'

'Can't be bothered faffing about with it.' His mother took a drag on her cigarette, screwing her mouth around the butt. She hadn't enjoyed smoking for years, but just like her reticence to any change she stuck with the habit rather than chucking it in.

'I was going to ask you if you could look after Mikey for another couple hours, Mam.'

She rolled her eyes at the boy. 'Didn't I tell you, Mikey,' she said to the boy. 'Looks like your mother thinks more of having a good time than she does coming home before your bedtime. That mother of yours needs to get her priorities in order, I'm telling you."

'Mam!' Richmond scolded.

'Aah, he doesn't know what I'm saying,' she said with a stab of her cigarette towards the wheelchair bound boy.

'Mam. He has cerebral palsy. He's not stupid, you know? He understands everything he hears.'

'I know,' she said. 'Misses nothing the little so and so.'

Exactly, Richmond thought, *which is exactly why you shouldn't be **calling** his mum near him.* He shook his head in defeat. There was no speaking to her.

'I can put Emmerdale on for you here,' Richmond said, understanding that his mother was as insensitive to Mikey's condition as Iain McCoubrey. 'I'll get you a taxi home after I get back. Get you a Chinese for supper.'

'When did you become Mr Money Bags?'

'I've got a couple of hours work. Pay's good. I'll see you right, Mam. Just keep an eye on Mikey til me and Trisha get back, OK?'

'Put the telly on for me before you go.'

'Thanks, Mam.' Richmond would have kissed her, but knowing her she'd shy away, maybe even push him aside. Instead he transferred his show of affection to Mikey, ruffling the little lad's hair. Mikey gurgled happily, offered Richmond some of his chocolate. It was slimy and hung in drools between his fingers and mouth.

Richmond refused a bite of the Mars Bar diplomatically. He patted his stomach and leaned in conspiratorially. 'No thanks, Mikey; I'm watching my weight. Don't want to be a fatty like your grandma.'

Mikey beamed in delight.

'I heard that,' Richmond's mother said.

'Y'know I love you really, Mam.'

'Get out of it.' She swatted at his forearm, but he was sure he noticed a slight tweak of the corner of her mouth. He wanted to hug her, say goodbye properly, because what he had in mind had no guarantees for a safe return.

He went through into the lounge and turned on the TV set. 'There you go. I've put it on ITV so you can watch Emmerdale. Corrie's on right after it. Just hit that button twice and you'll catch the beginning of Eastenders on the Beeb.'

While he demonstrated his mother walked away. She came back into the lounge pushing Mikey in his chair. Richmond shook his head softly. Then said goodbye. He ruffled the boy's hair again as he passed. On the way out, he went to a closet near the front door. Richmond wasn't much of a handyman, and was loath to do DIY tasks around the house. His toolbox consisted of a hammer, a Philips screwdriver, and a tin containing various rusty nails, screws and other odds and bobs that might come in handy one day. He left the tin behind but bundled up the hammer and screwdriver in a carrier bag.

When he came out of the cupboard his mother was watching him from along the hall.

'What kind of work you got on, Alan?' She was suspicious and rightly so. The tools amounted to a housebreaking kit and little else. 'Hope it's not what I think it is.'

'Mam, you know me better than that. Never burgled anywhere in my life.'

'You were brought up to be better than the other scrotes round this town,' his mother said. He smiled at her use of the scrote word. Something she'd learned from watching TV no doubt, with no idea what she was talking about. 'Don't start acting like them other deadbeats now. That lad in there might not be yours, but he's as good as. He needs you as much as his mother does. So whatever it is you're up to…don't get caught.'

Richmond blinked in surprise. She knew that Trisha owed Tonner money, and that Richmond had been at his bar to try to come to some arrangement. Well, obviously she'd sussed that the criminal hadn't agreed to him doing a little carpentry work for him in order to clear her slate. 'I won't,' he finally said.

'Pity your dad died,' she added. 'Tonner McCoubrey knew to keep a civil mouth around your father.'

'Like father like son,' Richmond said, wishing he were as confident as he made out.

He didn't look back. He closed the door behind him and walked back the way he'd came earlier. This time his eyes weren't red and his snotty nose had cleared up. He didn't walk with his head down either, and he decided against sparking up a fag. Better that he kept a clear head and clear lungs for what was coming.

As evening descended, the cops were out, prowling around in their squad cars looking out for likely lads. If they pulled him they might try and do him on a 'going equipped' charge. Burgling some spot was the least of it, though. If they knew exactly what he had in mind there would be some cops who'd silently applaud him, but it wouldn't stop them putting him away for years if he was caught. Rather than hide the tools, he carried the bag by the handles, all innocent like. The cops ignored him, as he hoped they would, and concentrated on the skinny-faced druggies skulking around in the shadows.

He made it back to The West Inn, Tonner's pub, without any hassle. He stood outside, on the opposite side of the street while he mentally geared up for what he had in mind. Earlier he'd thought a clear head was a good idea, but now that it came to it he understood a good old dose of red mist wouldn't go amiss. He took out his packet of cigarettes and thumbed a fag to his lips. He sparked up and drew on it. Could be his last cigarette ever so he may as well enjoy it.

As he savoured the smoke he watched the public house. In this day and age it wasn't unusual to see a small crowd gathered outside a pub. Since the smoking ban the front doors had become the gathering place of people who needed an extra hit of nicotine on top of the beer they were swilling down. But no one stood outside Tonner's pub. He made his own rules, and fuck legislation. Richmond knew that people still lit up inside, or used the old smoking lounge that was a feature of most pubs back in the days of workingmen. While he watched only one customer came out, and that was only to make a telephone call without having to shout over the top of Country and Western music. Even separated from its source by the pub's walls and the breadth of the street he could hear Johnny Cash growling about his ring of fire.

Richmond waited until the phone guy had gone back inside. He threw down the stub of his cigarette and ground it out under his heel. He felt a bit like Clint Eastwood or John Wayne, about to walk into a Wild West saloon and save the girl from the nefarious cattle baron and his gunmen. Only he didn't have a pair of shiny six-guns to do his talking for him. He took the hammer and screwdriver from his carrier bag, rolled the bag up and stuffed it in his pocket. He clenched a tool in each hand, took a practice swing of the hammer. Then he slid the handle of each into his sleeves and hid the business ends of the tools in his cupped palms. No sense in advertising his intention before he was more than a few feet inside the barroom.

79

He took a few short breaths, felt his pulse rate rise accordingly. Then he swore a couple times to get motivated. He was shitting himself if he'd to be honest, but he was past the turning back stage. Trisha was relying on him. Mikey was relying on him. Tonner and his sons weren't going to ruin their lives.

He pushed his way inside the pub.

The loud music continued unabated, but everyone in the place turned to face him. It was as if they were fine-tuned to the aggression he tried to contain. He didn't immediately see any of the McCoubrey's. But there was Trisha behind the bar, mid-way through pulling a pint for a wizened old man perched at the bar. Trisha was surprised to see him, and her mouth fell open in question.

'Trisha. You're coming with me,' Richmond said. He was slightly pissed that his voice was an octave higher than usual.

'What's wrong?' Fear flashed through Trisha and she almost lost her grip on the glass she was filling. 'Is something wrong with Mikey?'

Christ! He hadn't thought about how his sudden appearance would look to Trisha. She wasn't party to the discussion he'd had with Tonner, and it was obvious her first fear would be for her son.

'Mikey's OK, but you have to come with me now!'

A murmur of dissent went through the patrons in the bar. Someone, a skinny lad that Richmond didn't recognise, sloped off through the side door, obviously going to tell the McCoubrey's that trouble was brewing.

Trisha handed the pint of beer to the old lad and came out from behind the bar. She was a good looking lass was Trisha Jones, and it didn't surprise Richmond that Tonner would choose to take payment in kind from her. The bastard! Well, that wasn't going to happen. Trisha was his and Richmond would fight to the death for her.

'Get your coat and handbag,' Richmond said.

'Leave the lass alone,' someone said, misconstruing Richmond's command.

'What's wrong?' Trisha asked again.

80

'We're out of here,' Richmond told her. 'And you won't be coming back. Not ever.'

'I *need* this job,' she said.

'No. We'll get by another way. You're not working for the McCoubrey's any longer.'

Suddenly the skinny lad was back, and right behind him a stockier figure with flat eyes. Iain McCoubrey.

'What you doing back so soon?' he asked. 'You had until tomorrow afternoon.'

'Well I'm back now,' Richmond told him, 'and I'm not giving your dad anything. I'm taking my girlfriend. Go outside and wait for me, Trish.'

'But my bag and coat…'

'Forget about them.' There was nothing in her bag that she couldn't replace, and he'd been promising her a new coat for long enough.

'Alan?' she queried.

'Just go!'

From his left sleeve he allowed the screwdriver handle to slip into his palm.

A tremor of aggression went through the punters in the barroom. But none stood to confront him. None but Iain McCoubrey. He pressed the skinny lad aside and stepped into the space before Richmond.

'What's that for?' he asked with a nonchalant nod towards the screwdriver.

'It's for you or anyone else who tries to stop me taking Trisha home.'

Iain grunted out a laugh. 'You think that's going to stop me?'

'No,' Richmond said, and tossed the screwdriver at him. Iain caught the tool by instinct. 'It's for you. Don't want anyone saying I took advantage of an unarmed man.'

Iain's reaction was instinctive. He looked down at the worn screwdriver in his hand. By the time he glanced up again, a cold smile edging up his lips, Richmond was moving. He lunged like a fencer, at the same time whipping round his right arm in a short arc. At the last second he allowed the hammer to slip free and the solid nob of steel found Iain's left knee. The sharp crack of metal on bone was loud enough to be heard over Johnny Cash.

Iain McCoubrey was hard. But he won most of his battles by getting in with the first couple of strikes. A headbutt followed up by a smashing right around the ear hole. With his left knee buckling under him he could deliver neither. In fact, his reaction to the sudden blinding pain was to cry out, drop the screwdriver and clutch at his damaged kneecap. Richmond knew if he allowed the big guy even a second to compose himself then even armed with a hammer he was fucked. He swung it up over his shoulder and brought it down hard on Iain's right collarbone.

Enough was enough for Iain.

He fell to the floor howling in pain. Suddenly he didn't look such a tough guy any more, not crying out and holding out a hand to ward off any further blows from the hammer.

'Who's the fucking *cripple* now?' Richmond snapped at him.

The barroom erupted into movement. People trying to flee from Richmond in case he decided to take his hammering skills to their bodies. They were shouting and calling out in panic as they tried to exit the bar. Thankfully Trisha was carried out on the surge of bodies fleeing the scene. Richmond caught one disconcerted glance from her before she was pushed outside. He was happy to see her safely out of harm's way, but knew that he was going to have some explaining to do afterwards. For all she knew her boyfriend had lost it.

Davey McCoubrey was suddenly in the room. He stood off a few feet, looking from Iain to Richmond and then back to Iain again.

'Do you fucking want some too?' Richmond shouted, waving the hammer in the air.

Davey showed that the better part of valour was retreat. He ran into the corridor towards the private quarters shouting out for his father.

The best idea was to get the hell out while he had the chance. But Richmond knew that things couldn't finish there. He had to take the initiative, otherwise the McCoubreys would come for him and they wouldn't stop at smashing his knee and collarbone. They'd do the job right. So must he. He had to show the McCoubrey family that he was not someone to ever seek out again. He ran after Davey.

Davey tried to slam a door in his face, but Richmond was determined now. He thrust his shoulder into the door and almost took it off its hinges and Davey off his feet. As the thuggish son staggered away from the door, calling out to his kin for help, Richmond followed him into the room.

There was four of the McCoubrey clan in the room. Davey, his father, and two of the cousins. The cousins were no concern to Richmond, he could see they were indecisive about their blood ties and wished only to flee the room, but only their fear of the old man, Tonner, held them there.

Tonner was sitting at the same table as before. A china teapot and cup and saucer sat before him. His only reaction to Richmond's sudden appearance was to scowl down at his cup of tea.

Davey backpedalled away from Richmond, his words coming out in a rat-a-tat fashion as he explained to the old man about Richmond's assault and battery of Iain.

Tonner exhaled slowly.

'You're making a habit of disturbing me from having my cuppa,' he said.

'To hell with you and your fucking cup of tea!' Richmond pointed the hammer at each of the cousins in turn. 'You two. If you know what's good for you get the fuck out of here now.'

Tonner actually nodded at his nephews. 'Go on. Sounds like the man wants to talk business.'

Thankful of the reprieve the two cousins almost fell over themselves in their haste to leave the room. Davey stood his ground though, now that he was the only one between Richmond and his father. His fingers made fists, but flexed open again when the hammer was aimed at him.

'Take it easy, Alan,' Davey said. 'Just take it easy, OK?'

83

'Do you want me to smash you to bits as well?' Richmond growled.

'There'll be no more smashing of anyone,' Tonner said.

'Try me and we'll see,' Richmond warned.

'You've proved your point,' Tonner said, 'let things go at that.'

'I don't take too kindly to people threatening to rape my girlfriend.'

'Rape?' Tonner laughed. 'I'm sixty-eight years old. Even with a handful of Viagra I'd be no good to anyone. That was all talk, Richmond. To get you motivated like.'

'Motivated? You thought perhaps I'd go and rob a bank or something to pay you back?'

'I expected you to take some kind of action that'd make an impact. But not this. I hope you didn't hurt my boy too much.'

'Iain will heal. Not sure he'll ever be the same again, not now people know he isn't as hard as he made out.'

'None of us are ever as hard as we make out.'

Richmond settled the hammer in his fist: proof of Tonner's statement. But he added. 'My father was.'

'Aye. That he was. Good pal of mine too.'

'He was never your pal,' Richmond said.

'Oh, on the contrary. We were the best of pals.'

'You were frightened of him, you mean. Couldn't wait for him to die so you could step into his shoes.'

Tonner nodded. 'He was a scary bastard. Seems you have inherited his ways, Alan.'

'Aye.' Richmond stalked forward, brushed Davey aside and stood over the old man. 'I've tried my hardest not to be like my father, but here we are.'

'Glad I helped bring you out of your shell, son. Now it's all yours.'

'What do you mean?'

Tonner held out his palms.

'This place.'

Richmond squinted at him. 'What you goin' on about?'

'The West. The pub your father owned and that I've been holding for him til you came of age and proved your mettle.'

'My father owned this place?' Richmond was dumbfounded.

'Not just the pub, the entire business. *Everything*. It's yours for the taking, Alan. I promised your dad on his deathbed that I'd make sure it came back to you when the time was right. Well…you just proved yourself the type of man we need at the head of the firm.'

'This was *what?* A fucking test?'

'You'd been a little reticent to prove your true colours, Alan. You were beginning to look a little soft. I had to set you a task that'd bring the steel out of you. After what you did out there, I just bet there's nobody who doubts you now. Every one of those little shites that did a runner will be bigging you up to everyone they meet. You'll be the big man around town, just as your father and I always planned.'

'So all the talk of making Trisha work off her debt…'

'There's no debt. Don't you get it? How could she rack up any debt when the money was yours all along? Not unless you intend making her pay it back in kind.' He winked good-naturedly.

The hammer was forgotten in Richmond's hand. It slipped from his fingers and clunked to the floor.

'Was my mother aware of this?'

'Your mam, God love her, wasn't party to your dad's business dealings.'

'What about Trisha?'

'Totally in the dark. No one but me and my lads knew what was planned for you.'

'Hang on. After what I just did to Iain, why are you still giving it all back to me? Don't you want one of your sons to take over?'

'Alan, like I said, I'm sixty-eight. My lads are in their forties now. There's none of us as young as we'd like.' Tonner indicated the teapot. 'Who wants the day to day struggle of hanging on to an empire like your dad built when they'd rather just sit and have a nice cup of tea?'

Richmond shivered as the adrenalin began to deplete from his system and the magnitude of what he'd just learned hit him.

'Wh-what if I don't want to take it?'

'Then I sell the place, divvy up the takings and give you your cut. Me and my boys will need something to retire on, but there'll still be enough to see you right for a while.'

Richmond imagined pound note signs, but understood also that there was more to be made if he kept the business going.

'Before you make a decision think of the little lad,' Tonner said. 'Michael isn't it?'

'Mikey,' Richmond corrected.

Mikey was destined to be wheelchair bound for the rest of his life. He'd require more medical care and attention, nursing and assistance, as he grew bigger. Although Richmond had already committed to giving the little lad the best life he could, it wasn't about handing him the occasional Mars Bar. If he based it on what he could offer from his pitiful earnings from on-again off-again manual labour then neither Mikey or his mother would enjoy the kind of life Richmond hoped to give them. This was an offer he couldn't turn down.

Tonner could see the thought processes working behind Richmond's features.

'I can see that you're surprised and little wonder. You'll be confused by it all and won't have a clue what to say just now. But that's fine. I understand. And you needn't worry. I'm not talking about retiring today. We'll be around to keep you right til you've got your head around the business, then we'll just take a few quid and slip away quietly.'

'I don't get it. I just smashed your son's knee and shoulder yet you're still happy to help me like this.' Richmond offered Davey a grimace of regret.

'You weren't to know what we'd planned. None of us will hold it against you,' Tonner reassured him.

'Iain might see things differently.'

'Iain's tougher than he looks,' said a voice from behind him.

Richmond jumped at the voice, spun around and saw the big man hobbling in to the room. Once he was inside and the door closed Iain McCoubrey shook his leg a few times, worked off a kink in his shoulder. 'And obviously a better actor than I've ever been given credit for.'

'You're OK?' Richmond asked, genuinely concerned for the big guy.

'Glad you didn't use the claw end of the hammer,' Iain admitted. 'But you did the trick. Made me look a right twat, but I'm not one to hold a grudge. Don't worry, it was good work. Everyone in town will think you're the hardest bastard to ever walk these streets. You'll do well, Alan, believe me.'

Tonner smiled, and he looked like a genial old man instead of the hard-bitten gangster he'd portrayed for so long.

He picked up his delicate china cup. 'Anyone want some tea? Shame for it to go to waste.'

About the Author - Matt Hilton quit his career as a police officer with Cumbria Constabulary to pursue his love of writing tight, cinematic American-style thrillers. He is the author of the high-octane Joe Hunter thriller series, including his most recent novel 'No Going Back', published in February 2012 by Hodder and Stoughton. His first book, Dead Men's Dust, was shortlisted for the International Thriller Writers' Debut Book of 2009 Award, and was a Sunday Times bestseller. He has also contributed stories to various anthologies, and has self-published two stand alone occult thrillers, 'Dominion' and 'Darkest Hour'. Matt also collected and edited the ebook 'Action: Pulse Pounding Tales Vol 1', and is also editor-in-chief of the award winning webzine Thrillers, Killers 'n' Chillers.
Matt is a high-ranking martial artist and has been a detective and private security specialist, all of which lend an authenticity to the action scenes in his books.
www.matthiltonbooks.com

Get Carter
by
Nick Quantrill

I watched the blood flow from Dave Carter's head to the pavement. I wasn't sure what I should do, or what I should feel. Carter's routine had been easy to pick up, so I knew the route he would take through the estate. A concrete pillar at the top of the stairs gave me the cover I needed to do the job. The plan was basic, but it didn't require anything more. As he'd walked past me, I'd stepped out of the shadows and hit him with a cosh. It was as easy as that.

My boss, Mr Lewis, had called me up to the office a couple of days ago. It had been a first. I'd spent plenty of hours sat downstairs with the other drivers, drinking tea and reading the newspapers, waiting for a fare. But never in his office.

'I need you to get Carter for me,' he said. He explained about the rules and the territories. Carter had overstepped the mark.

'Can I leave it with you?'

He was the man who'd given me a job when no one else would. It didn't need saying that I owed him.

My lad, Stevie, has just turned two. Biggest surprise of my life, not least because Chloe was on the Pill. But what can you do? Shit happens.

'Things are going to be different for my kid,' I said to her.

'You're full of shit,' she said.

But I was serious.

The nine months flew by. Neither of us knew what we were doing, or what was going to hit us. I got some cheap paint off a mate in the pub and fixed up the nursery. I did Chloe's head in, always asking her if she was alright, if she needed anything.

'You're always under my fucking feet,' she said. 'Can't you just fuck off out somewhere?'

I wished I had fucked off somewhere else when she was in labour. It went on for twenty hours and she called me every name under the sun. And I'd stood there, helpless and unable to help. There was nothing I could do. And what I did do just annoyed her all the more. But the moment when Stevie slipped into the world? That was something else. I would have waited another twenty hours to see it. He was perfect and I'm not ashamed to say I shed a few tears when I first held him.

There and then, I said I'd do anything for the kid. I even gave up the cigs for him. I asked around and found myself a job in the local bacon factory. It was just sweeping up and packing things, but it was a job and we paid our way. Stevie got what he needed, but it wasn't good enough for Chloe. I was catching two busses each way to the factory and working shifts, but I was still the one who got out of bed when he was teething or being sick. And that was when the trouble started. She wanted to argue over anything and everything, but I never raised my hand to her. Whatever she threw at me, I took it.

'I've met someone else,' she said to me one day.
It was over. She wanted me out of the house. It was with the Council in her name, so that was that. I kissed Stevie on the forehead and walked away. Turns out the man taking my place was Dave Carter.

I lost the plot for a bit. Drinking too much, fighting too much. A walking cliché. Chloe wouldn't let me see Stevie, which broke my fucking heart. I moved from flat to flat, sleeping on settees wherever I could. Dave Carter was a big man on the estate. Everyone knew what he was, but he was providing for Stevie. He was doing the right thing. And then the factory started looking for excuses to make people redundant. Last in, first out. I got my P45 and a week's pay as I walked out of the gate.

'You're a fucking loser,' Dave Carter would shout at me when our paths crossed on the estate. 'Do yourself a favour and fuck off somewhere else.'

And what really hurt was the fact he was right. I was a loser. I had nothing, so I started to sort myself out. I moved back into my mam's and got a job. I'm not a man with many skills or qualifications, but the estate's taxi firm, A1, needed drivers.

'People are sick of them foreign drivers,' Mr Lewis said. 'Cheeky fuckers just stick an address into the Sat Nav and think it's good enough. People want a bit better, don't they? They want the local touch.'

The work was slow to start with. Just the occasional fare taking a pensioner to the supermarket. Chloe's still on my back for money, so I told him I needed more work. He'd stared long and hard at me before taking a package out of his desk drawer. It was well taped up with no address on it.

'I need this delivering,' he said.

I didn't need to ask what the package contained. Now he gives me one every other day and tells me the address it needs delivering to. It's that easy. Nobody stops a taxi with a pensioner in, that's his cover, and the extra comes in handy. I've started to build up enough money to think about a deposit for a flat of my own. But they still won't let me see Stevie.

I watched the blood continue to flow from Dave Carter's head to the pavement. I heard a scream. A teenage girl was stood at the top of the stairs, her hand over her mouth, staring at me. She was shaking. I waved the cosh in her direction and she ran away. My heart was already beating fast, but now I was fighting not to lose control of myself. I rolled Carter over onto his back and looked down at the man who Stevie now called his dad. I fumbled in my pocket for my cigs, took one out and lit it up. Get Carter? I hadn't asked the Mr Lewis what he'd meant by that. Hadn't really given it a thought. Maybe he'd just wanted me to take him in for a chat? Whatever. I inhaled the nicotine and slowly blew it back out again, listening to the sirens closing in on me. I looked down again at Carter and waited.

About the Author - Nick Quantrill was born and raised in Hull, an isolated industrial city in East Yorkshire. His Joe Geraghty novels are published by Caffeine Nights. A prolific short story writer, Nick's work has appeared in various volumes of 'The Mammoth Book of Best British Crime'. In 2011, Nick became the first person to hold the role of 'Writer in Residence' at Hull Kingston Rovers, contributing exclusive fiction to the match day programme and assisting with the club's literacy programme. For more information - www.hullcrimefiction.co.uk

Gregory's Girl
by
McDroll

She twisted her neck, trying to see her bum in the mirror, swung round for the close-up view. Scanned for new zits. Gave a few blackheads a squeeze, knowing that Linda, her best pal, would kill her. Pouted at herself, tried out some lustful looks, adjusted her high-waist trousers, fixed the collar on her navy and cream striped blouse, spread it out wide across her shoulders, cuffs turned up in the obligatory fashion, platforms on, ready to go.

Angela had been daydreaming in history class, planning the disco look for weeks, putting together the perfect outfit to catch Davie. Should have been listening to Wee Tooshie as she drew a diagram of the run-rig system on the blackboard but it was more fun thinking about running her fingers through Davie's hair.

"It's important that vegetables are rotated each year. Peas and beans one year, followed by potatoes and the ground must be left fallow for the final year."

Yawn, tuning out again, Davie gazed into Angela's eyes, took her face in his hands and kissed her strawberry lips.

"Get on with the task, twenty minutes maximum and no talking."

Tooshie! Spell broken, back to earth from her romantic haze. A glance over at Linda, no clue about the lesson, her friend's shrugged shoulders, head nodding at Wee Toosh.

"Angela, please get on with your work."

Not a clue but head down, started to write stuff about hundreds of years ago, not much coming to mind after the first sentence. Quickly sank back into daydreams.

Davie was dead gorgeous, all the girls, and probably some of the boys, fancied the pants off him, but not Angela; she was in love. Davie strutted down the corridor at school, leather bag slung over his muscular shoulders, long blond hair flicking to the side as he moved. A year older than Angela, fourth year. Sat on the benches out front with her pals, watched him walk across the basketball pitch with a Bowie album under his arm. Stopped and stared, drooling; never seen a boy with such long hair fluttering in the breeze as he strode out of sight.

Bit of detective work, Davie had a Saturday job in the electrical department of Fraser's, Angela hung out in the cafeteria, Viennese coffee, tried to look sophisticated while she spied on him.

He strolled past and winked at her, she loved him even more, not like the gawky boys at school, too affronted to ever speak to a girl, gazing lustfully from a distance like a pack of randy dogs, but not Davie. He was different.

Disco night, girls' tittle-tattle going ballistic; discussing the boys they'd get off with. Angela was worried Davie wouldn't come, church hall not the height of sophistication, minister parading around, kept a close eye on who shared hands and tongues.

"Linda, what if Davie doesn't come? I'll die."

"He will, I'm sure, been lusting after you for weeks."

"That's ridiculous, he has not." Nervous laughter.

"He has. Minki told me last night."

Minki, Linda's boyfriend, no subtlety there, not in his nature. Face of acne, putrid, lank mousy hair, cool in Linda's eyes. Angela didn't like him, weasely, looked at her in a way that made her feel dirty.

She lay on her candlewick in her bedroom, listened to Davie sweet talk her, gazed into his eyes. He held her hand and led her through a field of yellow buttercups as the sun shone high in the blue sky.

Idiot boys, ran up behind her, pinged her bra strap.

"Angela's a virgin! Never seen a hard-on! Angela's a virgin, big tits…" Guffawed in her face, ran off. Thought that drawing an enormous dick on the toilet wall was hilarious. Davie didn't do anything crude like that. He knelt down and picked a daisy for her as The Bay City Rollers shangalanged in the background.

Disco beat throbbed in the darkened hall, seats filled up around the edges. No dancing yet. No sign of Davie, too soon. Linda grabbed Angela's arm, pulled her into the toilets, shoved her into a cubicle. Bottle of vodka, long swig each, calm nerves.

"Are you ready for this?" Linda well gone, slipping off the toilet seat, fumbled for her ciggies.

Linda, knew her way around a boy, big breasts, star attraction. Looked at Angela and shook her head in dismay. Cigarette dangled from her lips, undid two more buttons on her friend's blouse, looked down at Angela's meagre cleavage. More laughs.

"Do what I tell you and everything will be fine, OK? Ignore him; don't run right up to him. Play hard to get."

Linda got out her kohl pencil and attacked Angela's eyes, black outlines.

"Are you sure about this? I don't want to look naff."

"Don't be daft, loosen up, less girl next door and more Debbie Harry."

Angela chittered with nerves.

Out of the toilet, hall filled up, crowds of sweaty kids pushing each other around, eyeing up the talent, planning their moves. Linda led Angela into the hall, heart pounding, scared to catch sight of Davie; terrified he wouldn't be there.

Minki waved, cigarette in one hand, comb in back pocket, pulled his other hand through his hair. Davie stood beside him.

"Linda, he's looking at me. What do I do?"

"Smile back, it'll be fine, I promise."

Heart stopped, tempted to look behind her. Was he smiling at someone else? Looked at Linda, gave her a shove as she went over to Minki. They stood there, two couples, boys with their arms around their girls. Davie nuzzled Angela's ear, tongue gently licking. Was this happening?

"You smell nice." He spoke.

"So do you." Terrified.

Davie pulled her onto the dance floor, smiled at her, occasionally gently kissing her lips.

"Want to go outside to cool off?" Good idea. Crowded room, vodka, excitement.

He led the way out into the cool dark air, beat fading in the distance, walked Angela around to the dark headstones. Silent witnesses.

Took her into his arms, kissed her hard, tongue thrusting, laid her down, hands pushing under her blouse.

"Davie…I don't know." Daisies, where were the daisies?

"Shoosh, everything's fine, trust me…" Hot, buzzing, hard.

Sucked, bit, undid her trouser button.

No. Squirmed. Pushed. No. Davie. No.

Tried to push him off. Stupid baby, told him to stop. Too far too fast.

"Shut up, you've wanted this for weeks. Don't change your mind now."

Grabbed her wrists, pushed her arms over her head. Heavy on top of her. Too strong.

"Stop it Davie, please stop it." Crying now. Pulled at her trousers, zip burst, hand inside her pants.

"Too fucking late." No daisies.

*****

She sobbed into the grass; no one came. Pulled up her pants and trousers, scrabbled around for shoes. Held onto the nearest gravestone, cool and smooth in the dark. Rubber legs. Hurt. Wet stickiness. Snot wiped, hands covered in mud.

"Angela, where have you been?"

Linda. She sobbed out loud at the sound of her friend. Told her what had happened, gulped in the night air. Longed to put her arms around her. Make everything all right.

"Stupid bitch! Thought you wanted Davie? Took me and Minki ages to persuade him. How's he going to feel now? Jesus Christ, you're just a stupid wee baby, what did you think he was going to do out here?"

Thought he was going to tell her she was beautiful. Thought he was going to pick her a daisy. Thought he was going to kiss her gently on her lips and tell her he loved her...

She felt stupid. She was stupid. A stupid wee girl.

About the Author - McDroll's crime fiction has a nip of noir and a splattering of Scottish humour and can be found floating around in the digital world, most notably in Shotgun Honey, The Flash Fiction Offensive and Near To The Knuckle. Other stories can be found in the anthologies Off the Record, The Lost Children, Burning Bridges and True Brit Grit.
McDroll is the author of the serialised crime novella 'The Wrong Delivery' and the short story collections 'Kick It Together' and 'Kick It With Conviction'.
Website: http://imeanttoreadthat.blogspot.co.uk

Eyes Wide Shut
by
Col Bury

Castro caught a red tear, trickling down the flushed cheek, with the muzzle of his Browning 9mm. "Aw… poor O'Shea. We all get our comeuppance eventually, don't we, Jack?"

The reply was muffled by a duck-taped mouth, but the panicky eyes and frantic head shakes translated as 'guilty' to Castro.

"That you begging for forgiveness, Jack? Well, you won't be getting any from me," Castro spat, his gold incisor accentuating a sneer behind the neatly trimmed goatee. "Fancy agreeing to come for a pint with me. As if I'd tell you anything. I'm no grass, ya fuckin sucker. Thought your lot always had your eyes wide open." Castro took a small bottle from his jacket pocket. "He-he. You'll know it as Rohypnol, but we call it 'Roofies'."

Jack O'Shea still appeared groggy, but his vivid blue eyes widened on seeing the bottle, the head-shaking more frenetic.

Castro thrust the single action Browning to O'Shea's left temple. "I see you've pissed ya pants too. Is that the piss of a guilty man?"

As he shook his head, O'Shea's eyes gestured desperately at his wallet on the adjacent desk.

"What? I've already taken the hundred quid. It'll come in handy that, thanks a lot, buddy. The credit crunch even affects us guys you know."

O'Shea indicated again, more pointedly this time by using his head.

"Oh, you want me to look inside?"

O'Shea nodded.

Castro used the muzzle of the pistol to open the wallet and studied the photo of O'Shea with his three children. Beaming smiles all round; his two young sons in their Manchester City kits, one with a foot propped up on a football. The older girl had headphones on, her long strawberry blonde hair lit by the sun glistening off the vast lake splitting a backdrop of two mountains.

"This you trying to convince me then, Jack?"

He shrugged, blinked exaggeratedly.

"Well, it's not working, man. The only thing this has done is give me a fuckin semi-on looking at your daughter."

O'Shea's eyes hardened.

"Tell me, Jack… does she take it up the arse?"

He wriggled on the wooden chair, jerking it briefly off the badly-tiled floor, the leg and wrist ligatures binding him and the chair as one.

"I'll take that as a 'Yes' then, buddy. Or at least she will do when I've finished with her." A throaty laugh revealed the gold tooth.

Muffled cursing followed, pleading eyes widening again.

"You really love 'em 'don'tcha', Jack?"

His head dipped.

Castro pointed at the snapshot with the pistol. "Look at you with your daft smile and that twinkle in your eyes. Aw, big daddy Jack O'Shea, the family man, eh? Hey, have you ever considered… you know… with her?" He pointed the gun at O'Shea's daughter.

O'Shea glared at him, fixedly.

"What?" Castro shrugged, chuckled. "You must've considered it, even for a split second. C'mon, man, admit it."

 Ignoring Castro, O'Shea looked up and scanned the room; desk to his left, the open window, a metal cabinet in front and the door to his right…

Another guttural snicker then he asked, "You gotta have seen her naked over the years… seen her maturing… an' then, a guy like you must've been tempted?"

He continued to scrutinize the sparsely furnished room, particularly the wide open window beyond the desk.

"Don't fuckin ignore me, ya low-life piece of shit!" yelled Castro, pistol-whipping him on both cheeks.

The chair jolted noisily off the floor and O'Shea shook his head violently, as if to clear the pain somehow. It didn't work. His jawbones throbbed like hell and he felt dizzy.

"So, let me put a scenario to ya, Jack... there's these two cops on patrol. It's late at night, not much happenin'. To relieve the boredom they cruise over to the red light district, near the arches on the edge of town. They see this fit piece of black meat and decide to have some fun, get her into the back of the van. She's cold, right? And she trusts the cops. They ask a few cop-like questions, but no worries, par for the course in her line of work, so nothin' untoward there, right? Then she's threatened with arrest cos she's already had her quota of street warnings. But she don't wanna spend the night in a cell cos she's rattling an' clucking, cold turkey, right? So they notice this, and the conversation turns to... 'What can you do for us?'... Right? One cop climbs into the back an' whips his cock out... an' she gets down to it. But, no, he's not happy with that... he wants to feel this whore, taste her. But she's not happy with that, and so the second cop pins her down. Then they both abuse their positions big time... and of course, the girl. Afterwards they just laugh and dump her back on the streets... the piece of meat she is, right?"

Jack motioned an emphatic 'NO' with his head.

"So, what do ya think of that scenario then?" he asks, almost casually, before ripping the duck tape from O'Shea's mouth.

"Aaargh! Fuck..."

"Bet that's what you said on the night, innit?"

O'Shea opened his mouth, stretching his aching jaw and stinging facial muscles. His mind still foggy, he tried to speak, but just croaked. He cleared his throat with a cough. "I didn't... do anything... I swear."

"Bullshit, bitch!" Castro forced the Browning into O'Shea's mouth, the muzzle clattering against his teeth making him heave. "Just cos some bullshit internal enquiry says you did shit, don't make it so, ya punk-arsed pig. I want a fuckin confession. Now!"

O'Shea just eyeballed him, had no choice. He could feel the metallic tang, the grind of metal on teeth. The sickly taste of the gun's

99

last discharge made him heave again. He wondered who it had been used on. Castro yanked the pistol from the cop's mouth, scraping a molar on its exit. A sharp pain was followed by a hint of blood oozing onto the back of O'Shea's tongue.

Ignoring the pain, and the banging headache, he tried to compose himself, think straight. With a deep breath, he said, "Believe what you want... but I know the truth."

"The truth? The fuckin truth!"

"Yeah... and I... did nothing that night."

"Nothin'?" Castro's dark eyes flared. "You raped ma fuckin daughter, ya cunt!"

"She was lying, Castro... and what the hell are you playing at anyway... pimping out your own flesh and blood like that?"

Castro suddenly became quiet, his eyes narrowing. He turned his back, shoulders sagging. Smoothing his braided hair, his voice hushed. "But times have been real hard. It's a fuckin jungle on the street, man. And, anyway, she was more than willing..."

O'Shea's senses continued to slowly kick in, and he realised just how musty the room was, increasing his nausea. He couldn't quite place the smell, but it was familiar. "Imagine how hard times will be... if you kill me. A life sentence, feller."

Castro pivoted, grimacing, pointing the Browning toward O'Shea's forehead. "Yeah, but it'll be worth it. I'd be a hero inside for killing a pervert cop."

"Whoa. Am not so sure about that, Castro. Pimps are classed as sex offenders in prison... just like the paedos."

"Don'tcha fuckin compare me to no nonce, man!"

"Well, my daughter's only fourteen, you know." He gazed at the photo on the desk.

"That's well different. You smartarse cops always twist things. This isn't about me, man... it's about you." Rushing forward a pace, he raised the gun, pointing it at O'Shea, whose head flicked edgily from side to side. Leering, he inched closer, pressing the pistol into the cop's brow.

O'Shea winced, thought of his family.

"Thirteen rounds in this magazine, Jack. Well, there was. Unlucky for some, eh?"

Was? O'Shea glanced at the wallet photo on the desk, he tried to stop his voice from trembling, being parched wasn't helping. "But... but what's the point, Castro, when I honestly did nothing wrong? The judge threw it out of court, remember?"

The gun remained pressed against O'Shea's forehead, creating a ringed imprint. "Rah, rah, everyone knows you all piss in the same pot. Confess or die, you cunt!"

"Pleeease! You know that's... not the case. Loads of bad guys get off with shit... including you."

Castro lowered the gun. "You're pecking ma head, man. You smartarse muthas do ma box in." He turned, picked up the duck tape from the desk.

"Look... before you do that... please, just let me tell you about that night."

Castro hesitated, glared. "It better be fuckin good, pig."

O'Shea glanced out of the open window, the view of roof tops in the distance telling him he was high up, the blue sky and wafting breeze teasing him. "Please, hear me out..." he began.

"It was a cold night, very cold. My partner, Webber, saw Shannice standing on the corner. She was freezing, had no coat on. He shouted her over. We took her into the van, flicked the heater on and chatted. Suggested ways she could get off the brown. Rehab programs, drugs workers and all that. I even gave her a coffee from my own flask to warm her up. We were with her for about twenty-five minutes, half hour tops, when she insisted on hitting the streets again, saying she was losing money for every second spent talking to us. So we dropped her off, told her to be careful. She even thanked us for caring... for God's sake."

"Not good enough, O'Shea. Nice touch blaming Webber for shouting her over, though. That lying piece of shit!" He noisily yanked duck tape from the roll, bit the strip off.

O'Shea briefly considered his partner. They spoke daily. Surely he'd be out looking for O'Shea by now. He had to keep

101

stalling. "Okay then. If it's as you said, then why did Shannice not get examined at the hospital? She refused remember?"

He held the strip of duct tape outstretched, aloft, his right index finger resting perilously on the Browning's trigger. "It was too late."

"Exactly. She left it too late. I mean, five days later she reports it."

He stepped forward a pace. "She was scared of repercussions."

"I'm not having that, as it's the easiest thing to do. Contrary to popular belief, and unlike with the public, if you accuse a cop of anything, he's guilty straight away, until proven otherwise. Because no one likes a dirty cop, including other cops. I've already been through hell these last eighteen months."

"Nice speech, O'Shea. Even I'm beginning to believe you. No wonder you got off with it."

"Okay, why didn't Shannice hand over the clothes she wore that night?"

"She'd already washed them."

"Surely it was worth a shot though, if not for DNA, then fibres."

"You're twisting again. Don't wind me up, you mutha! Or you'll end up like…" He fleetingly turned to the cabinet.

"Like what… who?"

Castro ignored him, screwed up the duck tape, went to the window and stared outside.

O'Shea's fuzzy mind drifted back to his children. They were too young to lose their daddy. He cursed himself for trusting this career criminal, saying he had 'info of interest to the police'. Should've taken Webber with him, dammit. He glanced at the door to his right, then back to Castro. He heard traffic below, emanating from the gaping window. He tugged on the ligatures. No use. *Think!*

He swallowed then said, "My guess is that Shannice, like many others, saw an opportunity. The chance of getting off the streets by winning a shed-load of compensation, and even selling her story to the papers then living happily ever after."

"Fuck this, man!" yelled Castro manically, passing the metal cabinet and banging the butt of the gun on it in anger. The left cabinet door slowly opened behind him, as he turned and forced the Browning into O'Shea's gob again.

This time Castro leaned in real close, his contracting pupils inches from O'Shea's. He was so close that O'Shea could smell his breath. It smelt like dog shit, a reflection of its owner.

O'Shea could just about see the left cabinet door, now fully open. His heart somersaulted and he double-blinked in a rush of panic. Webber was squashed inside, eyes staring like a dead salmon, but seeing nothing. The bullet hole in his forehead ensured that.

Castro seemed to notice what O'Shea had seen and glanced behind for a second. O'Shea bit down hard on the gun's barrel. With a twist of his neck he yanked the pistol from his kidnapper's grasp and flicked it overhead. The gun clattered on the floor. Castro's eyebrows shot up to his creasing brow, as O'Shea lunged forward, still tied to the chair. The cop's gaping mouth impacted Castro's neck, forcing him backward onto the desk. O'Shea clamped his teeth down, feeling the skin giving then splitting. The taste of blood, bitter and metallic, flooded warm in his mouth, spurted up into the air as he rocked his head side to side and ripped at the flesh like a Hyena on speed. He felt Castro's desperate punches thudding on his head. But O'Shea continued, tearing into the pimp's throat, survival instinct and desperation driving him on, until Castro's screams became a pathetic gurgle.

O'Shea was standing in a painfully awkward crouch, the chair sticking out behind him. He yanked repeatedly, ripping bloody tendrils out, feeling them rubbery between his teeth, Castro now offering silent screams, his vocal cords in bits. O'Shea re-clamped his aching incisors and dragged Castro inch by painful inch along the desk closer to the open window. Castro's dark, bloodshot eyes swamped with fear and tears, his leg kicking out like a giant, upturned insect. O'Shea struggled with the weight, so unclamped again and sank his blood-dripping teeth into the pimp's thigh, the punches hitting him now were like that of a child's.

Half out of the window, Castro's head jerked up and O'Shea looked into those dark, defeated eyes one last time, showing their true cowardly colours as they pleaded mercy. Ignoring the pain in his gums and neck, and the increasing weight of the chair, O'Shea swiftly switched his grip. He bit hard onto Castro's belt, before heaving him that crucial last few inches, the slippery blood-drenched desk O'Shea's ally.

Relief flooding him, O'Shea peered over the window's sill… and mentally waved 'bye-bye' to the cop killer, whose eyes bulged in disbelief as he plummeted.

Seconds later, O'Shea heard screams from below and sank backward clumsily into the chair still strapped to him, knowing his colleagues would soon be here.

Breathlessly, he surveyed the bloody scene; incredible how much of the fluid covered the walls, desk and floor. He, himself, was soaked from head to toe in Castro's claret. He prayed that the pimp hadn't dipped into too many of his girls. He spat sprays of Castro's sickly fluid repeatedly on to the floor in disgust.

His best mate, Webber, eyed him. How could he possibly tell Webber's wife and kids about this? His emotions bubbled and he saw his open wallet on the floor, the blood-splattered photo of his own three children staring back up at him. It was all too much. He cried red tears.

As he heard the sirens, he reflected. He knew the world would be a better place without Castro. And, as a vampiric smirk formed, he also knew that bitch, Shannice had enjoyed it. He could tell by her eyes.

About the Author - Col Bury is the crime editor of award winning webzine, Thrillers, Killer 'n' Chillers. Under the guidance of New York agent Nat Sobel, he's currently writing a crime novel series based in Manchester. Col's ever-growing selection of

short stories can be found all around the net, some winning online comps' and several being included in anthologies. His vigilante story MOPPING UP is in THE MAMMOTH BOOK OF BEST BRITISH CRIME 9, and FISTS OF DESTINY, from Col's eBook MANCHESTER 6, was selected for THE MAMMOTH BOOK OF BEST BRITISH CRIME 10. Col lives in Manchester, UK with his wife and two children. He's 'not a bad stick' at 8-ball pool and is an avid fan of Manchester City FC. He interviews crime authors and blogs here: http/colburysnewcrimefiction.blogspot.com/
Twitter: @ColBurywriter
Facebook: The Manchester Series by Col Bury
Website: http://colburysnewcrimefiction.wordpress.com/

Night of the Living Dead
by
Steven Miscandlon

Honour among thieves? There's no such thing.

Among armed robbers, even less so. Show me a man who's willing to shove a loaded shotgun in some young bank teller's face for their split of a few grand, then try and convince me that person has an ounce of what you'd recognise as normal human decency, let alone a sense of honour. No, that's just not how it is.

In this game, it's only a matter of time before one of your buddies will try to fuck you over. Always assuming, of course, you don't do it to them first. It might happen before the job. Sometimes it's while you're actually doing the bit of graft. Most often — as on this occasion — it's after the job's gone down, before you go off on your separate ways with your share of the loot.

And that explains why we're sitting here, the five of us. Around a table in Basher's lock-up garage, where we store the odd bit of moody gear. It explains why four of us look so bloody shit scared, why Basher is the only one holding a gun and why he's looking so properly fucking pleased with himself.

There's no denying we're a motley crew. Not really a gang, though, not the way folk on the outside might think of it. More a five-way marriage of convenience. We've done more than a few jobs together in the past, though it's beginning to look increasingly unlikely that we'll do any more together in the future. Not such a bloody convenient marriage after all, as it turns out.

The bare, cobweb-ridden light bulb hanging above the table casts each of our faces into stark planes of light and shadow, transforming some already pretty damned ugly mugs into something truly monstrous. Fingers Bob is sitting on my left, thin-faced and chewing his nails to the quick; looking like he doesn't know whether to cry, piss himself or run away screaming. I don't really blame him.

I've known Fingers for ages. Most folk assume his nickname comes from being a bit light-fingered, bit of a tea leaf. Well, light-fingered he certainly is, but I know for a fact that that particular nickname has more to do with a certain sexual molestation charge a few years back. I make it a point never to shake hands with Fingers Bob. You can never be sure exactly where his fingers have been.

To Bob's left is Italian Tony. Well built, olive skinned and he might have been handsome but for the massive, misshapen boxer's nose planted right in the middle of his mush. I remember when he first appeared on the scene a couple of years ago, Italian Tony tried to get people to call him The Rock, on account of him being from Gibraltar or something. I also remember Basher telling him to fuck off, saying all Mediterranean folk look and sound the same anyway, and that he was going to call him Italian Tony.

The name stuck, and we've called him that ever since. He still kicks off about it occasionally, but Basher just keeps saying "Fuck off Italian Tony" until he shuts up about it. Funny thing is, I'm not sure if his name is even Tony. Anyway, the guy can handle himself in a fight, he doesn't mind a bit of hard graft, and he doesn't scare easily. Looks scared now, though.

That would be on account of Basher, sitting opposite me with a look on his face somewhere between grim determination and rabid mania, grasping a sawn-off double-barrel shotgun like it's his best friend in the whole wide world. Which, come to think of it, it probably is. Alexei Bazhenov: known as Basher to his friends, while his enemies are more likely to be on the floor scrabbling for their teeth before they'd have a chance to call him anything.

You see, Basher is what you might call a proper psychopath. Or maybe a sociopath. Okay, I don't know anything about psychology but he's *some* kind of fucking path, that's for sure. His face, rendered now in harsh light and inky shade, is a pitted lunar surface of pockmarks and scars, and beneath his heavy brows he has the cold blue eyes of someone who doesn't care about life. Especially not yours.

The rumour on the street is that Basher is *Bratva*. Russian mafia. But I know that's not true. He's just one thoroughly evil fucker who got where he is by stabbing and strangling and slashing and shooting any poor bastard who ever got in his way. Without a second thought, without remorse.

He doesn't care about scale, either. Basher is equally happy whether he's punching a pensioner in the face for the twenty quid in their wallet, or knocking over a big high-street jewellery shop for his share of a few hundred grand. Which meant today's bank job was right up his alley.

Speaking of which, to my right sits Bullshit Billy. Ridiculous beanpole of a creature with a nose you could use as a ski slope and unpleasant, beady little eyes. He's a scrounger and a schemer and a liar but amazingly — and unlike the rest of us — Billy doesn't have a criminal record. This sterling character trait contributed to his unlikely coup, a few months back, of landing a job as a part-time "customer service assistant" in the big bank branch on George Street.

I'm sure Bullshit Billy has been far from the model employee, but in the past three months he's kept his great big nose clean and, he said, started to gather enough inside information to let us pull off a decent job with a good return, even split five ways. He told us that even as a lowly teller he knew how much the cash safe limit was at the branch, and how it was always higher on the Friday before a bank holiday. How the cash delivery came three o'clock Thursday afternoon, so the best time to hit would be just before closing time.

He knew there was no high-tech laser security system for the safe, no motion sensors or time lock; just two keys, both held by staff on the premises. Best of all, he knew that the bank's security training for staff recommended that if someone sticks a massive bloody gun in your chops and tells you to open the safe and hand over the money, then you should probably *open the fucking safe and hand over the fucking money*.

And there it was. Billy had a day off and stayed back here at the lock-up to keep out of mischief. The plan was that me and Basher would go into the bank, fully tooled up, quarter to five Thursday afternoon. Lots of shouting, lots of threats. Italian Tony tags along — he doesn't like guns but doesn't seem to have a problem waving his prized switchblade around like a lunatic — and takes care of getting the cash into the bag while us two concentrate on keeping the bank staff and any customers too scared to do anything daft. Fingers Bob is in the car round the corner, engine running.

Quick in, quick out. It isn't clever, it isn't pretty, and it sure as fuck isn't *Ocean's Eleven*, but it should do the trick.

And it went according to plan, more or less. Basher went a bit off script and took the butt of his sawn-off to the face of an old codger in the branch that he reckoned was looking at him funny. But other than that, it was fucking clockwork. The bank manager and counter supervisor remembered their training and were ever so helpful when the guns were pointed at them. Opened the safe and helped Italian Tony fill up the bag nice and quick. I reckon it's the best customer service I've ever had.

Out the bank, into the car. Fingers Bob, for all his faults, is a bloody good wheelman, and takes us quickly and efficiently on a carefully plotted route back to Basher's lock-up, while the rest of us in the car ride out the adrenaline buzz. Laughing all the way from the bank, you might say.

Then it all went a bit shit.

We're back in the lock-up, Bullshit Billy has joined the party and we're congratulating each other on a job well done. Tony dumps the bag with the haul in the middle of the table, and everyone is all smiles. All except Basher.

"I have idea," he says. His words, as always, are almost slurred through the thick Ukrainian accent. "We play game. For *money*." The emphasis he puts on this last word makes me suddenly wary.

"What do you mean, Basher?" says Italian Tony. "Have a game of poker or something? Now?" He grins. Tony isn't the sharpest tool in the box, but give him his due; he's a mean poker player.

"No, not poker," grunts Basher. "I have better idea. We stay here during night. Last one awake gets money. *All* of money."

109

"Hey, no, wait a minute," says Bullshit Billy. "We pulled this job off together. I mean, I know I wasn't there, mate, but I gave you the info. The deal was a five-way split." His brows furrow. You can tell he doesn't like crossing Basher, but Billy looks understandably pissed off.

"I have new idea," says Basher, reaching into his jacket and pulling out his beloved sawn-off shotgun. Before Billy can react, Basher swings the butt round, catching him firmly across the face. I hear a crack, and it's a pretty safe bet it's not the gun that's broken. Billy goes down.

That's when we should have reacted. I should have pulled my own gun. Tony should have gone for his knife or just thrown himself at Basher. But we just stand there, too shocked or too slow to move against him. Then he points his gun straight at me and indicates the inside of my own jacket.

I reach in, slowly pull out my own weapon and hand it to him. He takes it, then throws it into the far corner of the dim room.

"New idea is this. We spend night here, sit round table. You try to move, try to get away, I shoot you in face." He jabs the shotgun toward my face and, much as it might pain me to admit it, I flinch in fear. "You fall asleep, maybe I shoot you in face anyway." He chuckles; a gargling, throaty wheeze. "If I fall asleep, maybe you can get gun before I wake up and shoot you in face. Like I say, last one awake gets money."

Me and Italian Tony look at each other in horror. Fingers Bob has cowered into the background, in typical fashion. Billy is still on the floor, groaning in pain.

Basher's face splits into an ear-to-ear grin, and for a moment I think maybe he's having us on, that this is just his demented idea of a joke. But no.

"Come, sit down at table. Will be fun, like game show." Basher gestures to the chairs arrayed around the rickety oval table. Once me, Tony and Fingers are seated, he drags Billy off the floor and dumps him into a chair. Finally Basher sits, still grinning and relaxing back into his seat. Shotgun held firmly, finger resting on the trigger.

110

And here we are. I'm not sure how much time has passed. At least five or six hours, surely. Bullshit Billy is clinging onto consciousness, but his face is a state. The bruising below his left eye is horrendous, an ugly purple blotch contrasting with his otherwise deathly pallor. Definitely a broken cheekbone, I reckon.

Basher has made a couple of attempts at getting a conversation going, but for some reason the rest of us aren't really in the mood. He has now taken to gently humming something that sounds like it might be a Russian lullaby.

I can't speak for the others, but I'm flagging. Adrenaline can only sustain a body so far, and then the system starts to run down, trying despite everything to relax and gain rest. And we've been sitting here for hours, no food or drink, no stimulation other than blind fear. It's only a matter of time before one of us starts to nod off.

And what then? Out of the game? Shot in the face?

We're alive. And dead.

More hours pass, but little changes. Fingers Bob and Italian Tony look tired and glassy-eyed, sustained only by fear. I imagine I look much the same. Basher still looks thoroughly pleased with himself, occasionally humming his lullabies, every so often grinning or flashing a wink if one of us catches his eye.

Bullshit Billy is starting to look worse by the minute though. His cheek is swollen and bruised, his left eye closed up and weeping. The other eye flickers closed, then open, then closed again.

He pitches forward and his forehead slams onto the table, the sound reverberating sharply round the sparse room.

I brace myself for whatever might come next.

It isn't what I expect.

To my left, Fingers Bob leaps out of his chair, letting out a short cry of sheer desperation. He looks as though he's about to throw himself at Basher, David against Goliath, but hesitates just a beat too long. Basher snaps up his shotgun and, true to his word, shoots Bob in the face.

It would be an exaggeration to say his head explodes like a melon. But only a slight exaggeration. In a split second, Bob's drawn, ferret-like face is gone and a bloody, pulpy mess is there in its place. I'm just a little too close; bone and gore spray me.

Bob's body drops to the floor.

Italian Tony grabs his chance, lunging from his chair and slamming into Basher. The pair tumble to the floor as the gun is knocked from Basher's hands, skating across the room.

Basher is tough, but momentarily winded by Tony's bulk hitting him in the chest. Those couple of seconds make all the difference, as Tony pulls his knife from his pocket, flicks open the blade and buries it in Basher's neck.

Blood spurts as Tony keeps stabbing, frenzied now, plunging the knife again and again into Basher's chest and neck, and slashing at his face in fury.

I move quickly across the room and retrieve the shotgun, one barrel still loaded, then turn to survey the scene.

Bullshit Billy is still lying face-down on the table, not moving. It's impossible to tell if he's breathing.

Fingers Bob is a faceless mass on the floor, something from a horror movie.

As Italian Tony stands and moves away, a couple of gurgling breaths bubble through Basher's bloodied neck and chest. He's not dead yet, but isn't far from it.

Tony and I look at each other.

"Jesus," he says, his chest heaving. "Jesus fucking Christ. I knew he was a nutter, but …"

I nod. I always knew Basher would come to a bad end.

Tony looks around him, at the debris of the dead and dying, at the blood staining his own clothes. "Fuck. What are we going to do? It wasn't supposed to go like this. A quick job, he said. In and out then split the cash. *Fuck*."

I ponder for a moment.

Then I raise the shotgun and gesture with it.

"Take a seat, Tony."

"What?"

"Sit down at the fucking table. We've got a game to finish. Last one awake gets the money. *All* of the money."

Honour among thieves?

Don't make me laugh.

About the Author - Steven Miscandlon cut his writing teeth with various independent magazines in the early nineties, and by the age of twenty-one had been published in 'West Coast Magazine', the leading Scottish literary journal that helped launch the careers of writers such as Irvine Welsh. His latest release, 'Into the Shadows', collects a number of stories written and published over the past twenty years, in genres ranging from crime and horror to science fiction.

Dead Man
by
AJ Hayes

I was heading for the alley behind the fast food joints when the dead man called to me.

"Hey," he said. "Got a minute?"

"Maybe," I said.

He gave me a half-smile. It didn't stop the blood from the bullet holes in the front of his shirt though.

"Will you stay here a while? Just talk?"

Why not, I thought. Nobody but me and him around. The air was heavy with the smell of the rain that would be coming soon, so the ball game would be canceled or called early and I didn't really feel like a stripper bar tonight.

"Sure," I said and slid my back down the old bricks until we were sitting side by side. "What do you want to talk about?"

He was breathing low and hard now. A little blood trickled out of his nose and dripped down onto his tie.

"Who sent you here?"

I didn't see any harm in answering. It might take his mind off what was coming up fast and he wasn't going to be telling anybody anything after that happened.

"My boss, guy called Lenny B."

He turned his head and looked at me. The motion made his nose bleed a bit faster dropping bigger spots on his pale yellow tie. Too bad, I thought. That's a nice tie.

"What do you know," he said. "That's my boss too."

"Yeah, I know," I said. "He said you been skimming some money off one of his accounts."

He looked like I'd hurt his feelings. If he still had feelings that is. Maybe it was the copper jacketed slugs in his chest that hurt. A cold rain had started up, maybe that was what made them ache, the icy water seeping through his white shirt and into the bullets.

"He's wrong," he said. "I never--"

"Right or wrong, he told me where you'd be. And me? I always go where he tells me." I shrugged a little. "And do what he says."

He tried for a smile. It didn't work.

"Yeah, me too. I mean, I'm just an accountant. I don't know anything about this stuff. I told him that. He said I didn't have to know anything. Said all I had to do was wait until nine o'clock and step out into the alley and a guy would find me. Said all I had to do was fumble getting the papers out of my briefcase. Delay just long enough to distract you so the boys could get into position. I was going to try that, fumble around, you know? But you don't waste any time, do you?"

He took a deep breath, which I guess was a mistake because his face turned pale and he made a kind of grunt deep down in his chest.

I clocked the alley real fast. Nothing yet. But there would be pretty soon. I knew Lenny B. wouldn't send in a team just for poor old dead guy. If it had been only him, they would have just walked up and shot him, like I did. But they had to be a little more cautious with me in the mix. Take it a little slower. They were probably setting up the action just outside the alley mouth trying to catch me with the streetlights in my eyes.

Why me? Hell, nobody in the game ever knew why. We just knew what and where. That night, dead guy and me, we were the whats.

"Been nice, pal," I said. "But I gotta go."

I felt his hand come up under mine and started to jerk away.

"No, no. Here," he said. "This might help."

I looked down at the small oval of heavy steel in my hand. US military M67 fragmentation grenade. That'll do it all right, I thought. He bumped my hand again. Another one. Give the guy credit, he knew how to start a party.

"What the hell you doing with these, partner," I said.

115

"I'm not stupid," he said with that smile that cost him a lot of pain to make. "I knew something was wrong, so I thought I'd bring along a little insurance. Got these when I was an ordinance clerk in Iraq. I never got the chance to use them, though. You walked up and shot me so fast I never had a chance to grab them. Then you were here and you were listening and it made me feel better, maybe not so scared."

He looked at the rain and coughed red and died.

He didn't look bad. The small smile had stayed on his face. Maybe I helped with that. Maybe I did. I hoped so. Maybe I'd look like that when my time came. Hell, a guy's got a right to hope, doesn't he?

I sat with him for a minute, wishing I knew his name. I settled for saying, "Thanks for the party favors, man. I think they'll help a lot."

They did.

Later, I found the nearest truck stop and caught a ride with a cross-country trucker who needed a swamper and made it all the way to the West Coast where I got myself a new kind of life; a quiet one, with no guns. And that was that.

Except sometimes at night, when it rains, in the darkness I see dead guy's face and that shy smile and I smile right back at him.

About the Author - AJ Hayes lives near San Diego, California. His stories and poems been published in venues like Yellow Mama, Eaten Alive, A Twist Of Noir, Shotgun Honey, Black Heart Magazine's Noir Issue. The Hard-Nosed Sleuth, Apollo's Lyre, Flashshot, Skin Diver Magazine, Chris Rhatigan and Nigel Bird's Anthology: Pulp Ink. He's also in Off The Record and now Off The Record 2 (huzzah!) He likes to write about stuff and thinks it's nice to be able to fool some of the people some of the time—well, P.T. Barnum thought that first but AJ thinks so too.

The Graduate
by
Eric Beetner

Malone pushed the gun into Rodney's hand.

"It's your time, kid."

Rodney grinned. The moment he'd been waiting for since he was an actual kid. The chance to prove himself, to get inside.

The way it went in this organization was to wait it out until your turn. Your turn meant someone else had to die. Life expectancy in the business remained relatively low, whether from a disagreement with a business partner, the long arm of the law, or petty rivalries. To Rodney, the wait had been interminable.

No matter how your time rolled around, you had to prove yourself when it did. Never mind the past ten years Rodney spent doing anything and everything they asked. The slate was wiped clean. It was him, the gun, and whatever instructions came with it.

Malone let a sly smile move over his mouth. Seventy years old and he still loved the look on a recruit's face on the day they were about to get made. His three right-hand men took their cues from Malone and smiled out of reflex.

"You know what you gotta do with this?" he said, nodding toward the gun.

"Yes, Mr. Malone," Rodney said. "You say where and you say when."

"Don't you wanna know who?" Malone liked fucking with them a little bit.

Rodney swallowed. "Sure," Rodney said, correcting himself. "And who."

He'd only been allowed access to Malone's inner sanctum twice before, and only for seconds at a time. The dim lighting, rich wood and smell of decade's worth of Cuban cigars in the walls would have lulled Rodney to sleep if he weren't so keyed up and eager to get on with things.

"This time, we gotta make room, Rod."

Rodney nodded. Someone hadn't died on their own time. Someone needed a push.

"You understand what that means?" Malone asked, milking it.

Rodney nodded again, keeping silent for fear of putting his foot in his mouth again.

Malone pushed an eight-by-ten photograph, face down, across his desk. Rodney waited for a cue to move in and pick it up. Any sudden moves, especially toward the boss, would get him a knife in the back damn quick. And with three other men in the room he'd also be gifted with a knife across the throat and one in his liver. The inner sanctum was never to be disturbed by such din as a gunshot.

Malone gave an almost imperceptible nod and Rodney picked up the photo.

He nearly dropped the gun.

The face staring back at him was familiar. It was a face he expected in the room today. It was Stovall, the number two man in the organization.

Rodney unconsciously whispered, "Holy shit."

"You're okay with this?" Malone asked.

All part of the test. Rodney slapped his gaping jaw shut, did his best to man up. "No problem," he said. He set down the photo, turning it back over so Stovall's face wouldn't be staring at him anymore.

"You do this thing, you're in for good," Malone said.

Rodney nodded. He felt beads of sweat begin to form along his hair line. His stomach tightened, but he kept his best poker face on.

Malone pressed a button on the modern office phone / intercom system, an incongruous piece of contemporary technology in an otherwise old world office.

"Send him in."

Jesus H. Christ, thought Rodney. *They want me to bump off the number two man in the whole organization and they want me to do it right now?*

Malone steepled his fingers and kept a watchful eye on Rodney, looking for signs of weakness and hesitation. Rodney worked harder than ever to keep his expression neutral.

The face from the photo stepped into the room. Stovall wore his trademark three-piece suit, pocket square matching his tie, shine on his shoes. Professional all the way. Rodney wondered what the hell he did to make Malone so mad.

"What's up?" Stovall said, approaching the desk with ease. The second in command would have no reason to fear a trio of knives. His invitation into the inner sanctum was etched in stone. A bullet in the back he would never see coming.

Rodney took a firm grip on the gun. Stovall stood in front of him, between him and Malone. Rodney thought about the shot. If he fired now no way he'd miss, even with his jumpy nerves. If he did, he didn't fucking well deserve to get made. But, if he shot, he would aim for the head and if he hit Stovall in the skull then Malone would be covered with the brain of his ex-partner. That wouldn't look good for a debutante like Rodney, so he waited.

"Rodney here has some news for you," Malone said.

Stoval turned to face Rodney, not a hint of worry on his face.

Rodney's bowels rumbled. Why did Malone make the man turn to face him? A hell of a test. He never thought it would be this hard, and he'd thought about this moment a thousand times. Stovall's face never entered into it beyond being a spectator on the sidelines.

"What's up, kid?"

Rodney wasn't putting Stovall out of his misery, he was putting himself out of his own misery. He lifted the gun, tried for the coldest steel expression on his face for the benefit of his audience, and pulled the trigger – blood spray be damned. If this is what Malone wanted, this is what the boss man would get.

The gun clicked. He pulled again. Click. Empty.

Stovall was the first to crack a smile. The three muscles behind Malone knew better and waited for the big man to crack. When

119

he did, the whole room grinned in silence. It was the most unsettling sound Rodney'd ever not heard.

"You fucked up, kid," Malone said.

"But . . ." Rodney didn't see how it was his fault they gave him an unloaded gun. And why the hell was Stovall smiling when he almost got shot in the face?

"You never turn a gun on one of the family."

At once, the smiles faded, replaced by stony anger.

Rodney knew. He'd failed the test. Turned out it was a trick question. The right answer would have been to refuse the target. Show a pair of balls and stand up to Malone.

A trickle of sweat slid down across the bridge of his nose. Stovall stepped aside. Three knives were unsheathed. Rodney let the gun fall to the floor, closed his eyes, and waited.

About the Author - Eric Beetner is the author of The Devil Doesn't Want Me, Dig Two Graves and the short story collection A Bouquet of Bullets. He is co-author (With JB Kohl) of the novels One Too Many Blows To The Head and Borrowed Trouble. He has also written two novellas in the Fightcard series, Split Decision and A Mouth Full Of Blood, under the name Jack Tunney. His short stories have appeared in more than ten anthologies. For more info visit ericbeetner.blogspot.com

Unforgiven
by
Ian Ayris

My dad was a docker. And me granddad. Lived and died on the docks, they did. Both of em. Me, I never got the chance.

Most of the actual docks are still here, you know, the watery bits. But they turned em into places for posh boats and stuff. Rich boys paddlin pools, that sort of shit. The warehouses and the market and the clubs, and all the other stuff, all that stuff what made this place so special in the old days, it's all gone. Flattened. Levelled. Fucked. And where all that life was, they went and built an airport on it.

Who'd have thought it, eh. Round here. A fuckin airport. My dad would have laughed himself silly at the thought. Me granddad, he would've spit his stout all down his front.

But There it is. Right there. All big and shiny and new.

I only been there once, the airport. There was this job in the paper, see. Baggage handler. The docks was gone, but I'm thinkin, least I could carry on the family tradition, you know, workin where the docks was. Close as I was gonna get to followin me old man's footsteps, I reckoned.

So I phone em up and they send me a form. I send it back to em all filled in with me best handwritin. And I get this call they wanna see me. Cushty, I thought. I'm in. So I mosey on over in me Top Man suit and me twenty quid shoes, and a fair bit of hope in me heart.

Was bigger than what I thought, the airport. Huge. Me dad used to tell me the docks was massive in the old days, like its own little world. And walkin into this aiport, it's sort of like that. People everywhere. Millin about. Thousands of em. And there's shops and places to eat, and everything. A proper world of its own.

I take meself a deep breath, put me best foot forward and ask one of the security where to go. I show him the letter. 'Good luck,' he says, sort of like he means it but takin the piss at the same time. Couldn't work out which, if I'm honest. Too nervous, see.

But I let it go.

When I find the office, I knock on the door. 'Come in,' someone says.

There's two people when I got inside. All suited up, sittin behind a desk. A geezer and a bird.

They was all pucker, to begin with. Askin if I got there all right, where I see the advert, stuff like that. But then it gets a bit . . . well, you know, they starts askin me about me 'previous experience'. 'Other jobs'. Now I'm a bit touchy on that subject. I've turned over a new leaf since I come out the nick. All I'm askin for's a fuckin chance.

'Previous?' I says. 'Other jobs?'

That's right, they say.

'Mr Livingstone,' the geezer says, 'we only want to ascertain your suitability for the post.' Says it all posh. Like he could shit on me any time he wants.

So I'm straight with em. Tell em about me time inside and how I'm turnin over a new leaf. I tell em about me dad. How he was on the docks from leavin school, shiftin this and shiftin that. How he'd come home for his supper, knackered and filthy, but you know, settled for havin done a day's work. And I tell em about me granddad and how he worked the docks forty years, till a box of bananas fell on his head. Squashed him flat. Tell em I come here to follow the family tradition. Not the bananas bit. Wouldn't wanna go that way. But, you know, workin where they worked.

'You do know this is an airport, Mr Livingstone, I presume?' the geezer says. He's sayin the 'I presume' bit every time he says me name, like it's funny or something. Fuck knows why.

I don't get it, meself, but the bird next to him's smirkin every time he says it. I ain't in there much longer than another ten minutes.

'Thank you, for your time,' the geezer says. 'We'll be in touch soon.'

Two weeks later I get this letter sayin I ain't got the job. They wished me luck findin something else, and that. But it was too late for

122

fuckin niceties. If they'd have just listened. If they'd just understood, you know, about me turnin over a new leaf, wantin the job cos of me old man and me granddad, and the docks, and not took the fuckin piss, I'd have forgot the whole business. But they didn't.

So, I couldn't.

I give me old mate Danny a bell. You don't wanna know what shit he's into. Trust me. You don't.

But if you wanna make a difference, up the ante, so to speak, Danny's your man.

***

I'm on me way back there, to the airport, gettin out the station, me sports bag slung over me shoulder.

There's the same security guard. I give him a nod. He nods back.

'All right?' he says.

I nod. I don't smile. Puts the shit up him. I walk on.

Queues of people, whinin and moanin and grumblin and thinkin they're the most important fuckin people in the whole fuckin world. But they ain't worth fuck all, these sort. Standin there with their business suits and their mobile fuckin phones and their laptops. None of em would've lasted ten minutes in me old man's day. Five at most.

All the pretend's gone now. I went for that shitty job in good fuckin faith. I was tryin to go straight. I really was. But they laughed in me face.

I head for the karzi.

There's a geezer with his back to me, havin a shave at one of the sinks. One of the shit-houses is locked, but there's no-one at the pissers. I'm as good as on me own. Mind you, I don't care if no cunt sees me anyway.

I put the bag on the floor. Open it up. And I think of me dad and me granddad livin and dyin on the docks.

I take out Danny's piece of kit and feel the weight of it in me hands.

123

The geezer at the sink turns round as he hears me load up. I pop him with a quick blast, and watch him explode into the mirror. Then I'm out the karzi and into the airport proper. Stridin. Fuckin stridin. And I'm blastin away and there's people screamin and runnin and bleedin and dyin and I'm cutting em down like Clint Eastwood in that cowboy film where he goes mental at the end.

You know, that one where you know it's comin all the way through and when it does, when it does come, it's just so fuckin beautiful.

About the Author - Ian Ayris lives in London, England with his wife and three children. He is the author of almost forty short stories, including a story in the prestigious Mammoth Book of Best British Crime and his debut novel - ABIDE WITH ME - was published by Caffeine Nights Publishing in March 2012. More details of Ian's work can be found online at www.ianayris.com.

Kiki's Delivery Service
by
Gill Hoffs

The sound of the sirens gives me a buzz, as does the wind on my neck and the cool-box strapped to my bike. Someone else's organs mean I zip past Porsches and police cars, complete strangers willing me on with a peep as I nip round a bus and slalom through a junction. I'm leaving a human shell behind, a hollowed body stapled shut without rush or fuss, relatives grieving in the waiting room as the surgeon clips wounds closed without fear of a seizure or consideration of scars.

When a human dies, there are certain time frames one needs to bear in mind. Some faiths require the remains to be disposed of by the next day at the latest. Some expect a vigil, or a wake. All deserve respect, support, and no judgement.

Their organs need coolness and speed.

With kidneys, I can stop for lunch. Maybe dinner and a nap, too. Seventy two hours means I could probably walk most of the distances I choose to zoom through instead.

Hearts and lungs are trickier, four hours, tops. Sometimes, if it's not just a case of a quick dash across Glasgow and the central belt from corpse to cure, I have to pilot the helicopter instead of my bike. If it's windy, and it's Scotland, so it's *always* windy somewhere, I run the risk of becoming organ fodder myself or a burning splat in a valley or on a hilltop speckled with sheep. I don't even bother nipping to the toilet with trips like this. Every minute counts and I've a stash of waterproof pads and piss bottles by the pilot's seat in the cockpit for those occasions where I just can't hold out a moment longer. There's been more than one occasion when I've pelted through the hospital with a cool-box in my hand and a turtle's head in my pants, handed over the organ, and just kept running.

Like tonight. The heart and lungs sloshing next to me make me glad to be alive and gainfully employed, happy to act the hero, and break the speed limits to do it. They also make me regret the curry goat from last night and every mouthful of rice and peas that went with it.

If I was in the helicopter, I'd be crunching a bag of dry roasted now, remembering Laurel & Hardy in hospital and their 'hard boiled eggs and nuts' routine. But on the bike, that's not an option. Neither's a butt-plug nor a nappy. I'm pretty sure I'm touching cloth.

Our site says we go from 'theatre to theatre'. It's truer than Kiki might think. I heard her bitching a few months ago about costs and how she might need to cut my post just to keep the company going, go back to doing collections and drop-offs herself. Even though she gets bike-sick now, and has lost her nerve and her need for speed. Even though it would mean her taking calls and sorting details on a fucking Bluetooth while she was at it.

She said most of the donors were dying elsewhere now, places with their own courier services and crash teams who'd happily drop everything and take our business. From Stranraer to the Shetlands, Aberdeen to Orkney, some other outfit would do the job.

I don't want to be unemployed again. I don't want to sit on too-low chairs, security guards scowling around the place, waiting waiting forever waiting, on jobs and forms and fuck offs and come heres. I don't want to trail off for pointless interviews for jobs I'll never get and never want to, and sit in an MP's office while he talks shit about interview techniques and first impressions when everyone knows he got a leg up for getting his leg over with the boss's daughter, and later, his wife.

So I've fixed it.

More local lungs and possible pancreases, convenient corneas and trade for the funeral homes. A clip with the bike on a busy street, a shove into traffic or a knife wound in an alley beside the stage door, and suddenly there's a bundle of patients off the wards and waiting lists, back in jobs, and giving me work before they do it. Over forty organs can be harvested from a single body. Forty! That's three football teams and the substitutes, right there. Maybe enough for a referee too.

A card in their pocket with a smudge of a squiggle, an ambulance, and everyone's happy.

Well, everyone *I* know.

Including Kiki.

About the Author - Gill Hoffs, 33, lives with her family and Coraline Cat in Warrington, England. Her fiction and nonfiction are widely available online and in print, and her first book 'Wild: a collection' is out now from Pure Slush. All links are available at http://gillhoffs.wordpress.com/ but if you want to send her chocolate (Mars Caramels are her current favourite) you'll need to email scottishredridinghood@hotmail.com for her postal address.

Apt Pupil
by
Pete Sortwell

Boozers, I love them. The people, the layout, the décor — everything. Then there's the beer, of course. I fucking LOVE the beer. None of these new age alcoholic milkshakes that the student types who insist on coming to my local drink. Just beer for me.

I hate students. They don't do anything productive. They just sit there staring at the world and nattering to themselves about how great they'll all be one day. It's always 'one day' with this lot. There's just no get up and go in them.

I use my local most days. I ain't an alky or nothing, I just like the atmos. Except when the local adult learners come in to shake each other's satchels in celebration of spelling their name right.

I mean, I work hard six days a week — well four and a half out of seven. Call me a liar if you like, but I contribute more to society than these wasters ever will. The times I'm sat at home catching up when I could be in my local, I tell you; if I got paid for all the overtime, my salary would be doubled, I swear.

I saw one of them pay for three drinks with a cheque the other day. For god's sake! A cheque for under a fiver! Barry, the landlord, made them buy a couple of packets of crisps to make the money up. He hates them as much as I do. Mind you, he still takes their money. If I was him, I wouldn't. If it was down to me I'd ban the lot of the chair-stealing sad acts. In fact, I have actually made a few anonymous signs, but Barry always tells me to take them down, says there is more than one way to skin a toad, whatever the fuck that means. I hope he hasn't tried skinning one without me; I'd like to see that.

'What the fuck does that mean?' I asked Barry one night after he'd rolled out his favourite cliché.

'Well, Greg, I've got a plan to get them lot back for keeping on making my bogs smell of that Wanja leaf,' Barry told me, leaning in closely and lowering his already gravel-like voice.

'Can I put a hate poster up?' I ask hopefully.

'Give it a rest with the posters, will you Greg? You don't even spell them right,' Barry says, a little louder than necessary, making old Tom and big Jimmy Temple piss themselves at the other end of the bar.

'I bloody …' I start.

'Spastic!' Big Jim hollers, interrupting me mid-denial. Everyone in the pub laughed. Even the fucking students that were over near the pool table. I vowed to remember their public disrespect towards me.

'OK, so no posters. What are you going to do, Bazzer?' I asked, continuing to ignore big Jim who had started making spak noises.

'I think we should do what him next door,' Barry continued, with a flick of his head towards Stavros on the other side of the wall, 'does to everyone's chips, Greg.'

'Spunk in them?'

'Oh god! He don't do that, does he?' Barry asked, repulsed.

'I wouldn't put it past him, the filthy bastard. I haven't been in since I saw him sweating into the fryer. Smiling away he was. He must have known he was leaking into my dinner.'

'The dirty bastard! That's the last time I eat there,' Barry spat out in disgust.

'Yeah, don't eat there, mate. So, what's the plan to get the students?'

'Well, I was thinking about spiking the bastards with Kaliber and then letting them pretend to be drunk. But I might use Stavros's trick now and just gob in their drink.'

'Erggrrrrh,' Jim shouts out.

'Quiet, Jim,' Barry tells him, waving his shushing finger about and giving the students a sideways glance.

'You could gob in their Kaliber,' I offer hopefully.

129

'That's a grand idea. I must ask you though, Greg, why do you hate them so much? I mean, they're your students …'

About the Author - Having developed a love of telling porkies as a child, Pete now puts his bad habits to good use, and sticks to writing fiction instead of telling people he swum the channel. In ten minutes. When he was three. His debut Novel, So Low, So High will be published in 2013 (brace yourselves) and his new comedy e-book 'The Village Idiot Reviews' is out late September 2012 (again, brace yourselves) If you want to contact him Twitter is the best place. Unsurprisingly @petesortwell wasn't taken when he registered a few months ago.

Memphis Belle
by
Allan Watson

As the escalator shuddered on its steep ascent from the depths of the Turbine Hall, Bloomsbury glanced back at his boss a few steps below. 'So, Guv, you think we've finally got our man?'

John Stent bared his teeth like an old seasoned wolf about to feast on fresh meat. 'If Lily Weisler's sister is telling the truth, then Christian Haran will be leaving here tonight in handcuffs.'

Bloomsbury gave a low whistle. 'Nicking Haran in the Tate Modern at his own opening night? You do realise it's going to be teeming with media monkeys?'

'Poetic justice. Let's see how he enjoys being the prize exhibit in the dock of the Old Bailey, charged with first-degree murder.'

This would be Stent's last murder case before retiring and Bloomsbury knew the old warrior wanted to go out with a bang. He just hoped Stent wasn't so desperate to end his career on high note that he'd overlooked some vital detail that would leave him with egg on his face. Fucking up in front of a celebrity-strewn guest list with the press in close attendance wasn't the best way to bring the curtain down on an unblemished career.

A month ago, a design student, Lily Weisler, from Memphis, Tennessee, was reported missing to the police. They discovered Lily had been working for the shock-tactic visual artist Christian Haran. Her co-workers said Lily Weisler had been in love with Haran and it was an open secret the artist had rebuffed her advances. Perhaps a valid reason for her dropping off the radar? As far as the police were concerned Weisler was a responsible adult, and unless new evidence came to light, they wouldn't be pursuing the case any further.

Everything changed when Lily's blood-soaked handbag and clothing were found in a waste bin near the Tate Modern. Suddenly the police were falling over themselves to crack the case. Haran's design team were re-interviewed and Christian Haran himself was hauled in and grilled by DCI Stent.

Haran was a controversial figure in the art world, having been short-listed the previous year in the Turner Prize for his work entitled 'Dead Heads'. This entailed posing thirty human heads inside glass boxes. The heads were fitted with mechanical hinges allowing the jaws to move, giving the impression of speech. Concealed speakers completed the illusion by broadcasting monologues of actors reading passages from pornographic magazines. Haran had been branded obscene and godless by the British public, but he'd also become wealthy as a natural by-product of such notoriety. His latest exhibition was guaranteed to cause yet another uproar. Using a revolutionary new embalming process, Haran intended posing corpses in a display of carefully constructed tableaux to recreate iconic movie scenes.

The artist naturally denied any knowledge of how Lily Weisler might have come to harm, and in the absence of a body, even raised the possibility that Weisler herself had planted the blood-soaked clothing as a means of generating negative publicity for his latest exhibition. Without any solid incriminating evidence, Haran was released without charge and with no other obvious suspects, the investigation quickly ran out of steam. It looked destined to be filed away as a Cold Case until things took an unexpected twist that very afternoon. The missing girl's sister, Zelda Weisler, had turned up at the police station crying hysterically and claiming she had proof Christian Haran had murdered her sibling.

Zelda told Stent and Bloomsbury she had flown in that morning from Memphis, making the Tate Modern her first port of call knowing that Haran would be putting the finishing touches to his macabre exhibits. Not surprisingly he'd stuck to his tale of innocence, but when a gallery electrician had taken the artist aside to inspect a lighting problem, Zelda noticed one of the cadavers in his collection not only closely resembled her missing sister, but also had a tattoo of a rosebud decorating its left ankle, the very same tattoo her sister had inscribed for her 18th birthday. Without waiting to confront Haran directly, she had fled the art gallery, called the police switchboard and was directed to John Stent.

Leaving the escalator, the detectives followed the signs towards the Tate Modern's new star attraction. Stent was still shaking his head in disbelief. 'Hiding the victim in full view of the public and the press? Even the title of the tableau takes the piss. *Memphis Belle*? Can you credit the arrogance of the man?'

Bloomsbury still had a niggling feeling they had overlooked something important in the excitement of pinning the murder on Haran. But there was no more time to think about it as they arrived at the large doors emblazoned with 'A Night at the Movies'. Two security guards held the doors open as the detectives approached and both men were momentarily speechless at what their eyes beheld within.

The walls and ceiling of the darkened room were criss-crossed with blue and green neon tubes giving an unhealthy pallor to the milling crowd of people inside, the only islands of brightness in this neon gloom emanating from the half dozen flood-lit set pieces. These were what the crowd had come to gawp at and Tweet their friends about. The finishing touches to the eerie ambience included the cinematic whirr of a film projector running at high speed and the smell of buttered popcorn wafting strongly over the combined secondary scents of perfume, after-shave and human sweat.

Stent scanned the room, taking in the assorted tableaux dedicated to famous movie scenes. On the far side of the room a very dead Forrest Gump sat on a park bench, probably contemplating that death was a box of chocolates. Nearby, a necrotic Marilyn Monroe preened above an air vent that gusted her skirt above her cold, dead hips. He also spotted a macabre cross-dressing Tootsie, a bowler-hatted Clockwork Orange Alex leering through a triangular opening, and a female corpse posed on its stomach, crossed legs behind her and smoking a cigarette.

'Pulp Fiction,' prompted Bloomsbury seeing Stern struggle to place the reference. 'I think the one we're looking for is over there.'

Both men approached a low platform that featured a full sized nose-cone and cock-pit from a B17 Flying Fortress. Suspended by wires from the side of the cock-pit was a dead woman with long blonde hair wearing a bright red swimming costume, one thigh upraised to emulate the famous pin-up emblem of the US Air Force. Stent removed a photograph from his jacket and compared the likeness between the missing and the dead. It was difficult to be a hundred per cent certain, but if what the Lily Weisler's sister claimed was true…… Stent moved closer to inspect the cadaver's left ankle, experiencing a rush of blood to the head as he spotted the incriminating rosebud tattoo. It was half obscured as if a crude attempt had been made to disguise the tattoo with flesh-tone make-up.

'It's her, Bloomsbury. We've got the bastard cold.'

They found Christian Haran holding court with a large group of journalists. Pushing a photographer aside, Stent said loudly. 'I've a question for you, Haran. I'd like to know where you procure the bodies for your disgusting freak-shows.'

Haran smiled as if he'd expected this intrusion. 'I buy them, Chief Inspector. You've no idea how many poor people in Eastern Europe are only too happy to spare themselves the expense of burying an unloved family member. And it's all perfectly legal once the proper embalming and preservation treatments have been carried out.'

'What about that one over there?' Stent gestured towards the Memphis Belle set-piece.

The other guests had sensed there was a new event unfolding in the hall and began to congregate around Haran and the policemen. The artist looked like he was enjoying this. 'Ah, Memphis Belle. She was a very special acquisition. Such a good-looking young girl. I had to pay well over the odds to convince her family to release her into my care.'

'A higher price than you can possibly realise.' Stent flashed a glance at his colleague. 'Bloomsbury, place this man under arrest.'

Haran smiled even wider. 'You're arresting me? On what charge, exactly?'

'The murder of your former assistant, Lily Weisler.'

It seemed everyone in the room was now crowded around the three men, hemming them in while flashbulbs strobed through the gloom as the press gorged themselves into a feeding frenzy.

Haran still seemed unfazed by the accusation. 'And what proof would you have of that, may I ask?'

'We can go into all that later. Let's just say a certain distinguishing mark gives me just cause to make the arrest.'

'Then I'm sure you won't mind pointing out this distinguishing mark to the gathered company.'

Stent sensed the mood of the mob growing ugly as someone shouted out, 'Fucking police stitch-up!' Knowing that not to accede to the man's request might set off a minor riot, Stent reluctantly steered Haran to the Memphis Belle tableau. Once there, he pointed to the half-obscured rosebud tattoo on the cadaver's left ankle. 'There's your proof. Do you still deny it?'

The artist's only response was to beckon over a drinks hostess. Haran lifted a small glass of clear spirit from her tray and dipped his pocket handkerchief into the liquid before reaching up to stroke at the corpse's ankle. Instead of removing the flesh-tone make-up, the alcohol on the linen handkerchief also obliterated the rosebud tattoo itself so that the ankle now displayed only bare, discoloured flesh.

'Voila!' cried Haran. 'Looks like I'm once more an innocent man.'

Stern's face was white with shock and Bloomsbury noted with alarm that his superior was hyperventilating. Staring into the laughing mob surrounding them, one face in particular leapt out at Bloomsbury. He realised too late what their mistake had been. They hadn't thought to verify the credentials of the woman claiming to be Lily Weisler's sister. Taking hold of Stern's arm he led the broken man through the jeering throng towards the exit.

Hours later when the hall was cleared, Haran walked his personal assistant to the door and kissed her on the lips. 'I have to hand it to you, Zelda. You're one hell of an actress. I could get you into the movie business, you know.'

135

The girl stared at the grisly models across the room. 'No thanks, Christian. If you don't mind I'll pass on that offer for the time being.'

Haran grinned. 'I'll make sure your bonus is in the bank first thing tomorrow. The exposure from tonight's publicity stunt is incalculable.'

Once he was alone, Haran slowly made his way across to where Forrest Gump sat on his park bench. Taking a seat beside the corpse, Haran leaned down and gently lifted the left trouser leg to reveal a small rosebud tattoo.

'Thank you for this, Lily,' he whispered to the cadaver. And then just as gently he let the trouser leg fall to conceal the ankle once more.

About the Author - Allan Watson is a writer whose work leans towards the dark and disturbing realms of the fiction spectrum. He is the author of four novels and two collections of short stories. In between books, he wrote extensively for BBC Scotland, churning out hundreds of comedy sketches for radio and TV, in addition to being a regular contributor for the iconic 'Herald Diary'. When not dickering with stories he masquerades as a composer/musician with Candy Séance and Columbus Road, as well as collaborating with best selling crime writer Phil Rickman in a semi-fictional band named Lol Robinson with Hazey Jane II whose albums have sold on four different continents (Antarctica was a hard one to crack).
Allan lives and works in Glasgow, Scotland, but has never worn the kilt or eaten a deep fried Mars Bar. He is currently pretending to work on something new.

Weekend At Bernie's
by
Benoit Lelièvre

Fuck me. The boss is dead.

Bernie Lomax, scourge of Wall-Street, croaked face first into a batch of Chinese blow. It scattered in his hair, like shit-brown pellicles. White men who love Asia too much have a habit of dying before their time. Heat strokes, STDs, Russian Roulette, dick chopped off for debt settlement or in Bernie's case, overdose on shitty drugs. It truly is the land of a million dangers. Poor Bernie. I'm going to party over your dead body, just like I told you I would.

Lomax, you fucking asshole.

I call everyone. Larry, Gwen, the gay musclehead twins he hired as private fitness coaches. I spread the gospel of Bernie's death and everyone is happy. Good fucking riddance. Bernie was my boss for twenty-seven years, so I know most of the people in his address book. Better yet, I know the majority of them despise him. The old rat ran an insurance business for desperate millionaires. You're a flight risk? A degenerate Wall-Street gambler, a soulless adrenaline junkie with money to spare? Whatever your stupid projects are, Bernie Lomax is there to insure your ass and make you legit. For a fee.

Or was there. Bernie's dead. I love saying it. Dead. Dead. Dead. Dead. Bernie's dead.

I drag his body to the deserted kitchen freezer and make phone call after phone call. All afternoon. In six hours, I reach ninety-eight people and convince seventy-two of them to show up for 10 PM. It'll be a massacre. A party for the ages, just the way Bernie loved them. Except this time, it's at his expense.

I fantasize about what I'll do to him. Something symbolic? No, too easy. Too boring. He worked me like a dog, day and night, with my cell phone as a leash. Eighty hours a week, sometimes a hundred, at the market price for a contract analyst. No paid overtime.

One week of unpaid vacation every year, while still remaining on call. Whenever I threatened to leave (I did, several times), he was quick to remind me that what we were doing wasn't exactly legal. I knew it, he knew it and so did the IRS. I have a wife and a twelve year old son, so I never could walk out and cut a deal with the authorities. All these years, I dreamed of him in an orange jumpsuit, bunking with a three hundred pounds biker. Now that Bernie's checked out on his own, he needs more than petty vengeance. He deserves a spectacular send-off. Fireworks. Up his ass. Bernie's Butt Bacchanalia.

My mind wanders to strange places. Sick, twisted, dark horizons I never before dared visit. I'm seeing Bernie crucified behind the bar, or at least tied to a cross. Naked and covered in beer, eggs, paint, flour, whatever we can find around the house. People taking turns cutting off strands of hair.

Target practice with a nail gun? Why not?

Bernie's Bachelor Party.

I have other visions of Bernie's corpse all white and powdered up, propped up on the couch with a drink in hand, as if he were still alive. People taking turns sitting next to him, abusing him to their heart's desire. No holds barred. Punching, kicking, kneeing, spitting, peeing, anything goes. I would stay behind the couch all night long, putting him back in place for the next visitor, insulting him and vomiting all my frustrations upon him. Nobody ever fucked with Bernie when he was alive. He did all the fucking and never shared. It's all that mattered to him. Power.

***

We improvised. Bernie's propped up on his pool table, wedged between beer kegs like a drunk. He's naked, save for his stupid, Irish-flag golf socks. Cindy Bonilla, an ex-intern he brutalized at cocktail parties has put her lipstick to good use and inscribed: "GODSPEED, COCKSUCKER" on his chest. People take turns shaving off parts of his hair and mustache and engage in general mischief with his carcass.

Larry Wilson wrapped Bernie's hand around his dick.

138

Dan Moreira put stupid-looking shades on his face and a sun hat. He almost looks alive.

Linda Thornton poured two full buckets of sand on Bernie's fifty thousand dollars pool table.

We're tearing the place up, having ourselves a great time. Tomorrow, it's back to the wife and kid, but right now I feel like a new man. Everything is possible. I haven't drank and danced like this since my twenties. Since I accepted a certain job as financial analyst, in a certain controversial Manhattan insurance company. I have a lot to apologize for to my family. Wasted years. Wasted youth. A fucked up family portrait. But I feel alive, capable of tackling the challenge. I want to reclaim my life from the devil's hands.

Then it happens.

Nobody seems to notice at first. Bernie is being moved around by his former employees, so his position isn't always stable. Earlier tonight, he fell backwards twice and tumbled off the table, causing everyone present to laugh. The party slows down, but panic doesn't settle in until Bernie coughs. He has a terrible smoker's cough. He dry heaves like he's about to puke a lung out. It lasts forever. The room is frozen in terror and anticipation. Nobody can believe their eyes. I feel forced to say something.

"Bernie. You were dead, man. Holy shit."

This is not an excuse. Not for the boss. I suppose he's still the boss, now that he's back to life. What we did to him, you wouldn't do to a normal human being out of pity, respect, common sense, whatever. We wouldn't have done it to Bernie out of fear, knowing he could and would retaliate.

But he was dead.

Fuck.

"The fuck are you talking about, Parker? Do I look dead to you, bunch of motherfuckers? Could a dead man do this?" says Bernie, before delivering a swift back hand to a poor soul he wronged in the past. Guy goes flying backwards, flops on the floor, lifeless. Bernie finds the words on his chest. They are hard to miss. "Godspeed, what? What the fuck? What the fuck are you guys doing in my beach home?

139

You think you're clever huh? Bunch of fucking worms. I'll show you what it costs to fuck with Bernie Lomax. I'll fuck you all up, then I'll have you all arrested."

It's crazy how well he recuperates from death. He swivels his hips and jumps off the table in seconds. His legs are shaky, but he doesn't go down. Instead he walks behind the bar. People clear out of his way. Stares locked on the floor. Silence. A storm is coming.

Bernie disappears for a moment and I understand he's opening the trap door behind the bar. I noticed the lock on the floor years ago, but I'm not paid to ask questions.

Wasn't paid, anyways.

***

Bernie has been behind the bar for ten minutes, now. Or should I say, standing ON the bar. Still butt-naked and purple with anger, shooting at anything that moves with his .12 gauge shotgun. Not an old, raggedy hunting weapon. Some high tech shit used by the Russian Army. I've seen that weapon on "Deadliest Warrior". I guess Bernie's a fan too. Guests are hidden behind couches, under the pool table. The courageous souls who tried to leave are now dead.

Dead for real, not Bernie-dead.

I'm hiding behind the interior Jacuzzi (because there is an exterior one), trying to figure out how to save myself. I need to get to that gun stash.

"Bernie," I bark, from my hideout. Buckshot blasts through the Jacuzzi and comes close to amputating my liver. He's really lost it. "I always hated you, you arrogant piece of shit. You're not getting away with this. No way, man. You're going down. "

I watch my words sink in. His neck vein pops out and he aims for my head. I forgot this was a semi-automatic weapon. Once again, death eludes me by an inch and my skull becomes an echo chamber.

"You're a fucking worm, Parker. You always have been. I've been giving cock to that wife you've orphaned for the last six years."

140

"What?"

Bernie fires, but the gun is empty. Crazy Russian semi-automatic shotguns can inflict a world of damage, but they take time to reload. I move to the pool table, under which Wilson lays, catatonic with fear. Now, at least I have pool balls to defend myself. The plan is to get Bernie off the bar, so I can reach the gun stash. It's a stupid plan since I've never fired a gun, but it's the best I can come up with.

"Every Wednesday and Sunday, when I have you work on those bullshit contracts. What do you think I've been doing huh? Banging your wife and raising your faggot son."

He's trying to get under my skin. He must be. Evelyn is loyal. I've treated her and Scottie like dirt, but she's loyal. She's my woman. I've been loyal to her, after all. But Bernie has a point. He made me work twice a week on foreign contracts for clients I never met. Just plowing through a thick pile of contracts, alone at my desk. Housing development in Shangai for Mr. Wang Low. Import-Export deal in Abu Dhabi for Ahmad Muhammad. Doubt creeps into my spirit. Things were going so well.

"I stole two hundred grand from you, motherfucker," I say. "Maybe more."

His eyes bulge out. Then he shoots two more cartridges into the pool table. Wood splinters everywhere. It was a nice table.

"You lying cocksucker. It's impossible."

As my only answer, I throw a pool ball. Number 2, the solid blue one. I miss my target and the ball goes crashing into the liquor bottles. At least ten thousand dollars of damage, maybe more. Bernie shoots whatever he's got into the pool table. It gets so bad, it doesn't look like a pool table anymore.

"I've been stealing from you for years. How did you think I paid for my summer house in Montauk with the shit wages you gave me? You want to know the worst part? I've only been there twice. Because of you," I say.

"I should've known. I should've fucking known."

I whip the cue ball at him and this time, it hits his shoulder. His collar bone, I think. Bernie winces, reaches for his shoulder and loses balance. He falls to the marble floor with an almost comical thud. My chance. I need out of here, so I can make up with Evelyn and Scottie. For once, I'm fucking doing something for them.

Bernie is lying on his back, confused and searching for his shotgun above his head. His dick is as pea between his legs. I can't help staring at it. Men call each other gay for eyeing at each other's dick all the time, but whip one out and every man in the room's eyes will lock onto it. I make a play for the shotgun and step over Bernie to reach it. Bad move. He pops up from the floor like a wildlife predator and uppercuts me in the family jewels. Black dots flash before my eyes as I feel his thumbs digging into my throat.

"Parker, ya sonofabitch. What did ya do? How much did ya steal, ya cocksucking scoundrel?"

We back up against a low table and tumble to the floor. My throat burns, my junk hurts, this is the end of the world. I swing my arms at him as best I can, but life is leaving me. My vision is darkening around the corners. I feel like my throat is being crushed by a boulder.

Fuck.

After all this, I can't believe he's going to kill me.

***

I wake up. I'm surprised to still be breathing and that my crotch still hurts. I'm not in heaven. There aren't any naked angelwomen with wings, harps, fans and grapes. None of that. Next to me is a blown to hell, splintered pool table and the body of a young woman in a bikini. Her gaze is empty and there's a hole in her chest plate, where her heart used to be. Somewhere, I can hear Bernie's rage echo through his silent property.

We killed a man and awakened a demon.

People are fighting on the mezzanine. I can hear them grunt. Bernie, especially who grunts like he's breathing fire. This is my chance. God gave me a window of opportunity and if I survive this, I'm buying season tickets to Sunday mass.

I was right. The weapons stash had more than a shotgun in it. There was an AK47, grenades, a handful of handguns and even a rocket launcher. Hard to imagine what purpose Bernie foresaw for these toys. The rich and powerful sometimes do strange things with their money. There are over 140 personal apocalypse bunkers in California. When you don't have to worry about the bills, you worry about different shit. Maslow's pyramid and all.

I opt for the rocket launcher, because I don't want to leave Bernie any chance of survival this time. I learned my lesson in blood and testicular trauma. Bernie is indeed on the mezzanine, duking it out with Wilson. The poor sucker. He always tried so hard. Dressed sharper than anyone else (way too sharp for the office), laughed louder at the boss' jokes, worked weekends for no reason, etc. Stupidity of youth. Now he's failing miserably at hand-to-hand combat. Bernie has him in the same chokehold he had me in earlier, bent over the railing. He sees me taking aim.

"Parker, I swear to god, if you fire that thing, I'm going to fucking murder you."

"Go for it, Bernie. Do your worst."

I laugh at the irony as I prepare to pulverize his ass. As I press the trigger, he bounces up on the railing and jumps from it like a goddamn bat on National Geographic Channel. I see the rocket fly right under him and Wilson, poor Wilson, disappears into a ball of fire before Bernie latches on to me and sends me sliding across the room. My head bumps against the floor, then against a couch or something. I don't know where I am. I can't see too well because the room is spinning.

The smell of sweat is filling my nostrils as I feel Bernie's arms lock around my torso. His forearm slide across my neck and he says: "You can't kill the devil, Parker. I created you. I made you who you are. If men can't kill God, you sure as shit can't kill me."

About the Author - Benoît Lelièvre is twenty-nine years old and lives Montreal, Canada. His stories have been published in

143

Needle Magazine, Crime Factory, Beat to a Pulp: Hardboiled, Beat to a Pulp: Superhero, The Flash Fiction Offensive and the first Off The Record. He blogs about books, movies and pop culture at <u>Dead End Follies</u> and is a member of <u>LitReactor</u>'s news team. He's currently working on a novel project.

Silver Dream Racer
by
Paul D. Brazill

A storm shattered the early morning sky as Marcus Finch stumbled out
of *Blackjax Casino*, slurring a James Blunt song, a bitter grin crawling
over his face. His black Hugo Boss suit was quickly soaked and rain
slithered over his chrome-dome

Toby Finch shuffled out after him. Shivered. Pulled his
yellow t-shirt over his blond, curly hair.

'W … w … why are we … leaving now, Marcus?'

'Because I say so, Toby Juggs. Because I friggin say so.'

'Did we lose … lose a lot tonight?'

Marcus took out his car keys and unlocked his silver Aston
Martin with a near silent 'pop'.

'At the roulette wheels, quite a bit, yes. But not just there.'

'If you don't risk, you don't drink champagne, eh?' Toby
grinned.

Marcus gave a little growl, jammed the keys in Toby's hand
and shoved him toward the car.

They both got in. Toby shook his head like a wet dog.

'For fucks sake, Toby. Can't you at least attempt to be cool?'

Marcus looked daggers at his younger brother but Toby said
nothing.

'Drive,' said Marcus. He banged on the steering wheel and
Toby started up the car.

'Wagon's Roll,' said Toby.

They drove along Clerkenwell Road, the neon signs and
street lamps streaking the night sky. Marcus leaned forward and
turned up the radio. Fields Of Barley. Fields Of Gold. He lay back and
closed his eyes.

Toby stopped at a set of traffic lights and turned to Marcus. His eyes were still closed. His lips moving, silently counting. Keeping himself from exploding.

He was pissed off beyond belief. Another wasted night.

Marcus wasn't particularly fond of gambling, truth be told, and he'd actually gone to the casino to try and pick up the tall, blond croupier- Asia, Kasia, Dasia, whatever her name was – that he'd been hoping to bang for months.

But, it turned out she'd gone back home to Czechoslovakia, or somewhere, to visits a sick mother.

And then he'd lost a packet playing poker. A lot more than he could afford to lose, too.

A rage was burning inside him and there was only one way to put out the flames. Violence. Random, violence. The streets were full of victims this time of night.

The car behind sounded its horn.

'Twat!' moaned Marcus, opening his eyes.

Toby drove off and turned the car into Warwick Avenue. After a moment he pulled up outside the converted petrol station that was now an uber-expensive apartment block. Marcus and Toby's home.

'So, what's the plan, then?' said Toby, expecting the worst.

'What do you think? We're going hunting, Toby Juggs.'

Toby's heart sank.

'But …'

Marcus glared at his brother. Wagged a finger.

'STFU. Go and get the tools.'

Toby got out of the car and ran through the rain, indoors.

Marcus was getting excited, hard. Queens 'We Are The Champions' playing in his head.

And then his mood changed as he saw the dishevelled shape stuffed in the launderette doorway. That filthy stinking tramp was messing up the street again. Marcus would have to give him another kicking. Or maybe something more permanent, this time.

146

'Look at the state of him. Pissed as a fart,' said Tommy, as the yuppie staggered out of the flash car, and toward the launderette.

Ferret elbowed him in the ribs and made a shushing sound. Typical Tommy Trouble. Big mouthed twat always bolloxed stuff up. He told people he was called Tommy Trouble because he was so dangerous. Even used to sing that Elvis song called 'Trouble' at karaoke. Truth was, he was just a fuck up, though.

Ferret only used Tommy as muscle because he was cheap, and easy to push around. Needs must.

He tapped Tommy on the forehead and jabbed a thumb towards the yuppie.

'Git,' he whispered.

The yuppie was in his own world. Talking to himself. He didn't notice Tommy step from the shadows and bear hug him from behind, dragging him into the doorway of an Oxfam shop.

And he didn't know what hit him as Ferret stepped up and slammed a fist into his well-dressed gut, causing him to puke. Another punch broke his nose and Tommy let him drop to the floor.

'Right,' said Ferret, crouching over Marcus' blood and puke soaked body. 'Keep an eye out, while I have a gander.'

The streets were deserted. Always were at five in the morning. The clubs were closed up and nobody was heading off to work yet.

But, Tommy kept an eye on Ferret, instead. He didn't trust him not to pocket most of the good stuff. When he saw Ferret take a new Android phone from Marcus' pocket he almost salivated.

'Now that is a beauty,' he said, grabbing it out of Ferret's hand. He almost snogged it.

Ferret, emptied Marcus wallet and picked up the car keys. Handed them to Tommy.

'Home Jeeves,' he said.

Tommy just stared. Wobbled a little.

'What the fuck…' he groaned.

147

Ferret looked down. Marcus had stabbed Tommy in the balls with a knife.

Tommy doubled over. Ferret kneed Marcus in the chin, knocking him out.

Then, blam.

Toby slammed Ferret against the wall, stuck a screwdriver in his throat. And then Toby was pulled to the ground by Tommy, who started to throttle him

***

Even during a thunderstorm, the bang had been loud enough to wake the dead. Loud enough to wake Snoopy, anyway, who always slept lightly, just to be on the safe side. It was a habit he'd developed after living on the streets for over a year. There were always some drunks around who liked to give the homeless a kicking, piss on them, set them alight.

Snoopy peeled himself out of his sleeping bag. Folded it over and put it in his worn back pack.

He carefully walked over to the pile of groaning bodies jammed in the shop doorway.

'Can I help you?'

'Piss off you stinky tramp,' said Tommy. 'Or I'll …'

He screamed.

The curly haired bloke had stabbed him in the eye.

Snoopy backed off. He knew from past experience that helping someone out could land you in the shit. What was it dad used to say? No good deed goes unpunished.

The street light reflected against the car keys and mobile phone that were on the floor and Snoopy bent down and picked them up.

What a waste of a beautiful car, thought Snoopy. It was like the one in Goldfinger. His dad's favourite film.

He had a flashback to being a kid and them both watching Bond films on TV over Christmas. Before has dad had been made redundant. And topped himself.

Snoopy looked over at the writhing, blood soaked bodies. Another thunderclap. A flash of lightning.

And as he walked towards the Aston Martin he remembered another thing his dad used to say. It can be Christmas every day, if you want it to be.

About the Author – Paul D. Brazill was born in England and now live in Poland. He's had bits and bobs published in various magazines and anthologies, including The Mammoth Books Of Best British Crime 8 and 10. His novellas The Gumshoe and Guns Of Brixton will published soon. He has edited two anthologies: Drunk On The Moon and True Brit Grit - with Luca Veste- and published two short ebook collections, 13 Shots Of Noir and Snapshots. He is a member of The Hardboiled Collective and International Thriller Writers inc, and editor-at-large for Noir Nation. He contributes regular columns for Pulp Metal Magazine and Out Of The Gutter Online. His blog is at http://pauldbrazill.wordpress.com

Taxi Driver
by
Steven Porter

"Shocking. Makes you wonder what the world's coming to, doesn't it?"

Not really. These things happen every day. I couldn't give a damn about a murder somewhere down south to be honest. Doesn't affect me any, does it? Same old news stories over and over on the radio. Some passengers then seek approval with their self-righteous small talk. Everybody's a good cunt on the surface, aren't they? Was it really any better when we were younger? I seriously doubt it.

But let them think they're right. In another five minutes my shift will be over. This job wouldn't be so bad if it was only driving. But I've had just about enough of people's opinions. Look what happened to Travis Wotsisname. Went off his nut, didn't he? It's less hassle to agree with customers. If they're yappy they're happy, I always say. Take their money and get them out of the cab. Sometimes they even hold you up once you've parked. As if they believe I hang on their every word. Jesus Christ. It'll be the death of me this. This one's gob is opening and closing like a Muppet with a hand up its jacksy.

"You're spot on, mate," I say.

No worries about the van that's right up *my* arse. Can you not hear the horn? You're 50p short? Have a discount while we're at it. It's been a great honour.

"Thanks very much."

Close the door on your way out. That's it. Thank Christ. Another day over. And you can wait an' all! I've got a horn too, you know. Fucking hell!

Peeeep!

Removals van. You'd think there'd be some brotherly love between those of us driving for a living. Not a bit of it. As if you never park illegally. I fucking bet!

150

I'm on my way home now. Will the wife want to hear about my twelve hours at the wheel? Will she heck. But there's Chrissy's pressies to pay for on top of everything else. I don't have much choice except to work my never-minds off.

Hold on! One last fare maybe. Ease up. She looks quite stylish. Business-like, even in that white dress.

"In you get, love."

Hello, she's getting in the front. She's carrying something wrapped in fancy paper. A pressie I expect.

Might as well chat.

"All sorted for Christmas, love."

"Oh you're joking. Loads to do."

"Staying at home, like?"

"Yeh."

"Family coming round?"

"Very quiet this year."

"Just the husband? Kids?"

"My son's down south. At university. "

"Oh aye? You don't look old enough, love. What's he studying?"

"Philosophy. Useless degree if you ask me. But he seems to be enjoying himself."

These pedestrians think they own the zebras. Marching across at red lights like they're the bloody Salvation Army.

"For Pete's sake! Sorry about that. Oh aye? He'll be coming up to see his mum then?"

"A flying visit, I expect. I'll cook dinner . Do his washing. Most likely he'll be off on the 27th ..."

"No thanks, eh? Young uns!"

She's taking the item out of the bag. A scarf or something. Folding it neatly. Very tidy lady, I reckon. Maybe even a bit obsessive about cleaning. They've got a name for that now. It's a recognised illness.

"So, husband waiting for you at home, love?"

"Why do you keep calling me 'love'? Do you fancy me or something?"

"Not at all... I mean I wasn't...."

She laughs.

"It doesn't matter. I'm only pulling your leg... Well, do you fancy me then?"

"I'm not sure what you mean, love. Sorry, I mean... You're not...?"

"Oh, you're definitely on the pull," she giggles. "We're almost there. Just round the corner here... Come in for a drink if you like."

"I'd love to but… It's a bit awkward."

"A faithful husband? Huh! Makes a change. I respect that, driver."

"No it's… just it's quite difficult to get parked round here."

"Number 7 there. Yeh, this is it."

She offers a note for the fare. Probably a ten spot but it's hard to see in the fading light. I waive it away in any case.

"I'll leave the door open in case you have a change of heart, shall I? I owe you a drink... at least."

"Give me fifteen minutes."

She winks. Her heels scrape the pavement. Kitten heels. Meow! I'm not fussed about a few quid but what about the night's takings? This might be some kind of stunt to get more cash. Not worth the risk. I'm a bit sweaty too. Maybe that did the trick. Some of them like that, I hear. Better spray on some deodorant from the can I keep in the glove compartment for emergencies. Just to be on the safe side, like.

Then I drive a couple of blocks round to Dave's. I'm in luck again. He's at home. Quick chat. I leave the takings with my mate and ask him to keep an eye on the motor.

"Sound, Dave. There'll be a pint behind the bar for you on Thursday. Put me down for the darts."

Am I doing the wise thing here? It's not too late to change my mind. I could forget all this, go home, pour myself a Scotch and wind down with that porn website I like. A tug on the old John

Thomas and this little episode would soon be forgotten... Nah, that's not true. I'd think about it for days, if not weeks. It would prey on my mind and I'd kick myself for passing up the chance. You have to take what's on offer in this life. Isn't that what I always say? It's too late to stop now, to quote Van the Man.

The front door is slightly ajar when I get there. I'd better mind my manners and ring the bell... Just the once, so she knows it isn't the postman.

"Come in. First on the right."

She's sitting on the sofa with her legs curled under her. Red paint is visible on her bare toes. She has the new scarf thing around her neck. It's obviously for decoration rather than winter. Her drink looks pure as water but she's got the confident smile of someone who's had a couple of sherbets. There's a bottle of gin next to the tonic.

"Relax. Take your shoes off. Pour yourself a drink. Sorry there's no beer but there is some Scotch in the cabinet."

My stocking soles sink into the shag pile carpet as I go over to pour myself a large whisky.

" Lovely place," I say, taking off my combat jacket and rolling up my shirt sleeves. Everything is immaculate. Just as I'd expected.

"It's alright. Come and sit down. You're pacing about there like a caged animal."

I park my arse on the sofa. She ruffles my hair.

"So what's your name, lover boy?"

"Call me Rob if you like... or Bob."

"Oh, yeh? I think I prefer Robert... It's more sophisticated. Am I safe with you, Robert? I won't end up with blood all over the place, will I? Hee hee. Even my husband would probably notice that."

"He's not around is he?"

"Don't worry, he won't be back... not for a few days anyway."

"What does he do? It's quite nice around these parts."

"Actually, Ron earns less than me. Probably the main reason he's still living here. But that's not really any of your business."

"Sorry."

153

"Oh, don't apologise. It makes you sound weak. I want a *strong* man. Reckless even. That's why you're here, isn't it?"

"I'm game."

"You know, I liked you as soon as I saw your eyes in the mirror. Properly lit up they were. You don't need headlights on that taxi."

Jesus. Speechless I am now. Isn't it me who's supposed to do the chat up lines? The whisky hasn't had time to get to work its magic yet. So I just smile like a moron.

"And you've got that cheeky grin too. Makes you look a bit rough round the edges."

I almost say, "Likewise", but manage to hold my tongue.

"You're the quiet type, aren't you? All that chat in the car. It's just part of your job. You know what I like best about you? Personality-wise, I mean."

"Go on."

"You're not going to tell me your life story or bombard me with opinions. That's such a turn-off."

Fuck's sake. She's treating me like a brainless gimp and I'm going along with it.

"Suits me. I have to listen to other folk all day long. It's tiring."

She approves. Clicks her tongue on the roof of her mouth.

"Great... But you're going to have to look the part. Tell you what. Why don't we give you a new look?"

Bloody hell. The next thing I know she's got the clippers out and is digging away at my scalp. What the hell is she doing? And more to the point, what the hell am I doing?

"Ron's got a good shaver. Though I don't know why he bothers. Bald as a coot he is. This won't take long. Then you'll be able to have your wicked way with me, Robert."

It takes long enough. I feel like a right clueless gimp. But at last she says, "Go take a look in the mirror".

Fuck me. The hair is shorn into the skull at the sides. My head looks smaller, my face longer. I can already feel a few razor bumps coming up. What's the wife going to think when I arrive home like the last of the Mohicans dragged through a hedge backwards?

"Perfect," she says. "Very sexy."

The whole thing's ridiculous. I might be dreaming so just go with the flow. She asks for her hands to be tied with the new scarf. No problem.

She's drunker than I thought. She's pissed her Alan Whickers. I'm not really into water sports. As we get down to it, I expect her husband or son to walk in at any minute. Every little sound from the street sets me on edge. For some people, all that might add to the excitement but it's hard to focus on the task at hand.

The shagging is fine but I don't come. She does – twice, I think. It's pretty much a waste of time if you don't shoot your load. Only last week I was saying that to Dave and the other lads.

She soon nods off on the sofa without finishing her gin. Her scarf has fallen onto the carpet. It's more of a neckerchief really. I think about putting it in my pocket. A silky souvenir to hang in the car. It'd make a change from furry dice but would also be a reminder of a hollow victory. I place it back round her narrow shoulders then help myself to a second large Scotch. Watching her asleep, I'm still hard. I go to find the downstairs bog and have a quick ham shank.

I stay on a bit longer to give the whisky a chance to wear off. Flick through the TV channels. Might have dozed off myself. She's still sound asleep anyway. I leave without saying goodbye.

The chilly air assaults my head as I go to pick up the cab. It's just getting light as I drive home. I take the back road past the golf course where there's less traffic and not much chance of the cops lurking with their Christmas special – the breathalyzer test.

I run over some possibilities in my head. I half-think about heading back into town to wait for the barbers to open. But that would mean getting home much later when the wife might already be off to work. Then it would look like I had stayed out all night. I'd better just try to sneak in and shave this silly Mohawk off myself. I've had skinheads before, so I could say I'd gone for a haircut first in the afternoon and started my shift later than usual. Then near the end of

155

the night I'd got a fare all the way to Manchester. Couldn't turn that down, could I? It's was a pretty shit excuse but she might buy it. I'll worry about filling in the details later.

A black and white flash slips out from the side of the road and under the car. It grinds to a halt under one of the wheels. I stop, reverse back and get out. A bloody badger. This is the first time I've ever seen one properly. Blood is gushing out of its head as if it has a blowhole on top. Poor bastard. The fella's white neck is twisted to one side as it rapidly turns red. The eyes are staring at me. It looks kind of humiliated with that stripe down its forehead. Join the club, mate. I think it's dead. If I had a gun handy, I'd blast its brains out just to make sure. I drag it off the road by its still warm tail.

It begins to rain heavily as I restart the engine. I don't exceed third gear as I go over the story I plan to tell the wife. I can't get the animal's eyes out of my head. But the rain will soon wash away those bloody traces of life.

About the Author - Steven Porter was born in Inverness in the year man first stepped on the moon. Some say he inhabits another planet. His versatile output includes novels, short stories, poetry, memoir, travelogues, reportage and sports writing. Taxi Driver is his first published story since the collection Blurred Girl and Other Suggestive Stories. His offbeat tales have also appeared in other anthologies, such as Byker Books' Radgepacket series and True Brit Grit. See Steve Porter's World of Books blog at http://stevenjporter.wordpress.com/ for more info.

Don't Look Now
by
Keith B Walters

Villiers Street was its usual crowded Saturday night self, full of the sights and sounds of those heading to catch last trains out of London from Charing Cross or black cabs to seek out further entertainments until the small hours.

Battling against a tide of people heading in the opposite direction, Detective Inspector George Haven made his way down the hill towards Embankment underground station, trying to ignore anything around that looked like it might flare up into a situation requiring Police intervention.

Up ahead, by the entrance to the ticket hall, stood Jon Sutherland, his DS and friend of over ten years. Jon raised a hand half-heartedly in welcome on seeing his approach.

'Sorry to have to call you out on this one, George, but the top said you were close by.'

Haven placed a hand on his colleague's shoulder and they walked into the station ticket office hall to head straight through to the Thames' embankment. The lights of the riverside were glaring before them and, ahead of those, the glow of the Royal Festival Hall from the other side of the river.

'It's fine, Jon. Just having a meal with the family in Haymarket - we were about to leave anyhow. So, what do you know?' They paused as a cycle rickshaw wobbled past, its passengers giggling and waving as they passed by, then crossed the road just to the side of Hungerford Bridge. A line of emergency service vehicles and a white forensic tent being assembled on the narrow stretch of riverbank indicated where they needed to go.

'No name as yet. A young couple spotted her as they walked along the embankment after their evening out. Must have been a hell of a shock, looking over and seeing her floating there.'

Sutherland reached the railings first, pushed open a small gate and began to climb down the rusted metal ladder.

'It's okay, Tide's out!' He quipped. 'But, watch this ladder, George, it's bloody slippery.'

Haven let his colleague get a few rungs down before starting his own descent.

'So, a jumper then? From the bridge here or maybe further upstream?'

'No, George. Not a jumper.'

Haven looked down as he stepped the last few rungs, to see who had answered him and saw the familiar face of crime scene investigator Alec Newman.

'Good evening, Alec. So, what DO we know then?'

Newman lifted the side panel of the tent that was still being set up around the body and gestured for the two detectives to look inside.

'I'll have to ask you to stay stood where you are, gents. Don't want you screwing up my lovely crime scene by the waterside here. But, as I'm sure you can see, even from there, this poor lass didn't choose to end up here tonight. But somebody sure meant her to.'

The girl's body lay face down in the mud beside the steadily sloshing water's edge. Her face was turned slightly on the ground but masked with the matted locks of her long blonde hair which, pulled up and across her face, gave a clear view of the dark bruising around her neck. Her bright red party dress, despite being muddied, still managed to add colour to the grey scene.

Haven looked a while longer, willing the girl to stand up as though from a drunken stupor and smile the smile of a happy Saturday night party girl, but she remained still before them.

He turned away, looked back towards the street, his eyes scanning the small crowd that had formed and who were staring back at him.

'Got a name, Guv.'

Haven turned his head.

One of the forensic team was walking towards him. In his hands he held a small silver handbag and a travel card wallet.

'Kate Hanbury.' Haven muttered as he read the name and looked at the photo on the travel card. 'Somebody really hurt you, Kate, didn't they, love? I wonder if it was someone who once really loved you too. Though, I doubt that.'

He repeated the name over in his mind as he continued to watch the crowd that was watching him. Kate Hanbury. Hanbury. Hanbury. The name resonated with him, but he couldn't place it.

'You okay, George?' Sutherland asked.

'Fine.' Haven came out of his trance-like state. 'Just fine, Jon. But best you leave me to go back up alone. Don't look, but I think I've just spotted our perpetrator stood over there and getting his kicks watching the soco's at work. Let me see how close I can get to him. You follow on in a few minutes, okay.'

Sutherland nodded, couldn't quite resist a quick scan of the group of people, but saw nothing to suggest the killer was amongst the group assembled there.

'Right you are.'

'Hanbury. Hanbury?' Haven muttered as he moved away, his eyes sweeping across the group of people up ahead. Carefully he took hold of the metal ladder and began to climb, knowing that for the briefest of moments the man he had been watching was out of his sight. He quickened his climb, reached the top and slowed again, pushed open the gate, scanned the crowd.

'Everything okay, Sir?'

A young PC at the gate lifted the Police line tape, that he'd only just tied to the gate, to allow him through.

Haven looked quickly in each direction, desperate to see the one face he'd picked out from below, realising with every passing second that there was every likelihood he'd had the killer in his sights just moments earlier.

159

'There was a man. Stood just over there, towards the back of the crowd, white shirt, dark jacket?'

The PC looked about the crowd.

'Sorry, Sir. Can't say I noticed him.'

Haven stepped away from the crowd and to the edge of the road, looked both ways along the embankment, scanning the half-light, looking into the shadows, but seeing nothing.

He heard heavy footfall and turned to see Sutherland running up to him.

'No need to hurry, Jon. He got away. Bastard got away.'

Sutherland removed his glasses and wiped his brow. He was out of shape and he knew it.

'You're sure? Sure it was him, I mean?'

Haven nodded solemnly, still looking all around in the hope that he'd still see his prey.

'Oh, yes. It was him. And the worst part is, other than the fact he strangles them, I think he's doing this by way of a tribute.'

'What do you mean, trib – ' But that was all Sutherland managed to say as Haven pushed him hard in the chest, sending him hurtling back against the embankment wall, as he rushed forward.

'There!' Haven shouted, his heavy brogues pounding on the pavement as he ran on in the direction of the lion statues at the foot of Cleopatra's needle.

Sutherland pushed himself back from the wall, took a breath and focused on the image of his colleague rushing towards a figure crouched behind one of the lions.

'George! Wait!' He started after him, but knew that he could never make up the distance and that Haven would be upon the man before he got close.

Haven could see the figure beginning to rise from his position on the concrete plinth, preparing to jump down to flee. With his heart hammering in his chest, he forced himself on and reached the man just as his feet hit the pavement.

The two men went down together hard onto the ground, Haven's hands tight around the man's throat and pinning him against the side of the embankment wall.

'Hanbury. Kate Hanbury!' Haven snarled. 'How long did you think it would take us? Huh? Wasn't enough to take names, too obvious I suppose. You had to go one better – or so you thought.' His hands tightened, the man's pale white face staring back at him as he struggled to catch his next breath, his feet kicking out in desperation, his hands pulling at the stronger man's arms to try to release his grip.

'George?'

Haven turned to look up at Sutherland.

'She wasn't his first, Jon. The girl in the waste chute at the back of that restaurant in Seven Dials? She was his too.' He turned back and stared at the man. 'Tell me I'm wrong.'

Sutherland thought for a second, looking back over his shoulder to see if any other officers had followed him.

'Laura Berner?'

'Yes.' Haven moved to place his right knee on the man's chest, holding him firmly in place, his hands still wrapped around and crushing the man's windpipe. 'Berner. As in the street, Berner Street. Hanbury Street. This sick bastard was working his way through finding girls with the same names as the streets where the ripper dumped his victims.' He squeezed harder still, directly under the man's jaw line, forcing his head back against the wall. 'Tell me I'm wrong!'

'Jesus!' Sutherland knelt down and placed a hand on Haven's shoulder. 'Okay, George, okay. Ease off him now, let me hold him. You step away and call it in, okay?'

Haven said nothing at first. He just remained there, pinning the man to the ground, slowly shaking his head, and then, from the movement in his shoulders, Sutherland realised his superior officer was weeping.

'George?'

Haven looked around at Sutherland, his eyes filled with hatred and sadness.

'I have a daughter, Jon. A daughter and a beautiful grand-daughter. Those girls – the girls he took – they were someone's daughters too. If I wasn't holding him now, he'd be on his way to finding his next one. Maybe he'd become as bad as the man he's trying to emulate. Maybe he hasn't got the balls to use a knife just yet, so he's using strangling and drowning – but we can't allow him the chance to try out new things.'

The man was still in his hands, staring up at the Detective Inspector in total horror, with the sudden realisation that he had been stopped from his project.

'Okay, but let me call this in now, okay George. You just hold him steady there.' Sutherland reached inside his jacket for his mobile.

'Jon. You leave that phone where it is! I want you to walk away from this right away. Do you understand? Just go back to the station, write up the scene notes and that's all. You weren't here, okay?'

Haven began to get up, keeping one hand tight under the man's throat until he was upright.

'Okay, you sack of shit, let's have you up.'

He grabbed at the man's right arm and forced it high up on his back as he hauled him to his feet, holding him around the neck with his other arm.

The man said nothing, as though accepting whatever was to come next. He simply stared out across the Thames.

'Open the gate, Jon.' Haven nodded towards a small metal gate beside the statues. Beyond it were stone steps which led down to the riverbank.

'George. I can't – what are you doing?'

'Open the gate, Jon. Just do that. You know as well as I do that we're better rid of scum like this, better to not let them enter the system. Better just to finish things here and now. Open the gate, and then walk away, Jon. Please.'

Sutherland looked at Haven for a moment longer, then reached across and unbolted the gate, pushing it wide before them.

162

Haven pushed the man forward, forcing his arm higher up his back.

The two men began their descent down the steps, glancing over to their right, to where Kate Hanbury still lay amongst the circus of the emergency services parade ring.

Sutherland leant on the wall and watched as the two men reached the bottom of the steps and stepped onto the riverbank, Haven pushing the man on towards the inky black water of the Thames.

Haven turned and looked back at him.

'Jon. You weren't here, Jon. You didn't see this, you don't need to see this. It's better that way. Don't look now, Jon, don't look. Walk away, please.'

Haven waited until he saw his DS turn from the wall and begin to walk away. Not until he was out of sight did he continue on his way, leading his prisoner towards his watery grave.

About the Author - Keith is married with two children, two cats and lives in Kent in a house made almost entirely of books. He has written book and film reviews since before the internet (despite his youthful looks) and, in recent years, has been book blogging at booksandwriters.wordpress.com and his daughter handles YA reviews at booksandwritersJNR.wordpress.com For two years he has been Blogger in Residence at the Theakstons Old Peculiar Crime Writing Festival in Harrogate, covering the event for his own blog and for the first year for Culture Vulture in Leeds. This is his second anthology appearance in 2012 - following on from his flash fiction entry in the 'Once Upon a Time: Unexpected Fairytales' collection, edited by SJI Holliday. Detective Inspector George Haven appears regularly in Keith's crime fiction short stories and so far in one, as yet unpublished novel, 'A Long December', which he takes from the bottom drawer and dusts every now and again.

Keith's new blog, where he is putting up his short fiction, author interviews and book reviews is keithbwalters.wordpress.com and can be found on Twitter @keithbwalters

Priscilla: Queen of the Desert
by
Graham Smith

The bite of the plasticuffs on my wrists did nothing to dampen my
spirits. I'd had my revenge on the greedy, grabbing claimants who'd
ruined my life. I should feel shame. Regret. Or a whole host of other
emotions. All I felt though was elation at ridding my life of a nuisance.

***

I was driving along at a steady fifty five when this arsehole shot
sideways out of a junction. He was driving a typical boy racer's car. It
was all tinted windows, lowered suspension and fake exhausts.

The anti lock brakes kicked back at my right foot but I didn't
have enough time to stop.

My Mondeo hit him square on the driver's side. There was
just enough time to see the look of shock and disbelief on his acne
ridden face before impact. My airbag exploded filling the car with a
choking white dust. I was unhurt though.

Climbing out of my car I went across to see how young Mr
Schumacher was doing. Not good. He was out cold with blood leaking
from his forehead. The skanky girl in the passenger seat was
screaming fit to burst. Shock had already laid its clammy fingers on
her.

Hauling on the door handle, I gripped her arm and pulled her
out of the car and sat on the kerb. Turning my attention to the driver,
I checked his pulse and breathing. Nothing. No heartbeat. No life
giving breaths. Nothing.

Remembering the first aid training the Army had given me, I
dragged him out of the car and shouted at the girl to call an
ambulance. While she fumbled a mobile from her pocket, I started
compressing his bony chest, while trying not to look at the needle

marks on his arms. His ribs cracked as I pumped his sternum. Gritting my teeth, I took my life in my hands and blew two deep breaths into his lungs.

It seemed like the ambulance was never going to come, but I was later told by bystanders that it arrived less than ten minutes after the crash.

Two paramedics ran over with a portable defibrillator. Relieved that professionals were here to take over, I moved away and sat down exhausted with the effort of trying to keep him alive.

Three shocks later a paramedic announced, 'there's a pulse.' With help from the traffic cops who arrived, the paramedics loaded the driver onto a spinal board, which they secured in the back of the ambulance before rushing away with lights and sirens in full "get out of the fucking way" glory.

The next hour and a half was spent giving statements to the police. The copper who cross-examined me was a decent sort. He passed on a message from the paramedics that they'd reckoned I had saved the other drivers life. Now that the adrenaline was gone from my body, I was pleased I'd saved the driver while furious with him as a motorist. He could easily have killed me or his passenger as well as injuring himself.

Six weeks after the crash I had a very rude awakening as to how low the human race can stoop. Four times I read that letter.

The driver's family had hired an ambulance chasing lawyer who was suing me for assault. The driver's spinal cord had been trapped between the third and fourth vertebrae and he was now paraplegic.

What's the fucking world coming too? The little shit had been driving like an idiot to impress a girl. He'd caused an accident in which he'd nearly died and his greedy bastard family were suing me for saving his miserable drug addled life.

A doctor – who I suspected was on the lawyer's payroll – had written a statement saying that I shouldn't have moved the driver.

What utter bollocks. If I hadn't moved him, then I wouldn't have been able to do the CPR which saved his bloody life. *Hadn't he heard of the Hippocratic Oath?*

I had a meeting with my solicitor who advised me to sit tight while she built my defence case. When I protested there was no case to answer, she warned me that this was a civil case and that I would have to go to court to defend my actions regardless of how noble they had been.

This was unbelievable. The police had laid all the blame for the accident at his door. He had two bald tyres and his blood had shown traces of heroin. Yet I got sued.

***

An out of touch judge acknowledged that while I had undoubtedly saved the life of Mr Tyson Bridges, I had taken unforgivable liberties with his well-being while moving him so I could perform the necessary resuscitation.

The deal breaker had been the weasel faced Doctor whose testimony damned me and the actions I had taken that day.

I was apoplectic with rage and only my father clamping a hand over my mouth prevented me from hurling a string of abuse at the lying bastard. The two paramedics who had attended that day were so nervous at being in court that their stammered testimonies were shredded by the lawyer representing the driver's family.

The judge found me guilty of grievous harm, and ordered me to pay recompense to Mr Bridges to the tune of one hundred and fifty thousand pounds, with a further award of ten thousand pounds per annum towards the specialist care Bridges would require for the rest of his life. *I saved his life you moron. Without my help he'd have died.*

The solitary journalist present that day had had a field day snapping away at me. When the weekly paper came out he'd unearthed a picture of me from my Army days. The picture showed me in desert fatigues underneath the headline

"Priscilla Kennedy: Queen of the Desert, Sued for Assault".

My house would have to be sold to pay Bridges. Paul had left me six months ago, claiming I had changed. My hair had ten times more grey than a year ago and I was surviving on a diet of hard liquor and anti-depressants.

I would have to sell up and start all over again. Not easy for a woman pushing forty whose only saleable skill was killing.

I spent two days flipping between gut wrenching sobs and outraged tantrums before deciding on a course of action.

**

Four days after losing the court case I bought a nurses tunic with matching trousers from the internet. I had my hair cut short and dyed blonde instead of my natural mahogany.

When the tunic and trousers arrived, I slipped them on and set off for the hospital where Bridges was still being treated.

Arriving at the hospital I grabbed an abandoned wheelchair and pushed it with an unhurried gait until I found Bridges' ward. A glance at the layout plan by the nurses' station told me he was in a room of his own at the end of the corridor. Walking down the corridor my heart was trying to pound its way out of my chest. I was terrified of failure. Of being stopped. Of not completing my mission.

Swapping a mop and bucket for the wheelchair, I entered his room. The mop handle went through the loops of the twin door handles.

There, lying immobile on the bed, was the cause of my woes. My nemesis. The man I hated enough to kill. The man I was going to do time for.

Bridges' head was constrained in a neck brace. It soon hit the floor and I tilted his head back to expose his Adam's apple.

I swung the edge of my right hand down onto the lump in his throat. Fuelled by outraged anger I made certain of the damage by repeating the blow nine more times.

168

The crunch of cartilage was sweeter than a thousand whispered sweet nothings. I could feel the smile on my lips. The weight lifting from my shoulders.

The damage I had done to his throat was so great that even the fact he was already in hospital would not save him this time.

Even so I planned to wait by his bed for an hour to make sure that no rescue attempt could be made. A rattle at the door warned me that I was about to be discovered. A real nurse was trying to enter the room. She called out. I sat in silence as she peered through the glass at me. Thwarted by the makeshift barricade she ran off to find help.

A man's face adorned with a security guard's cap appeared at the window in the door. A shake to test the nurses claim, was followed by a crack as he shoulder charged his way into the room.

I grappled with him as a delaying tactic, without inflicting any serious damage. It was not my plan to harm innocent workers.

As we rolled on the floor, a bunch of doctors tried to resuscitate Bridges without success.

My mission was complete so I stopped struggling with the guard and allowed him to capture me.

I would plead guilty to Bridges' murder as soon as the police arrived. Offer no defence. Create no lies. I would let them sentence me. I reckoned I would get seven years max. Be out in four and a half if I kept my nose clean…

About the Author - Graham Smith is married with a young son. A time served joiner he has built bridges, houses, dug drains and slated roofs to make ends meet. For the last eleven years he has been manager of a busy hotel and wedding venue near Gretna Green, Scotland. An avid fan of crime fiction since being given one of Enid Blyton's Famous Five books at the age of eight, he has also been a regular reviewer for the well respected review site Crimesquad.com for over two years.

He has three collections of short stories available as Kindle downloads and has featured in anthologies such as True Brit Grit and Action: Pulse Pounding Tales, as well as appearing on several popular ezines.

For more information visit his blog
http://grahamsmithwriter.blogspot.com/

Natural Born Killers
by
Court Merrigan

Lacan Clintock made it big and be damned if he wasn't going to let the valley know it. He built a stark white house atop Spider Ridge, its vast square footage supported by an unwieldy system of beams and columns, visible fifty miles off. From his front veranda, Lacan could look down on the valley where he had grown up white trash. A short walk across the Greathall carried him over the spine of Spider Ridge to the back veranda with its plummeting view of rocky Mug Creek filling the pristine fishing pond he now owned, where as a boy he had often been chased by dogs and finally fired on by an irate landowner, a pellet of birdshot entering his shoulder and slowly migrating down his arm until years later it formed a sticky abscess at his wrist which was removed in an operation he cracked a molar enduring since he could not abide the sight of a needle. He named the pond for his daughter, Lucy. His plans called for a lot of fishing, but various construction waste materials leeched into Lucy Pond, killing off most the fish. The Game & Fish man said restocking had to wait till spring. That was fine by Lacan. He hated fishing.

He dismissed his advisors when they prattled on too long on teleconference and invited his cousin Gainerd (Gain) Wilson to come live with him. They'd grown up together but Gain had had made it nowhere until Lacan called him. Gain crowed to his cronies at the Pike & Crown he was finally getting to where he deserved and walked a quarter way up the long switchbacks of the drive to the house before collapsing with the heaves, unaware that Lacan employed a chauffeur in a modified military ATV.

***

Lucy Clintock, seventeen, felt like the whole world was staring at her perched up on Spider Ridge. When her father proposed the house be named in the grand tradition of grand manors everywhere in the civilized world, Lucy suggested Spread-Eagled Honkey. She was banished from the supper table and ran from the hated house down the long staircase to the side of algae-slicked Lucy Pond where she sat slapping at mosquitoes which no one can do with dignity until the jerking stitches in her chest subsided, pistol across her knees. She was a champion sharpshooter. At one contest she had potted a bull's eye at five hundred feet with the hand cannon that now sat on her lap. After entertaining the usual teenaged fantasies of wild leaps from great heights (the Greathall verandas providing convenient settings), she began potting rocks that sat at the water's edge.

What she really wanted was escape, and in this her fervour matched her father's in his own youth. She also wished her mother was still alive; naturally she blamed Lacan. Also she hated school. Owing to Lacan's nomadic fortune-hunting, Lucy had started kindergarten late and was three years before she would finish high school. It was a part of Lacan's plan for mastery of the (local) universe that his chauffeured daughter graduate with full honors and recognition from the high school that had expelled him. No amount of pleading on Lucy's part for boarding school or at least her own car altered Lacan's mind. She went on pulverizing rocks with the hand cannon.

***

Lacan spent his days brooding violently in his as-yet unnamed mansion, fingering his collection of firearms, staring at the flickering flat screen. That prison riot in *Natural Born Killers*. He couldn't stop watching it. His fantastic wealth was consolidated into a row of figures even a child could understand and his brain crawled with schemes. But all his acquisitions had been calculated as revenge on the valley below. For many years he had cherished images of sundry offenders (the kids from Richfield Heights who made him eat dog shit in the parking lot, the history teacher who observed to the class that one ought to bathe

172

before making a presentation, the baker lady who shrieked when he touched the display case) parading up to the house begging for forgiveness and favors, which he would thoughtfully consider while the supplicants waited in an agony of suspense. However, the only supplicants who appeared were snivelling drinking buddies of Gain's, one of whom puked in the interior of the ATV. He threw these from the house and time weighed like molten lead on his brain.

Fortunately, Gain had a ready remedy. It was the sole innovation of his life, a concoction of boiled local snortables that produced a mist potent as bull balls. Gain modestly called it do-juice. He nursed a few hurt feelings that do-juice had not caught on, attributing this to a lack of imagination on the part of the crankheads in the valley below. In the small west wing study where he spent increasing chunks of daytime, hazed-over Lacan would shove a pistol out of the way going in for another hit and agree.

**

Winter came on. Lucy made daily pilgrimages down the slick staircase to the pond, which sported a thin sheen of blue ice. The house staff repeatedly warned her of the dangers, admonitions they were too terrified by Lucy's hissed threats to repeat to Lacan. Likewise they were powerless to report Lucy's sometimes spending whole schooldays cruising the town in the limo, shooting out mailboxes and porch lights from a rolled down window with her hand cannon, hissing more threats the instant the chauffeur got slack on the gas. Her stumbly father and staggering cousin seemed only intermittently aware of her existence. The house staff increasingly shrank from all three, especially cousin Gain, who got very feely with the maids when Lacan was incapacitated with do-juice in the study.

Towards evening one day, the snow let up, the clouds cleared, and a resplendent sunset pearled the sky in golden-ochre streaks, setting the valley and mountains off in a cascade of sparkles. Lacan, pacing the Greathall, saw none of it. The do-juice had given out midmorning and Gain was down in the valley procuring more makings, an errand which was taking a devilishly long time. Lacan was coming down, a freefall of trembling chills, nauseous shivers, and a splitting brain ache. Though wearing only a light kimono and slippers, he was sweating as though it were tropical midday.

Leaning his forehead against the cool glass of the back veranda, he nearly toppled through when a spidery network of cracks suddenly spread across it. He fell backwards as the window collapsed in a shower of shards shivering to the marble and stared flabbergasted at the unblinkered evening sky. Then he heard a thin wailing voice and gingerly stepping over the slivers of glass, he peered down into the abyss. Just visible in the retreating light was a tiny figure, planted in the snow at the edge of Lucy Pond, waving both arms.

"DAAAADDY," came a thin wail, "HEEEEELP MEEEE …"

It was Lucy. Then Lacan remembered overhearing a maid saying something about ice and snow on the stairs, which made him remember that in irritation at the same maid's wheedling tone (honed in constant efforts to evade cousin Gain) he'd peremptorily given the entire house staff the holidays off. He was all alone.

He tried to call out to Lucy down below, but his mouth was cracked and stuffed with cotton, so he managed only a raspy whisper: he was coming, he was coming. Then he dashed out of the Greathall, kimono flying around him, to collide into Gain stamping his bare feet against the cold he'd just left. They piled to the floor.

Unfazed, Gain said, "I had to drive that rig myself. Asphalts slick as bug snot. I thought she would …"

"Lucy," croaked Lacan. "Down below. Got to help."

"Hell, you can't do nothing if she's down there already. Doubt you could even find her. Wonder how she got down the drive … well, it don't matter. Come on. Let's get us juiced."

He helped up Lacan, rasping and pointing towards the Greathall and shivering so hard he looked to be having a seizure. Gain looked vaguely that way and felt the draft.

"Turn up the heat, for Christ's sake," Gain said. "No Eskimos live here I know of."

Lacan, eyes fixed on the familiar wooden shoe polish box Gain kept the supplies in, obediently followed Gain to the study. *Natural Born Killers* was on the TV.

"Look at those crazy fuckers," said Gain, gesturing to the screen.

"They know how to do it," said Lacan.

Half an hour later, freezing Lucy came tromping into the study, where she found her father exactly where she expected. It took him a long moment to get her in focus and another to cover himself up where his kimono had flapped open.

"Lucy," he said, thinking of her mother. "Baby."

"You were going to leave me down there to die?" said Lucy. "Your own daughter?"

"What the christ is she talking about?" asked Gain.

"Oh," said Lacan, memory returning in a heavy soup of golden hilarity, "She was down by the pond. Shot out a picture window." He grinned.

"Now there is a hell of a shot. That deserves a hug," said Gain

He removed his bare feet from the desk, lurched to a standing position and reached out to Lucy in very unfamilial fashion. She sidestepped him and Gain's momentum carried him into the hall.

"Hell, I'll just have to go see for myself," he said, and went off towards the Greathall.

Lacan was trying to keep his daughter in glazy focus. Runnels of melting snow trickled off her parka.

"I am going," said Lucy. "And I ain't never coming back to this shithole."

"Don't you talk like trash to me," said Lacan, raising his head from the plush couch. "Not now or never."

"Never's goddamn right," said Lucy, "cause it's never when I am coming back."

Then she was gone. Rousing himself to give chase, Lacan bashed his shins on the coffee table, overturning it and falling. This knocked the wind out of him and on his belly he watched the precious pot of do-juice seep into the carpet.

When he finally did get up, he followed a trail of wet boot prints to Lucy's room where he found only a stripped-off scarf. Nothing apparent to an intoxicated inattentive father appeared missing, though in fact Lucy had taken a carefully packed bag of essentials devoid of sentimental trinkets. Hollering round the house till his voice was gone, Lacan decided he couldn't leave his daughter out in the cold a second time, much less surrender her to the blood-sucking valley. Still in his kimono, he climbed into the ATV. Gain had failed to set the parking brake and when Lacan depressed the clutch it rolled off the drive down Spider Ridge.

Later, investigators gave up on the jaws of life and used blowtorches to cut the mangled wreckage open; the same investigators found the concussed and frozen corpse of Gainerd Wilson, Esq., in a snow bank eighty feet below the shattered picture window, where he'd fallen after a couple howling hops on feet perforated with broken glass.

It was surmised Lucy left the house by means of the conveyor belt which brought supplies up to the house. She never materialized to clarify and the deteriorating house remained a eyesore the valley lacked the resources to renovate or remove. The Clintock fortune was held in public trust the requisite number of years before being donated to the Valley Home For Boys & Girls.

About the Author - Court Merrigan's short story collection MOONDOG OVER THE MEKONG is forthcoming from Snubnose Press and he's got short stories out or coming soon in Thuglit, Needle, Weird Tales, Plots With Guns, Big Pulp, Noir Nation, and a bunch of others. His story "The Cloud Factory," which appeared in PANK, was nominated for a Spinetingler Award. Links at http://courtmerrigan.wordpress.com . He also runs the Bareknuckles Pulp Department at Out of the Gutter. He lives in Wyoming with his family.

American Beauty
by
Erik Arneson

'Beautiful Bobby' Ferrari balanced himself on the top rope of the
wrestling ring, his energy surging with the wild cheers of the sold-out
crowd at Madison Square Garden. The fans chanted, "Bobby, Bobby!"
and he felt the familiar rise of goose bumps as he stretched his arms
wide, showing off before he jumped.

This, Ferrari thought, was his moment. He was about to
defeat the World Champion, the legendary "Nature Boy" Ric Flair. He
crouched slightly, then pushed off and flew across the ring. Time
moved in slow motion until his sculpted body crashed onto his
opponent's chest.

"One! Two! Three!" The 20,000 fans counted the pinfall in
unison with the referee. They screamed even louder when Ferrari
stood, squeezed his eyes shut and raised his hands in victory.

When Ferrari flicked open his eyes, reality smacked him in
the face. The fans, they were on their feet cheering, that much was
true. But they numbered in the dozens, not the thousands. He had
defeated a flabby jobber called Jack "The Mauler" Morgan, not Ric
Flair. And this was the Elks Lodge in backwater Lebanon,
Pennsylvania, not the mecca of professional wrestling, the Garden in
New York City.

Ferrari ignored the calls of fans clamoring for high fives and
autographs as he swaggered back to the dressing room, a repurposed
storage area populated with pro wrestler wannabes, never-gonna-bes
and has-beens. His only thought was how soon could he be snorting
the precious white powder that awaited him back in his hotel room.

It was just after 11 p.m. when Ferrari hurried through the
back door into the Elks' parking lot, where half a dozen fans were
loitering to shake his hand and get another chance for an autograph.

"Great match, Bobby!"

"You should still be the champ, Bobby!"

"Damn right," he said while again ignoring the autograph seekers. Ferrari made a line straight across the parking lot to his 2002 Cadillac Escalade, a vehicle with 292,000 miles on it. He'd loved the SUV when he bought it at the pinnacle of his popularity. Now, he hated it for reminding him how far he had fallen.

Two men, one white and one black, were leaning on the SUV. "Sweet ride," said the white guy, whose tight white T-shirt revealed he spent a lot of time in the weight room. He was tall, had maybe four inches on Ferrari, and wore fingerless black leather gloves.

"Or used to be," said his buddy, a slightly shorter musclehead who also wore jeans and a tight T-shirt, but his was pink with vertical turquoise stripes. "Back when you were somebody." The two men laughed, a practiced kind of laugh like they'd worked on the joke over and over preparing for this moment.

"Good one," Ferrari said. "Funny as that Miami Vice shirt you're wearing. Now get the hell out of my way."

The white guy stood still, blocking his path to the driver's door.

"You deaf? I said, get the hell out of my way."

The black guy moved to trap Ferrari between them. He reached behind his back and pulled a .38 revolver with a wooden handle. "You have any idea who I am?" he asked. Ferrari shook his head. "What I thought. Get in the back."

Ferrari looked over the musclehead's shoulder to see if any of his fans remained. The parking lot was empty, a single dirty light illuminating it from the far side.

"What do you want?" Ferrari asked.

"The Eagles to win a Super Bowl and fucking world peace," the black guy said. "Right at the moment, I'll settle for your worthless ass in the backseat with Bubba."

Ferrari thought about running, thought about fighting, then remembered the .38 and got into the car. Bubba pulled his own pistol and pushed him across the backseat. "Give your keys to Linwood," he said. Ferrari complied.

Linwood started the car and asked, "Which way to your hotel, *Beautiful?*" Drawing out the nickname, mocking him.

***

Not a word was spoken on the ride, Ferrari trying to figure out who these two worked for. There were many possibilities -- promoters he'd screwed by not showing up, one-night stands he'd left without saying goodbye, husbands and boyfriends of said one-night stands ... and that was before considering the many drugs dealers he owed some serious cash to.

Ferrari's hotel was a two-story dump on the main drag west of Lebanon, less than five minutes from the Elks Lodge. No one would mistake it for the luxury hotels he'd stayed in when he was a top draw. Roach traps like this survived by cutting unnecessary costs like cleaning the bathrooms and bed sheets and by catering to a crowd that rents by the hour. Only a few cars sat in the parking lot, each one begging for a trip to the body shop.

"Which room?" Linwood asked, turning off the ignition. Bubba shoved his revolver into Ferrari's head.

"212," Ferrari said. "Opposite end from the office."

"Perfect. Let's go." Linwood's cavalier tone turned Ferrari's stomach.

The three of them walked up the concrete stairs and down the exterior hallway to Ferrari's room. Ferrari handed his room key to Linwood, who unlocked the door. Bubba went inside first, switching on the lights and closing the heavy curtains as Linwood casually shoved Ferrari inside and onto the bed.

"You not curious about who we are?" Linwood asked.

"Figure you'll tell me when you want me to know," Ferrari said.

Linwood nodded. "Bubba, tell him."

Ferrari turned to face Bubba just in time to see the gloved fist hit his temple. *Fucker must have something in that glove*, Ferrari thought as he fell, unconscious.

179

When Ferrari woke, he was naked and handcuffed to the headboard, his legs tied to the bottom of the bed. He did not take any of this as a good sign. Before he could focus his eyes, he heard Linwood laugh.

"Look at you there, Bobby. Gonna look real pretty when they find you. A real American beauty, right?"

"What the fuck's going on?" Ferrari asked.

"I'll give you one chance," Linwood said, lifting a meaty finger and pacing on the worn carpet at the foot of the bed. "One chance to apologize to me and we all walk away from this right now."

"Apologize? Sure, yeah. I'm sorry. Now let me go."

Linwood chuckled, but cold, no emotion. "What are you sorry for, asshole?"

Ferrari stared at him, trying to guess how he had wronged the man in pink and turquoise, but … nothing. "I'm sorry for … that night I spent with your woman?"

Linwood shook his head. "Bubba, correct the man."

Another punch from a gloved fist, this one to the ribs. Ferrari groaned as he heard and felt the cracking bone, contorting in pain as much as the restraints allowed.

"Maybe some coke will help your memory," Linwood said. He grabbed a small mirror with two lines of cocaine from the nightstand and held it beneath Ferrari's nose. "It's okay, *Beautiful*, it's from your own personal stash. I knew you'd have plenty here. Help him out, Bubba."

Bubba put a small straw up Ferrari's left nostril and pinched the right nostril shut. Ferrari snorted, almost instinctively. The powder had an instant euphoric effect.

"Go ahead, the other line, too," Linwood said, and Ferrari did.

"Feeling better?"

Ferrari nodded, quietly rejoicing in the high.

"The name Linwood Guns mean anything to you?"

"Linwood … Guns … Nothing."

"More coke."

They forced Ferrari to snort two more lines. He didn't resist much.

Linwood leaned right into Ferrari's face and gritted his teeth. "Linwood Guns. You remember?"

Ferrari's heart raced and he felt sweat forming on his forehead and face. He had OD'ed more than once. This was what it felt like when he needed to stop with the coke.

"Linwood Guns, motherfucker. Remember?"

Ferrari shook his head. "I want ... I want to remember. I can't."

"How about Mega Summer Bash 7, Philly, 2007? You remember that?"

Ferrari nodded, slowly. "Maybe. A little."

Linwood slapped him. "Come on! You and Joey Nightmare wrestled a tag team ..."

"Yeah," Ferrari said, nodding. "Yeah, we did, we did. The Vice ... something."

"The Vice Squad. Me and Elroy Guns, God rest his soul. You remember what happened in that match?"

"Yeah ... Oh, fuck. Fuck, I'm sorry, man."

"Last match I ever wrestled, motherfucker. You were wired on coke and screwed up a suplex. Broke my damn neck."

"Jesus, I'm sorry."

"I'm afraid that moment has passed, *Beautiful*," Linwood said. He turned to Bubba. "More coke."

"Shit, no, no, no," Ferrari said, shaking his head wildly. Flecks of sweat flew from his forehead. His heart raced faster, his whole body trembled, his vision blurred. He knew what more coke meant.

Bubba went to the bathroom. Ferrari heard water running, then Bubba returned with a full glass. He poured cocaine into it, a lot of cocaine, and stirred the mixture with the coke straw.

"Elroy killed himself last week," Linwood said. "You know that?"

181

Ferrari shook his head. Swallowed.

"He was my best friend, but he was Bubba's daddy."

Bubba held the glass at Ferrari's lips and said, "Time for a little drink. Open up, *Beautiful*."

Linwood squeezed Ferrari's cheeks, forcing his mouth open. Bubba poured the cocaine-laced water into his mouth. Ferrari tried to scream, tried not to swallow, but he couldn't stop the liquid's passage to his stomach. In less than a minute, the glass was empty. Ferrari thought his heart was going to explode.

Linwood nodded to Bubba. "Another one."

Halfway through the second glass, Ferrari passed out. In his mind, he flew. Flew across the ring one last time, heard one last crowd cheering, relished one last moment of glory. On the filthy bed in the shithole hotel, he convulsed and then his body lay motionless.

About the Author - Erik Arneson lives in Pennsylvania, U.S.A., and dreamed of becoming a professional wrestler until he realized how many of them died noir-worthy deaths. His crime fiction stories have been printed by Shotgun Honey, Near to the Knuckle and Mary Higgins Clark Mystery Magazine. He blogs at http://erikarneson.wordpress.com and tweets @erikarneson.

The Window
by
Steve Weddle

Paul stood at the window, a little removed, and watched the teenage boy step into the woods. Paul was a landscaper, recently unemployed, and had nowhere else to be.

A few minutes later, when the tea water whistled across the quiet house, Paul finished making his wife's breakfast, set the toast, the tea, the two eggs poached just so, and walked it up the stairs to her, put a pillow under her casted leg, walked back downstairs to the window.

He watched the road in front of their home, the comings and goings of the morning.

The blue Volvo with the Outer Banks sticker, a half dozen grocery bags piled in the backseat.

A white work truck, ladders, water cooler strapped to the side, slowing through the curve.

He took the black and orange afghan from the back of the rocking chair, set it on the chest next to the wooden bowl of decorative pine cones. Turned the chair to window and waited for the boy to come out of the woods.

After a half hour of watching the cars give way to the joggers, the woman bicycling with the twins, the old man with hairless legs walking and stopping, walking and stopping, Paul got up from the window to check on Amy, again.

"Do you remember that time in Memphis?" Amy asked.

He said on the edge of the bed. "Yeah."

He looked at her toes, the cracked nails, flecks of leftover red polish.

She reached for his arm, looked off to the blank wall where he'd wanted to put a TV. "Remember how we went to see the ducks at

183

that hotel and the man in that captain's hat and how we had key lime pie in the café."

"Right."

They were just married, the whole world a map of options, of little dots waiting for your "We Were Here" pushpins.

"Remember how we had to split a piece? Do you remember that? That pale little piece of pie and the crust all graham cracker crumbling and all?"

He said he did. This house was third they'd lived in the past fifteen years, one they'd expected to fill with children and birthday parties and dogs and barbeques. In the basement was a stack of photos they'd not yet unpacked. Magazine pages from places they'd wanted to visit. A shoebox filled with plans.

"We've come a long way since then," she said.

"About a thousand miles, I guess."

"Oh, come on, goof." She swatted his arm. "You know what I mean."

He took her hand in his, held it to his mouth, said he knew what she meant. He tucked a sleep-matted clump of hair behind her ear.

She looked to the windows. "Will you open the curtains on your way out?"

"You need to rest."

"I know. I just want to look outside this morning."

"Too bright."

"Please. I just want to feel the sunlight. On my face. Just a little bit."

He got up. Slid one of the curtain panels to the side. "There. That's enough. Now close your eyes and go back to sleep." He took the cup of tea she hadn't touched, the tray of food, carried it downstairs to the sink, and walked back to the front window to look for the boy.

***

184

When her sister knocked on the front door, Paul left his sketches and walked her upstairs. She had short hair that she wore bobbed, rectangular glasses she didn't need but had gotten after she'd seen them on someone else. She had flowers in her arms for Amy. Irises. Daylilies. Purple and red and yellow. The types of flowers Paul enjoyed working with, the burying of the bulbs in the fall, the harsh winter, the surprising blooms in the spring. Amy's sister walked up the stairs, cut flowers held in the fold of her arm. Childlike. Paul stayed downstairs to look for a vase.

When she came back down a while later, she said Amy had fallen back asleep. Said Amy needed to rest.

"I know she needs to rest," Paul said. "I'm the one who told her to rest."

"OK. She just needs to rest now. That's all I'm saying. I didn't mean anything."

"I'm sorry," Paul said, sitting back down. "Been a long, I don't know," he looked off somewhere else, "however long it's been."

Her sister smiled just a little bit. "Did the doctor say anything about," she started.

"No. The doctor didn't say anything." Paul walked her to her car, nodded as she drove off.

After she was gone, he walked across the street to the woods. Paul had often thought of Amy's sister, in many ways. Then she had twins and he didn't think of her as often. The twins going into middle school next year. And Amy's son from her first marriage now grown, living in Cincinnati.

After Amy's sister had gone, Paul gave her a few minutes in case she'd forgotten something, needed to come back. Then he put a hand on the front door, eased it open, and crossed the road, stepped across the ditch, into the brushy weed before the trees where that boy had disappeared. The Lot For Sale sign, faded red and white, still against that tree, hanging from one nail. A new name and phone number nailed against the old one.

Paul walked into the woods, stepped across the fallen pine limbs, the brown and browning leaves along the ground.

Twenty feet from the edge of the woods, he found the boy's hideout, a slight depression in the ground, maybe two feet, covered with a sort of lean-to of limbs and an old blanket. Paul leaned underneath, saw a pile in the corner—a garden gnome, a peeling cigar box, a small trophy with what must have been a tennis player standing on top of it, stubs of arms reaching up like some forgotten piece in the corner of a museum.

No whiskey bottles. No cigarettes. No rain-soaked, clumpy pages of naked women he'd never be with. Just fragments from the nearby houses. Glimpses of neighbors. The flyers wedged into mailboxes in the Spring: "If you see any suspicious activity." The emails going back and forth. Neighborhood watch. The county deputies adding Mallard Place and Bufflehead Boulevard to their daily routes. All because this boy had taken this Made In China ship's lantern fitted for votives from the deck of that brick house with the front-facing garage everyone complained about.

Paul leaned under the roof of the place, started to ease a shoulder in. Then he stood up, rolled one of the logs back, and slid through the wider opening, slid the log back behind him.

***

When he got back to the house, Amy's sister was back, sitting in her car, cellphone to her ear.

Paul walked over to the driveway, knocked on her window. She shook, dropped the phone, rolled down the window.

"I was just trying to call Amy," she said. "I knocked. You didn't answer."

He said he was out. He might have made an explanation to someone else.

"Did you fall?" she asked, stepping out of the car. "Your shoulder, the mud."

"No," he said. "I'm fine."

He walked her down the sidewalk, through the overgrown mint and lavender, to the front door.

186

"I brought Amy this book," she said, pulling a crinkled paperback from her shoulder bag of a purse. She offered Paul the book.

A mystery novel by a woman he'd never heard of. He turned the book over. Costa Rica. Where Amy and RJ, her first husband, had honeymooned.

"You'd love it," she told Paul once when he'd walked in on her looking at photo albums. "It was like Eden."

Paul held the novel. "You can come in if you want or I give it to her," he said to Amy's sister, who said that was fine, that she needed to get back to the twins.

Then he waited behind the front window, watched her get back into her station wagon, back down the hill, turn and leave the development.

Paul thumbed through the novel, reading the place names. Nicoya. Cartago. Oh, you should have seen the rains in San Pablo, she'd said. Drowned rats, she'd said.

She had told Paul they should go back, that he would enjoy the landscapes. The exotic plants, though she couldn't remember any of their names.

She called down the stairs to him. He set the book on the yard sale table by the front door, walked up the stairs.

"Five weeks," she said. "That's all I can think of. Then the soft cast. Then we can go somewhere, do something. We can go back to Memphis."

He said it was too late to go back.

She said maybe someplace new. Someplace neither of them had been.

He said he hadn't been many places.

"You always say that," she said. "You always make it sound like I'm some world traveler."

"Aren't you?"

"Don't be like that," she said. "I said let's go someplace. Me and you. It can be old or new. It doesn't matter."

"What's wrong with here?" he asked. "We can get the garden back. Start that grove in the back. Some place to put a swingset in a few years."

"Is that what this is about? Jesus, Paul. Can we not talk about that? Please? Jesus God, Paul."

He swallowed. "It's fine. It's just that," he started.

"I know it's 'just that,' sweets, I know. You heard what the doctor said. This time didn't work out. You heard what she said. We can try again."

"I know."

"Just not now. Let's not talk about it now. Let's talk about where we want to go. What we want to see."

Paul said maybe they should stay close to home for a while, just in case.

"We can 'try' anywhere," she said. "And if it happens, it happens. Sometimes," she stopped. "Well, we're not getting any younger."

He said he knew that. "What do you mean? We already talked about this." Paul looked at the photo on her nightstand, of her son in Cincinnati, the Get Well card he'd overnighted her. He looked across the bed to his nightstand, the lamp, the magazine.

"You just can't imagine how difficult it is to get up at two in the morning to feed a baby, to keep up with the shots, the flu, the diapers, all of it. I mean, at twenty it was hard enough. You just can't imagine, Paul. You really can't imagine."

He said he could imagine that. It was all he could do.

"I'm just tired. That's all. I'm sorry, Paul."

He said that was fine, pulled her covers up to her neck. Said he was going downstairs to watch the game, to let her rest.

When he got to the bottom of the stairs, he took the novel off the table, eased open the front door.

As he crossed the street, he waved to a mini-van with a woman inside. He didn't know her and she didn't wave back. When she'd gone around the corner, he crossed the ditch into the woods.

He opened the book, peeled the last few pages out, then set the novel against the little trophy, at a slight angle, leaning like a family portrait on someone else's mantle.

About the Author - Steve Weddle is the editor of NEEDLE: A Magazine of Noir and a co-founder of DoSomeDamage.com. His website is www.steveweddle.com

The Conversation
by
Eva Dolan

"A man walks into a bar – see you're bored already."

Mason grinned. "I'm not, go on."

"A man walks into a bar," Lorna said, smiling back, showing him teeth. "And he meets this girl..."

"Getting better. Is she attractive?"

"Naturally. He's a good looking guy."

She wasn't lying. Six-two of clean-cut bastard in a Saville Row suit and handmade chestnut Oxfords. Mason was forty-five but wore it well. He'd have no trouble picking up teenagers still, she guessed, bring them somewhere like this, discreetly lit and reeking of effortless money, all grey walls and velvet chairs and ironic rococo flourishes.

"Now he's a speculator of sorts and he tells her that the reason he's so good at his job is his ability to read people. She thinks he's full of shit."

"He sounds it."

"Doesn't mean he's unlikeable."

"Do you think the audience is going to like him?"

"Men will want to be him, women will want to be with him?"

Mason nodded, sipped his Hennessey XO, blue eyes steady on her across the rim of the glass.

"I like him," Lorna said. "That's a good start."

"So..."

"So he bets her a thousand pounds he can guess what she does for a living."

"He's rich."

"Croesus envies this guy's yacht." Lorna recrossed her legs and watched his eyes drop. "She gives him five guesses and he goes through the usual bullshit flattery. Are you model? An actress?"

"High class whore?"

"That's his fourth guess, after nuclear physicist."

"One more then." He gestured at a passing waitress for more drinks; one manicured finger making a lazy circle in the air. "I really thought he had it with the whore."

The pianist at the back of the bar launched into Stormy Weather and Lorna ran the lyrics in her head as Mason scrutinised the height of her heels and the way her hair fell, trying to decide what kind of woman looked that way.

"Serviette or napkin?" he asked.

"Seriously?"

He smiled, capped teeth, crow's feet. "No, you ambitious urchin types always learn the patois."

"Who's talking about me?"

The waitress brought their drinks over, iced Snow Queen for the lady, another cognac for sir. She was unobtrusively pretty, slight and blond and east European. The owners knew how to keep their city boy clientele happy. Mason checked her out as she walked away, a reflex straight from his balls.

"She's a hack," he said.

"No. Not a bad guess though."

"So what is she?"

"She doesn't tell him."

He wagged his finger at her, a little drunk already. "See you have a problem there now. You've led the audience to expect a pay-off and you've not delivered."

"I'm working the delayed gratification angle."

Stormy Weather ended and the pianist picked out the opening bars of Round Midnight. It wasn't quite that late but getting there fast. Late enough that Mason wanted to wrap up the negotiations and proceed to business.

"She offers him double or nothing that she can guess what he does."

"Because she already knows who he is?"

Lorna nodded, shot him another smile.

"Is she stalking him?"

191

"In a professional capacity, yes, you could call it stalking."
Mason went for his glass. "It's getting dark."

"You better brace yourself then." Lorna leaned forward in the chair, gave him an eyeline down her top. "At this point the story moves across London to a high risk cell in Belmarsh. I'm seeing a nice swooping shot here, I want to communicate how far apart the two men are; we've got our murder suspect, raddled, emaciated, old before his time, and our corporate big dick with his ostentatious charity work and his armour-plated reputation."

Mason put his glass down very deliberately but the tremor in his hand still showed.

"She's a solicitor," he said.

"You're smarter than him anyway."

Lorna called to the waitress, told her to make them trebles. A couple staggered past their table, drunk and glowing, the man holding his date upright, carrying her small gold clutch and the shoes she'd taken off, inevitable red soles flashing like a warning.

The colour had risen in Mason's lightly tanned cheeks. "What do you want?"

"I just want your opinion. A lot of the work now is how to show the audience the link between these men without giving too much away. I want to finesse it."

"I think they'd prefer you to cut to the chase."

"There isn't a chase. It isn't that kind of story."

"If she's going after a powerful man he'll defend himself."

"No. He doesn't have those kinds of connections."

"Are you sure?"

"I've worked his back story through very thoroughly."

Their drinks came and he took a long swallow, fighting the urge to down it at a single draft. Lorna expected more composure from him, this self-professed corporate psychopath who'd boxed at Cambridge and climbed K2 solo on his fortieth birthday.

"Our solicitor has been assigned to the prisoner by legal aid. He's inside for murdering his business partner, which makes it sound more glamorous than it is; they have a taxi firm working around the

192

square mile. Some accounting mistakes were made..." she waved her hand vaguely. "Violence ensues. That part's quite gory, we might need to tone it down for a fifteen certificate. Bolt cutters are applied to some sensitive areas."

Mason sat rigid with his hands placed just so on the arms of the chair, his posture in lock-down.

"The prisoner confesses everything to the police – that isn't our primary focus – but he wants leniency. He's getting on, he's not well. One of those obscure cancers. So he tells his solicitor that he's got something to trade and tells her where to find the evidence."

"That old chestnut?" Mason said.

"It gets even hoarier. The evidence is in a safety deposit box and we have a very atmospheric scene in this old bank; the solicitor going into the vault and opening the box and we'll really draw this out. Because she doesn't believe the guy's got anything at that point."

Lorna sipped her vodka, like licking snowflakes off chrome.

"The only thing in the box is a CD with a date printed on it."

Mason watched her with a blank expression that looked painful to maintain. He was running down his bad deeds now, trying to figure out if any might have been recorded, if some quiet fraud was about to be exposed. Maybe the one which paid for the knighthood he was rumoured to be receiving in this year's list.

Lorna flicked her hair and made eye contact with the man on the next table for less than a second.

"Is it holding your attention?" she asked.

Mason nodded. "What's on the disc?"

"Our solicitor leaves the bank and climbs into a cab and puts the disc in her laptop and we get this moment of dislocation as the screen fills with the interior of an identical hackney cab. People come and go, she's got all their conversations on there. Isn't it strange how everyone asks cabbies what time they're on till?"

"Humour isn't your strong suit."

"I'll subcontract the jokes."

His mobile phone vibrated on the low glass table between them but he ignored it.

193

"Your middle's sagging," he said.

"That's why I put another murder in."

His jaw tightened but it couldn't have been much of a surprise to him. Two weeks since the body was found, wrapped in a cashmere blanket and stuffed into a recycling bin on a quiet suburban street. Front page news for a couple of days, weeping family members brought out for the cameras and appeals for information which yielded nothing.

Contempt flickered around Mason's nostrils and he cleared his throat noisily before he spoke,

"A dead brunette?"

"I believe blondes are more traditional."

"I'd prefer a brunette. About your size."

"I don't photograph well," Lorna said. "The camera loves you though."

He smiled thinly. "Whatever you think you have – "

"Check your phone."

"What?"

She gestured towards his mobile and watched the slow play of realisation as he ran the video clip he'd just received. His eyes narrowed, then widened and he looked away sharply, as if the actual crime was on there.

It wasn't though.

"I don't like it happening off camera," Lorna said. "It feels like we're cheating the audience. They want to see the couple get out of the cab – it's a nice street in Little Venice, white mansion houses, clipped privet. Very upscale. It could be quite a sexy scene actually, they can't keep their hands off each other in the back of the cab can they?"

He held his mobile face down on his thigh. Like that would contain his problem. He glanced around the bar, trying to figure out who'd sent it. The black guy in the razor tailored suit or the Russian looking pair in the booth opposite them, tattoos and shaved heads and bulges under their jackets that might be guns.

194

"The problem is certain audiences can be very conservative about man on man action." His attention snapped back to her. "No, let's maintain the integrity of our story. Two men, lovers, there's an intimacy between them, this isn't just about sex."

He drained the last of his cognac.

"I've got a bit of a gap here – it's still a work in progress you see? I don't actually know how the young man goes from over-the-clothes action in the back of a taxi to being battered so comprehensively that the police could only identify him by the tattoo someone tried to burn off his back after he died. "

Mason took a deep breath.

"How much do you want for your story?"

"You don't know how it ends yet."

"If I'm buying it I get to decide the ending."

"So he buys her silence?"

"Isn't that what she wants?" he asked and laughed suddenly, the tension breaking out of him. "Jesus Christ, don't tell me you're on a moral crusade?"

"Morals?" Lorna said, reaching for her glass. "They're those little French mushrooms, right?"

Mason nodded. "Exactly. Now, how much do you want?"

"Two hundred thousand."

"Don't be ridiculous."

"I'm not bartering with you. The price is two hundred, non-negotiable."

"In unmarked bills?" He smiled faintly.

Lorna took a slip of paper from her bag, placed it on the table between them. "In this bank account. By close of play tomorrow."

"I don't even get twenty-four hours?"

She stood up, smoothed her hands over her hips. "At one minute past six the recording will go on YouTube. And don't get any stupid ideas about introducing third-parties. I'm not the only person in this."

"What about the prisoner?"

195

"The prisoner's a McGuffin. You know what one of those is, right?"

Lorna tucked her handbag into the crook of her arm.

"By close of play, Mr Mason."

She half expected him to follow and she held her breath as she walked out of the bar, nodded goodnight to the doorman and climbed into the back of a waiting cab.

The camera was small, a discreet black lens tucked low on the metal grille. She couldn't blame Mason for missing it, distracted as he was that evening, all loving words and hard on.

"Will he pay?" the driver asked.

"Of course he'll pay."

About the Author - Eva Dolan lives in the only part of Essex where a spray-tan isn't mandatory and you can go for weeks without hearing the word vajazzle. She divides her time between copywriting and poker, with mixed results at both. You can read reviews, interviews with authors, and short fiction at her blog Loitering With Intent.

Everything You Always Wanted To Know About Sex (But Were
Afraid To Ask)
by
James Everington

`

Throughout the period when Macy had been trying to save his
marriage, the killer had been on the news. The discovery of the first
body had coincided with their first row; the dead prostitutes had
continued to be found as his wife found more and more to disliked
about Macy; and the press had first given the killer an alliterative
nickname on the day Rachel had first said the word "divorce".

Her final departure left Macy stunned - he was a meek man
and had thought his meekness would give Rachel less to be angry
about, but in the last weeks his meekness had seemed to infuriate her
the more. It wasn't until he watched her struggle with her suitcase to a
waiting taxi (he'd offered to help, as if a final gesture of obedience
might make her stay) that Macy felt the first stirrings of anger; of a
need to refute some of the things she'd said about him.

Not knowing how to achieve such a thing, he'd turned on the
TV.

"... another body," the TV said. "Twenty year old Stella King
had come to the city to..."

The photo they showed of the dead girl was full of life; Macy
thought she looked very young and very pretty. He didn't allow his
conscious thoughts to go further than that.

You're a coward, Rachel had said near the end. *You haven't
touched me for months but I know you haven't the balls for an affair.* He hadn't
felt it fair that his twenty plus years of fidelity had been used against
him, had been made pointless.

"... showed signs of strangulation," the TV said.

Macy had always know that his home town had a red-light
district, but the knowledge had never seemed quite real, nothing he
could ever have acted upon. He'd seen the prostitutes on the odd

occasion he'd had to drive through the area, their poses in his headlights like flashes from something he'd repressed. He'd seen men handing tenners to the girls who then led them off somewhere or got in their cars, but the idea that the tenners in *Macy's* wallet could be used in such a way had never seemed plausible. Macy was embarrassed by sex *and* money (and even talking to strangers). And besides, what would Rachel have said if she'd known?

The TV was showing stock footage of a faceless prostitute, flicking ash to the pavement on a street corner. Macy stared at the image and his fingers drummed nervously on the table top, coming away with a thin patina of dust. He felt sick with something that felt like shame even though he'd not done anything, and it was as if Rachel's voice was in his head mocking him for that.

***

His first attempt was a failure.

It had taken him weeks to even pluck up the courage - the idea of going to a prostitute had obsessed him even as it had terrified him. Sex acts he'd never had the guts to ask Rachel to perform seemed even more outrageous imagined with a stranger. Every time he thought about it he felt sick with nerves; but he didn't stop thinking about it.

He'd walked to the outskirts of the red-light district on foot - the idea of coming with something so identifiable as a number plate for all to see had been too much for him. He'd taken out a hundred pounds cash; he didn't know how much he'd need but that seemed ample. He was glad it was dark but Macy still felt exposed, as if the obscene images in his mind were being broadcast for all to see; for Rachel to see.

He'd started to cross the road but then the sound of sirens sent him panicked into the pub on the other side, rather than up the hill into the red-light area. He felt like a sheep herded into a pen. His heart was still hammering as he looked round the rough and dirty pub. The thought of pushing through the crowd and ordering a drink in such a place was *almost* as scary as going back outside and up the hill.

He didn't want to order a pint, for he knew it would hit his bladder just at the time when he might not want to be distracted by such things. Knew too that he couldn't order wine in a pub like this, so he asked for whisky. Feeling reckless and knowing Rachel would disapprove, he ordered a treble.

He seemed to hear the sound of mocking laughter somewhere in the pub bar, although there were no women present.

He had the whisky neat and it tasted rough and gritty with something as he downed it. Macy went to the gents to wash out the taste at the sink, but the water from the taps tasted gritty too, and he felt like he was spitting dust into the washbasin.

Outside the pub he heard more sirens and saw a police car hurtle up the road that he had wanted to take. "He's killed another one," he heard a passerby say. As he scuttled home Macy's thoughts beat a complex rhythm of shame and relief.

***

Three days later and he left the same pub spitting the same taste of whisky from his mouth, and headed up the tree-lined road that cut through the heart of the red light district. A each junction with a side street a woman stood. As he walked past he heard them call to each other, or worse to Macy as he passed.

"Lookin' for business love?" - their voices were loud and brash and Macy felt his face flame each time. He'd heard somewhere that most prostitutes were scared immigrants (a fact he'd tried to keep from his mind these last weeks) but these women were all local judging by their accent - the broad working class accent that always intimidated Macy, whether from shop assistants or mechanics... The women wore gaudy mini-skirts and their unsubtle attempts to catch his attention - "have you got a light love... have you the time on you?" - made him feel as uncomfortable as when someone cold-called him at home.

There were more of them than he had thought there would be - if the killer had struck again the other day these women were obviously too brave or desperate to care. Despite the excitement he

199

felt when he glanced at their bosoms or fishnet thighs, Macy couldn't even make eye contact with any of them, never mind ask them to do the things Rachel wouldn't (or hadn't, anyway - he'd never dared ask *her* either). But for some reason Macy didn't turn round but walked head down past all the women as if daring himself, while his hands squirmed uselessly in the dust and lint of his jacket pocket. Behind him he heard a cocky male voice bargaining successfully for exactly the thing Macy wanted, but he avoided looking round. The voice acquiescing sounded like Rachel's.

When he first saw the girl, coming down one of the side roads that bordered the red light district, he didn't think she was a prostitute for she was dressed so ordinarily, so unflatteringly - tracksuit bottoms and a hoodie. (And besides there had been something *familiar* about her.) So Macy glanced more openly as she neared him than he had any of the other women earlier - she was young, he thought, and pretty, and sad looking. Walking slowly, as if lost. When she asked him if he had the time at first he thought her genuine, and nervously checked his watch...

Her next words startled him.

"Yes," he heard himself say in reply, "yes." The fact he'd plucked up the courage exhilarated him, a savage exhilaration like revenge. He felt the whisky thud in his head now, and it made him tremble.

Somehow, he dared ask the girl for what he wanted.

She just shrugged, named him a price less than half of that he had on him. As if sensing his nerves she took his hand and led him through an unlocked gate into the deserted yard of a deconsecrated church. Gravestones for removal were piled up at one side. Is it really this easy? Macy thought. He felt flushed with triumph even though he hadn't done anything yet; he was already thinking of return trips and further requests...

The girl let go his hand to dig in her hoodie pocket; she pulled out a dusty looking condom packet.

"Ah," Macy said, "yes. Better safe than sorry." He was gabbling somewhat; he never had been good with strangers. "But *without*, perhaps...?"

The girl shrugged again, named another figure. Macy pulled out more tenners from his pocket. He didn't seem to be able to stop talking. "I mean I understand if you'd *rather*," he said, "better safe than sorry, yes. Lots of unsavoury characters around I imagine." She didn't reply and he felt the ridiculous urge to show some empathy. "Not to mention that murderer..." he said.

He'd no idea why he'd said such a thing, and the girl looked at him directly for the first time; her eyes had cleared of their dazed look and the force of them made Macy step backwards. There seemed to be lines on her face he hadn't noticed before, and they twisted her expression into one of hatred.

Macy realised he was involuntarily wiping one of his hands (the one she had held) against his trouser leg, because it was so dusty. For a second he almost turned and walked away.

But then it was if he had imagined her look of malice (and of age) for the girl was coming back to him, making cooing noises of reassurance. Her hands were all over him, and Macy tried not to think about what marks they might be making on his clothes. Hadn't that been exactly the kind of thing Rachel had left him for - fussing over trivialities when he should be enjoying himself?

The girl tugged at his belt; she bent her head. Her hair fell away from her neck as she did so and Macy thought he saw smudges of grey blue dust curving from her throat to nape. But they weren't smudges of dust, he realised, but bruises.

"Oh Jesus!" Macy said. He made the girl stand. "Have you been attacked? That killer... did *he* try and..."

She looked at him directly again, and her eyes held the same hatred, her skin the same dead-weight. Whoever it was hadn't just *tried*, Macy realised.

The girls hands clawed, as if she meant to strangle him.

"No of course not," he said swiftly, "silly me." The hate faded from her face (slower this time, but it faded) and the young girl came back to him, tugged again at his belt, which Macy had done back up in the interim. Her movements threw up small clouds of dust and to Macy the smell carried the faintest trace of old meat. *She doesn't know she's dead,* Macy thought in horror, *or doesn't want to be reminded at least.* He thought of the hate seething under the surface of this dazed looking girl's face. The hate and the dead flesh already turning to dust. To avoid that hate returning he had to act like he didn't know, he realised.

But his whole body felt shrivelled with fear, and as she unzipped him and stroked him, all he could feel was the sensation of grit-like dust. He wanted to flee but knew he couldn't back out, for then surely she would realise that he knew, and he had no doubt this murdered thing could murder him in turn. But surely she would realise soon anyway, if his body remained as unresponsive?

Macy closed his eyes and tried desperately to think of all the sexual fantasies and imagined, unknown pleasures that had led him here, to this abandoned church yard. But they all seemed ridiculous and unrealistic to him now. The only thing that came to mind, the only thing that *worked* on his reluctant flesh, was the thought of *Rachel,* memories of the safe, comfortable, lazy, boring, nice sex he'd had with Rachel. He hadn't wanted any of those other fantasies, not truly - hadn't wanted *this.* In truth, Macy's libido was lukewarm as glowing embers, gradually turning to ash. Only when he thought of his soon to be ex-wife did it spark.

The girl seemed satisfied, took away her hand, and knelt to do what he'd paid for. Macy risked opening his eyes and saw again the hand-shaped bruises ringing her slim neck. He shut his eyes quickly again. *Just think about Rachel,* he thought in a panic, *think this is Rachel...* As long as he could continue to pretend that then it would be okay.

He thought it was going to work and that the girl would let him live, until the moment her mouth touched his flesh, and he realised it was as full of the cold dust of her death as the rest of her.

About the Author - James Everington is a writer from Nottingham, England who mainly writes dark, supernatural fiction, although he occasionally takes a break and writes dark, non-supernatural fiction. His first collection, The Other Room, contains both. He is also one of the four Abominable Gentlemen behind the Penny Dreadnought e-anthology. You can find out what he is currently up to at his Scattershot Writing blog (www.jameseverington.blogspot.com). He drinks Guinness, if anyone is offering.

From Here To Eternity
by
Adrian McKinty

At midnight all the agents are asleep and on the beach there are only
disaffected, cold policemen silently sharing smokes and gazing through
binoculars at the black Atlantic, hoping to catch the first glimpse of
the running lights on what has become known to the ironists in Special
Branch as the *Ship of Death*. My journal says that it is October 12th
1985. Reagan's the President, Thatcher's the PM, some chinless
wonder is new Secretary of State for Northern Ireland. The number
one album in the UK is Madonna's *Like A Virgin* and Jennifer Rush's
torch song *The Power Of Love* has just hit the top of the charts where it
is destined to remain for a dispiritingly long time. . .

   Drizzle. Static. Oscillating sine waves of sound. A fragment
of Dutch. A DJ from RFI informing the world that "Euro Disney sera
construit a Paris." Grey air until finally the constable in charge of the
shortwave finds the shipping forecast: "Rockall, Malin, Hebrides,
Bailey, light drizzle, fair, calm."

   The weather is perfect, the moon is down and the tide is on
the ebb.

"If they're coming, they'll be coming soon," a Chief Superintendent
says, voicing the consensus of all the old hands.

   I say nothing. I have been brought in by Special Branch
purely as a courtesy because one of my informers contributed a tip to
this complicated international operation and it is not my place to
speak. Instead I pat my revolver and flip back through my journal to
the place where I have taped a postcard of Guido Reni's Michael
Tramples Satan. I discreetly make the sign of the cross and, in a
whisper, ask for the continuing protection of Saint Michael, the
archangel, the patron saint of coppers. I am not sure I believe in the
existence of Saint Michael the Archangel, the patron Saint of coppers,
but I am a member of RUC, which is the police force with the highest

mortality rate in the Western World, so every little bit of talismanic assistance helps. I close the notebook and light a cigarette for some evil eyed character who says he's from Interpol but who looks like a spook from 140 Gower Street come to keep an eye on the Paddies and make sure they don't make a hash of the whole thing.

He mutters a thank you and passes over a flask which turns out to contain high quality gin.

"Cheers," I say, take a swig, and pass it back.

"Chin chin," he replies, takes a swig himself and puts the flask in his raincoat pocket.

A breeze moves the clouds from the face of the moon. Somewhere in the carpark a dog barks.

The policemen wait.

The spooks wait.

The men on the boat wait.

All of us tumbling into the future together.

"So are you based in Lyons?" I ask the 'Interpol' man and he gives me a puzzled noncommittal nod of the head. *He's MI5 or I'm Rudd Gullitt.*

Time crawls by. The wind picks up.

We watch the waves and the chilly, black infinity where sky and sea merge somewhere off Malin Head. Finally at 12.30 someone shouts "There! I see her!" and after this is confirmed by another sighting we are all ordered off the beach. Most of us retreat behind the dunes and a few of the wiser officers slink all the way back to the Land Rovers to warm up over spirit stoves and hot whiskies. I find myself behind a sandbar with two women in raincoats who appear to be Special Branch Intel.

"It's exciting, isn't it?" I say.

"Who are you?" the brunette, the prettier of the two, asks.

I tell her but as soon as the word 'Inspector' has passed my lips I can see that she has lost interest. There are Assistant Chief Constables and Chief Superintendents floating about tonight and I'm a lowly Detective Inspector?

205

I wave to the MI5 goon with the flask of Tanqueray. "I'll take another hit of that, mate," I tell him and he reluctantly passes it over.

"About time!" someone says and we watch the *Our Lady of Knock* navigate its way into the channel and towards the surf. It's an odd looking vessel. A small converted cargo boat, perhaps, or a trawler with the pulleys and chains removed. It doesn't really look seaworthy but somehow it's made it all the way from Boston, across three thousand miles of Atlantic Ocean.

About two hundred metres from the shore it drops anchor and after some unprofessional dithering a Zodiac is lowered into the water. Five men climb aboard the little speedboat and it zooms eagerly towards the beach. As soon as they touch dry land the case will come under the jurisdiction of the RUC, even though all five gunrunners are American citizens and the ship is registered in the Bahamas.

Skip, skip, skip goes the little Zodiac oblivious of rocks or hidden reefs of which there are many along this stretch of coast. It miraculously avoids them all and zips up the surf onto the beach. The men get out and start looking around them for errant dog walkers or lovers or other witnesses. Spotting no one they shout "Yes!" and "Booyah!" One man gets on his knees and, emulating the Holy Father, kisses the sand. He has dedication this lad, the tarmac at Dublin Airport is one thing but this gravelly, greasy beach downwind from one of Derry's main sewage plants is quite another.

"We made it!" one of the men yells.

"Whoo-hoo!" another one replies.

They open a bottle and begin passing it around. It is clear that they are pretty young guys. Young American men who have come across the big sea to bring us death in the form of rocket launchers and machine guns.

"Look at those eejit Yanks," one of the female Special Branch goons says.

"They think they can do what they like, don't they?" her pal replies.

I resist the temptation to pile on. It isn't really my case and although these Irish American gunrunners are undoubtedly naïve and ignorant I understand where they're coming from. Ennui stamps us all. Vietnam has cured America of foreign adventures for at least a generation so you have to get your kicks where you can find them. Northern Ireland is as good a place as any. Few women, I suppose, will ever understand men's need for aggro. It's in our DNA. One of the mysteries of the Y chromosome.

The men on the beach begin to look at their watches and wonder what to do next. They are expecting a lorry driver called Alex McCready and his son Joe, both of whom are already in the Castlereagh Holding Centre in Belfast getting the third degree. One of the men lights a flare and begins waving it above his head which, when you think about it, is just ridiculous. It's hard not to feel something for these patriots but this level of carelessness robs you of your compassion pretty quickly.

"What are they going to do next? Set off fireworks?" someone grumbles behind me.

"What are we going to do next?" I say back, loud enough for the Chief Supers to hear me. I mean how much longer are we going to have to wait here? If there are guns on the boat, we have them and if there no guns on the boat we don't have them, but either way the time to arrest them is now.

"Quiet in the ranks!" someone says.

If I was in charge I'd announce our presence with a loudspeaker and spotlights and patiently explain the situation to these patriots from Massachusetts. *You are surrounded, your vessel cannot escape the lough, please put your hands up and come quietly. . .*

But that is not what happens. This being an RUC-Gardai-FBI-MI5-Interpol operation we wander off the straight and narrow into the realm of the epic screw up.

A high ranking uniformed policeman begins walking towards the men on the beach.

"What the hell is he doing?" I mutter to myself.

"All right chaps, the game's up!" he announces to the gun runners in a brisk *Dixon Of Dock Green* accent.

All right chaps, the game's up?

207

Christ on a Kawasaki.

The Americans immediately draw their weapons and run for the Zodiac. One of them takes a pot shot at the uniformed peeler, making him hit the deck. *This is not cricket,* he's probably thinking as he crawls for cover behind some driftwood.

"Put your hands up!" another copper belatedly yells through a megaphone.

The Americans fire blindly into the darkness with an impressive arsenal of weaponry including shotguns and what must be M16 rifles.

Some of the policemen begin to shoot back.

We have now well and truly crossed the border into the land of clusterfuck and within seconds the moonless night is lit up by phosphorescent flares and radiant muzzle bursts and red tracer.

"Lay down your arms!" the copper with the megaphone bleats with an air of desperation.

A police marksman brings down one of the Yanks with a bullet in the shoulder, but the gun runners don't still don't give up. They're confused, sea sick, exhausted. They have no idea who is shooting at them or why. They reach the Zodiac and begin pushing it towards the surf. They don't realise that they're outnumbered ten to one and that if by some miracle they do make it back to the *Our Lady Of Knock,* they're just going to get boarded by the Special Boat Squad and them boys don't mess around.

"Put your guns down, this is the police, you are surrounded!" the men are told through the megaphone.

But blood has been spilled and the men respond with a fusillade of machine gun fire that sends us all ducking for cover.

"Jesus!"

A hand on my shoulder.

I turn to look into the grim face of the Assistant Chief Constable. Black eyes, grey buzzcut, heavy handlebar peeler tache.

"We can't let them get back to the ship! We don't want the navy getting them. This is our operation. What's your name?"

"It's—"

"Doesn't matter. Come with me!"

"Where?"

"We're going to arrest them!"

"With all due respect, sir, no fucking way."

"That's an order!"

I am pulled up by my collar. I'm in plain clothes: jeans, jumper, rain coat. No body armour, no bullet proof vest. . .

"Sir, be reasonable I—"

"Right you lot, come with me!" the ACC yells to the cowering policemen and runs down the dunes towards the escaping Americans.

It's such an absurd atavistic World War fucking 1 manoeuvre that half the coppers follow him. I find myself following too.

The Americans are still shooting.

The policemen fire back with revolvers and Sterling submachine guns.

Its madness. Complete madness.

Bullets are whizzing everywhere, mostly missing people, instead slamming into the dunes or arcing off into the black night.

Another gunrunner goes down. A box of ammo on the Zodiac catches fire.

We reach the bottom of the dunes and begin running across the wet sand.

In five seconds we're all exhausted.

Suddenly the box of ammo explodes with a deafening blast and shrapnel and white fire. I dive for the sand and when I look up I see the Zodiac overturned and burning and all the Americans on their backs.

I run towards them. Two are dead, torn apart by the explosion and one lanky bearded Jesus is wandering in a daze, scorched but apparently unhurt.

Another longhaired guy is face down in the surf.

I turn him over.

It's a she.

209

She's seventeen or eighteen. Red-haired, freckled, pale, beautiful. Blood is pouring from a wound on her scalp.

"Medic!" I yell back at the disorganised shambles on the dunes.

A wave breaks on top of me and the surf knocks me over. I take off my raincoat and put it in behind her head. But then I see that it's too late for that. The sea all around her is red. I notice a gaping wound in her abdomen from which blood is pouring by the pint.

"Medic! For God's sake! Medic!"

She begins to convulse.

"H-hold me," she says.

I cradle her in my arms.

"What's your name?" I ask.

The surf rocks her.

I can see the starlight in her eyes.

"We did it," she says.

"Yeah you did it," I tell her.

About the Author – Adrian McKinty is the author of twelve novels, with his latest being 'The Cold Cold Ground', released in 2012. More information can be found at his blog http://adrianmckinty.blogspot.co.uk/

Vertigo
by
Maxim Jakubowski

I kill people. That's my job.

I get paid for it. Well, I try not to worry about the moral implications of my trade, and I know that in the majority of cases the people I am eliminating are bad people if only because my employers are bad people themselves. Makes sense, no? Although I have actually never met the people who settle my bills. For security reasons, it's all done at one step removed, through the phone, the Internet or by coded messages and left luggage lockers in train stations or other places which attract discretion.

The little I see of my victims, whether on the photographs in the dossiers I am supplied with beforehand or, in the flesh, when I first track them down, observe their goings on and plan the hit, normally confirms my assumptions: they look shifty, dishonest, dangerous and tick all the wrong points. And in some cases, they just look perfectly normal. It doesn't bother me either.

I do have certain rules and I stick by them.

No children, no witnesses, no one under police protection.

I entered the hitman profession by accident. But then isn't that how most careers develop?

I needed some cash fast. I have some expensive hobbies and collecting rare books is one of them. And when a title I lust after appears in a dealer's catalogue and if my funds are insufficient, that's when I indicate that I'm available for a job. In between books, I lead a normal life. I am not a greedy man, you see. I am pragmatic, dispassionate, logical. That's what keeps me out of trouble.

I even sometimes think of myself as something of an artist.

There are so many ways to kill a person. Many of them are vulgar, I find. If the client wishes the hit to be loud, spectacular, sometimes in order to make an impression, I comply. But in most instances they leave the minutiae to me, and that's the way I prefer it. I never use the same weapon twice, vary my methods. There are even cases where I can manage to make the death look accidental. Depends on my mood, the circumstances, the location. As I said, I'm a pragmatic sort of guy and I get a real kick out of improvisation. Which doesn't mean I'm neglectful when I make sudden changes to a plan. I still remain careful and go by my rules.

On this occasion, a dealer in Belgium was advertising a first edition, not only in perfect condition and with dust jacket but also signed by both authors which was pretty rare, of Boileau-Narcejac's D'ENTRE LES MORTS. I actually do read French, not that I soil any of the books in my collection by actually reading them. I already had a reading copy, a later paperback reissue of the title. The film is actually better than the book in my opinion. But my principal motivation was the fact this thriller novel had later become one of my favourite Hitchcock movies and, actually, one my favourite films altogether. The price the dealer was asking for was outrageous, but as I said neither of the now-deceased authors were in the frequent habit of signing copies of any of their titles and once I saw the listing, my lust for the book could not be sated.

Her name was Madeleine.

Normally I don't wish to know too much about the reasons behind the jobs. Makes things easier. But in this instance the dossier (which I had of course destroyed Mission Impossible-style after first carefully noticing its contents) had spelled it all out. There's nothing new under the sun. Rich husband, unfaithful wife, money involved. The usual shitty reasons.

She was in the habit of cruising the plush hotels that circled the airport where she picked strange men up in bars. She didn't do it for money, which she was not short of. No amateur whore, she. She did it for the sex or whatever else she was after. Never went with the same man twice.

It didn't take much planning.

I followed her in my hire car from the moment she drove off from the mansion in which she and her husband (conveniently away that week at a trade convention in St Louis, Minnesota) lived in the plush suburbs of the city.

I'd been tracking her for a few days, checking her habits, the hotel she liked to frequent. She flitted between a half dozen four star establishments and I'd booked rooms in all of them beforehand under an assumed name and a credit card which couldn't be traced to me.

When I saw her drive her hybrid Prius into the underground car park of the Royal & Golf, I rang to cancel my other reservations pretexting a flight delay and parked across the Boulevard and was already checking in at the reception desk and picking up my electronic door card by the time she emerged from the elevator which connected the hotel lobby with the parking area. She went straight to the lounge bar.

I entered the dimly lit room in which a mediocre jazz pianist was tinkling the ivories in a corner with a repertoire ranging from Gershwin to Cole Porter and back to Gershwin again. Someone should have put a contract out of him long ago, I felt. But I didn't do jobs for free.

She was sitting at the bar and seemed familiar to the bartender. She never drank much, I knew. Just nursed a couple of glasses over a whole evening unless she connected with someone, usually businessmen passing through the city and stuck in the particular hotel between flights. Mostly gin and tonics, which was sort of more European than American.

I sat on a stool across from her. There were barely half a dozen people in the bar; it was still early in the evening. She was daydreaming. From observing her over the last few nights I knew she never took the first step. Which reassured the punters who might be nervous and feared they were dealing with a professional. She dressed elegantly but conservatively and did not look like a woman of the night, which was why she was not bothered by the barmen or hotel security staff. She could have been any business executive in town for meetings halfway between the coasts. Bored. Available.

She had style, did not throw herself at men. But there was an air of sadness about her, an emptiness that made you want to call her over and get her to lay her head on your shoulders while you stroked her long, lustrous dark hair.

"A drink for the lady," I beckoned the barman.

She acknowledged me with a faint smile.

Looked at me, the smile broadened. I was acceptable.

"Thank you..." Took a glance at my own glass. "What's that you're drinking?" she asked.

"Just Pepsi," I said.

It was always a good gambit to begin a conversation. A man who didn't drink alcohol. I never quite figured out whether the fact I did not drink made me appear more reliable or more remarkable. At any rate, I knew there were no rumours circulating about a Cola drinking killer at large.

Her eyes were ebony black, deep wells of melancholy. Her lipstick just the right, discreet shade of red. Her cheekbones prominent and rouged to elegant perfection against the white tundra of her skin. She reminded me of Snow White. Her tailored suit top was open just one button down so you could catch a glimpse of the thin alley of her cleavage and her breasts appeared to be milky white. Her voice was husky, a bedroom sort of voice. She didn't wear her wedding ring.

Normally, one would have conversed and quickly raised the subject of the unhappiness in her marriage, but I was aware she was on the prowl and knew all the normal preliminaries were quite unnecessary. I was the only willing male in the bar right now and I had passed her initial test of acceptability it seemed.

"We could have a last drink up in my room, " I suggested.

She agreed.

We were by now speaking the same language of things untold.

As we entered the elevator, I caught a whiff of her perfume. Anais Anais. I'd always had a nose for fragrances. Sometimes that's how I remembered women. Not just their bodies, but also their perfumes. Call me sentimental.

Her ankles were a thing of beauty, thin, firm, curvy, like a delicate sculpture of flesh and the shoes she was wearing, heels just right, neither too short or too high, like a showcase.

Constrained within the thin grey material of her suit skirt, her arse swayed gently over strong hips.

We had already kissed before we reached the top floor where the room I had booked was situated.

Yes, we fucked.

Some of you might feel that was taking undue advantage of her. That I could have done the deed without going to bed with her (although to be technical about the whole thing not all of it actually took place on the bed…).

I disagree.

Now, I might not be God's gift to womankind but I did feel she deserved more than a peck on the cheek before I got around to the business of the night. If you feel that was an act of selfishness, then you are entitled to your own opinion and I won't come after you with a Sig Sauer or a dagger drawn if you persist in thinking that.

We made love.

She drew a deep sigh as I entered her for the first time and her fingernails raked my back as she held tight to me while I thrust inside her. Her legs circled my buttocks and gripped me in a vice of desire, inviting me to go ever deeper and reach her furthest sexual connection points.

When I came, and opened my eyes and looked at her face, I caught a few tears pearling down her pale cheeks.

"Are you OK?" I asked.

"Yes, I'm fine," she reassured me. "It's silly. I always cry a little when I'm fucked. Just the way I am. Don't let it bother you." And she attempted a feeble smile.

We lay together in the darkness a long time.

Madeleine didn't want to talk.

Neither did I.

Maybe this surprised her, as all the men she picked up on her lost evenings no doubt bombarded her with the customary questions

215

as to why she did this, why she was unhappy, if they were sensitive enough to the situation, or just treated her disdainfully once they'd enjoyed the fuck they were seeking and found her eminently disposable.

She gave me a few curious glances, peering through the penumbra of the room, expecting some form of reaction.

I was different.

It was the middle of the night by then. Soon, I knew, she would want to leave. She never stayed with any of the men she slept with until morning. It would have been too intimate.

"You know, the view from the balcony is incredible. Did you know you can see the whole city and its lights. It's really great. Let me show you."

She hesitated one brief moment then consented and rose, regally naked, from the bed. At the sight of her body, my heart seized a little. She now looked smaller without the heels, the clothes, like a little girl lost in a deep, dark forest,

I took her hand, slid the window open. It was a summer night.

"It's OK," I said. "No one can see us this high. Know we are naked." I kissed her neck as we stepped across to the balcony rail. My hands held her waist. Her skin was warm and ever so soft.

"It is beautiful," she agreed, taking in the view that stretched for miles until the horizon of night and electricity just faded into nothingness. She shivered a little, as the breeze caressed our undressed bodies.

"Good," I said as my hands left her waist and rose.

One sharp push and she tumbled over the balcony rail and fell into the void.

Her white body flying downwards through the night was like a broken butterfly in flight.

She didn't even scream.

By the time she reached the ground I was already back in the room and it only took me a couple of minutes to dress, gather her clothes, her bag and the bed's crumpled sheets, dust the few surfaces I knew I had been in contact with and make my way to the ground floor through the service stairs and find my car. It hadn't even been ticketed.

I scattered her belongings in dumpsters throughout the next city fifty miles down the highway and caught the first morning shuttle flight out to the East Coast after returning the rental car.

In all likelihood it would be reported as a suicide.

Job done.

And if you were expecting that on my next assignment I would meet another woman in a bar who would have looked just like her but wearing her hair a different way and in a different colour, and calling herself Judy you'd be sadly mistaken. Life is not that ironic.

Death is.

And if you really want to know about the next hit, well it was a slimy Cuban in the drugs business and I slit his throat.

About the Author - Maxim Jakubowski is the author of 9 novels under his own name, the latest being EKATERINA AND THE NIGHT. He is an ex-publisher and editor, owned the Murder One bookshop for 20 years, and reviewed for Time Out and then the Guardian. A winner of the Antony Award and co-director of the Crime Scene Festival, he is also currently a judge for the CWA John Creasey First Novel Dagger. He occasionally updates his website at www.maximjakubowski.co.uk

The Piano.
by
Victoria Watson

"She's trying to kill me" hissed my father as my mum was in the kitchen boiling the kettle. "Please get me out of here".

"I'm sure she's not trying to kill you."

"She is, the bitch held a pillow over my face this morning."

"Dad," I sighed. "Mum's not trying to kill you."

"Mum? Who's Mum?"

"She's my mum." I said, feeling the tears cloud my vision.

"That woman in there? That's not your mother."

"Who is she, then?" I often did this, rather than argue, let him to think about something in the vain hope he'll realise he's confused.

"I've no idea who she is, she just appeared and now she won't leave."

Just as he said that, I heard the tea tray in my mother's hand, shaking as she approached the front room. Dad got up when Mum walked in, her face red with the effort of holding her tears in. I thought of how difficult it must be for Mum, having to live with my dad and his confusion day in, day out. It must be so frustrating, especially when he had been such an erudite, talented man.

Dad walked to the grand piano, stroking the mahogany wood. The lid of the piano was always down now – there was no point propping it open, after all, Mum didn't play and Dad was in no fit state. The piano, though, remained the focus of my dad's attention even after he'd lost the ability to play it. One day, I'd popped in to drop off some shopping and I found my father lying on top of the piano, asleep. Another time, he'd taken a fork to the piano lid, carving indiscriminate patterns on it. Every so often, he'd press the keys haphazardly. That action was the one that hurt me most. Only two years ago, he was still lecturing at the university and playing piano in concerts at least once a month and now he was pressing keys as though they were the most alien thing in the world to him.

I noticed my dad unbuttoning the plaid shirt he had on. I saw the vest he was wearing. It was white when I had bought it for him but it was now grey. I despaired inwardly, wishing mum would say if she wanted me to pick up some new clothes. I didn't know whether she was just refusing to accept that my father, this brilliant musician and academic, was no longer the man she married or whether she just didn't want to ask for help from me. They'd been self-sufficient all of my life, encouraging me to go off to university and live my life. They supported my wild ideas about building orphanages in Kenya and my teaching efforts in the villages of Vietnam. But now, my dad didn't know who I was and my mum wouldn't acknowledge that she needed help.

Sipping my tea out of the china cup, I thought about Sebastian. How would I feel if the man I had pledged to love forever didn't know who I was? How could my mother not be bitter about having her companion taken away from her? How could she smile at church every Sunday and tell the nosy Christians that Dad was "fine, never better"? Surely if they were true Christians – or friends for that matter – she could tell them and they would offer sympathy and help? Maybe I'm the wrong person to be saying that, I don't know how these relationships work. But aren't they wondering why they never see my father at church? Don't they ask at the fundraisers and the little get togethers why he's no longer socialising with them? Do they think someone's upset him? Well, in a way, God must have upset him, giving him this horrible, unfair disease. Well, not my father, he's upset with everyone and no-one all at the same time. But how could my mother still worship this supposed omnipotent being who allowed my father to no longer be able to hold a conversation?

I looked up at my mother, whose eyes were darting from my father to me and back again like a never-ending tennis match. I followed her nervous pupils, only to see my father's plaid shirt laid out over the piano lid and my dad with one leg out of his trousers, struggling to free the other. He was bent forward, wrestling his ankle

219

out of the trouser leg, his bottom in the air. His greying briefs had a couple of holes around the waistband and when he turned around, I noticed a couple of small stains on the front of the briefs. I felt sick. I began to sweat. I thought I was going to faint. My father continued piling his clothes onto the piano, my mother remained in her seat, her face impassive.

I noticed, while trying to compose myself, that he was wearing one sock on his left foot. It had a reindeer on despite spring being in full bloom. On his right foot was a white sports sock with one of my mother's flesh-coloured pop socks over the top, pulled halfway up his calf.

"Dad," I said quietly. He didn't respond.

"Derek!" Yelled my mother, her voice high-pitched and angry. I looked at her, in her blue floral two-piece with her hair set in a tight perm. I remembered being a teenager and finding out she'd read my diary. She'd been absolutely furious that I had compared her to Hyacinth Bucket from 'Keeping Up Appearances' although I was sure she had no idea who that was. It made me smile for a split second. I got off my chair and held my dad's arms down by his sides. I noticed an unpleasant odour coming from my dad. I felt embarrassed on his behalf.

Dad had the vest in his hands, ready to take it off and add it to the growing pile of garments on the top of the piano.

"Dad, come on, you must be cold. Put your clothes back on." My voice caught in the back of my throat as I tried to chivvy my father along. I could feel my mum's eyes on me, watching the pantomime unfold in front of her.

"Aren't you cold, Dad?" I continued, hoping to bring him back from the alternate reality he was occupying more and more.

"I don't know pet. Are you cold?" He said and it occurred to me that my father could no longer tell how he felt. He didn't know if he was hot or cold. He didn't know if he was relaxed or angry. I had been wondering for a while if he only ate and drank when things were given to him and now I knew he was unable to identify the feelings of thirst or hunger.

As I helped my dad back into his clothes, I noticed some small blue and purple bruises on the backs of his legs.

"What's happened here, Dad?" I asked.

"She did it." He said certainly, pointing at my mother. My mother, in response, rolled her eyes dramatically and sighed.

"Really Erica, I don't see why you ask him. You could ask me and I would be able to tell you without all of this silliness."

"So what happened then, Mum?" I was irritated at her insensitivity to my dad. He may have dementia, but he wasn't deaf.

"He fell over the other day" she said quietly, as though she was ashamed at admitting it. Her face was scarlet and her eyes avoided mine.

"Oh mum, why didn't you tell me?" I softened, trying to imagine how I'd feel in her situation.

"I'm just so ashamed, Erica. I just want to protect him and I can't."

"Why won't you let me help more then?"

"You've got a baby on the way love. And your work and Sebastian. Frankly, I don't know how you do it."

I glanced at my dad, who was now pulling the shirt back on, his fingers fiddling with the buttons. His fingernails were brittle and jagged.

"We could get people in. There are people we can pay to help around the house and with Dad. Then when you went to WI and book club, there'd be someone here sitting with Dad."

"I don't want strangers in here." My mum was quiet but assertive. "I can manage, he only needs me." I knew how protective my mum was, she liked to be needed and the thought that she'd have to admit she couldn't look after her own husband would kill her.

"But what happens if he falls and you can't lift him up? Look at how much bigger than you he is. Will you at least think about it Mum? I'm worried about you too." I felt so helpless and ill-equipped to become a mother myself. I couldn't even look after my parents for god's sake.

221

"Will your young man be waiting for you my dear?" My father sensed the tension and spoke up. The irony of him calling Sebastian a young man wasn't lost on me. When I moved in with my former dissertation supervisor, my parents were less than impressed to say the least. I remember my mother crying and my father ranting about "abuse of power" and "in loco parentis". Neither one of them could understand why I was choosing to be in a relationship with a man nearer their age than my own.

"Well, dad, Sebastian is at work. He's trying to get ahead of himself for when the baby comes." I smiled.

"Baby? I don't like babies. I hope it's no-one I know bringing a baby in here." He hadn't noticed my eight-month bump or didn't understand what it meant. My dad sighed and rubbed his forehead. That was when I saw the scabs on his hand.

"What's happened to his hand, Mum?"

"His hand? I don't know." My mum looked surprised, nervous even.

"They look like burns." I eased myself up and approached my dad. He shrunk back when I put my hand out to him.

"Where did you do this, hey?" I asked him as gently as I could.

"She did it, she burned me. She puts hot spoons on me." My dad pointed at my mother again and she burst into tears, running out of the room.

"Oh Dad," I sighed. I pulled him into a hug, the bump keeping us at a distance. The baby kicked and he jumped away, looking scared. He glanced down at the offender and smiled. He put his hands onto my tummy and waited. He closed his eyes and started to hum a tune. He turned away, lost in a reverie and put his fingers on the keys. It wasn't Debussy or Beethoven but it was the most wonderful sound I'd ever heard. My father played the opening bars of 'Greensleeves' and my heart leapt. My dad was still in there. The shell was not completely empty. I felt the baby kick, as if knowing to dance to its grandfather's playing.

As I carried the tea tray back into the kitchen, I found my mother sitting at the dining table staring out into the garden.

"I have to go, Mum, I've got an antenatal class at three." I kissed the top of her head.

"Ok love. Would you like me to come?"

"No, I'll be fine. You stay here and enjoy the music." I smiled and walked out of the back door. I would have skipped down the path if I could. It was only when I'd walked a few metres down the lane to my car that I realised I'd left my handbag in the house.

I walked back into the kitchen. My mum was no longer at the table. There was no music coming from the front room. Short-lived but better than nothing, I thought.

"Bloody baby brain!" I said cheerfully as I stepped through the door to the front room. Just as I stepped into the room, my mother brought the key lid down onto my father's hands with all her might.

Searching for the Wrong Eyed Jesus
by
RJ Barker

Bal O'Reilly were twenty one, a year older than me and he scared us
more than anyone I'd ever met, including me Dad and he were a right
bastard. Bal were small and wiry, like a ferret, his skin rough and his
hair tight ginger curls, greased till it were almost black. In his cheap
suits he was easy enough to spot and keep away from when I were
walking around the Blades Edge estate. I'd always done me best to do
just that. Since he'd started shagging me Mam though, weren't much I
could do about seeing him more regular than I wanted, like.

We were sat in the front room, Bal sipping from a can of
Tenants, when he got the wrong eye on. It were slightly less
uncomfortable having him down here watching TV rather than
listening to him calling me mam a dirty slag while he gave her one
upstairs. When the wrong eye started I wished me Mam'd come home
quick, feeling randy and drag him off for a session.

The wrong eye meant Bal wanted something, weird stuff
usually, not money or a jewellery like a normal would. It were usually
something he wanted to have in his hands. Then he'd smash it, so no
one else could enjoy it. He'd done for my Playstation like that. At least
the wrong eye weren't coming in my direction, if Bal gave a person the
wrong eye that meant a kicking or worse was in order. Everyone knew
Bal'd cut off two of Derek Barnes fingers but no one knew why, not
even Derek or if he did he weren't saying. Just said he got in the way of
Bal's wrong eye.

Bal'd say it were all about the anarchy and then sing a bit of
that song by that grandad who advertises butter, 'I wanna be anarchy.'
Cept it weren't anarchy he wanted cos that were something to do with
politics and Bal always switched off the TV and said he were bored
when politics came on.

No, the wrong eye were shining for Jesus. We were watching the local news and Bal was twitching, moving about the couch and scratching his balls when they started talking about a celebration at Calfley church, one of the rich villages where I used to go robbing when I were younger and stupider. As the Vicar talked Bal pointed at the screen.

'I'm fucking havin' that.'

'The Vicar?'

'Are you calling me queer, Roddy? Do you want me to fuck you up the arse?' his green eyes didn't look wet like normal people's and the left one never quite looked at you. 'I will you know, then you'll never call me fuckin' queer again you fuckin queer.'

'No Bal,' I moved me sen further down the couch, 'I just didn't understand what you meant.'

'Thought you were meant to be clever, eh? Eh?' he said and his eyebrows shot up each time he said 'eh', fighting eyebrows, we called them. 'Like to read fucking books y'queer.' Bal shook his head slowly, all the time keeping one eye locked on me. 'I'm talking about the fuckin' Jesus.'

The news show had moved on, talking to an old bint about a community garden on the Blades Edge. Wouldn't last five minutes before someone drove a car over it.

'What does you want Jesus for, Bal?'

'None o' fuckin' yours,' he tapped the side of his nose, 'me and you, we'll go get it, right' He gave me a ratty smile showing the brown lines on his teeth from smoking too many rollies.

'But I'm not allowed out after six,' I told him, 'I'm on probation, if we get nicked I'm going back to jail.'

'Fuck off,' he said, staring at me.

'They'll send me to prison Bal.'

'Fuck. Off.'

There was no arguing with Bal O'Reilly when he got an idea in his head but I tried anyway.

'Bal, it's church, you can't nick stuff from a church.'

225

'You don't believe in God,' I hated this about Bal, he'd take stuff you'd said months ago and store it away in his head turn against you later on. 'I remember,' he said, 'you saw it on TV, dead clever you fuckin' thought you were, Charles Manson said there's monkeys you said, so there can't be God, you said.'

'Why don't you take Big Terry? He thinks he's the devil. He'd love this.'

Bal pointed at me, his fingernail dirty and the last joint of his finger was bent so he really pointed at the door not me.

'Big Terry isn't here, you are. Besides, Big Terry stinks.'

'But Bal me mam'll' he didn't let me finish.

'Fuck off,' he said then grabbed his crotch, 'I know how to shut yer fuckin' mam up.'

It was a half hour drive to Calfley and it started to rain the moment we left the house. I spent the time staring out the window while Bal drove and smoked. Didn't dare look at him cos I could feel the tears clawing at the back of me throat like I'd smoked twenty fags made from ashtray leavings. I couldn't cry, if I cried Bal'd make sure everyone on the estate knew and I'd be a target for everyone who felt like doling out a kicking for months. I can hold me own in a fight but I couldn't afford to get arrested. Jail had been a bad place and I weren't going again.

I'd been to Calfley church before, when I was fifteen. I'd come with me Dad so he could work out where to park when he nicked the lead from the roof. We never went inside. I'd only ever been in the church on Blades Edge and it were like a schoolroom except it leaked more, smelt of old people and had nothing worth stealing.

It was old, like an important building that should be in the centre of Leeds not some little village but posh people get good stuff don't they? It were big too, when you looked up at the square tower you felt like it were going to fall on you and it made you dizzy. Bal pushed me and I nearly fell.

'Stop fuckin' gawpin', you prick. Here take this,' he shoved a crowbar into my hand. 'Doors, he said loping off and I followed him

226

through the drizzle. The doors were thick wood inside a stone porch and even that felt more solid than the council house I'd lived in all me life, I didn't need the crowbar to get in, doors was open.

'Silly fuckers,' said Bal and walked in ahead of me, hands on his hips, head bobbing. I thought he looked like a chicken and had to fight back a nervous laugh. Bal didn't like it if you laughed unless he'd made a joke.

It were cold inside, and big, bigger than it looked from the outside. I can't explain. The building did something weird with sounds. The noise of us footsteps on the stone floor seemed to go on and on into the gloom as if there were other people here walking about. Dim lights hung from the ceiling and the only thing that was properly lit in the whole place was the statue of Jesus on the cross. It looked just like a real person but whoever had made it had got the face wrong, he didn't look in pain. He looked like he was, I dunno, not happy or anything, he wasn't smiling, smug, maybe but that's not right either. He didn't look pissed off and the weirdest thing was that the painted on eyes seemed more real and alive than Bal's.

'This is wrong, Bal.' I said and my words came out as a whisper.

'Fuck off,' he said, then grinned a dirty grin, 'dunno why yer fuckin whisperin either, no one's ere.'

'There is actually,' I jumped at the quiet voice and took a step nearer to Bal. We'd not noticed the man sat at the front of the church looking up at the statue. He stood and walked slowly up the path between all the benches to meet us. He were right old, small, bent over and his hair was mostly gone.

'You're wearin' a fuckin dress,' said Bal.

'It's not a dress, it's a cassock,' I said, 'he must be the Vicar.' Bal gave me a slant eyed glance that sent a shiver through me.

'It is indeed a cassock,' the old man smiled and it seemed to light up his face, 'but I am not the vicar, how can I help you boys?'

'If you're not the vicar,' said Bal, 'why are you wearing a fucking dress? are you a queer.'

227

It was as if the old boy couldn't hear the threat in Bal's voice and he carried on smiling.

'I'm the sexton.'

'You don't look very sexy to me, you look like a fuckin pervert.'

The old man laughed.

'You're funny,' he grinned.

'Am I?' Bal took a step forward, puffing himself up, jerking his shoulders all spiky and violent, 'fucking funny am I?' he rolled his neck.

'What's a Sexton?' I raised my voice, Bal turned to me and glared but he backed off from the old bloke.

'Yeah,' he said, 'what's your job, sexy.'

'I look after the church, do maintenance, dig graves, things like that,' I noticed he'd left a shovel leaning against a bench a little further down the aisle. 'I just came in to get out of the rain for a while.'

'Then you'll know how to get that statue down,' sad Bal, pointing up at Jesus hanging above us.

'Why would I want to do that?' he looked right confused.

'Because I want it,' said Bal, 'and if you don't get it down I'll hurt you.'

For the first time the light left the old man's face and he shook his head.

'I'm afraid not, we have some silver candlesticks if you're really bent on robbing us.'

'I'm not fucking bent you old queer,' spat Bal and then dragged me forwards by my arm. 'and you can keep your fucking candlesticks, get me Jesus or Roddy will fuckin' do for you.'

'We shouldn't be her, Bal,' I said, trying to break away but his grip on us arm were like a vice.

'Listen to your friend,' said the old boy calmly, 'you can't sell the statue, it's too big to get out the church without being taken apart...'

228

'Shut the fuck up, I only need the head anyway,' said Bal and he pushed the old man sending him staggering back against the benches.

That was when I saw, when us stomach did a flip and I wanted to be sick. Bal was giving the sexton the wrong eye. Then he turned it on me.

'I came for that statue,' he pointed up with his bent finger, 'and I'm fucking having it,' he wrong eyed me again, 'hit him, Roddy.'

'What?'

'Unless you want to deal with me, fucking hit the old bastard, with that,' he pointed at the crowbar. 'Do it.'

The crowbar seemed to double, triple, its weight in my hand.

'But he's only an...'

'He knows our names and I am not leaving without me fucking statue. Hit him, or I'll hit him with it and then I'll hit you and I'll go back fuck your mam and hit her.'

I looked to the old man and he gave me a tired smile. As if he understood the situation I was in, as if he didn't mind. Knew what I had to do.

'Fuckin do it,' said Bal.

So I did.

The old man closed his eyes tight and the opened them in surprise when the crowbar landed with a dull thud. I put all my weight into the blow, wanting to make sure I did it first time, I couldn't bear to have to hit him more than once.

The Sexton stared down at Bal's body, a pool of blood spreading out across the stone floor. I dropped the crowbar and it sounded impossibly loud in the quiet church.

'Sad,' he said, 'sad that such things should happen.' He looked at me and gave me a slow smile. 'Idle hands make the devil's work, young man.'

'I'm fucked,' I said sitting down on the bench. 'I'm going to spend the rest of my life in jail.'

The old Boy put his hand on my shoulder, it felt light, like a bird.

229

Ever dug a grave?' he said and walked away down the aisle. 'Only I'm getting a bit old for it,' he glanced back over his shoulder. 'And you strike me as lad in need of a job.' He walked away, pointing at the spade as he passed it.

I stared at Bal's body for a moment, unsure what to feel or even how. I didn't feel guilty though. I looked up at the statue of Jesus and realised that I knew the word for his expression, he looked serene, as if all were right in the world.

I picked up the spade and followed the old man.

About the Author - RJ Barker is slightly eccentric and lives in Yorkshire with his wife, two year old son and a constantly growing collection of poor quality taxidermy. His short fiction has been published in all manner of places and received three honourable mentions in, 'The Year's Best Fantasy and Horror'. RJ's illustrated poems (together with Mikko Sovijarvi) 'Interment' and 'The Social Diary of a Ghoul' have received a slew of good reviews and are available through Amazon for electronic readers. A paper version is planned at some point. When not writing, RJ dreams of growing a huge pair of antlers and hiring himself out as a novelty coatrack. You can find RJ on Twitter as @dedbutdrmng or read more of his work on his blog at http://wah-wahwriter.blogspot.co.uk/

The Bride with White Hair
by
K. A. Laity

Usually it was an advantage, her hair that is. There's no one more invisible than a middle-aged woman. Add a few pounds and shock of white tresses and then eyes just passed over her like the glaze of rain on a window. She would ease in, find her mark and knock him off before he'd even clocked her existence.

Only last week, she had managed to locate her target, follow him back very nearly to his doorstep and walk up to his car window without the slightest notice on his part—though he had given the hairy eyeball to any male who passed him in his wanderings and ran a lascivious searchlight up and down the two young women who had crossed his path. When she stopped beside his Land Rover, his expression betrayed only annoyance.

Perhaps he thought she had been collecting for Oxfam.

Surprise came belatedly as she put the Glock up to his neck and fired it. He died eyes wide, looking somehow cheated, as if she didn't fit the arc of his storyline. She smiled to herself later remembering it and celebrated with an expensive bottle on the way home to her tiny flat, feeling a smug satisfaction with her ability to remain unseen.

Not this time.

The penny dropped as soon as she stepped through the door. She'd done her research, following up on the sketchy details the client provided, tracing her mark's schedule and movements. He had a routine of unerring predictability that showed his age. Men tended to draw the threads of their lives closer as they got older, avoiding change and surprise. They had habits.

Women, on the other hand, often chucked the known and sought out the unexpected. As she had done: after all, it wasn't easy living on a former teacher's pension. Her invisibility had been a positive boon, as had been her dad's early instruction in ridding the farm of rabbits. Her reflexes remained speedy and she could be justly proud of her sharp shooting skills.

Lately, however, all the work had been at close range, which required a rather different set of skills.

When she started out, her primary fear had been that she would feel too much empathy to carry out the assignments. She found that channeling all the frustration of years of budget cuts, pointless bureaucratic regulations and an endless stream of resentful kids—all convinced that education was a mug's game because all you needed was to get on a reality show or make a viral video to get rich—provided her with ample ammunition for this new line of work. Her marks were precisely the kind of people who sneered at education, who had nothing but contempt for learning, erudition and knowledge. Would-be thugs and thugs right enough, many of them were engaged in simply knocking one another off.

Why not help?

She had a modicum of natural empathy for any living thing, but had to admit there was a frisson of joy in bringing to an end a few lives that delivered nothing but pain, crime and poor grammatical skills to the world. *You're something of a snob*, she scolded herself upon feeling grim satisfaction dispatching a particularly vile gold-chain clad lad in a shiny track suit with "ASBO FOR LIFE" tattooed in a Gothic script along his arm.

She performed a charitable service. And the pay proved extraordinary. While she did worry occasionally about the way it inured her to the humanity of some, those ponderings could be reserved for quiet contemplation over a glass of good single malt, which had given her a good philosophical problem with which to wrestle.

At the moment her primary problem was slipping into the pub without drawing any more notice. A pub was a pub was a pub—except when it was one of these old geezer pubs where a woman never darkened its threshold. Many small pubs remained largely the province of men, it was true. Women might appear on Friday or Saturday night without alarm. Before Geoff died, she had often gone with him to the local, but only at the weekend. He had always joked about sending her into the women's snug, though it had usually been full of laughing young people who treated it as their own club room.

This place, though; she knew if she asked for a Guinness the barman would give her a half without even asking. Waves of hostility emanated from a couple of the men, indifference from the rest. This changed the dynamic.

She walked up to the bar, turning alternatives over in her mind and decided 'in for a penny, in for a pound'. Maybe she would have to pass the mark to another, but she wasn't ready to give up just yet. Scanning the shelves she saw a dust-free bottle of Lagavulin and asked for a double when at last the barman deigned to notice her and leave his murmured conversation down the other end of the bar.

The perfume filled her nose as she sipped the golden liquid and her confidence returned. Popping open her bag on the bar—which drew a raised eyebrow of displeasure from the barman—she pulled out the battered Moleskin she used for notes and turned to a fresh page. The other two men at the bar studiously ignored her as she began to make a list. After a moment, she paused, looked around and then moved to a small table under a one of the few lights. Returning to her list, she stopped now and then to savour the single malt and smiled to herself.

Luck smiled upon her fairly soon. "Not too common to see a woman with such exquisite taste."

She looked up. Double luck; it was the mark. "I assume you mean the scotch and not my impeccable taste in Marks & Sparks." The smile she offered sprang from the memories of other bars and younger days.

He held up his glass. "People come and go, but a good single malt will always delight." His smile seemed genuine. It had warmth, too, unexpectedly so. She motioned for him to sit opposite her.

"Making a list?"

"Checking it twice." She looked up at him. The pictures didn't do him proper justice. It seemed particularly unfair that people considered the crags and wrinkles of a man's face to enhance an older man's looks, but handsome was the only accurate word for this one. "Figuring out how much longer I need to save and be nice, before I can spend and be naughty."

He chuckled. It was a nice sound, one she hadn't heard in some time. Since Geoff died most of her concern had been managing their finances and figuring out how to leave the dreary north for a wee villa or condo in Spain, where she could let the sun leech the ache in her joints that she somehow woke up with most days now.

"I've never seen you in here before," he said, a mild look of surprise on his features. She noticed his suit had an expensive cut, though he wore it with the ease of one long accustomed to its comfort. Born to money—or just successful so long that it had become second nature? Judging by the bonus offered for this little commission, he was something of a heavy weight, but clearly all class.

Mr. Land Rover last week; now there was tacky new money. From his shiny tracksuit to his ridiculous Burberry cap everything shouted, "Look at me! I'm rolling in it!" A lot of the kids dressed like that, hoping to be taken for the real thing. The last years of teaching she had found the loud boasting and posturing set her teeth on edge. It wasn't just manners—though the art of them seemed completely lost—it was the jangling noise of all the attention seeking, as if they had regressed to toddlers.

"I've never been here before," she said with a genuine laugh. "That sounds dangerously like a cliché, doesn't it? 'Do you come here often?'"

He smiled, showing nice teeth that were nonetheless not Hollywood bright. She'd always found those too white teeth unsettling. His showed his years without embarrassment. "I think I'm too old to try that sort of line. Or any sort of line."

"It's one of the few advantages of age. You don't have to bullshit anyone." She looked at him over her glass as she took another sip, pleased to see his reaction to her words.

"A time saver that," he agreed, swirling his own glass. "And I've done well enough that I really only accept the very best these days, too."

"Ah, the lost art of compliments," she said with mock sorrow. "Although I notice there's a good bit of confidence in there, too."

Her sharp observation did not daunt him. "I think a woman of quality appreciates a man who's confident."

"And drinks good Scotch," she added, sipping her elixir with pleasure.

They had a second drink together and exchanged little tit bits of truth. His ex, her Geoff, his disappointment with his son, hers with her students. They traded stories like old war heroes, showing their scars and medals.

Inevitable perhaps that she should be tempted. It had been some time since she had had the least interest in pursuing such a thing. Geoff had left the bar high behind him, not only as a lover but as a companion, too. The truth was that she got more excitement from her new employment than she did with the pursuit of the mostly tedious old men who would be willing to bed her. She found something gauche in the idea of a young lover and filed the thought away for Spain and later days.

Yet she found the adrenaline charge of her new pursuit quite entertaining. Tracking, dodging, getting close and then dispatching them with consummate skill. Unlike teaching there was a sense of closure and completion. She enjoyed the feeling of striking the latest name off the "to do" list with a flourish of her pen. So different from the endless grading grind! It really brought a sense of accomplishment to her day.

This man confused her, however. She found herself attracted to him. She had already blown the hit by miscalculating the pub's nature. If she had to pass the lucrative pay packet on to someone else, why not get something out of it for herself?

"You are an unexpected development," she told him.

"You are an unexpected treasure."

"I feel I should steal some sophisticated badinage from Coward or Wilde," she said downing the last of her single malt.

235

"I could pull you into an elegant dance like Astaire and Rogers, but I forgot my tuxedo."

"We would shock the regulars anyway," she said with a glance around the pub where the regulars in question were studiously ignoring the two of them.

"Or we could retire to a rather nice boutique hotel around the corner and decide just how much we would like to get to know one another." He almost looked abashed at his own boldness, a faint hint of pink in his cheek betraying the very real investment in his words.

She put her hand on his and smiled. "I'm glad we're too old to need a lot of folderol before getting down to what we want."

"So you do want it, too?"

Her smile assented and a nod fixed their fate. She insisted on paying for the hotel room, one of the cards from her employer—insurance if anything should go wrong. She would reconcile it somehow.

In the room, he paused before touching her. "I love your hair," he said at last running his fingers lightly through it as if afraid to find out she was too delicate. She wrapped her arms around his waist and lifted her face to be kissed. He put his hands on her cheeks and gazed into her eyes before at last touching his lips to hers.

What a wonderful feeling. It had really been too long. She found herself eager for more and reached up to unbutton his shirt.

"I think I'm old enough to demand darkness for undressing," he said, smiling but serious. Yet later, after they had made love, he did not mind when she opened the curtains to let the moonlight caress their skin.

"This night is special," she whispered as they lay side by side.

"Magical," he agreed, his voice choked with rare emotion. He fell asleep in her arms and she thrilled to the familiar warmth and weight of him. It really had been far too long. The moon cast a silvery sheen over the bed like a spell.

She awoke well before dawn, the internal clock set too many semesters ago. Her purse had a lipstick but no makeup, which she regretted, but a shower restored her confidence. Dressed once more, she stared at the figure under the sheets. Removing the pillow from his face, she admired once more the handsome lines of it, then sighed at the blood seeping into the mattress. A good man was hard to find—and vice versa. But a condo in Spain was for life.

About the Author - K. A. LAITY is the author of Chastity Flame, The Claddagh Icon, Owl Stretching, Unquiet Dreams and many more. Her stories have appeared in Drunk on the Moon, Spinetingler, Near to the Knuckle, A Twist of Noir, Pulp Metal Magazine and ACTION: Pulse Pounding Tales. See a complete list of her publications at www.kalaity.com

Pretty Woman
by
SJI Holliday

I noticed her straight away.

Partly because she didn't look like any of the other girls working in FreshCo but mainly because she was shouting her damn head off about the uniform being made of nylon and how it was irritating her sensitive skin. Probably a fair point, because she had the sort of soft, milky white skin that was almost transparent, spidery blue veins floating under the surface. But her face, when she wasn't scowling, was only one notch higher than plain, to tell the truth.

She thought differently.

They put her on tills straightaway, which was a bit unfair, because I'd been there six months and was still stuck in the warehouse, only getting out to trundle my massive trolleys full of bog rolls and cleaning products to shelves that never seemed to stay fully stocked.

Popular item, bleach.

She got put on tills because she demanded it, and the manager was a weak-willed loser who couldn't say no. Except to me. No amount of asking was going to get me on the shop floor during store opening hours. Discriminatory bastards. Even the Human Resources woman didn't want to help me. '*You've got to understand our position, here, Alex,*' she'd said. '*You're doing a great job behind the scenes. You're one of the cogs that turns the wheel. Remember that, eh?*' Bitch. But what could I do? It was the only place in town that had agreed to give me a job.

Anyway, this new girl, Melissa. Long, over-bleached hair and over-caked mascara. Tight skirt and high shoes – too high for work, but I suppose they *did* make her calves look good. She was the kind of girl that everyone thought was gorgeous, at first glance. The full package. Until you looked – I mean, actually *looked,* at her face. *No oil painting,* my mum would've said.

I didn't expect her to notice *me.*

I was sitting out the back, eating my sandwiches on one of the cheap plastic chairs they'd stuck outside the staff entrance so that people could sit out there for a fag or a tea or just a bitch, or whatever. I'd brought tuna and cucumber on a roll that was a staff freebie from the bakery the night before. Can of Fanta and a packet of cheese and onion. I was quite happy, eating there on my own. I mean, I was more than used to it. Anyway, she comes outside, pulls a packet of gold B&H from the pocket at the side of her overalls. Then she starts patting herself, swearing under her breath. Finally she turns round and sees me. For a second, she just stares then she catches herself and decides to speak.

'Got a lighter?'

'Sorry, I don't smoke. There might be some ma—'

She flared her nostrils; reminded me of a bull getting ready to charge.

'Fuck's sake,' she said. 'It's all right for *you*.'

I was genuinely confused. All right that I didn't smoke? I suppose, but…

'You don't have to put up with it like I do.' She sounded agitated; she was pacing about, one hand on hip, the other waving her unlit cigarette.

'What?' I said, carefully as I could. I wasn't really up for listening to her rant but I didn't seem to be getting a choice.

'Everyone fucking coming *on* to you all the time. Pawing at you. Smacking your arse…'

Now I was intrigued. 'Who's smacked your arse? Someone here?' I instantly suspected Paul, the trainee butcher. I'd heard other girls complaining about him before. He wasn't particularly nice to me either, but that's another story.

'Yes!' She shouted it, which was unnecessary as I was only three feet away. 'Some of the staff are bad enough, you sort of expect that in a place like this… but not the bloody customers too. That old bloke that always buys a tin of mince and one potato… that he doesn't even put in a *bag* for fuck's sake… he asked me what I was doing tonight – the cheek – he's about… *fifty*, at least…'

239

I knew who she meant. She had that typical young person's view of age. The man was seventy-three and his wife had died last year. I saw him at the bus stop sometimes. He told me all he could cook was a baked potato in the microwave and put the heated up mince on top. I felt sorry for him.

'Maybe he was just being polite? Asking what you were up to—'

She shook her head violently. 'As if *you* would understand.' She gave me a look that would unblock a drain, shoved the unlit fag back into its packet and stormed back inside.

'Bitch,' I muttered. What did she mean, as if *I* would understand?

I paid more attention to her after that, which I'm sure was the opposite of what she'd expected. I made my breaks coincide with hers, as much as I could without anyone getting suspicious. I listened to her bitching and whining about her hard, hard life.

'It's so bloody stressful looking like this!'

'Why don't they just leave me alone?'

'Sometimes I wish I was ugly.'

Others sympathised with her plight. Nodding sagely. Giving her advice.

'Maybe you should wear a bit less make-up to work?' someone said. One of the girls from the deli counter, I think. One of those 'nice' girls, you know the type.

Melissa had replied with: 'But I'm still a bloody babe without it, aren't I? It's a fucking curse! I can barely walk out of the shop without getting accosted by blokes...'

I seriously doubted that; both parts of it. She was no babe, and without her mask of make up, I doubted you'd even be able to make out her bland features. *And* I'd seen her leaving work many, many times. There was never anyone waiting to *accost* her. At times I felt sorry for her. Clearly she was lacking in self-esteem, despite her outward display of the opposite. I would have talked to her, given half the chance. I was the resident expert on self-esteem issues in that place. I even started carrying a lighter in my pocket in case she ever asked me for one again. She didn't though; I was invisible to her.

As time went on, I grew bored of her.

Until she came outside on her own again one day; no hangers-on in tow.

I was having ham, cheese and mayo that day. Packet of salt and vinegar and a can of Sprite. Just normal white bread because there hadn't been anything left over from the bakery the night before. I still had the lighter in my pocket.

'Alex!' she said. Gave me a big smile. She had her hair pulled back in a too-tight ponytail, her eyes were like coin slots on a vending machine. Her roots were dark and carried a slight oily sheen.

She knew my name.

I smiled back. 'Hi Melissa,' I said.

'Got a light?'

This time I was ready. I stood up and pulled the lighter from my jeans pocket, handed it to her.

Another smile.

'Thanks – you're a life saver,' she said. She lit the fag and pulled hard on it and I noticed the little wrinkles as she puckered her lips. Her mouth was like a screwed up crisp packet. She handed the lighter back to me and said: 'You are *so* lucky, you know?'

This threw me. Lucky wasn't a word I could ever imagine applying to myself.

'Why's that?'

She laughed then, a horrible cackle. I'd noticed it before but it seemed more horrible than usual. For a girl who rated herself so highly, she had a hell of a lot of faults, in my opinion – but who was I to judge.

'Because you're so… unattractive… I mean, aren't you? You don't have a clue what it's like to be me. You should count your blessings, you—'

I swallowed hard. My tongue had become a useless flap of leather. 'What?' I said. I could taste salt at the back of my throat.

241

She cackled again. 'I don't mean that *badly*… No offence… I'm just saying, you're lucky you can just get on with your normal life without anyone bloody *pestering* you all the time. I'm telling you, being beautiful is a nightmare, it really is! Sometimes I wish I didn't even *have* a bloody face.' With that, she ground out her fag with the heel of one of her stupidly high shoes and flounced back inside.

I was speechless. My *normal* life? She wished she had *no face?* Did she really think that would make her invisible? I swallowed back the tears and was thankful no one else had heard what she'd said. I couldn't stand the pity.

Maybe the HR woman was right. Telling me I needed to stay in the warehouse. Keep away from the customers. *'We're happy to have you working here, Alex. We do like to keep up the quota of 'equal opportunity' employees, you know,'* she'd said. Since when was being transgender a disability, for Christ's sake. I wasn't a freak… I wasn't even ugly. Okay, I wasn't the best looking 'bloke'. Not yet. But once I started on the hormones and I got a bit more *masculine*, I'd look better, I knew I would.

I'd never been pretty as a female – my mum thought that was why I wanted to be a boy. She couldn't understand that I *was* a boy. I'd just been born into the wrong body. The psychological assessments had come back 'borderline'.

Whatever that meant.

They'd refused me surgery until I'd lived as a male for three years and had another psychiatrist assess me. My family couldn't understand. Wouldn't.

Told the doctor I needed 'help'.

Of course I needed help. I was dying inside, trapped. I moved away to where no one knew me and tried to start again, but I faced the same prejudices over and over. I taped up my breasts until they ached and I could barely breathe. Cut my hair and grew my eyebrows. Tried to lower my voice and change the way I walked; but I wasn't fooling anyone. I got laughed at in the street. By everyone. Except for that old man who's wife died. Somehow he saw through the mask and saw the real me. That's why I knew he wouldn't have said anything inappropriate to Melissa. He'd have known she was bad to the core.

Yes, Melissa had a good body, and a decent enough face. But no, she wasn't beautiful – not in my eyes anyway, because I've always believed that beauty comes from the *inside*. There was hope for me, I really felt that. But there was no hope for Melissa.

Not unless I helped her.

I left work early that day, said I had a stomach ache. The useless manager just waved me off with a 'whatever'.

No one saw me take the bottle of drain cleaner from the back of the trolley.

I waited in the bushes behind the bus stop, knowing she'd be walking home that way, knowing because I'd watched her before. Followed her. I knew there'd be no one waiting, despite all her bullshit and bravado.

I twisted off the cap and crouched down behind the bushes, bottle in hand.

Poised.

Waiting.

'I wish I didn't even have a bloody face.'

Be careful what you wish for.

About the Author - SJI Holliday is a lover of all things crime and horror and has several short stories published in places such as What the Dickens? Magazine, Six Words, The Rusty Nail and Ether Books. She has a story in the upcoming Crime Factory 'Horror Factory' anthology and is currently working on her first novel. You can find out more at: www.sjiholliday.com.

Un Chien Andalou
by
Christopher Black

By the time I came out of the shower the old box-style radio was playing some kind of classical Spanish jazz. I pulled on clothes that smelled of old sweat and watched her through the screen door. She was still out on the wooden veranda, watching the sun as it turned big and orange and sank towards the horizon. Her skin glowed bronze in the fading light. Denim shorts, a bikini top and a straw cowboy hat that hadn't left her head since she snatched it from a stand outside a small store, next to the postcards and the inflatable beach balls. How long had it been? It seemed like a long time. It seemed like the end of time, here on the edge of the continent, sitting and drinking and looking at each other, looking out on the beach, and looking at each other again.

I rubbed my face, scratching at where the stubble had been an hour ago, and found blood from the nick on my chin. Last night I'd been on a drunk. Really drunk. She was still out there, sipping at that grappa shit, or cheap Pernod or whatever the hell it was. She said nothing, but drank that shit and stared out on the beach, and then stared out into the night as it covered us. I took a cigarette from the packet by the bed and turned off the radio. The scream of the cicadas filled the silence. Last night's whisky bottle lay empty, so I held a cold beer from the fridge against my neck, feeling the condensation drip down my chest.

As my cigarette burned low she rose to her feet, holding onto the wooden railing that edged the veranda. She came inside and walked past me, took a cigarette from the packet and put out her hand. I clicked the lighter and held it for her. She puffed a couple of times and turned away, and turned back again. She glared up at me with the cigarette hanging from the corner of her mouth like Marlene Dietrich.

"What?" she said.

I had nothing to say. She took her cigarette back outside and sat down, and poured herself another drink. Through the window and the screen door the sun sank lower, grew bigger, burned with a fiercer orange-to-red, ready to dip itself into the sea. And I watched her.

Even with the sun gone, the air outside was not much cooler but I sat out with her on the veranda anyway. The insistent sound of the waves drifted up to us, endlessly repeating like a bad joke, like a bad memory. Already, I could hear some of the local boys. All the time, the local boys. They took boats across the bay every afternoon and played football or fooled around on the wide flat beach over the dunes. Some of them returned in the evening. They laughed and drank and played guitar around a fire, and you could tell what they were doing by the pitch of the laughter. Sometimes they talked and sometimes they joked and sometimes they chased each other through the surf. Sometimes they came up on the dunes, and they watched her sitting out, drinking her grappa shit in a bikini top and a straw cowboy hat. They spoke to her. I heard them from the room, but they talked in Spanish and when I appeared they would drift off again, over the dunes. So I listened to them now, a bit of guitar and low talk and high laughter, and I knew she heard them too, but she didn't say anything. Not about them. Instead she said, "It's hot. It's hot is all it is."

"It's hot," I said.

I looked over at her and I could see the sweat on her arm and her brow and her chest. I drank some beer.

She finished her drink and poured another. One from the bottle, one of water. It turned from oily clear to cloudy white in the light from the cabin. In the trees behind us the cicadas still screamed like they were on fire.

"I might take a walk," I said.

She sipped her drink and put the glass down on the wicker table and watched the stars come out over the beach and listened to the sound of the night and the sound of the local youths over the dunes.

"You do that," she said, her stillness blending with the dark. I listened to the waves and tried not to remember.

245

Reaching up to my face I rubbed the nick on my chin. It had stopped bleeding now. "I'm going for a walk," I said again, and finished my beer, setting the can down next to her glass on the sand-and-salt-blasted wicker table. She didn't say anything, didn't even watch me leave. I walked away from the local boys, away from the dunes and up the beach and towards the wooded hill and the trees. But the cicadas followed me all the way, although I couldn't see them.

***

Not so long before, she was a vision on the side of the road, wearing not much more but without the cowboy hat because she hadn't stolen that yet. She asked me where I was going and I said south. I only said it because that's the direction the road was taking me. I looked over at her as she sat in the passenger seat. She wasn't over thirty but her eyes were older, hardened, and not by a life of travelling. She said she was going south, too, and I nodded, and we sat in silence for a while as I drove. Her only possession was a small duffel bag that she clutched tight to her chest.

After a while I said, "Are you leaving someone behind?"

She looked at me, and said, "Are you?" I didn't answer and she smiled, and I felt her eyes linger on me as I stared at the road. "I don't know either," she said. "How can you leave anyone behind if you have nowhere to go?"

"That's okay," I said. "As long as you keep on moving, they must be getting further away. Right?"

We didn't talk for a while, then, but the wind from the desert roared through the open windows. When the sun began to draw down I told her that I had nowhere to stay the night. I told her I'd been sleeping in the car. "That's fine," she said.

We stopped for a bite to eat and picked up a couple of cheap bottles of wine. I didn't tell her that it took almost all the cash I had. For a couple of hours outside town we drove up into the mountains until I pulled over by the side of the road. It was dark by now, and a million stars filled the sky over our heads. We sat out on the hot bonnet of the car, taking big hearty swigs of cheap Spanish vino and watching for nothing. It was much cooler up there in the mountains and soon she was leaning on me for warmth. It felt like time was standing still for us, but it wasn't. Not really.

Out of nowhere she said, "I killed my husband."

I had nothing to say to that, so I let her words carry to the mountains and the stars.

"I shot him." Still I said nothing. "You don't believe me?"

"I believe you," I said, although I didn't know what to think.

She didn't say anything more. Instead she took the wine bottle and emptied it into her mouth and threw it into the desert where it bounced around and dinged off rocks and disappeared without breaking. She got back into the car. I looked up at the stars and wondered what I was doing here, and followed her. She was looking through her small duffel bag, and when she pulled out the gun I flinched away from it, but I believed her.

It was an old revolver, long and cumbersome. It looked like something from the civil war.

"I told you," she said, and pointed the gun through the windscreen at some imaginary man in the night. "I shot him. Do you believe me now?"

"I believed you from the start," I said.

"But now you know I'm not lying," she said.

"I never thought you were lying," I said. She put the gun back in her bag, and she kissed me.

***

As I reached the top of the hill, I felt the breeze coming in off the sea. For a moment it chilled the sweat on my body, and I wished I could sit up here all night, if only I had another beer. Until the cicadas started up again, driving me crazy with the buzz buzz buzz that never stops. From way up here, I could see the fire that the local boys had started on the beach, where they can party far from their parents who hid in the safety of the small town. I could see the light of our hut, as well.

247

Money was due, or we had to move on. But where? Not so long ago I could barely imagine this place, and now I couldn't imagine anywhere else.

By the time I returned to the cabin she was gone. I grabbed another beer from the fridge and settled on the bed, to stare at the wall and listen to the noises of the night.

The next morning she was beside me, sprawled over the covers. The sheets beneath me were damp with sweat. I stumbled to the sink for a glass of water, and kicked the straw cowboy hat out the way in case I stood on it. A headache pounded behind my eyes.

I scraped together the last of our cash and drove into town. There'd been an accident up ahead. Some girl was lying in front of a car, her shopping bag spilled across the road, apples rolling into the gutter. I sat in the traffic and watched, just like everybody else.

***

After that first night, we drove through the mountains to the next little town and I stopped to fill up the tank. I scraped up every coin I could find, searching behind seats and on the floor for any form of money.

In the store I took out the cash to pay. In Spanish, she asked for cigarettes. I told her I didn't have enough. She said it was okay, and grabbed a handful of snacks and dumped them on the counter, and took a bottle of water from the fridge, and added that to the pile. The old man behind the counter totted it all up on a calculator, and told her the price.

She asked the old man to repeat it and he did, and she reached into her little duffel bag and pulled out the gun. I flinched away from it again, as I had the night before. The old man did too, but as she asked for the cash from the drawer he slowly took out the notes, eyes flicking from the barrel of the gun to her face, back to the gun. He bagged up the groceries and the cash in silence, and we just walked straight out and drove away. She was happy for a while, smoking out the window and humming softly to herself.

248

I turned off the highway and took a back road for several miles, and turned north again and found my way to another road headed south. I tried to twist and turn the car, checking in the mirror for the *Guardia Civil*, but she hummed away and smoked and sometimes she looked over at me.

***

In the town I waited while an ambulance pulled up. As a policeman directed the traffic around I couldn't help rubbernecking. An African girl-- young woman, really-- lying still and frightened as the paramedics whispered to her, attached things to her, wrapped a thick brace around her neck. The ambulance lights flashed red and blue and I thought about my boy. I couldn't help but notice the girl's sandal, dropped in the street, and I worried that nobody would remember to pick it up, that it'd lie there, on the side of the road, a forgotten reminder.

***

We took the long way round after that, and robbed another couple of stores for cash and water and cigarettes, then used the money to fill up the car and buy whisky and wine and hotel rooms. We doubled back constantly, since I figured the police must be getting a bead on us, trying to figure out where we'd be turning up next. I kept to the small places, the family-run places which were less likely to have cameras. She didn't worry about any of that. She just hummed tunes to herself and drank and in the evening she laughed at me and then she'd kiss me, and the next day she'd do the same thing, waving the gun around like a toy, like a cowboy, like it didn't matter.

I checked the gun one night when she was passed out drunk in a motel. There were four bullets in there, and two empty spaces. There were no spent cartridges. Maybe she'd removed them before.

As we left a small town up the coast, she yelled for me to stop. We skidded to a halt on the side of the road, and the cars behind us swerved and honked. She jumped out of the car and ran back to the

249

small store we had just passed. Next to the postcards and the beach balls, and the snorkels and t-shirts, was a stand with straw hats. She searched through them quickly, scattering discarded and unwanted ones onto the pavement and the street. Finally, she picked out one shaped like a Stetson and ran back to the car. As she jumped into her seat she yelled, "Drive, drive drive!" and we rejoined the traffic headed for the coast road.

As we pulled out onto the cliff top highway, and the sun glinted off the sea and the radio played happy music, she yelled and cheered out the window and jammed the hat onto her head. She pulled the gun out and waved it around, like a toy, like the movies. Sometimes I think that was all she wanted, to be someone else, like an actress who plays different roles in different films. As if she never before had the chance to figure out who she really was.

***

In town I tried not to think about the girl in the road, or my boy, or anything else. I tried not to think about guns or car accidents or the past. I meandered through the supermarket and spent the last of our money. On the way back to the cabin, as I passed the pedestrian crossing, there was no sign of the girl, or the accident. I couldn't see her sandal, so somebody must've picked it up.

As I pulled up outside the cabin I saw a couple of the local boys hanging around on the dunes. She was on the veranda, smoking. As I walked up to the cabin she hummed along to the radio blasting from indoors. There was another bottle of cheap grappa shit on the wicker table. She must've got it on credit at the local store. I couldn't do that because I didn't speak Spanish.

She stood and gave me a kiss on the cheek, and put the cowboy hat on my head. I walked inside and tossed the hat on the bed, poured myself a cheap whisky and added a dash of water from the tap. I kicked the cowboy hat onto the floor and turned off the radio, and looked through the screen door at her as the local boys looked on from a distance. Time didn't move in the afternoon heat haze, but still

I could feel the weight of the past. It pressed up behind me and it didn't stop coming, no matter how many times I filled my glass.

***

When we arrived at the cabin, we paid for a long time and no questions, and then we made love, and then we made love again. And then we found the long hours of the day, the sun glaring down at us, and the longer hours of the night. And we made love, and we drank, and we drank, and we sat and stared at each other, for day after night after day. And I wondered where we could go, now that we'd reached the end of the land, the end of the world. We stopped having sex and started drinking more and staring out at the light and the dark as they slipped quietly by. And she slipped away from me, too, into the darkness. Once or twice, then most nights, and I didn't ask where she went.

***

I woke to the smell of cooking. She leaned against the wall, watching me and twirling the cowboy hat on a finger. "I made dinner," she said. She slid the food out onto one plate. The sun was just sinking to the horizon. On the veranda she'd set up a candle on the wicker table and opened a bottle of wine, so we sat out there and ate, and drank the wine and listened to the waves. The youths were just starting up their noise, and the stars were edging out nervously.

When she was finished eating she sat back in her chair, and the smoke from her cigarette curled around the roof of the veranda and disappeared. She said, "What happened to your boy?"

I washed down the last of the wine and was silent, gazing out at the fading orange glow where the sun had been. I didn't answer the question because I didn't have any answers. Nobody does. You can pretend you have a reason for what you do, but you don't. It doesn't matter what happened in your life, every moment is a chance to make something new. And we always, always, let those moments slip away,

251

like smoke on the breeze. In the end you learn to stop asking questions.

I went back inside and when I came out I had the bottle of whisky. I walked past her and I walked up into the hills, away from the cabin, and I sat up there with the whisky and I heard the party starting on the beach. I heard the noise and the voices as they laughed and joked and chased each other through the surf. I saw their fire, and I saw couples hugging close around it, and guys playing guitar, and other figures disappearing towards the water or into the shadows.

I sat there staring at nothing and knew that time had stopped. I had stopped moving, stopped running, and time had stopped with me. But the past never stops. It flows on, relentless, and I knew the past must catch me soon; the memories already filled my head. I knew when it caught up it would hit me in the back like a train. I smoked cigarettes to chase off the mosquitoes, and the other insects buzzed around me in the night until they filled my ears, and my thoughts drifted on whisky to other times and other people. I remembered the things I didn't want to remember. And I knew what I had to do.

In our little shack I reached into her duffle and pulled out the gun. It was heavy and long and awkward. Cumbersome. I sat on the bed and faced the door and I waited, trying to hold back the memories for as long as I could, but still I felt the tears dripping slowly down my face. Nothing moved but the tears. The waves were still, the cicadas silent. There was no time but the tears of the past and the stolen future. Until she walked in through the door, and I raised the gun.

I feel like she smiled. Like she understood. Like she knew that it was time for both of us to move on. But all that was shattered by the gunshot. The present, and the future she could never possess, all gone in an instant. And my mind was clear, and I was free again.

Afterwards, I stood on the empty beach in the early light, and I gazed up at the stars but they were the same. So I threw the gun into the sea, and climbed into the car, a straw cowboy hat on the passenger seat, for company. I drove, and I didn't stop.

About the Author - Christopher Black is from Bristol, England, but works out of Seoul these days. His short stories have appeared at A Twist of Noir, Thrillers, Killers 'n' Chillers, and in Pulp Ink 2. Every now and then he pops into availableinanycolour.blogspot.com for a coffee and a chat.

Once Upon A Time In The West
by
Richard Godwin

VIOLATION AND VIRGIN LAND

No mercy in this land. A bloodied sheet flapped like a flag from a nail on the deserted farmhouse in the back of beyond as I rode away. Nowhere to go except towards the past, the sound of my horses' hooves thundering across the landscape. I rode through the dust and emptiness. This land is full of gods, not the Christian God, that impostor in this place of heartache, genocide and guilt. This was before Hollywood and the creation of myth. The myths were already there, like the slaves Columbus said he discovered. They were there deep in the virgin soil I cut my hands on. I travelled hard through the blood shot night.

It was a restless slice of earth in the middle of a battle. The pioneers were men who were little better than killers, maybe that's why we had so many wars, the account of them mythologized on the big screen. Heroism. A dirty word. I was there for my own reasons. I do not try to moralise. We all want to own something, somebody. And some of us want to take back what we fought for from the men who were blind to our struggle and violated our lives.

They were building the future. The railroad broke their backs, as they slaved in the sun, their skins blackened to leather, their pay little more than enough for bread and water. To give a life to their wives alone somewhere where savage cowboys raped them. The frontier was an invitation to that kind of thing.

I played my note like that train whistle in nowhere, my harmonica in my mouth a shrill alarm.

Sweetville. What a lie that was. Nothing sweet about it. A virginal slice of lawlessness full of killers and whores. And one whore in particular with eyes that seared you. They were all trading, dealing in something, flesh, corruption.

I stayed away, in the shadows, and killed them one by one. I watched them fall. I found Jack there. His eyes looked like they were bleeding and some murderous light shone inside them. There was a fight going on. For a railroad and a whore. Norris's men wanted him dead and I helped him out. I wanted him for myself.

Ever since it happened it was like a spring coiling up inside me. I knew he'd forgotten. He'd killed so many. I waited until the duel came.

And as I stood there looking into his animal eyes I remembered my brother on my back. Holding him there beneath the creaking rope, the harmonica in my mouth, until I couldn't hold him anymore and his neck snapped beneath Jack's rope.

I wasn't going to miss.

I blew two yards of flesh out of Jack's guts, ragged loose flesh that showered blood onto the dry desert. And I walked slowly across the space between us and he looked up at me.

"What's your name?" he said.

I just put my harmonica in his mouth.

He nodded and I rode away.

The train was coming into Sweetville and it was an ending. Civilisation was being brought to a lawless land and I watched Sandra take water to the workers. Even she represented something softer than that town. And I saw it was all about to change and there would be no place for men like me.

Marco was bleeding, he'd been shot by Norris's men. I looked around at that place of railroad, and I took Marco out of there and rode away on my horse, like the time I'd ridden there, but with Jack dead and my brother avenged. Law doesn't belong there. The railroad would try to change that but the land knew. The men who'd killed out there went to kill in other countries.

All those years waiting for him, waiting to kill Jack, and that harmonica. All those times I'd made that note, sounding like the train, they echoed in my head as I rode away, looking for the frontier. But

255

the frontier was gone. It was nothing more than men like Jack and Norris killing and trying to make money.

That's what the business was built on, bloodshed and rail track. I rode, I looked for a place. Men like me had nowhere to go, so we went to remote places to slug it out, shoot or be shot in desolate saloons on the edge of nowhere. It took killers to make what we know as civilisation. The railway delivers men and women to places where they would never have survived in the old west.

Jack thought my brother was nothing. He thought he could kill him and leave me, like he left all the people he'd violated and murdered, and ride on. But I remembered and he forgot and that was the difference. That was how I killed him, out there in Sweetville with the track laying crews coming, and the train on the horizon and the virgin land bleeding with all the crimes forgotten and remembered.

Devil's Advocate
by
Darren Sant

A Daimler caressed the streets and cruised almost noiselessly by two
scruffy kids playing kerby. When one kid raised a foot and made as if
to kick the ball at the car, the driver grinned and wagged a finger in
mock admonishment. A cloud of cigar smoke drifted around from his
fat stoogie. He took a long puff and the end momentarily grew
brighter. He exhaled and added to the already dense cloud. Further
down the street was a sign that read *Welcome To The Longcroft Estate*.
Underneath this some wit had written *Abandon hop all ye who enter here.*
Frowning the man stopped the car. His handmade Italian loafers
kissed the dirty pavement gently and shaking his head he walked up to
the sign. His disapproval was clear. A glint of sunlight reflected from
his Armani sunglasses in the early evening light. He ground the
remains of his stoogie under an expensive heel and withdrew a small
spray can from his jacket. With a quick spray and a flourish *hop* became
hope. The man smiled and nodded his approval before returning to his
car.

As he drove along the quiet streets most people were inside
eating their evening meal and watching the soaps. A few pairs of
envious eyes watched the cars progress. To some of them it was worth
more than their houses.

The car finally slowed and turned into a pub car park. A sign
swinging precariously on rusty fixings declared that it was the Rampant
Horse. The sign depicted A heraldic beast rearing magnificently up on
hind legs, it's dignity was stolen by an out of proportion spray painted
penis between its legs.

The man in black stepped into the pub. With a simple fluid
gesture he removed his shades and slipped them in his breast pocket.
For a moment, just a precious second, time seemed to stand still. A fly
feasting upon a cheese sandwich behind the bar stopped and regarded

257

the newcomer. Multi-faceted eyes saw only the darkness behind the shape.

A Beatles track on the aged jukebox stopped for a fraction of a heartbeat before the sad tale of Eleanor Rigby continued as if nothing had happened. The newcomer snorted.

"I was always a Stones man myself." He muttered.

Shane Cullen, aged local hard man, looked the man up and down. He admired the expensive clothes and dryly said.

"I think you came to the wrong place lad. We're a little low rent for your kind don't ya think?"

The man stepped forward and regarded Cullen with a clinical eye. For a moment Cullen gave an involuntary shudder. He smelled predator and his instincts were telling him to run. His pride however said "Don't you fucking dare sunshine!"

The man in black placed a hand upon Cullen's shoulder and said.
"I've come to collect from a debtor Mr Cullen. They always pay…in the end."
With this the man ordered a pint of best bitter and then sat alone at a table. Cullen felt a tingle on his shoulder and saw that a hole was burned in his shirt where the man had touched it. It was only later that it seemed important to him that he had never actually told the man his name.

An hour later and the man was looking at his watch with an impatient frown. The amused smile had long since left his face as he watched the regulars. A woman for whom the expression mutton dressed as lamb could have been invented suddenly sashayed across the room and sat across from him. She'd been nursing the same drink for a while and had decided that desperate times called for even more desperate measures. A girl had to take a chance now and again. The well-heeled stranger looked like an easy mark.

"Alright luv?" she slurred. In her head to Ivy it was the most seductive tone she could muster.

The man looked up from his phone and casually placed it on the table with the kind of deliberate slowness you rarely see but that is always a precursor to trouble.

"No, my dear I am not alright. Someone will be paying a very high price for his tardiness." His language was precise and educated. Not the kind of language heard often around the estate.

A thought occurred to Ivy, "Hey are you a brief like?"

The man slapped the table and laughed with genuine mirth.

"My dear I am called many things in many languages. I wonder if you could guess my name?"

With this comment a familiar Rolling Stones track suddenly thundered from the jukebox. Ivy looked bewildered for a moment. It looked like the bloke was a bit of a nutter. Maybe she could exploit that.

His brown eyes seemed to burn with a dangerous ferocity and Ivy felt herself drawn in, seduced. She felt that she could lose herself forever in them. For the first time a stab of fear gripped her. However, the strange connection was broken just as suddenly as it had started. Ivy giggled but was clearly unsettled.

"Listen, I'm skint like and I really wanna stop here a while longer. If you give us a fiver I'll show you my tits in the alley behind the pub."

The man smiled. The smile contained no warmth. His expression conveyed an ancient malice too deep to be understood by human kind.

He reached into his wallet and withdrew a twenty. He placed it in Ivy's sweaty palm and leaned forward.

"You have a divine night on me Ivy and in my darkest hour just *imagining* your saggy tits will keep me going."

With this he winked, placed his phone on the table and walked towards the gents. Ivy suddenly decided that she had business elsewhere and left the pub as fast as she could totter on her high heels.

As the man in black walked towards the gents two figures in the corner nodded to each other. The first got up and walked by the man's table, casually pocketing the phone before leaving the pub. The other figure slipped into the gents behind him. The man in black stood at the urinal his back to the door. The figure slipped behind him and pressed a knife into his back.

"Fucking wallet now rich boy or you're going to get hurt."

The man in black tutted audibly. Steam rose above his head, more steam than there should have been from a short piss.

Suddenly the knife grew red hot in the assailant's hand. He dropped the knife and ran to a washbasin. The cold water felt like bliss and he turned it up to maximum in an attempt to take away the pain. The man in black turned to face him and suddenly the room darkened. The walls slid away and he felt as if he was tumbling ever downward. He landed and his hand throbbed, the pain intensifying. He hand grew redder and redder. All the flesh boiled into a blackened mess and he screamed in agony. All around him was lava and writhing naked bodies. People were begging for mercy as wispy wraiths spun around them, clawing and defiling them. Everywhere he looked was decay and corruption. The smell of burning flesh and excrement made him gag. Suddenly and without warning he found himself back in the bathroom of the Rampant Horse. The man in black just smiled at him and held out him wallet.

"Still want to take it? Now you know the cost?" he opened the wallet, it was stuffed with money. More than he'd ever seen.

"Go on take itttt…." The word it became a serpent's hiss.

The man who then ran from the pub screaming would spend the rest of short life drooling and ducking from horrible visions that were with him twenty four hours a day. His friend who had swiped the phone died of a stab wound two days later, whilst arguing over a price for the phone with a fence who didn't take kindly to the bartering.

***

The man in black walked calmly back to his table. He shook his head when he saw that his phone was gone. Taking a final sip of his pint he swallowed an unsuspecting fly that was having the time of its life in the dark fluid. He bought another drink. In the following hour he had to endure an accidental pool cue in the face, the random ramblings of Tourette's Ted and Daniel O'Donnell on the jukebox. When Westlife came chirping like rabid chipmunks out of the jukebox he could take no more punishment. His eyes aflame he strolled up to Big Dave the barman.

"If John Faust comes in tell him Abaddon is truly pissed off and that I'm going to make him suffer an eternity of agony."

The man in black stalked from the bar. Old Pete who sat on his usual barstool hiccupped and laughed.

"Get the diva. His boyfriend stood him up." He said dryly.

Big Dave had grabbed a pen and paper. He shouted after the man, "Here mate, how many D's in Abaddon then?"

***

The car park was a more foreboding place in the darkness. A single weak orange street lamp cast a feeble light upon the glass strewn car park. Silhouetted in the pub doorway briefly the man in black looked to be aflame. His black coat blew dramatically in the breeze as he stalked across the car park. His sleek and flawlessly elegant Daimler now sat neatly on four piles of bricks, incapable of even the shortest of journeys. The Longcroft's latest victim threw back his head and bellowed at the moon with all the primal rage of the blackest of fallen angels.

About the Author - Darren Sant is a 42 year old writer who lives in Hull. His writing often features dark deeds that are offset with humour and the odd uplifting moment. He is pleased to have been published by Byker Books, Pill Hill Press and such classy online fiction sites as the Flash Fiction Offensive, Thrillers Killers 'N' Chillers and Shotgun Honey. He has an ongoing series of stories called Tales From The Longcroft Estate with Byker Books.

Jaws
by
Chris Rhatigan

I have a list with five names on it. Wrote it in blue ink on the back of a napkin while I was having a cocktail at the hotel bar.

The names are people I'm going to fire. Today. In a matter of hours, maybe less if I have any say about it.

I selected those five from a much, much longer list. These were the names that called out to me, that said, "I have no value, I do no real work. Please, release me."

Corporate wanted to fly me in, but I told them to save their hard-earned cash—any excuse to let my Five Series out of its cage is a good one. I burned through 300 miles in under four hours, checked into the Hyatt late last night.

I leave before sunrise. Want to get to the parking lot of the regional branch as early as possible.

I'm sitting on the hood of my Five Series, sipping a thermos of coffee, when they start shuffling in—the office drones, hundreds of them, exhausted before they've even arrived at work, luggage sets under their eyes weighing them down. A couple of them notice me and—quick as they can—avert their eyes.

Word's out. They know what's going down.

I smoke a cigarette, then another, drop the butts on the ground just to let them know what's what.

It's quarter after nine. I tighten my Windsor knot and I'm about to go in, end the delicious suspense, when an old Geo rattles into the lot. Its driver is a man—if you want to call him that—of such stunning, thorough mediocrity that I find his existence thrilling. How anyone could be so devoid of vigor is beyond me.

We lock eyes and the truth is plain: Very soon, I will cross his name off the back of that napkin. His windows are rolled up, but I smell fear.

I breeze through the lobby and nod at the receptionist. Cute face, but probably has an ass the size of a fridge and cankles that would put Monica Lewinsky to shame.

She says nothing, just smiles and lets me pass without checking my ID or asking me to sign in. Being good-looking gets you wherever you want in this world. More than smarts, more than height—more than even money—a pilot's chin and a chest to match is what you want.

I wander into the first vaguely important looking office. According to the nameplate on the door, it belongs to Fred McDuffy. He stands when I come in, slides around his desk.

"Mr. Powell," he sputters. Shakes my hand with all the enthusiasm and authority of a soiled adult diaper. "Welcome to—"

"I know where I am."

He blinks, readjusts his glasses. I really wish his was one of the five names. "Of course, of course. Please, sit down. My team has assembled a detailed file for your perusal—"

"None of that will be necessary." I put my arm around him. He's about six inches shorter than me and I got him feeling every bit of that right now. "Listen, Frank—"

"It's Fred."

"Here's what I need. I need a desk. I need two chairs on opposite sides of that desk. I need an IV drip of strong, preferably drinkable, espresso." I shove the napkin into his palm. "And I need these five people to see me, in order, with five-minute breaks between each. Think you can handle that?"

He nods like a bobblehead doll.

***

Most people in this job fuck it up. They try to let them down gently. "I'm *so* sorry. This was *such* a difficult decision. We don't want this any more than you do." Then, the biggest lie of them all, "This decision was not based on merit." What a fucking joke—if some idiot is laying off people *not* based on merit, that dude deserves to have his ass

263

canned yesterday. And not having a choice? Bullshit! They had plenty of choices—like everyone else who works there!

Most people, they this miss the point. They think they're firing a human. But really what they're getting rid of is a unit of production. After all, that's why companies hire employees—to produce. Companies don't hire employees so they can put food on a family's table or pay for a trip to Disney World. Companies hire employees because they believe those people will help their bottom line *so much* that it will make up for paying their salaries and health care and pensions—and then turn the company a profit on top of that.

But very, very few employees do that. Which is why my job is so easy. Why it's so essential.

So I don't tell these losers that "I'm sorry," or "This was a difficult decision." I tell them the truth—and deep down, they know it's the truth—that they're frauds. That they don't work as much as they should, or as well as they should, and the scam they've been running for years is finally over. Yep, it's been a good run, you've stolen a lot from the company—*and you get to keep all that*—but this is the end of the line.

You'd be amazed at my results. Production increases at the offices I visit by an average of 30 percent.

***

The first one in is a guy from IT, youngish with a moon face and the delicate hands of a porcelain doll. I don't think he knows how to turn on a computer let alone fix one. He seems unsurprised that he's there and pleasantly surprised by the company's severance package and the prospect of collecting unemployment. I predict he'll be on the government teat for two years, minimum.

Next is the receptionist, and I must say I'm a bit taken aback. What person younger than 40 is named Ethel? Jesus Christ. And she's considerably better looking than I originally thought—toned legs, solid C-cup, classic bottle-shaped figure.

No matter—I tell her that her job can be done by a computer or shipped overseas, both cheaper options for the company, and either one will do a better job than her. Tell her that she's lucky—she's still young, she can switch career paths no problem.

Not that being a receptionist is a career path, but that's just semantics.

The next two sail by uneventfully and I'm starting to doubt myself. Where's parking lot guy? He has to be on this list of names. But he wasn't Barney Stickling or Eugene Morgan. Really thought he would have been Eugene Morgan...

I'm flipping through an old issue of *Time* magazine, killing the five minutes between jobs, when in slumps Martin Feesbender.

Or, should I say, parking lot guy.

I smile, take a long swig of lukewarm instant coffee, and crack my knuckles.

"So, Mr. Feesbender, tell me why you think you're here today."

He exhales and his lips flap like a horse's. He's got that 1,000-yard stare.

I snap a few times in a vain attempt to reconnect him with reality. He blows his nose into a handkerchief, keeps his gaze fixed on the Thomas Kinkade print behind me.

Maybe he's retarded, or he's a genius, exerting complete control over the situation.

Either way, my job remains the same. I skip my standard speech, move right to the nitty gritty. Feesbender says nothing throughout my bit about the two weeks' severance pay, how he can file for unemployment, his eyes glassy, his expression as if this is happening to someone on another planet.

He stands and leaves while I'm explaining how he can cash out his 401k.

***

265

It's only one-thirty and my work day is done. I'll catch a nap at the hotel before taking the redeye back to corporate. Figure I've earned it—I've saved the company about $200,000 in salary alone today, not to mention tens of thousands in annual benefits.

Fred McDuffy smiles and waves, clearly relieved his name wasn't on that napkin.

I say, "See you again soon," and erase that smile immediately.

Feesbender is outside with his box of personal belongings, not doing anything, just standing there, that aimless look now stuck on the Perodex building and the leafless trees. I say nothing to him—what is there to say—and get in the Beemer. I back out of the space and Feesbender puts the box down on the ground, takes a couple of steps toward the curb.

That's when I see it—he's going to step in front of my car, take the hit, collect the insurance money. It's a half-baked plan at best, but still, not a bad option for a guy with no marketable skills who just lost the only real job he'll ever have.

But I'll be damned if I let him escape that easy.

So I floor it. The Five Series purrs, completely in its element. Speedometer ticks up—twenty, thirty, forty.

It's like the games of chicken I used to play in high school—a pure adrenalin rush no drug can match.

Feesbender stays planted on the curb, tunnel vision on the speeding car coming toward him.

At the right moment, he takes his dive. Hits the hood, head cracks against the windshield, rolls off. ABS kicks in, I shudder to a stop.

I stand corrected. Now *that's* an adrenalin rush.

Unfortunately, his blood's all over the car and that could cause some problems.

I glance at the rear-view. He's twitching, looks like he might even be able to get up if he put his mind to it. I picture cops showing up at the hospital, Feesbender describing to them how I hit fifty in a parking lot and mowed him down.

We can't have that.

So I throw it in reverse, back up over his body—*thud thud*—and speed out of the lot.

***

I keep it at a steady sixty-five on the highway, signaling between lanes like a responsible citizen. No reason to call more attention to myself. I figure if the cops pull me over, I'll just tell 'em I hit a deer or something.

I call up an old buddy from my Exeter days and, as luck would have it, he knows a guy who can fix my beautiful machine on the DL. Comes at a price, of course, but I tell him not to worry—with a fat bonus coming up, I got money to burn.

After all, I've got the best job in the world.

About the Author - Chris Rhatigan is the editor of All Due Respect and the co-editor of the anthologies Pulp Ink and Pulp Ink 2. His short stories have appeared in Beat to a Pulp, Needle, Pulp Modern, and other venues. His novella, 'The Kind of Friends Who Murder Each Other', will be released by KUBOA Press.

Lost Highway
by
R Thomas Brown

The pitted and uneven road gave way to broken chunks of asphalt as Hap Callahan drove out toward the beach. His aged but proven truck bounced over the terrain, stopping only when he reached a large pit just in front of a field of wild grass.

He turned the truck to drive toward the sandy lane that ran along the gulf before slipping it into park and hopping out with the engine still running and lights still on. Hap took a moment to admire nature reclaiming its territory. Undoing the damage. Or at least trying to make things right.

His moment of quiet contemplation was shattered by the sound of the approaching sedan bottoming out over some of the broken road and scraping its way toward him. The headlights bounced around the shoreline beyond and Hap shook his head at the choice of vehicle.

As the old man stumbled out of his car, Hap looked off toward the coast. The few other cars that shared the night had drifted along the shore and their lights blinked out in the distance. He took a necklace from his pocket and gripped it before turning back.

"Hell of a place to want a meeting, Mr. Callahan."

Hap watched the man's uneven gate over the rubble, weeds and sand. "Why'd you hire me, Bergstrom?"

Alan Bergstrom cleared his throat. "The police quit looking. You came very highly recommended."

Hap nodded. "Maybe, but I'm no PI. There's better people for that."

"I was told you solve problems and find people. I have a problem and need someone found. Did you find her?"

The necklace felt heavy in Hap's hand. The thin metal links and few gemstones weighed little, but the confusion and conflict added substance to the delicate jewellery. He'd carried the necklace and the conflict for a month. The month since he found her.

Grace Bergstrom had vanished a year before. Story was she headed out in her car on the way to college and never got there. Mom and Dad said their good-byes, but didn't hear from her that night. Called the police the next morning. Figured she got tired and would call the next day.

Police looked for a few months. Scoured the whole way between the house in San Marcos and the university in Houston. Never found a damned thing. Other cases came up. The search stopped.

Mom didn't want to give up, so Mr. Bergstrom called Hap.

He knew how to find people. Wasn't limited to the same methods as the police, or any other talented people who felt like obeying the law was part of the job-description. He found her. And the necklace.

"Yeah. I found her." Hap ran his hand through is thinning hair. "You still didn't answer my question. Why me?" He let the necklace dangle from his fingers.

Bergstrom swallowed. "I was also told that you were a man loyal to your employer."

Hap looked away. Loyalty. It was about the only thing like a virtue he hung to anymore. Someone paid, they were the boss until it was done. Some guy getting blackmailed, Hap didn't care what he did, just that it didn't get out.

He found Grace in an old ghost town outside New Braunfels. A few building scattered throughout along a single road. Biggest one left was a bank. He knew she'd be there. There, out of the way, but still close. He couldn't let her get too far away.

Hap saw the picture of the bank in Bergstrom's office. Sat right on his desk. The old building behind he and his daughter, well, step-daughter. She was six when he married the misses. Hap saw the picture in Grace's room too. Behind the desk. Crumpled. Torn. Trashed.

269

He asked Bergstrom about the picture. Didn't mention Grace's copy. Step-dad was proud. Said they went there a few times. Was one of the happiest days of his life. Hers too, according to him. Said he'd always wanted to take her back there.

Hap let the necklace fall to the ground and pushed his hands into his pockets. "Yeah, that's right. Always loyal. Person that pays is the boss."

Bergstrom exhaled. "Good. Then I guess we're done."

Hap pulled out a piece of paper from his pocket. Unfolded it and held it out toward Bergstrom. Sweat poured from the man, darkening his tailored shirt.

Hap found the note with the girl. It was clinched in her hand. She was slumped behind the old teller window, note in hand, strangled with the necklace Hap had let fall to the floor.

He'd read the note a few hundred times. It was short. "Alan, I can't do this anymore. I'm going to tell Mom." That was it. Two sentences. Two little thoughts that broke Bergstrom's life apart and ended a little girl's life.

"So, I'll let everyone know she's been found and you'll just vanish. That how it works from here?"

Hap shook his head. "No. Not this time."

"What?"

"The note, Bergstrom. The note's really giving me trouble."

"Oh, you have a conscience now? I was sent your name by a guy who was being blackmailed with photos of him killing a homeless man. You kept his secrets."

Hap just nodded. Moral ambiguity wasn't just an asset in his line of work, it was all he knew anymore. Just who he was. There was no insult to be taken.

"Yeah, I did. This, though. Stuck with me."

"How so?"

"It's almost like she's begging for help. Even from beyond, she's pleading for someone to help her tell everyone about you."

Bergstrom stepped closer. "Look, I paid you. This is done."

Hap looked down at the necklace. "What's that worth?"

"What? Twelve grand or so. Why?"

"So, a little more than you paid me."

"Yeah."

Hap gripped a knife in his pocket. Kicked Bergstrom in the stomach. "Well, I figured I took that from her for payment. Decided to work for her instead."

Bergstrom fell to the ground, clutching his gut. "You do this, Cunningham, and I'll make sure everyone knows about it. And, it's not like you have any proof of anything. Just a dumb note that doesn't even really say anything."

Hap nodded. "You're probably right." He took out the knife. "So, I figured I just kill you and get it over with."

"What? Think about this, Hap. When people find out, you'll never work again."

"Look around. Look where you are. You think anyone's gonna find you out here? At the end of a piece of road no one drives?"

Bergstrom stepped back. Hap rushed and shoved his knife into his stomach. Dragged the knife across before pulling it out.

He watched Bergstrom fall to ground. Saw the life in his eyes fade until he only saw little pools of death in his face.

He took a shovel from his truck and dug a shallow grave in the thick wild grass at the end of the old road.

As he drove away, he hoped nature would reclaim that piece of damaged humanity in the ground. Sooner rather than better. He fiddle with the necklace. He'd picked it up before he drove off, but it still felt wrong. He tossed it out the window.

He left the broken highway behind and drove toward the nearest bar in Galveston. Figured he'd send the note to the mother in the morning. Let her decide for herself what to believe.

Right then, though, Hap had too many things on his mind. He needed a few still drinks, and a six pack, to stop those thoughts in their tracks.

271

About the Author - R Thomas Brown has been a story teller as long as he can remember. Many of those were devised to escape punishment of one form or another. He has over time turned his creative energies toward crafting stories he hopes will both entertain and provoke thought.

You can follow him at rthomasbrown.blogspot.com

Memento
by
Tracey Edges

He cried the day I gave it to him.

Turning it over in his hands he splattered it with big, hot
tears. He didn't wipe them off though and the inky words ran in
rivulets into each other, stretching spidery fingers across the page.

"Dammit, John." I said. "Stop it. Look what you're doing."

He couldn't look. He couldn't see through the past or his tear
frosted lenses.

I gently pulled the paper away from his trembling hands and
replaced it with my firm ones.

We stayed there for a long time. Silent and still.

Traffic on the road outside the open window rumbled noisily
past, a horn blasted and children shouted above the din, to make
themselves heard. We didn't notice.

After rush hour a calm fell outside but, inside, the lack of
movement belied the tumult and the turbulence.

We were there for three hours or more. I knew not to speak
and he couldn't talk. I waited. I got cramp but I bore it and tried not to
move. Tried not to disturb his process.

He would deal with this. I knew he would, he could, but he
needed this time of stillness. I couldn't break down his wall but I could
be there when the bricks came tumbling down. I just held on. Tightly,
so he knew I was there. So he wouldn't forget and think he was alone.

It gradually grew dark. Day to dusk to night. It was never
dark in the town. A red aura hovered below a pitch sky. Tonight the
dark, dark, blue was studded with the eyes of angels.

That's what Tilly had always called the stars. She liked to feel
protected and safe.

We used to laugh with her and make up stories about the different angels. Venus loved chocolate but the boy angel, Mars, didn't. Ironic.

Tilly had a dog; a funny mongrel called Angus. We used to guess what he was made up of. It was quite hard. His paws were huge but the rest was medium, except for his eyes. His big, blue eyes. Everyone though they made him particularly special. Tilly called him her guardian angel as he never left her side, where possible. If she left the house without him he would sit at the window and wait for her. Never moving until she arrived home safely. We put a comfy cushion there for him in the end. Mainly so we didn't have to listen to his bones grinding against the hard windowsill.

Until Tilly came home, Angus wouldn't eat, or wee, or chew his favourite bone. Nothing but wait. Maybe he did know how special she was too.

Miranda had died giving birth to Tilly. Maybe that was Tilly's saving grace; never knowing a mother to grieve for. Only John. John was lucky, well no he wasn't, as his precious wife had died, but he was lucky in that Tilly was a perfect child. Always slept through, always happy, always loving. Tilly always had someone or something in her arms. She'd have been the perfect nurse for a Vet; caring, not cutting.

John stirred. Just a little. Stiff in body and manner. Awkward. I didn't know what to say. No words would ever be the right ones. I stayed silent and kept looking at him.

No more tears. They had dried up a while ago, leaving patches on his face and on our hands where they had fallen. Heavily for a while, then slowly easing, until, eventually, none.

I was thirsty and I knew he must be too, even if he didn't know it himself.

We had had afternoon tea. Just the two of us. Outside. It had been a beautiful day. Warm, blissful, relaxing. I'd baked some scones. They looked flat and wonky but were delicious and we ate more than we should have. Too good to resist straight out of the oven. Their steamy hotness melting the yellow butter into little pools which swirled into the jam. We didn't have any cream. It didn't matter. Earl grey tea perfumed the air from our cups and we moaned a lot with the simple pleasure. Smiling at each other. Big, silly, soppy grins. We were happy.

That seemed a lifetime away now.

I came in to find a teaspoon that I had suddenly remembered. It was pretty, delicate, and I wanted to put it in the sugar bowl as I liked using it to put a spoon of sugar in John's tea. I didn't take sugar so it was nice for me to spoon it into his so I could use my little spoon that would, otherwise, have just been no more than an ornament.

Frustrated at its unexplained disappearance. I was rifling through a drawer in the dresser. You know the type – full of batteries and tiny bulbs, business cards and rubber bands. Fuses too.

It was there right at the back, that I found it. Half jammed into the crack at the base of the drawer. I pulled it out carefully, as I did not know what it was and I was curious.

It was from Tilly. Dated the third of February 2003. The last day she was in our lives. Not the last day that we felt life but it was a good while before it began to creep back in and we never forgot. Not for a minute, but we did have to give ourselves permission to live and feel. Eventually.

John eased to his feet. Stiff. He stretched and touched my face.

"Thank you," he whispered, "I love you."

"I know. I love you too." I held his hand not wanting him to move it. We looked out of the window. The stars were shining brightly, despite the air pollution.

The angels had not been looking that night; the third of February 2003. It was stormy and wild and we were all bundled up against the cold, the wet, the biting winter wind. Even Angus had his coat on. Red tartan to match his name. Tilly had chosen it. She liked things 'right'.

We don't know what happened, what Tilly saw. A man bumped into us. Possibly drunk, possibly ill. He dropped his carrier bag and the contents spilled across the wet pavement. Oranges rolling around. Vivid against the dark, wet. John and I rushed to pick them up for him before they got ruined. As we turned to bend down, Tilly ran

275

across the road. What she had seen to make her do that, we will never ever know. Angus barked, pulled and won. The lead slipped from John's hand and Angus shook out his wings and flew after Tilly. The big, red, double-decker bus got them both and that was that. Life extinguished in a squeal and a bang and a thud. Deep silence before the screams from me and the lone passenger. Screaming in stereo. The driver, vision blinded by the rain, didn't have a chance. Never even saw them. Never drove again. It wasn't his fault.

John hadn't seen the piece of paper before. Neither had I. It was probably stuffed in the drawer; a surprise in hiding. The drawing was in felt tip pens. Colourful. It was us. Our family. Tilly had honoured me by calling me Mummy. The first time made me cry and she gave me a hug, not understanding why I suddenly couldn't talk to her.

There we all were in the clothes and hairstyles (roughly) of 2003. Tilly in her red coat, to match Angus', of course. John in his long, grey wool coat and me in my, fashionable for that year only, flowery duffle coat. We weren't dressed for the picture weather. A big yellow sun dominated one corner and flowers and hearts filled the spaces between. Black ink scribed our names: Daddy, Mummy, Angus and Tilly on a nice walk. A headline declared. I love you forever my angels.

Later, much later, we framed it. Black rivulets, crumples and all. A memory, a message, a lovely memento from our little angel.

About the Author - Tracey Edges is a Professional Fine Artist, who is now also a Writer. She's rather pleased about that as she has always written but kept her outpourings to herself. After being encouraged to start a story-blog, she found that people quite liked reading said outpourings and now there is no stopping her. She is unleashed. Her story-blog, PI GY (Private Investigations Grimsby), is a mix of fact and fiction. If you ask her nicely she'll happily spill the beans but most of the disasters, especially those involving animals, did actually happen to her. PI

GY has been read worldwide and has already been made into a Radio series of 8 episodes with series 2 already in production. You can read the series from Part 1 "The Beginning," in the May 2012 archive at www.traceyedges.blogspot.com and her short story blog is at www.alittlebitoftraceyedges.blogspot.com Originally from Lincolnshire, Tracey has lived in Oxfordshire, where she studied Art, and Cornwall, where she owned a Village Shop and Post Office and was the rather unlikely Sub-postmistress for a few years. Returning to Lincolnshire she built up her acclaimed Art profile and has exhibited widely. You can hear Tracey talking about her Artwork and varied life in this interview by Estuary Radio: http://www.youtube.com/watch?v=5depLM8R6RU Her work can be found in her photo albums on Facebook: Tracey Edges or on her in-dire-need-of-an-update website: www.traceyedges.co.uk She is also on Twitter: @tedges Tracey is always happy to be distracted from whatever she should be doing, especially updating her website, by a good chatter or a walk on the beach with her dogs.

Dead Man Walking
by
Mel Sherratt

Trevor Rowley looked up as he heard muffled laughter. He might have
guessed it would be coming from Cheryl Latham. He watched as she
rammed another sandwich into her mouth. It wasn't a hard task, he
supposed, given how she easily had the biggest mouth around. One of
these days he'd ram his fist in there too. That would shut her up.

He glanced around the bar, eyeing all the greedy fuckers
scoffing his food like they'd never had a decent meal in their measly
lives. It was always the same, every funeral he held there. They all came
crawling out of the woodwork. Still, it was good to get everyone
together under one roof now that The Crook's Nook had been
spruced up. All leather settees and low tables, bright colours and art
deco. It looked more like a wine bar than a local pub. Trevor was
proud of it. And if any one of the punters so much as ripped a beer
mat, there'd be trouble.

'He was a gentleman,' he overheard someone say. 'Had a
heart of gold, did our Freddie.'

Trevor collected a few glasses and walked back to the bar.
What a stupid thing to declare. He hated funeral talk. Everyone saying
what a great guy Freddie was; how he'd died too early. Freddie Marcs
was forty-three: most of Trevor's mates died early in this game.
Occupational hazard: lose your bottle and you were a goner. Simple as.
But Freddie hadn't lost his bottle. He'd got what was coming to him
instead.

Trevor had seen to that.

Over by the window, Tommy Latham perched on the arm of the sofa
next to his wife. Too busy trying to steal the limelight herself, she
didn't even acknowledge his presence.

278

'I suppose it won't be long before Conor Rowley comes sniffing around,' Cheryl Latham said, checking over her shoulder to see if Freddie's widow, Vicky, was in hearing range. 'And we all know he'll be after more than just money. I often wonder if he had anything to do with Freddie's fall.'

Tommy wished he could put his hands around her neck and squeeze real hard. Not that it would make any difference. It wouldn't stop her from spouting her mouth off. But she was right in some respects. It couldn't be anything other than murder yet the police had no evidence of foul play. Or rather they weren't concerned with finding any. All they seemed to be pleased about was that another of the boys was off their patch, less for them to deal with. But Tommy knew Freddie would never stumble and, besides, he'd seen what had really happened. He had eyes everywhere nowadays. And one thing was certain: Trevor Rowley wasn't going to get away with murder again.

The door opened and a few people came in all at once. Tommy raised his chin when he noticed Derek Bourne amongst them. Any minute now, his manner said but Tommy wasn't ready to make a move yet.

Trevor surveyed the room again. Freddie's family were sitting in the middle, congregated around one table. People were mulling around them. He watched the grieving widow, Vicky Marcs, as yet another woman gave her a hug and she held back tears, taking their sympathy as she dabbed at her eyes. Trevor knew it was all for show: she was another one who liked to be in the thick of things. Despite the circumstances, he knew she'd be relishing in the glory. And everyone knew how she was shagging around behind Freddie's back anyway – he knew because he'd been there too. Nothing much to write home about. Just another desperate housewife. He sighed. Fuck, even he was getting irritable. It was like a morgue in here.

'Come on, everyone,' he shouted from behind the bar. 'Freddie wouldn't want to see anyone moping. The drinks are on me. Conor, turn up the music. It's time to give the guy a proper send off.'

279

'Bloody typical of him to think we should celebrate death,' Emma Bourne said, pinching a pickle from Cheryl's plate and stuffing it into her mouth before she could protest.

'Yeah,' Cheryl agreed. 'After everything he's put us through, you'd think he'd want to keep quiet and not make a fuss.'

Derek left his wife to it and moved over by the dart board. He leaned on the back wall, hands in his pockets, hidden away for fear he'd use them too early as he waited for Mickey Peters to arrive. His shoes were uncomfortable: he wanted to kick them off but knew it was impossible. He hated funerals – couldn't believe this was his fourth in the past year. Couldn't wait for the fifth, if truth be told.

To his right, Conor Rowley sat on a stool at the bar. Surrounded by his mates, his laugh was loud, fearless and menacing, telling everyone around him that he thought he was untouchable, just like he believed his father was. Silly little fucker. Derek knew that Conor was responsible for a lot of the ill-feeling among the men he used to call his friends. He was still beat up about it. But Conor wouldn't be able to hide behind his father forever. Soon he'd be alone. That would make things just about even.

That laugh again. Conor glanced his way but didn't acknowledge Derek, looking right through him even. Where were his manners, the little scrote? An icy mood fell over him. It was so frustrating not being able to lay a hand on him.

Finally, Mickey Peters arrived with his wife. As Maggie made her way to sit and gossip with the women, Mickey moved through the crowds of people. People he used to associate with; people who used to look up to him. Now they didn't even see him. That was down to Trevor Rowley. Rowley had hit him for everything. He was still haunted by it; couldn't wait to get his revenge.

'I was beginning to think you weren't showing,' Emma said to Maggie as she squeezed in between them on the settee.

'I suppose we have to look out for one another now.' Maggie's voice was cold.

Conor Rowley shook his head as he made his way past the women on his way for a slash. Stupid bunch of bitches, the lot of them. Thank God he wasn't married to any of them. In the toilets, he pressed his head against the tiles as he relieved himself, welcoming the chill on his flushed face. Man, he was wasted. But he still managed to take a quick snort of coke before stumbling back into the hallway. Right smack bang into his father.

'I told you not to get hammered,' Trevor said as he righted him. 'Calm it down.'

'Okay, okay,' Conor slurred, shrugging off his hand. 'I'm fine!'

'You'd better be. If your mouth runs away with you, you'll have me to answer to.'

Trevor left him leaning on the wall in the hallway and made his way to the cellar room. Christ, that boy was a fucking liability. He had to see to it that Conor kept his mouth shut for a few more hours at least. Then, for now, he'd be home and dry.

It hadn't been easy planning all of the murders but it seemed to have worked out okay. He knew all the fuckers out there who were scoffing his ale and drinking his food – by now pissed beyond getting their words in the right order too – were aware that he'd killed them all. But there had been no proof. There was never any proof.

Tommy Latham had been the first to go. There hadn't been much of him left after an electrical fault set his car alight with a boom. Getting rid of Derek Bourne had been a bit dodgy though. Trevor had lost his temper when he'd found out Derek was on the take, so he'd given him a good seeing too. He'd wanted to savour his death, take his time over it but instead it had to be quick. Still, there were no witnesses to a mugging that had gone too far – and no CCTV cameras seemed to be working that night. Trevor had seen to that.

Mickey's death had been the easiest. Hit and run. Trevor's car had been fixed by the time the cops came calling – strange, they hadn't even mentioned the smell of fresh paint. So when it came to pushing

Freddie off the roof – well, it felt like child's play. 'He was larking about, officer. I tried to warn him but he wouldn't listen.'

Trevor laughed to himself. It had been such a hoot taking over their businesses one by one. Making their widows realise they had no choice but to hand them over. Mickey's run of doormen; Derek's massage parlours; this place, Tommy Latham's gaff.

Now they was all his.

Outside, Conor paced the hallway. He was sick of being told what to do; he'd stop drinking when he'd had enough and not before. And if his old man thought he was going to be top dog now that all the gang had gone, then he was going to put a stop to it right now. He spied an empty pint glass that someone had left on the window sill. Without hesitation, he picked it up and followed Trevor into the cellar room.

Starting to get hot under the collar back in the bar, Tommy wondered what was taking Freddie so long to changeover. And then he saw him in the distance. Back to the wall in his best bib and tucker, standing near to his family – shaking his head as he watched his wife being comforted yet again. Tommy wondered if he'd been there all the time, only wanting to reveal himself at the last minute. Watching, waiting, listening in. Freddie never fell for anything.

Tommy signalled to Derek. Derek nodded at Mickey. Mickey gestured to Freddie. It was show time.

Trevor decided to grab a bottle of something special from the rack before heading back to the bar. He wanted something mysterious with a fine body, a touch of class and a sexy little nip to it. Pretty much like his women, he mused. He picked one out and read the label. He felt a wisp of wind across his face and shuddered; saw a shadow out of the corner of his eye. He turned suddenly but there was no one behind him. Then he laughed to himself. Shadows giving him the creeps? Grow up, Rowley.

The door opened and Conor staggered across the room. 'I want a word with you,' he slurred.

'Get back to the bar, son.' Trevor took note of the glass in Conor's hand. 'Go and play with your stupid mates.'

Conor charged towards him. A swift upper hand sent him staggering backwards. Enraged, Conor ran at him again, running them both into the wall. Trevor pushed him away with such force that he fell into the rack before crashing to the floor in a drunken heap. Flat out on his back, a groan escaped his lips. The rack swayed violently, its contents too. Trevor saw a car battery rise up into the air and fall, landing on Conor's face, a corner squishing into his eye before smashing down on his forehead. He frowned in confusion: he couldn't remember that being on top of the rack. What the…?

Freddie Marcs was standing in front of him.

Hands to his head, his breathing laboured, Trevor gulped. Fuck, what was happening? Had Freddie moved the car battery? Had he *thrown* the car battery? No, he couldn't have. Freddie was dead. He looked down at Conor's still body, a pool of blood forming around his head. Shit: he had to get out of there and fast.

He turned round just as Tommy Latham came through the door. Derek Bourne appeared after him, followed by Mickey Peters. And then Freddie joined the men, as if he was alive and kicking and not recently buried less than two hours ago. As if they were *all* alive and kicking.

Trevor closed his eyes tightly. He opened them again. They were still there. Four men in a line. Four men he had killed to become number one. What the fuck? Had he been drugged?

'Well, well, well.' Freddie shook his head before passing through Trevor to check on Conor. 'We'd come today to sort out your young one but it seems like you've done the deed for us.'

Trevor shook his head to rid it of confusion. Had they come to kill Conor? Fuck, was Freddie *talking*? No, he was imagining it. Hearing voices, that's was it was. This couldn't be happening.

A deathly chill ascended as the men moved towards him. Trevor stepped backwards. Losing his footing, he fell down the stairs. Arms flailing, his head took the full force of the fall. Sickening thud after thud after thud.

283

People say that Trevor Rowley died of fright after seeing what was left of his son's face. It was the only explanation the police could come up with. There wasn't a mark on him to indicate foul play.

Besides, no one could explain the look of terror on his face. He looked as if he'd seen a ghost. Or two… Or three… Or four…

About the Author - Ever since she can remember, Mel Sherratt has been a meddler of words. Right from those early childhood scribbles when she won her first and only writing competition at the age of 11, she was rarely without a pen in her hand or her nose in a book. Born and raised in Stoke on Trent, Staffordshire, Mel used her beloved city as a backdrop for her first crime thriller novel, TAUNTING THE DEAD, and it went on to be a Kindle #1 best seller in three different categories. Mel has a new series out, THE ESTATE, and is currently writing a psychological thriller. It seems she's always ready to commit murder and mayhem. You can find out more at www.melsherratt.co.uk

Mermaids
by
Patti Abbott

It was particularly hot that day so we ditched summer school. Creaky ceiling fans had pushed the heavy air around all morning, almost making it worse. At break, we decided to take off. I don't remember who came up with the idea, but there was some discussion of going downtown to see a movie.

"Let's go to Mermaid Lake," Tina suggested.

It wasn't really a lake by 1970. As toddlers, we'd squished slimy mud between our toes in Mermaid Lake. Sharp rocks had once cut up our feet and stained our suits green with algae. But eventually, someone installed an Olympic-sized pool, a food stand, a tennis court. The namesake body of water sat unused except for boaters, ducks, and an occasional kid who got tossed in.

Anne and I looked at each other.

"Do we even know how to get there," I said. During car trips, we usually reclined in our backseats reading *Archie* comics or movie magazines, never noticing the roads.

"I think you just go up Skippack Pike," Anne said, pulling out a cigarette.

"Take a bus?" I asked.

"I don't think SEPTA buses leave the city." Anne took a deep drag on her cigarette and considered it. "We'll have to hitch."

"You mean stick out a thumb," Tina asked, her eyes growing large. "Are girls allowed to do that?"

"I doubt it," Anne said, offering me a drag. I shook my head. "But it's probably the only way to get there."

"What will we do for swimsuits," I asked. "We don't even have a towel."

"We hardly ever go into the pool anyway," Anne pointed out, patting her hair. "We can lie on the chaises and sun ourselves. If we get too hot, we can stick our legs in."

"The boys will think we have—you know," Tina said.

"Good," Anne said. "Maybe they'll leave us alone."

Of course, none of us really wanted that.

Twenty minutes later, we found a shady place to stand on Skippack Pike and put out our thumbs. When a Chevy carrying an older couple pulled up, we scrambled in. The back seat lacked springs and had the musty smell of cheap perfume, cigarettes, and something else.

The woman saw me wrinkle my nose and said, "Our Whiskers use to sit back there."

"Where you girls going?" the man asked, looking at us through his rear-view mirror.

"Mermaid Lake," Anne said. "But you can drop us off anywhere along the way." She waved her arm expansively.

"Mermaid Lake, huh? Figure you can get another ride if I don't wanna go that far?" he asked. His eyes were red-rimmed and bloodshot. "Mermaid Lake must be ten miles north. Right, honey? A hoity-toity place now, right? Ever since they put in the pool."

Nodding, his wife turned around. She wore a straw hat and her hair poked through in several spots. "Do your mothers know you're hitchhiking?"

We nodded simultaneously.

"Ha!" she said, shaking her finger. "No mother would let her daughter hitchhike. Still it's a hot day and I guess you wanna swim." She took a handkerchief from her pocketbook and mopped her cleavage. "I can understand that. Wouldn't mind a quick dip myself."

"You girls have any idea what could happen if the wrong person picks you up?" the man said, turning halfway around as he stopped for a light. "And there are a lot of nasty people in this world." His wife smiled her agreement.

"I'll tell you what can happen," he continued when we didn't say anything. "You can be molested, you can be kidnapped, and you can be sold into slavery. Think of this," he said, warming to his subject. "Maybe some jerk will think it's funny to drop you off on a lonely road far away from that Mermaid Lake. It'd just be a big joke to him." His eyes were on us in the mirror again, and we nodded simultaneously. "And just last week, I heard about a girl some guys took inside a deserted house in Ambler." He paused. "You don't want to know the rest."

But his wife decided to tell us anyway. "She was in there for hours with boys taking turns. Lying on a bare wooden floor, not even a pillow for her head. Do you know what that means, girls? Taking turns? She wasn't even hitching either. Just walking down the road with a bottle of milk and some SOS pads near dusk. You might've seen it in the newspaper. They found the grocery items on the road. That's how they found her."

None of us read newspapers.

"You can also be arrested for hitchhiking in the state of Pennsylvania," the man said. "Imagine what your parents would say if they got that call. Had to bail you out of a jail cell in the middle of the night like a juvenile delinquent."

"Mind if I smoke?" Anne said, pulling out her cigarettes.

"Aren't you awful young to be smoking?" the woman said. But she pulled out a cigarette of her own and held the lighter up to Anne.

"Have to be real careful about what car you climb in," the man said. "Now choosing a couple—like you kids did— was a good move." He paused for a second or two. "But even so—did you ever hear about that looney couple over in England? She lured in children for him to murder. Just a few years back, this happened," he said. "Mona something. She was worse than him. He couldn't help himself, but what was her excuse." He looked at his wife and she shrugged. "Man-crazy," he finally decided. "Do anything to keep her fellow."

"Of course, we've had our own murders right here in Norristown," the wife said. "Someone murdered elderly Italian folks. Went on for a few years." She paused. "We're not Italians, of course, but one of the couples lived right down the road."

287

"Norristown is full of Eyetalians," the man said. "Guy killed them with some gun he picked up at Sears. Can you believe it? Just sauntered into Sears and bought a gun instead of paint. Thought the old folks were giving him the evil eye. Another Eyetalian thing—evil eyes."

"A complete crazy," his wife added.

"There are a lot of crazies," he agreed. "Doing stuff decent people never even thought of."

"You two seem to know a lot about crime," Anne said, cranking her window down far enough to toss out the cigarette. "Kind of a hobby for you?"

"Which is why you have to promise us you'll call your parents to come pick you up," the man said, ignoring Anne's remark. "Or get a ride home from someone you know." He paused. "I'd come and get you myself but we have chores to do."

"We have animals that need feedin." The woman tossed her cigarette out the window too. "We keep chickens," she explained needlessly. "And a cow."

"My Dad'll come get us," I promised. "He gets done work early on Thursdays."

"Today's Wednesday," the woman said.

"He gets done early on both days," I said.

Anne and Tina were choking back laughs.

The swimming pool at Mermaid Lake was awash with sweaty humanity that day. It would've been nearly impossible to swim two strokes without banging into someone. There were no chaises to lie on and the concrete was scorching. We sat on the pool's lip, our legs in the water. Every few minutes some boys, younger than us by at least two years, would come by and splash us. An hour passed before the problem of how to get home came up.

"We can't call our parents or they'll know we ditched school," Anne said. "Anyway, mine are at work."

I looked around thinking there'd be someone we knew. There always was.

"I think I see a neighbor," Tina said. She stood up, hand-visoring her eyes. "Nope. That's not Mrs. Mellon. Too skinny."

"There must be someone," I said.

"I keep thinking about the stories those old people told us," Tina said. "Think they made them up?"

"So what if they were true. One happened in England. The other one was about killing old Italians. Anyway, there's three of us." Anne trailed a hand in the water. We all watched as a boy cannon-balled off the high dive. A lifeguard's whistle immediately blew. "Who'd try anything with three of us?"

"So you think we'll have to hitch a ride home?" I said.

"Go check out the picnic tables, Susan," Tina said. "But it's pretty hot to be sitting out in the sun."

The story I thought about as I walked toward the picnic tables was the one with the girl tied up in a shack somewhere, a long line of boys waiting their turn. I wasn't exactly sure what a turn meant, but Anne probably knew. It'd never occurred to me that sex was something that could be quickly repeated. I always imagined it was followed by a deep sleep or a shower. That's how it looked in movies at least.

The only picnickers were a bunch of girl scouts building a fire in a pit, probably trying to earn their pioneering badge. The leader looked up, and when she saw I wasn't one of her scouts returned to her thick handbook. "Next we need to look for some kindling," she was saying as I turned back toward the pool. The wind was picking up, but it was a hot wind. An empty swing swung wildly in the breeze.

"Nobody over there," I told Tina and Anne. "Hey, you guys better get out of the sun. I think you're starting to burn."

"Take a look in the mirror." Tina said. "What time is it anyway?"

Anne looked at the clock over the locker room entrance. "Nearly two. We should get going."

"Get going how?" My voice quivered a bit.

She shrugged. "We'll just look for another old couple. Easy-peasy."

289

"I don't want to hear stories like theirs again. A carload of boys might be better."

Anne glared at me. "We're not taking a ride from any carload of boys."

Within minutes, we stood a few feet from the entrance road to Mermaid Lake. The traffic seemed scant for girls used to city traffic.

"If we don't get home soon, they'll know we cut school," Tina said, waving her thumb at a white convertible. A long beep was her only answer. "Same to you," she hollered after him.

"That was a man, Tina," Anne said. "Women or couples."

"Three of us can handle one man," Tina reminded her.

"I think I better call my Dad," I said.

"He'll call my parents," Anne said.

"No, he won't" I promised. "He's not like that. He won't care if you cut school."

"He'll care that we hitched a ride up here."

"We can tell him a friend gave us a ride. He'll go for that."

Anne shook her head. "It's too chancy. Plus by the time he gets all the way up here, I'll be late."

"I think this truck is stopping," Tina said suddenly. "Oh, look he has chickens in the back. A farmer. Just one man too. And he's older than my Dad."

"Where you goin', girls?" the man said as he eased onto the side of the road, his tanned arm resting on the open window. The chickens, in cages, were squawking in the heat. He wore overalls with no shirt. A large dog sat next to him.

"Toward Philly," Tina told him. "You headed that way?"

"I am indeed," he said. "But the cab won't hold all of you. My dog sits up front. Right, Manson." The dog barked in a kind of a growl. "You girls will have to get into the back—with the poultry. There's room along side of their cages."

"That's fine," Tina said. We all nodded, glad to have it settled.

He got out, opened a gate, and we climbed in.

290

"Now don't stand up," he told us. "You could fly out like a dog of mine did once. Keep your heads down too. Huddle up."

A few seconds later, he pulled out.

"What kind of person names their dog after someone like Charles Manson," Tina whispered as if he could hear us above the noise of the squawking chickens and the noisy truck.

"Maybe it's another Manson," I said hopefully.

"Or maybe he said Mason," Tina said. "I think he said Mason."

Anne and I shrugged.

A few seconds later, the truck turned left, heading north, away from Philadelphia. None of us noticed, huddled in as we were with the chickens. Not then and not for a while.

About the Author - Patti Abbott is the author of more than 100 stories, a quarter of which are collected in her ebook MONKEY JUSTICE. Forthcoming stories will appear in PANK, SHOTGUN HONEY: TWO BARRELS, MYSTERICAL-E, NIGHTFALL, and CRIME FACTORY-THE HORROR ISSUE. A novel in stories (HOME INVASION) will be published by Snubnose Press in 2013. You can find her in Detroit or at http://pattinase.blogspot.com

Victor Victoria
by
Andrez Bergen

I do believe my first bona fide blunder of the war was when I shot a
goddess between the eyes.

Unforced error number two came into play the moment I
took note of said mistake. Having yanked up my goggles, I perched in
the seat of my plane, stunned. With my head turned around, searching
for her descent, I obviously wasn't looking where I was going, and the
next thing I knew I'd collided slap-bang up the arse end of a 530-foot
dirigible.

The propeller of my Sopwith Pup punctured the rubberized
cotton fabric, the nose went in, the biplane shuddered, and then we
hung there, conjoined in the clouds several thousand feet up. The
name *L.19* was written in big gothic letters on a ripped flap that waved
above my head, and beneath that "Kaiserliche Marine".

I'd buggered a bloody zeppelin.

Hence, it wasn't long before the Huns on board started
taking pot shots at me, having positioned themselves on an iron trellis
built into the rear-engine gondola. They were so close I could see the
rifles poking out—standard issue 7.92 mm Mauser Gewehr 98s—but
the dunderheads were such poor marksmen that I continued to sit
there, strapped into my open cockpit, unharmed and reasonably
unfussed.

Eventually I got tired of the fun, games and projectiles. I
unholstered my Webley Mk IV revolver to fire off three rounds in
return. The soldiers ducked for cover. Then I glanced around,
wondering what the devil I should do.

"You know, that *hurt*."

I peered over the side of my aeroplane, past the words "Sea's
Shame" that my batman McPherson had stencilled onto the canvas
fuselage, to the jutting-out wooden wheel frame beneath my Pup.

What I discovered alarmed me far more than the pointy-headed fools only yards distant.

Winged Victory, or whomsoever this was, hung there one-handed. In her other hand, the left one, the woman was armed with a trident and shield, and on top of her head she wore a centurion's helmet that was at an accidentally jaunty angle—probably because it had a couple of dents in it, courtesy of my machine gun. Golden hair poked out from under the hard hat, and this fluttered in the breeze. Her ocean-blue eyes, however, remained fixed on mine. They were anything but flighty.

"So, are you going to offer assistance? Or would you prefer to sit there and stare while those men continue shooting?"

"Can't you fly?"

"Do I look like I have wings?"

She had a point. There was nary a feather on her body.

"She's younger than me, too."

"Who is younger?"

"Your Winged Victory."

I certainly hadn't expected things to turn out in this squalid manner—they'd started out innocuously enough. There had been heavy fog the evening before, when a fleet of zeppelins took advantage of the cover to bomb a string of inconsequential towns in the West Midlands.

The next afternoon—today—one of the intruders was spotted over the North Sea, which explained away my current mission flying a spot of reconnaissance. Having flown out from Freiston Airfield in Lincolnshire and spent the past frigid, unproductive hour in empty skies, I'd decided to return home to a jolly good cup of warm cocoa, with a shot of Dalmore whisky, when directly ahead in my flight path—in the midst of a bank of clouds and silhouetted by the setting sun—I spied Winged Victory.

Before I could think, I was triggering my Vickers machine gun, the woman tumbled, and I crashed. This surely smacked of something of a feat.

293

"I do wish you would desist with the Winged Victory nonsense," called out my unwilling passenger, as I unstrapped and leaned over to give her a hand. "She's Greek," that voice nattered on, "and, dare I say it, has no arms and lacks a head."

A bullet whizzed close by my ear. "Would you stop that?" I yelled, directing my words at a stout sergeant in a greatcoat and a rather dangerous Pickelhaube spiked helmet. "Can't you see I'm busy?"

The man lowered his rifle to act sheepish. "*Es tut mir leid!*"

"Not a problem. Be a good fellow and go fetch your commanding officer."

At least the gunplay ceased. I encircled the woman's wrist with my gloved fingers and proceeded to haul, although I had a bugger of a time. I barely managed the exercise, what with the heavy armoured trinkets and her Amazonian stature—at about six feet, she was at least as tall as me, and had broader shoulders.

Finally, she propped herself up behind the cockpit, powerful, stark naked legs straddling the canvas for balance. While I'm hardly one to gush, the woman's face was something precious—chiselled, athletic, magnificently bewitching.

"Is there a way down?" she asked, while I rudely gawked.

"You mean to terra firma?"

"No, I mean the moon."

"Ahh, you're joking."

"Bravo." She breathed out in loud, overdramatic fashion, apparently annoyed. I suppose I would be too, if I were god-like and recently gunned down by an overzealous aerialist. "Now, about getting down..."

"I think we're stuck until this zeppelin lands. I heard the Huns have introduced a device called a parachute, but we haven't anything like that in the Royal Flying Corps. I suppose you could jump. You are, I take it, some kind of deity?"

The young lady held up a majestic chin. "I am. I have been worshipped by people since the Pritani, well before the Romans invaded Britain two thousand years ago, and in all that time nobody ever shot at me before."

"Hold on. If you really were some kind of patron saint-cum-goddess, why didn't you kick the Spigs back to Italy?"

"We choose not to interfere in human affairs."

"Well, that's bloody convenient. Why, then, do you bother lugging about the military gear, and what's the story with the Roman helmet?"

"It belonged to Julius Caesar. I liked Gaius. After he invaded, he named the island after me, Britannia. Claudius I loathed—he had no respect for foreign figureheads—but Hadrian was marginally better."

"Oh, I see. Britannia. Of course. I do apologize for the Winged Victory bon mot. I'm known as Wilks. Might I call you Brit?"

Since I was leaning out of the cockpit, I felt something tap my buttocks.

"Are you forgetting the trident?" the woman reminded me. Thank Heavens; she resisted using the sharp bits. "Britannia shall do nicely. If you're searching for something earthier, you may call me Frances. I prefer Britannia."

"Speaking of Earth—given that you're a god, well, I would venture to guess that jumping will not be a problem."

She looked down through the clouds and I would swear I saw a grimace. "How high are we?"

"About three or four thousand feet, the last time I checked."

"Then it's a problem."

"You have height restrictions?"

"Something of the sort." Britannia shivered. No wonder, since she was wearing only a light shift of linen material that barely came down to her thighs, and the woman had a lot of cold metal pressing against her.

After I took off my leather coat, I reached across to place it on her shoulders.

"What are you doing?"

"Attempting to be a gentleman."

295

"Well, stop it. I reside on a completely different plane. I don't feel the chill. Put the blasted thing back on."

"Right you are." It was my turn to play annoyed as I buttoned up the coat. "Anyway, I thought Britannia was a nymph of some kind."

"Hardly."

"And aren't you supposed to have a lion? What were you doing, prancing about on top of a zeppelin?"

"Attempting to help—you looked like you were going to fly straight past, so I decided to intervene."

"Against your better nature?"

"I do that sometimes. These people dropped bombs on my native soil. I was cross." She smiled. "I left my lion at home." Touché.

I resisted a spot of laughter, and again instead looked over the side of the aeroplane. I decided the sea was closer than it had been only a quarter of an hour before. "We're losing altitude."

"Quite possibly it has something to do with the giant hole you ripped in their side. Gas must be escaping."

"True—which means we'll end up in the drink in the North Sea, not the best idea in February. It's probably around forty degrees Fahrenheit this time of year."

I heard somebody discreetly cough nearby.

There was a new addition to the open window of the gondola. With the monocle, a Luger 9mm in his hand, the soft hat and the pencil-thin moustache, this man was a stiff-necked caricature of the German officer class.

"I say, Englander, my name is Kapitänleutnant Wilhelm Klink."

"Charmed, I'm sure. Flying Officer 'Wilks' Wilkinson, 287 Squadron, RFC, commanded by Major William E. Johns."

I heard him click unseen heels as he bowed. "We are currently throwing excess baggage into the sea in order that we might gain some height and make it to the continent. Your blasted *flugzüg*—your aeroplane—is not helping matters, Herr Wilkinson."

296

"Sorry, Herr Klink, but the crate is here to stay. Your men shooting at me has not been much fun—it makes it difficult to come up with a viable plan."

"Well, you *are* the enemy."

"There is that. But tell you what; I have a woman here with me."

Klink adjusted his monocle. "Ja. Quite the *fräulein*."

"Eyes off, Fritz."

"My apologies." While he inclined his head, Klink's stare remained affixed to my hitchhiker. The man was incorrigible. "You know, I always envied you English your Britannia. The Americans have Columbia, even the Italians have their mundane Italia Turrita, but we Germans... ahhh, and we are sadly lacking in the allegorical personifications."

"Er... yes." I frowned. "Once the balloon—"

"Zeppelin. It is a zeppelin, not a balloon."

"All right. Well, once the zeppelin gets lower, Britannia and I will bail out, jumping into the sea and thereby lightening the load up to two hundred and eighty pounds."

"I beg your pardon," the girl behind me grouched, "just how chubby do you presume me to be?"

"Well, you are six feet and wearing all that armour."

"Pfft."

Klink rubbed his chin. "To tell the truth, I am more concerned with the aircraft—not that I do not appreciate the gesture."

"Every little bit helps, am I correct, Kapitänleutnant?"

"Ja, Ja, in getting my crew safely home."

"Then we have a deal? Toss me a lifesaver, there's a good fellow."

I hadn't counted on Klink lobbing the contraption so damned hard, and I can't fault the officer for accuracy—the lifesaver struck me on the forehead and, being unstrapped, I fell straight out of the plane.

I recall nothing thereafter, until I came to in darkness in the shallow water of a cove. I was saturated, half-drowned and mostly frozen. Flashes of memory—a flapping dirigible, the burlesque German officer, Britannia in a dimpled helmet and very little else—played a merry jig across my mind and I deduced that an aeroplane crash must have conjured up the whole fiasco. Since I had no plane, I could only assume I'd crashed at sea.

Turned out, I was on the coast of northern France.

A helpful farmwoman named Marianne, who carried a rowdy rooster tucked under her arm, got me safely to British lines. While she spoke no English, this woman was remarkable for her height—she towered over me in her Phrygian cap—and an impressive stamina, since she never tired once during our ninety-mile hike.

Two weeks later I discovered myself back in Blighty, at company HQ. I was informed by my commanding officer, Major Johns, that a zeppelin earmarked *L.19* had in fact gone down in the North Sea, with a loss of all hands, and he was putting the kill on my record sheet.

"Jolly good show, old chap," the major decided as he shook my hand.

So. There *was* a balloon. But what about the balance of the featherbrained dream? I returned to my quarters and allowed McPherson to mix up a drink. I continued seeing the girl's face in the sights of my Vickers, right before I pulled the trigger, as I stood first in front of the fireplace and then wandered over to a bay window. It was dusk outside.

"Restless, Sir?" McPherson inquired as he handed me a tumbler.

"Vaguely." I bowed my head. Was she dead too? Or was she some figment of an overactive, semi-concussed imagination? "I think I'll hit the sack, old man," I decided. "Take the evening off. Sally forth and enjoy yourself."

I trudged slowly up the staircase with the drink between my fingers. I felt inconceivably dismal. Probably, it had to do with touching god—or, in this case, a goddess—and losing her. Never good form to do that kind of thing. One might as well try manhandling the sun.

When I entered my room I switched on a lamp, and straight away noticed the Corinthian helmet on the desk. It had been hammered back into shape. Next to it—slouched unmajestically on my favourite leather armchair, with her feet up, sans armour, and showing far too much leg—was someone I recognized.

"You."

"Me." She straightened up, stretched her back, and smiled. "You recall that that my name is not Winged Victory?"

"I do seem to remember that. It was a Victorian fancy—and, to be honest, I thought you didn't exist. That you were only up here." I tapped my right temple, but this acted as the woman's cue to stand up and slip out of the miserly frock she wore.

"Perhaps you should put down your glass?"

I realized I was spilling the drink, and did as suggested.

Britannia stood before me, without even her shield, her head at an angle, blue eyes close, golden hair framing her face, and I realized she pipped my height by two inches.

"I like you."

"Where's your trident?" I responded. I had no intention of accidentally sitting on the bugger.

"It was on extended loan—now returned to its rightful owner." I could feel her cool breath on my neck.

"Shield?"

"Beneath the bed. You're stalling."

"Not at all. I believe you said you didn't interfere in human affairs."

"Nobody ever shot at me before. C'mere."

About the Author – Andrez Bergen is the author of the novels 'Tobacco Stained Mountain Goat' and the forthcoming '100 Years of Vicissitude'. More information can be found at http://andrezbergen.wordpress.com

In The Heat of the Night
by
Stuart Ayris

There's nothing harvest about this moon, nothing crescent about it
either. It's not blue, it's not full and there are no beams anywhere near
it. From what I can tell, what I can feel, it's hot and it's yellow and it's
just about as big a ball of melting wax as you could ever envisage.
Every time I look up it seems to have fixed its gaze upon me just a
little more intently. It's a spiteful moon, a smug moon, a grinning,
searing monstrosity. Just me and the hot moon right now. Just me and
the wild hot moon.

I decide to shelter awhile in a duckdown alleyway – dank and
dark and all shadows. I can hear water unseen dribble down the walls
as if the bricks themselves are spattering the ground with a drunkards
piss. But I sigh and realise it's me. I've urinated against a wall in every
town and city and country I ever lived in or visited. It's not as simple a
thing as marking your territory like a dog or cat might. It's more
primeval than that, more necessary and significant. I've pissed up
against bus stops in Barcelona, against a tree on the Champs Elysees
and into the Danube from a bridge in Budapest. And I've done the
same in about every street within a two mile radius of my flat in
Romford. It's not that I'm proud of it. Just something I do. When I
need a piss, I take a piss. Never been caught yet. But then the moon
has never been this wild and this hot before.

Two girls walk past the end of the alleyway. One of them
giggles. The other one calls me a dirty bastard. They both run off
clattering the pavement with their pointy nightclub shoes and breaking
the night with their shriekings. The youth of today – I say to myself –
no respect. I ponder for a moment, staring at my black boots, trying to
see something profound in their perfect unremitting darkness. The
gleamy shine has gone for a moment and I'm loathe to allow the
cunning moon a chance to wink at me from the metal toecaps that

have given me such good service. But a man like me, doing the job I do, cannot linger too long in the alleyways of this godforsaken town. As the time ticks towards midnight I know that girly giggles will seem like sparkle spangles in a few hours time when the real nutters fall out into these dirty Essex streets.

"Boyd, mate. Come on. You're like a fucking elephant. We need to get going."

It's my colleague, Stebbing. He's a bit younger than me and not nearly as experienced in the ways of the world – even less so in the game we're both in. Has a habit of rushing things, of always being disappointed and never satisfied with a slower pace. He'll learn though. I was like him once. Probably up until that Danube piss – and that was only a few years back. You calm down as you get older. I think it's a sort of defence mechanism, something in your brain telling you that you need to start being a bit smarter, less reckless, if you're going to last the journey. Like I say, Stebbing's okay. He's a good lad. Could just do with slowing down a bit. That's all.

"Keep your hair on, son." I have to look up when I speak to him. It's not that he's much taller than me; just he has this way of filling himself out, stretching himself, when you talk to him. It used to really irritate me but I guess he can't help it. Just gives me more opportunity to bring him down a peg or two. "If you spent less time ogling hussies and more time shining your shoes you'd give yourself more of a chance when it comes down to it."

"'Ogling hussies?' Mate, how old are you really? Three hundred?"

Now a real man doesn't smirk. Smirking is for idiots. Sometimes I think Stebbing must be an idiot just on account of his tendency to smirk when he thinks he's been funny. In my book you either laugh or you don't. Simple as that. Smirking is bad for you. That's what the lads in Newcastle tell me anyway. One of them even told me they have No Smirking signs in all their offices and in their cars too. Good on them, I say. Good on them.

I did not dignify Stebbing with an answer. In truth, it would have taken more than a reply from me to dignify Stebbing at all.

Different generations can at times have varying definitions and perceptions of things such as dignity, respect, honour and the like. Our job, in my view, is about upholding values that, to many, have long since passed.

The night is just getting hotter, this Saturday night Sunday morning scene that is probably playing out the same all across the country – drinks drunk, drunks drunk and pavements full of slobbering, slavering tossers. They make Stebbing look mature and respectable. Now that's saying something.

"You hungry?"

"If you want, something Stebbing, just go and get something. Make it quick though. Midnight is not a time to be messing around. You should have learned that by now at least."

"Yeah, yeah. Walk with me to the Kebab shop and I'll just nip in. You can watch me through the window if you like. If it makes you happy."

He quickens his pace but I keep mine. Dignity. After a few years you learn how to walk so as not to scuff your shoes. You also learn that there is now way of walking whilst eating a kebab that does not culminate in chilli sauce blood spatting your white shirt.

"Fuck me. Gets everywhere this stuff."

I nod as Stebbing makes an idiot's attempt to clean his shirt up. A couple of young lads walk by, unseen by Stebbing. One of them coughs whilst simultaneously uttering the word 'wanker.' I pay it no heed. Small fry. The night may be hot but it's still early.

And then it starts – the crash of glass followed by the bravura roars of jacked-up fucks. Stebbing turns to look at me before running off high speed to the site of the action. I follow, shaking my head at all this. There's heat and there's heat. You have to respect that to stand any chance at all.

When I arrive at the scene, Stebbing has his foot resting heavy on the once cool jacket which is being worn by a once cool man. Little does he know that the dirty alleyway ground into which his cheek is pressed was just a while earlier awash with my piss. He wouldn't be grinning like he is if he knew – and I have no intention of

302

telling him. Always best to show first – tell later if they don't get it. That's the old way. None of this new-fangled bollocks where the customer, the consumer, the citizen is always right. They're right when I say they're right. So I let this grinning miscreant smell the leather of my shiny black boot before kicking him in the face. The thud shudder quakes through me, adrenalin bursting and justice, true justice beats its fabled beat. I stand back as Stebbing applies the handcuffs and drags the bleeding, piss-stained fuck to the squad car.

I feel a sweat coming on.

It's us and them.

In the heat of the night.

About the Author - Stuart Ayris is the author of three novels - A Cleansing of Souls (written when he was 22 years old) and the first two books of the FRUGALITY Trilogy - Tollesbury Time Forever and The Bird That Nobody Sees. He is also the author of a collection of poems called Bighugs, Love and Beer. His blog can be found at www.tollesburytimeforver.blogspot.co.uk

The Umbrellas of Cherbourg
by
Vincent Holland-Keen

The arbiter of my life and death: a white umbrella dotted with circles from every colour of the rainbow.

I only had myself to blame.

I knew how long it took to get from Rue du Chateau to the Rue de Neufbourg and I knew how little time remained before the sun rose, yet I dallied at the shops, losing myself in a dream of a life transformed by the purchase of a new mug. By the time the shutters came down, the streets were empty around me. I knew I was in trouble.

I ran as fast as I could, but I am not a fit man. As my pace slowed, the sun's ascent appeared to quicken; the sky turning from black to gold with alarming speed, the claustrophobic town I was used to, transformed into a nightmare of open spaces by the light of day.

A fresh attempt at a sprint achieved only a jog and my lungs complained about that before I'd made fifty paces.

I looked around for shelter. I saw only windows criss-crossed with bars and doorways blocked by steel. You'll have heard the stories – everyone has – about the friend of a friend caught out after curfew. They take desperate refuge in the meagre shadow of a doorway and then watch that shadow gradually diminish as the blazing sun arcs across the heavens. Inevitably, the feet are first to burn. The acrid smell of shoe leather melting into boiling flesh only becomes worse as the legs catch fire. Everyone at work figured this friend of a friend would be dead before the searing light reached the chest, but these stories defy logic. They always end with nightfall and a passer-by finding the charred husk slumped in the doorway with eyes alive enough to deliver one last pitiful blink.

Keeping going, home isn't far.

I crossed the Avenue Amiral Lemonnier moments before the sun crested the horizon. A hiss rose at my back – the night's rain rising in a cloud of steam. I stumbled on into the shadows.

Desperate thoughts turned back to that new mug, tantalisingly solid and pristine in the shop window. My only mug at home was held together by masking tape, the many cracks still big enough to leech away coffee almost as fast as I could drink it. The coffee didn't go to waste; I collected it in a bucket for recycling. But as that bucket also served double-duty as my toilet, the allure of a new mug was great indeed.

So great I'd thrown my life away.

The shadows were shrinking too fast, the gaps between them growing too large. The bleached sunlight was a rising flood promising to drown me in fire. I wasn't going to make it.

I began to cry. Tears blurred my vision. Spluttering sobs made it even harder to breathe. It really wasn't helping at all, but I couldn't stop. I couldn't choke back my gutless fear of an imminent death.

And then I saw it.

The umbrella.

My first instinct was to recoil, to look away, but the bloody panic in my veins focussed my gaze and whispered a dream of salvation.

The owner was dead. They lay beside the umbrella in a short alleyway, fingers still grasping the handle, their gaily coloured clothes further enlivened by lashings of red spilled from a skull smashed to a pulp.

I felt no pity for them. I didn't have time. I had to make a choice.

***

My apartment was ten foot square. The major furnishings were a rotting mattress and collapsible table. The only light came through the

305

inversion filter on the window; an insipid yellow staining the tiled floor and papered walls.

I sat on a stack of books and sipped my coffee. Drips fell from the cracked mug into the bucket between my knees. The umbrella lay open on the table. Since rushing in through the door and setting it down, I hadn't been able to touch it.

Instead, I stared.

It clearly did not belong here. Its colours remained vibrant despite the dingy surroundings. The dots on the canopy were almost hypnotic. They wavered under my gaze as if about to break free and dance across the room. The crook handle was black, topped by a studded collar. The perfect silver of the extendible shaft was marred by flecks of dried blood splattered along its length. And it was humming to itself, which was disturbing.

I couldn't leave it lying there.

Tentatively, I reached out. When I touched the handle, harmonic vibrations ran up my arm; a thrilling tingle that almost over-rode my fear. I felt the urge to sing, but a sudden knocking at the door forced me to choke it back.

I snatched up the umbrella and desperately tried to collapse it. I brushed a stud at the top of the handle and a jagged spike sprang out from the ferrule tip, almost puncturing my shoulder.

Another round of knocking.

Merde!

The catch holding it open was stiff. The metal bit into my thumb as I pushed against it.

The knocking stopped, but the visitor did not depart – the tell-tale floorboards remained silent.

The catch finally relented. I folded the umbrella away and hid it under my mattress.

I answered the door.

The stranger in the corridor wore the traditional policeman's garb – red ceramic armour hanging from sloping shoulders like a scaly dress. His helmet made no allowance for a face.

"Good morning, citizen. May I ask you a few questions?"

***

The guys at work were shocked when I told them.

"I've seen a man gutted in the street for his boots," shouted Marc over the racket of the production line, "I've seen a mob tear apart a filling station looking for a last drop of gasoline, but the only time I've ever seen a policeman was when they line the streets on Midsummer."

"Consider yourself lucky," shouted back Nino. "You see a policeman any other night, chances are you'll never be seen again." He looked sideways at me and nodded his head. "What brought them to your door?"

"An umbrella got himself murdered."

Their shock at my reply could be counted by the number of shell casings that passed by on the conveyer – eighteen.

"Now I hate the umbrellas as much as the next guy," said Marc, "but I kinda liked the idea of folk living above the shit the rest of us are buried in. Meant there was a chance of getting lucky, finding an umbrella and—"

"Getting executed for grand larceny," snapped Nino. "Scum like us don't get to join that club."

"I know," said Marc, "but just getting to step outside in daylight…"

Then dancing across green, green grass and marvelling at the bluest of blue skies – it was a horrible, impossible dream and one I now woke from every evening. The cheery humming reverberating through my mattress told me why.

The umbrella's song was a death sentence for someone like me. I knew I should throw it away, but never took the chance; always convincing myself now was too risky and later would be safer.

She proved me wrong.

***

307

The market was always worse in the summer. The short nights left little time for shopping after shifts ended. Fighting for scraps alongside hundreds of other tired and starving souls meant sharp elbows and grim determination became as important as the coins in your pocket. The rain made things worse – lashing down, soaking the unprepared to the bone, adding bite to the capricious wind that whipped back and forth across the square.

On this night I was after food, but I was too late. Only rotting vegetables were left. I struggled on toward the grain stand.

Everyone knew the umbrellas were there. Their songs drifted down from a rooftop. The umbrellas themselves could not be seen, but that was always the way.

Only four bags of grain were left. I swear those bags were half the size they used to be and twice the price. I was trying to snare the vendor's attention when someone bumped into me from behind.

Custom dictated I respond with questions about their parentage, but more jostling interrupted my insult. A disturbance was pushing everyone back. I struggled to keep my footing as bodies barged past.

Close by, a woman cried out in alarm.

I pushed forward, foolishly thinking I could help, but in going to her aid I was left exposed at the front edge of a retreating crowd.

The woman was on the ground, a bag of shopping spilled in front of her. On either side: a column of three policemen. She didn't dare move and neither did anyone else.

Beyond this frozen scene was an alleyway, where a flight of steel steps led up to a rooftop.

Down those steps came a pair of high-heeled boots.

The boots were made of emerald green leather and decorated with skeletal leaves traced in gold. They stopped just beneath a pale-skinned knee. No more of the leg was visible due an ephemeral dress of paler green that ghosted tantalisingly about feminine thighs and hips and waist and then came the line of the umbrella, hiding the rest of her from view. This umbrella was also green, but printed on every other panel of the canopy was the picture of a white penny-farthing. The umbrella emitted a luxuriant glow that fell brightest from the underside, casting those boots in their own private spotlight. They skipped off the last step and then… her walk was not simply a walk, it was a promenade; leisurely and graceful and captivating to all who watched.

The umbrella's pool of light fell upon the fallen woman and stopped.

The crowd's fascination turned to dread.

As one, the policemen drew their truncheons and lifted them high… but a gesture from a slender hand stayed their violence.

That hand then reached down and, one by one, gathered up each item of spilled shopping. They were returned to a bag and the bag returned to its owner.

The fallen woman gazed up at her benefactor in wonder. Words of thanks came as a faltering whisper. If the umbrella smiled, the rest of us could not see. If she spoke, the rest of us did not hear. But after the umbrella walked away with her police escort, the rest of us surrounded the woman.

"What did she look like?" One question asked a dozen different ways by a hundred different voices.

"Beautiful. An angel," replied the woman, staring into space.

I glanced round at the departing procession – one green umbrella followed by six men in red armour. For reasons I cannot readily explain, I decided to follow.

***

We travelled streets I knew well, but I felt like I was walking them for the first time. Street-lighting was banned in Cherbourg and citizens were only permitted to carry lux-restricted lanterns. We never saw more than a few steps of the city at a time, but the glow of the umbrella spilled onto adjoining streets and reached up two or three storeys to reveal aged signs and window boxes unseen by human eyes

309

in over dozen years. The rain too was changed; no longer an elemental trial, but a glittering spectacle that tempered my unease.

But still I hung back, out of sight. I hadn't completely lost my senses.

Eventually we passed into an area unfamiliar to me. I kept glancing back, keen to remember our path, but there was little point – nothing but blackness lay behind.

We entered a garden square. The paving underfoot was nothing special. The houses on three of the four sides were unremarkable. The tower rising from the fourth side, however, was like nothing I'd ever seen. I don't know how tall it was, but it stretched up beyond the light of the umbrella. What I could see was decorated with black and green diamonds. Narrow windows were placed randomly across the wide, curving frontage. A flag bearing the penny-farthing emblem billowed over a giant, oaken door, which slowly opened to admit the umbrella and the retinue of policemen.

The door closed just as slowly.

Slow enough to tempt.

Slow enough to tease.

But I turned my back. I went home. And then did something even more foolish instead.

***

A dream is just an impression of an experience. You can't pin it down, you can't breathe it in; it's something you're supposed to forget.

That's why I don't regret taking the umbrella out from under my mattress and stepping outside in daylight. That moment of delightful terror, waiting for someone to shout imposter or the sun to burn me to a crisp was one I always want to remember.

The moment passed. The street remained silent. I felt pleasantly cool beneath the umbrella. When I finally dared to move from the doorway and the angle of the shade exposed my foot to direct sunlight, I realised the protection of the umbrella was not limited to its shadow. Its magical technology generated a climate-controlled bubble that I could only breach by extending my arm and fingers to their fullest.

The price of this experimentation was a set of singed fingertips. The pain stayed with me as I walked. I had only one destination in mind, but I pretended otherwise, taking my time to explore a city I hadn't seen in daylight for thirteen years.

It wasn't the same.

Back then the city was alive. Cars filled the streets, pedestrians went about their business and there was always noise – voices, engines, sirens – whatever the time of day.

The Change came at half past three in the afternoon. A pleasant summer's day became a furnace in the space of ninety seconds. Everyone outside turned to ash. Those near windows burned. Those further inside screamed.

No one knows why the buildings remained untouched. I was working a shift at the factory. We didn't even know anything had happened. The air inside stayed hot and muggy, but safe. When word came round, no one believed it. We stopped doubting when they let us out after sundown. The carnage in the streets took weeks to clear.

I don't remember when the umbrellas first appeared, but I know it was well after the change. First I heard rumours, then I saw one pass my window during daylight hours; a nonchalant figure turned spectral white by the inversion filter. At first I was spellbound, but when they sauntered from view and I was left to my own petty thoughts I became jealous and angry and in a fit of rage smashed my one decent mug.

Those memories made me suddenly self-conscious.

What if someone watched me now from a darkened window? Was furious resentment bubbling behind their eyes? What had I done to deserve this privilege?

Nothing.

Dumb luck brought me here and if that luck turned, my life would end.

Far too late for it to make a difference, I searched around for sight or sound of police. All was quiet. I needed to get home quickly.

I tried to orientate myself. The buildings around me were unfamiliar. I tilted back the umbrella to search the skyline for a landmark – a church spire or office block. Instead I saw a tower, but not the green and black tower I'd seen in the hours before daybreak. This was painted with diagonal lines of white and purple. I had to lean back to see the summit. It reached hundreds of metres into the air and was surrounded by a criss-cross of vapour trails. To my further amazement, there were airships up there, dozens of them. Each bore an umbrella's livery. They travelled between other towers or off into the far distance. I spun round. There were eight towers in total, each with a different pattern. Together, they dominated the city below.

There were no towers thirteen years ago.

Thirteen years also brought another change. It blazed fearfully bright in the sky and drew a burning nausea up from my stomach into my throat:

A second sun.

***

I'd set out in the hope of finding out what manner of face was hidden beneath that green umbrella.

That question remained unanswered, unimportant.

I kept my gaze fixed on the path in front of me. I did not look up. I didn't want to see those ominous towers, their airships or that terrible second sun. For all these years I had been oblivious to their presence and now I knew they were there, my world was irrevocably transformed. Into what, I did not know. I did know that come sunset I would head back to work and factory full of people living in ignorance. How could I tell them without mentioning the umbrella? If I did tell them, would they believe a word? And say they did, say they accepted enlightenment – what then? Our eyes open to the realities of a new world, would our lives still go on as before?

Bleak.

Bitter.

Broken.

312

I was a man with an umbrella, alone, staggering across a road and into a lamppost. I clung onto it, desperate for something solid to shore up a mind racing with fragile, feverish thoughts.

A click of fingers snapped me out of it.

I was not alone.

Click.

Someone was nearby, unseen, and—

Click.

Ahead lay the Place de la République. I ventured forward.

Click.

There was whistling too – a jaunty tune that kept time with the rhythmic clicks. The umbrella in my hand hummed a soft counter-melody.

I reached a corner and cautiously peered round. The Place de la République was not a grand sight. Parking spaces separated parallel roads. Two memorials were surrounded by overgrown vegetation. Flanking the roads were more parking spaces and a dozen fancy terrace houses. I'd arrived to the south. At the far north, a mounted statue of Napoleon pointed back the way I had come.

The whistler leant against a tree midway between the two memorials. His umbrella was light blue and printed with the eager eyes and lolling tongue of a cartoon puppy.

The second umbrella was decorated with the image of a playing card – the Jack of Spades. Its owner had his back to me. I could see white and black boots, chequered trousers and a hand snapping finger against thumb.

The second umbrella approached the first.

The first replied with a song.

"Who is this noble figure, gracing my sight? My cousin, no less, intent on a fight."

The Puppy Dog's words were accompanied by a chorus of woodwind. The Jack of Spades' response continued the tune with a swell of strings.

"A fight for justice, my dearest cousin; I bear only regret for what must be done."

313

"Speaking the truth is my only crime—"

"No! Speaking lies, time after time."

The Puppy Dog pushed himself clear of the tree and straightened up.

"Then there is nothing more to be said."

The Jack of Spades stopped in front of him.

"Not till one of us is dead."

A shotgun blast from the tip of one umbrella was deflected by the canopy of the other. A gout of flame fired back, but the Puppy Dog was already clear, somersaulting high in the air, his umbrella suddenly lined with blades and spinning like a circular saw.

He struck the ground and cut a swath through concrete, sparks bursting up around him.

The Jack of Spades skipped backward, pulling loose his umbrella handle to produce a sword. The canopy slipped onto his arm like a shield.

I saw no faces. Both fighters wore a glowing mask.

The Puppy Dog raced forward. Saw-blades clashed against sword steel. Strike was met by counter-strike. Parry became thrust, dodge became slash. Their moves were almost too quick to follow. Their leaps and flips were beyond human.

The fight tore chunks of masonry from the surrounding buildings. The tree was sliced in half. Bullets shattered windows. Fire burned back the overgrown grass.

The music continued to play; woodwind and strings describing the furious ballet, building to a deafening crescendo that stopped abruptly when Jack of Spades' sword pierced his dearest cousin's heart.

***

Back at the factory, I kept my mouth shut and focussed solely on the work; the tedious, brainless work. It was the only thing I felt capable of dealing with. And there was the irony. In learning about the wider world, I closed my eyes to the troubles in front of me. They were

314

opened again by Nino slamming his tray down against the floor of the canteen.

The other diners looked at him in stunned silence.

"We all know, don't we?" shouted Nino. "We all know, yet what are we doing? Sitting here, moaning about the food, bitching about management, slagging off the government. Same as it ever was. Except today's different, isn't it? Today one of us is missing and no one's talking about that. No one's bitching or moaning or complaining, and I can't… I can't understand why. Marc's gone. Marc's *gone*! Does nobody care? Or… or is that it? Is it because nobody really cares about that other stuff? It pisses us off, of course it does, but it doesn't hit us here, right in the gut. Not like this. This is about one of us, snatched off the street on the way home from work and shoved aboard the next submarine bound for the killing seas. And however cut up I feel about the fact I'm never going to see my best friend again, I bet I'm like the rest of you, thinking: for That's the terrifying thing, isn't it? Something like this happens and however much we fight back we'll always lose. That's why we're not talking about it, isn't it? We complain about the food because it kind of makes us feel better, but nothing can make us feel better about living a lottery where all the prizes only make things a million times worse."

I hadn't even noticed Marc was missing. If the fact had registered in some dim corner of my brain, I would have guessed he was off sick.

Not *gone*.

Nino didn't return to the production line after lunch. I was left working alongside Henri, who I could tolerate more readily if his constant chatter came from a position of age and wisdom, but he's seventeen and thinks he knows it all.

Henri told me about the workings of a Vauban-class submarine and how the navy no longer bothers to stock them with food for return trips. He talked at length about the gout in his mother's right big toe. He explained how to tie a Catspaw knot and how best to marinade a decomposing rat. He spent an age reciting an alternate version of Les Misérables that featured himself as the hero.

315

For all this I should have been grateful. His verbal diarrhoea distracted me from thoughts of Marc and the invidious sense that if anything could have saved my friend from the press gang, it was a man with an umbrella who dared to use it for more than self-indulgent walks in the sun.

"… and then are the cards," continued Henri. "If we assume Lévesque's theory is correct – that complexity of design represents a higher status within the social structure – the Cards must be one of the powerful houses, with those canopies representing royal cards marking out individuals of particular consequence."

"Wait, stop," I said. "Are you talking about the umbrellas?"

"What else could I be talking about?" asked Henri.

"You were talking about mustard as a cure for head lice a moment ago. But that… that's not important. The stuff about the umbrellas – where did you hear all that?"

"I didn't hear it. I read it."

"Like hell you did. They took all the books."

"You think that stopped people writing? Have you even been to the library recently?"

***

I went during the day to avoid being seen by anyone I knew. I wanted to avoid the awkward questions that might follow. Of course, awkward questions were nothing compared to the consequences of getting caught out after curfew by the police or an unfriendly umbrella, but my brain was much better at blotting out the terrible than it was the inconvenient.

A grand redevelopment of the Cherbourg's cultural quarter transformed the municipal library into an airy, modern establishment that brought the extensive book collection together with multimedia and social facilities. The Change did not hit the library as hard as the scourging of Rennes two years later. The government, fearful of how quickly our cultural heritage could be lost, came and took the books away for safe-keeping. The library became a refugee centre for a while,

316

then, as the refugees succumbed to hunger and sickness, a morgue. The morbid stench drove a community-minded citizen with a drinking habit and a packet of matches to conduct further redevelopment. All that remained of the old library now was a twisted steel skeleton, piles of concrete and thousands of charred bones.

The library's replacement was a collection of three bookcases on the upper-level of le Café du Théâtre. This was a place where those so inclined could listen to avant-garde music, drink Calva and read whatever their fellow citizens cared to place on these dusty shelves.

I counted thirty-two books, but my definition of book was generous. There were rolls of cloth scrawled with words, ragged sheets of paper tied together with string and old school exercise books. There was a faded copy of Henri Charrière's 'Papillon', apparently untouched, while a classic edition of 'Asterix and the Big Fight' had every page defaced with a barely legible poem lauding The Change as a divine test to separate the pure and worthy from the undeserving masses.

Pure and worthy were not words I would use to describe the umbrellas.

That thought focussed me on the task at hand. Where was this book claiming to know all about them?

It took me two weeks to find it.

Like any other library, books were borrowed and returned. On my first visit, 'Umbrellas: Observations and Remarks' by Armin Brandt, was checked out. I came back each day thereafter, searching the shelves without any luck.

I tried reading the other books. Most were personal accounts of life after The Change. I gave up a few pages into most, but kept going for one man's account of life after the death of his wife. Each day was described in a matter of fact tone, without trace of melancholy, but his increasingly difficult quest to find a different kind of flower to place on his beloved's grave each week fascinated me up to the blank final page, whereupon the tale simply stopped.

I abruptly became aware of how alone I was. This stranger had kept me company with his words, and now he was gone. I hoped his quest continued. It seemed a far more worthy endeavour than my own, which was driven by shallow motives. If I knew more about the umbrellas, I might learn more about her and if I knew more about her, then maybe…

I hadn't been back to the green and black tower. I didn't need to see her face any more. If I closed my eyes I could see her luxurious blonde hair and sparkling blue eyes. Her delicate lips were always quick to smile. She would blush a gentle pink if I complimented her.

I was chasing a dream. Reality couldn't possibly match the picture in my head and anyone who approached an umbrella would probably be dead before they could say hello.

Armin Brandt's book confirmed as much.

There were eighty-seven recorded incidents of citizens being executed for inappropriate contact with umbrellas. This meant Brandt could only observe and speculate from a distance. The other sources he quoted were in the same boat. None of them really knew the truth. Levesque's theory of canopy complexity and social standing came from two years spent staring out through binoculars. When umbrellas passed in the street, he recorded the degree to which they dipped their umbrella in greeting. Yet in the whole two years, he'd only seen umbrellas pass each other a grand total of fourteen times.

There was nothing about the towers. Nothing about the airships. Nothing about the second sun or umbrellas duelling in the streets. Brandt and his fellow scholars couldn't even tell me why the umbrellas communicated solely via song.

This exercise had been a waste of time.

I kicked over a bookcase.

I threw a chair down the stairs.

I picked up my umbrella and pressed the stud that made a spike jut out of the end. I did some stabbing. First a dusty cushion and a painting of King Louis XIV, then on around the room – my rage became a pointillist statement writ large across the floor and walls. And when I was done – my blood cooling, my feeble panting an embarrassment to my ears – I chose not to reflect upon my actions, preferring instead to try pressing a second button on my umbrella.

The spike immediately shot across the room trailing a silver wire. Hooks sprang out from the tip. When it struck a distant wall, the hooks bit deep into the concrete.

I raised my eyebrows. Then checked for witnesses. As ever, there was no one around.

Giddy with the excitement of scientific experimentation, I pressed another button. A crackle of blue light shot down the wire and when it reached the spike, a ferocious pulse blasted outwards and caused the whole far side of le Café du Théâtre to explode.

***

Three blocks of running later, there was no sign of pursuit. My run became a skip; the child in me still giggling at the memory of accidental carnage. Perhaps the remaining un-pressed button on the umbrella would unleash similar destruction.

Then the skipping slowed to a walk. I was an adult. I knew actions had consequences. People would arrive at the café come nightfall and start asking questions. The sensible course of action was to hide the umbrella away and never touch it again.

I returned home to find an envelope slipped under my apartment door. I spent ten minutes debating whether or not to open it. When I did, I found an invitation inside printed with the following words:

'You are cordially invited to the 11ᵗʰ Annual Summer Ball at La Cité de la Mer on June 21st. The jollity and festivity will commence at five of the morning clock in time to celebrate the rising of the midsummer sun shortly after six. All umbrellas wished for and welcome.'

June 21ˢᵗ – tomorrow.

If that on its own were not disconcerting enough, there was a handwritten postscript:

You are one of us now. It's about time you joined the party.

319

***

I had no intention of going. That said; I didn't want to deprive myself of the opportunity to change my mind either, so I left for work with the umbrella wrapped in tarpaulin.

Before I reached the factory gates, I broke off from the dispirited procession heading in and found a little-travelled alleyway with no other lanterns in sight. Of course, there could have been countless observers hiding in the pitch black beyond my own lantern's pitiful glow, but anyone who'd travelled the streets for any length of time was well-practised at ignoring that kind of thinking.

I located a crumbling ledge high enough to remain in shadow if anyone else passed by with a lantern. I stashed the umbrella there and then hurried on to work.

I spent my entire shift regretting my behaviour. I wasn't going to go to the damned party, so what was the point in bringing the umbrella? What if someone found it? What if they traced it back to me?

Those weren't difficult questions to answer. Far more difficult was this: what if the anonymous soul who'd invited me to the party carried a green umbrella printed with a white penny farthing?

Of course, the chances of that being true were too remote to be worth considering, but human thought is not bound by the realms of possibility, especially when egged on by a starving libido. So of course I brought the umbrella.

But that still didn't mean I was going to the party.

***

The significance of the day didn't register until I stepped outside the factory gates and my lantern's light fell across red armour – Midsummer, the one day of the year when you were guaranteed to see a policeman.

The police did not carry lights. They were illuminated only by the lanterns of the workers they channelled away down authorised routes. This annual ritual had been a mystery until today. Now I knew they were keeping us from intruding on the umbrella's party.

My umbrella's hiding place was not on a permitted route. I ran for it anyway, taking a chance I could leave the street unseen.

"Stop!"

A left turn, then a right. Twelve paces and right again. A blast of light chased me round that last corner. I felt searing heat at my back.

The ledge was up ahead – a few feet more.

I hoped the umbrella was still there.

I leapt up to grab it.

The policeman rounded the corner and stopped. The truncheon in his hand still glowing red, ionised vapour reeling from its tip. The face plate of his helmet was typically blank and expressionless.

"Apologies, your grace, I was…"

"Chasing down an errant citizen, is that right?" I felt untouchable in the light of my open umbrella, at least until I realised my mistake. A mistake that became more obvious and painful with every passing second, but my mind was frozen, able to think of nothing beyond its own inability to come up with a simple rhyme. But then a hum from the umbrella sparked a flash of inspiration. "He came by here; gave me quite a fright. Sad to say I reacted without much thought; your errant citizen no longer exists to be caught."

The policeman hesitated only a moment before nodding his helmet in deference.

"No less than he deserved, your grace, I'm sure. Now I must get back to my duties."

"And I must be away to the party." Oh, why didn't I keep quiet? What rhymes with party? Arty? Farty? "May both our evenings be hearty."

Good grief. He should have shot me with that truncheon and then beaten my smoking corpse to a pulp for that. Instead, he walked away. I headed off in the opposite direction, wiping sweat from my forehead.

Moments later I saw the parade.

A citizen-issue lantern gives off a pale white glow and the market is the only place where more than five citizens can legally gather their light together. Yet now I stood staring with shock and awe at bright yellow streetlamps strung with bunting and adorned with flags to celebrate the march of the umbrellas – hundreds of them, their canopies a riotous collection of colour, patterns and pictures, their clothes more ostentatious than ever – billowing silks, golden threads; buttons and buckles glittering with reflections of the grand procession.

This is what errant citizens were not meant to see.

Naturally, I wanted to see more.

***

La Cité de la Mer used to be a museum housed within the old transatlantic liners' terminal down on the Dock of France. Now it was the destination for the umbrella parade. The party-goers half-walked, half-danced up Allée du President Menut. Catherine wheels spun sparks at the side of the road. Banners sewn with metallic sequins welcomed one and all to the ball.

The revellers were too preoccupied with what lay ahead to notice me trailing behind.

The northern frontage of the Terminal's former train station was a monument to art deco design; two-tone brickwork mixing hard edges and soft curves. My heart jumped when I saw acrobats performing between the two towers – there were regular people here too!

Then I saw the wires. These were no more than human-sized puppets, masterfully choreographed by umbrellas sitting atop the roof.

Slowly, casually, the attendees made their way inside.

I groped for a reason to follow while hiding behind a bush outside. It wasn't fair that I should be denied this. I had an invitation. I was one of them now.

Except I wasn't. I was an imposter. I owed my allegiance to those I lived and worked alongside; all of us consigned to the austerity of darkness.

322

Then I saw her and thought: 'screw that.'

I entered a vast reception hall. Marquees housed all manner of food. No rotting vegetables here. There were silver bowls stacked with fresh fruit, fish cooking over open grills and giant squid cut open so the innards could be sampled alongside the fine wines on offer.

Umbrellas were everywhere. I kept my own tilted low so no one could see my face. I glanced up only occasionally to navigate the crowds.

She was with a group of other umbrellas. One shared the same penny farthing motif, but was black instead of green. A second carried a canopy of red and yellow stripes, while the last was marked as the ten of hearts. The quartet moved beneath a walkway and into The Great Gallery of Men and Machines.

I quickened my pace and the music filling the air increased its tempo to match. All of the umbrellas sang to its tune, but each with different words; the notes serving as hooks upon which they hung their conversation.

Archaic submersibles hung from the roof. Across the floor, umbrellas whirled and twirled in a well-practised ballet until the music suddenly stopped and the sing-song conversation died away.

"Indulge me a moment and listen up one and all, for our honoured guest has arrived at the ball."

The hall grew dark, save for a spotlight that pinned me in place. I shrank beneath the cover of my umbrella.

"He carries the rainbow spots in his hand, a fact that leads to one simple demand: that the charges against my name be dropped, and the persecution that followed, stopped."

The speaker was the Jack of Spades. He stood atop a flight of stairs. A clock above him showed twenty minutes left before sunrise.

"Yes, none can object when faced with such evidence. I was not the killer of our beloved Eminence. That crime falls upon the man in the spotlight – a man desperate to join with us tonight." The Jack of Spades descended the steps toward me. "Which leaves a problem that needs to be solved; should this man be punished… or absolved? From a pitiful life he wishes to ascend, a wish I'm sure all here rightly commend. Given his Eminence is dead with no hope of return; I say the future alone should be our concern. I say give this man his chance in the sun. And that's all I shall say, now I am done."

I was a little confused. First he accused me of murder, then he argued for my life. There was some greater game being played here.

Whispers surrounded me. Even they followed a melody, albeit a furtive and sinister one.

I kept my head down, my umbrella low. My eyes were fixed on the floor. I didn't know what to do.

A pair of high-heeled shoes stepped into my limited view. They were an emerald green. Dark stockings traced statuesque legs with golden leaves. It could only be her.

"You need not say a word in reply." Her voice was deeper than I'd imagined, but no less sensuous. "I ask but this: look me in the eye."

I couldn't refuse.

I tilted my umbrella back, revealing a dress that caressed her curves with shimmering grace – diamonds running in a line from her right hip, up around her left breast and then back around the right of her slender neck to form a glittering necklace.

But the haute couture was nothing compared to her face.

It shone.

The light was so bright at first I could only blink with embarrassment until my eyes adjusted and I could make out that perfect nose and inviting lips.

And then my eyes adjusted fully.

Her skin *crawled*.

This was not a face of flesh; it was made of writhing worms that formed an approximation of human features. I could not tell if there was muscle or bone beneath. I could not even find eyes to look into.

I felt sick.

"Did you kill the husband promised to me, desiring an umbrella's life so fervently?"

I shook my head; an excuse to look away as much as express my innocence, but in doing so I saw the rest of them, staring at me with their glow-worm faces, every one void of both eyes and humanity.

The lady in green leaned close. I resisted the urge to back away.

"I believe you," she whispered, "so best hold on tight."

"But… but you didn't rhyme. That's not right."

She didn't have eyes, but managed a wink. Then she grabbed my hand and pointed my umbrella upwards. Her thumb hit one of the buttons.

The spike shot out from the tip and embedded itself in the ceiling.

Uproar from the crowd.

"What do you think you're playing at, Cicely?" shouted a voice.

"She's playing at foolishness, quite obviously," snapped the Jack of Spades.

Cicely swung her umbrella down so the handle hooked under her heel, then she pressed another button and detonated the ceiling.

We shot upwards as glass and masonry rained down, the falling debris brushed aside by the twin canopies.

On reaching a giddy altitude of about two hundred feet, Cicely shifted her umbrella's handle from foot to hand and directed us down toward the town. I clung to her; my natural revulsion choked back by an instinct for self-preservation.

I glanced back. We were being followed.

Some rode their umbrellas like a witch's broomstick, others held the handle while the canopy carried them along like a sail. Those that could not fly were running out from the old terminal building and shooting with their umbrellas into the night sky.

Cicely deftly evaded the arcs of tracer fire before swooping down between the buildings of Cherbourg and into pitch blackness.

My sense of speed came only from the wind in my face and the sight of illuminated cobbles rushing past below.

325

I almost screamed when a wall sprang up before us, but Cicely was already turning. My flailing shoes kicked against a window. I heard someone inside start a complaint about trying to sleep, but we were long gone before they could finish.

We swung left.

I tried to get my bearings. It took only a moment. The light ahead could only come from the market. A line of armoured police blocked the way.

Cicely's umbrella smashed them aside like skittles, then she had to brake and pull upwards sharply to avoid the stalls.

We hung for a moment above the square, the shoppers below staring up at us.

I looked down, both hopeful and fearful that I might see a familiar face. But all those faces were mired in gloom; my eyes now used to far brighter sights.

A bang heralded a brilliant flash that lit up the market and two blocks on every side. The startled citizens on the ground shielded their eyes and ran for cover.

The flare fell slowly to earth, still burning brightly. Its radiance picked out flying umbrellas homing in on our location and, high above, the bloated shapes of airships coming about.

Cicely swept down and away, skimming the paving stones as we left the market far behind.

More flares exploded above us.

LIght washed across roads and buildings, striving to expose us to the hunters above. Cicely clung to the shadows, brushing against brickwork that crumbled away at our passing.

A juddering boom sounded close by, then another came from further off. I guessed they were speculative shots into the stricken town. I wondered how many innocent people were caught in the blasts.

We reached the garden square as the sky began to turn from black to orange. The first rays of day fell upon the heights of the green and black tower.

The door opened before us. Cicely took us smoothly from flying to walking as we crossed the threshold.

The tower's reception was a high-ceiling, circular room. The tiled floor formed a penny farthing mosaic. Seven doors led off this chamber, each a different colour, each with a golden dial set in marble above.

Cicely led me to a green door.

Her heels clicked across the tiles.

"I'm sorry," I said, hurrying behind.

The door opened to reveal a lift. There were one hundred numbered buttons inside, but Cecily pressed another marked with a heart.

"I was running late," I explained as the lift ascended sharply. "The sun was coming up. He was already dead. If I hadn't taken the umbrella…" I closed it down, staring at my hands as I did so. "I know I should have handed it in, but I was scared. Someone like me isn't supposed to have something like this."

The lift slowed and then stopped. The doors opened. Cecily walked out.

"I wish your fiancée were still alive," I called after her, "then I wouldn't know about you and the towers and the second sun and I wouldn't have gone chasing after answers…"

And chasing after you.

You with the alien face.

I exited the lift into a fantasy of a library. Oaken bookshelves ranging across several floors nestled into curving walls. Luscious vines coiled around balustrades and flowers blossomed beside white stone sculptures. The volumes on display were pristine and ranged from leather-bound Shakespearean folios to the complete, unspoiled adventures of Asterix. Two chairs waited at a table set for tea and scones, but Cecily waited by a spiral staircase. She walked back over on seeing my awed expression.

"Understanding the whys of the world is a laudable ambition," she sang, "but less important now given its current

327

condition. This broken society wrongs us both, my friend. I propose this sunrise signal its untimely end."

She touched a gloved finger to my lips, then turned on her heel and hurried up the stairs.

We emerged onto a sprawling balcony near the tower's summit. Peculiar winged bicycles were moored to a railing I was reluctant to venture near, but Cicely took my hand and dragged me forward.

"See there, at the horizon, the progenitor sun does rise. Now witness the rise of its burning brother with your own eyes."

The second sun rose into the sky from a field to the east of town. It was a bank of circular grills attached to the side of another airship. I watched the grills turn from red to yellow to a blazing white and then was forced to look away. Artificial light seared the streets of Cherbourg below while the true sun remained cool and hazy behind strands of cloud.

"You and this umbrella were meant to be," Cicely whispered in my ear, "a fated chance to set your race free."

She pushed me onto a bicycle. An airbag inflated above my head. A kick sent me drifting out into space.

A moment of confusion was followed by blind panic. I hunkered down against the frame and gripped the handlebars tight. My feet missed the pedals several times before finding purchase. The rooftops of Cherbourg were dizzyingly distant below.

I clumsily turned my head to ask Cicely what on earth she expected me to do now, but she was busy spinning round and around, arm and umbrella outstretched, the tip belching forth a great cloud of smoke that rapidly surrounded the tower and then rolled past me, billowing outward until all I could see were the dim lights of the two suns.

And then I knew what I had to do.

Awkwardly, I began to pedal. The wings on either side of the bike started flapping up and down, driving me forward.

Operatic music trilled through the burgeoning cloud accompanied by the sound of diesel-driven propellers.

328

"Why do you think me so wicked, dearest Cicely?" sang the Jack of Spades. "All I ever wanted was to love you tenderly."

"Your love lies, cheats and kills in my name," she shouted back. "That I inspire such acts fills me with shame."

"Let shame not sully a clear and rationale head. Soon I shall rule; best accept my bed."

"Better to kill myself and have your madness cease..."

"If only I could permit you such an everlasting peace."

A terrifying crack sent a wave of force thundering through the cloud. The bicycle juddered, but remained on course.

I glanced back. Lightning flashed where I knew the tower to be.

I pedalled on.

While one sun remained distant, the other grew larger and larger, rising up to meet me. I thought of Marc and his dream of stepping outside in daylight. Hopefully he was still alive out there somewhere.

The sun drew dangerously close. I could feel the heat even through the protection of my umbrella. I pulled on the brakes. The flaps they triggered barely slowed me at all.

I was headed straight for those inferno lights.

I tried turning, but couldn't turn sharply enough. A lever controlled the bike's elevation. I pitched it downward.

One wing caught fire, then the other.

I looked up fearfully at the airbag. The silver fabric was beginning to blister and boil.

The false sun continued its ascent and with inches to spare my aircraft passed below, but the tortured airbag snagged on a grill and finally burst.

I grabbed at a rope binding the airship's envelope.

My fingers took hold as the bicycle plummeted earthward. It was immediately lost to Cecily's smokescreen. Then it appeared again, a forceful wind unravelling the cloud and showing the bike as a speck still falling toward a stark landing.

I was not surprised to see the wind came from another umbrella, who stood on the prow of an airship decorated with playing cards. The Jack of Spades was there too, Cecily beside him. He held her arm tightly. Her umbrella was conspicuously absent.

"I gave you the chance to be somebody," he sang to me, "yet you've chosen to die a nobody."

All I could see of Cecily's face was that alien glow; a glow that didn't seem so frightening any more. I smiled up at her.

"This was never about me or you," I replied. "It was about a man with an umbrella and what he can do."

First button: the spike, rammed through the envelope.

"Shoot him!"

Second button: the wire shot, firing me backwards and downwards.

"Kill him!"

Third button: the crackling blue light lancing up and away.

"No more rhymes," sang Cecily. "Now everything changes."

The explosion filled the sky above me; the roar rapidly becoming the roar of air rushing past my ears as I fell.

Time slowed.

For the first time in weeks I could think clearly. I wondered what would become of Cherbourg now. Things would surely be different after today. That was good. Different could hardly be worse.

The second thought exercising this crystal clarity concerned my broken mug. I could now appreciate its cracks and leaks. They were not a frustration, they were an inspiration. They were the reason I found this white umbrella with its rainbow dots, this arbiter of my life and death.

Which brought me to my final thought:

There's still one more button left to press...

About the Author - When asked to write a biography, Vincent Holland-Keen types his name, pauses thoughtfully, notices how

mucky his keyboard is and diligently starts cleaning it. While this typifies his approach to writing, he has one published novel to his name - 'The Office of Lost and Found' - and both scripts and directs the book show 'Un:Bound Video Editions'. Occasionally he produces cover art for other books. His official website is: http://www.vincenthollandkeen.co.uk/. He is, at the very moment you are reading this, using a combination of cotton bud and tissue to remove the grime that has inexplicably built up on the sides of his keyboard's keys.

The City of Lost Children
by
Sean Cregan

It is 11:05. Jenny stands at the junction near the little row of empty
cafés. The big clock on the tower across Evergreen Park tells her it is
11:05, and since neither she nor most of the other kids in the City have
a watch, she has come to rely on it. As she does at 11:05 every day, in
this place without true days, she stands there and watches the ghosts,
hoping with all her heart, as she does at 11:05 every day, that this time
she will see her parents.

Later, when Scott never shows, Jenny's first thought is that
maybe her best friend has managed to escape without taking him with
her. He's been talking about it for weeks — whatever those counted
for in the City — but she's never actually believed it would work.
There's no way out, that's what he used to insist. *The City just goes on*. He's
taken her with him a few times, long hikes out of Batterytown, where
they've both settled, to far-off parts she'd never even heard of.
Neighborhoods that look a bit like she imagines Paris or Rome or
Moscow, but that was crazy because you couldn't just walk to those
places and they weren't *there* anyway, they just looked like *there* and
maybe more of the kids there talked in other languages or with other
accents, but that was all. It didn't matter anyway because it was all just
part of the City.

"It just goes on," he said. "I've talked to kids all over, and
none of them know of an edge. Like wherever you are, you're in the
middle of it all."

"So why are we here?"

"Because maybe the way out is anywhere you look for it, and
maybe if I learn enough from all over, something will tell me how.
Then we can go home, Jen."

Home. Home *then* for her was Brooklyn, originally, and Scott
came from some part of London. Yet they both ended up, eventually,

in Batterytown, home *now*, two kids from thousands of miles apart. Distance in the City was like time in the City: there but not so it made much sense.

Scott helped her when she first found herself in Batterytown. Two twelve-year-old kids, lost. She can't, now, remember exactly *how* she found herself there, not all of it, but what she still knows of *before* she figures she knows because of him. "This place does things to your memory," he said. "Everything blurs if you let it. You need to find something, concentrate on something, that's *you*, and stick to it no matter what. Keep a focus."

Which is why she went to that junction, one that most reminded her of *before*, every day. It was one of the places where you could see the ghosts. Here and there in the City, where the world was *thin* enough, if you let yourself defocus, sort of look *past* the City, you could see people, grown-ups. Barely there, hard to see like ghosts, but walking the streets, going about their lives back in the world. One of her few clear memories of what had happened was a clock reading 11:05, and she knew she was out with her parents then. And if her parents were out at that time once, no reason they wouldn't be again. Maybe she could see them and maybe they could see her and then... and then she doesn't know what. It doesn't matter.

Scott's focus, she learned over time, was more practical. He wanted to escape the City. He never said anything about his *before*, but he wanted away from *now* for definite. Maybe, she thinks, he's done it, and that's why she's sitting alone on the landing outside the apartment she's taken as home, waiting for a boy who's an hour late and counting.

If he hasn't escaped, then something has happened to him, and for a moment she feels a spike of fear that maybe he's just *gone* instead. But that only happened when kids started drifting, ones you saw less and less, ones who stopped bothering or caring, until one day they just *weren't* any more, like they'd faded into nothing. Scott is a long way from that; he couldn't be more *there* if he tried.

By the time she's come to the conclusion that there's something wrong, it's too late to do much about it. There's no night any more than there's day in the City — the sky is always grey, too dark to be proper daylight and too light to be night time — but the big clock all the way across Batterytown by the park is tolling ten and she's too tired to look for Scott now.

"You're worrying too much," Duncan tells her in the morning when Jenny finishes explaining. She's helping him forage in the cupboards of the tenement building he occupies, usually alone. Food and other things just sort of *happen* in the City. You can clear a place out, and then a day or two later, it'll be like it has restocked with groceries. None of the children ever see it happen. Scott once forced himself to stay awake for nearly three days, watching Jenny's empty kitchen, waiting to catch the mechanism that brought them fresh food. Nothing. The day after he gave up, the cupboards were full again. It's the same everywhere: houses, stores, cafés. No one restocking them. No one looking after anything. Just the kids. The only adults you see are the ghosts.

The way it goes, no one ever seems to get any older in the City. You just sort of *feel* older in your head. Except for the really young kids, who seem to go backwards, become more childish. But they mostly *went* before long. It was the older ones like her and Scott and Duncan who stuck around.

"He promised he'd meet me," she says. "He's never failed to make it before."

"Scott's always going away. He's travelled more than anyone I've ever met here." He passes her a can of soup. "Hold onto this for me. I think there's Oreos back here."

"He always *says* when he's going away, though. What he said this time was that he'd see me today at two and he was real excited about something. I think he might have found a way out."

"And?" He turns to look at her. "Look, Scott's been trying to find a way out for ages. I've seen him get worked up plenty of times. You should check his place. Whatever it was probably just didn't work out and he's moping."

"I checked his place before I came here. He's not home."

"Which place, though?" he says. A grin on his grubby face.

334

He wants to take her to Scott's *other* place, his secret place he never told her about, but the morning is wearing on and she has an appointment she must keep. She makes him promise to find her afterwards and then they can go to Scott's.

It is 11:05. Jenny stands at the junction near the little row of empty cafés. The big clock on the tower across Evergreen Park tells her it is 11:05, and since neither she nor most of the other kids in the City have a watch, she has come to rely on it. As she does at 11:05 every day, in this place without true days, she stands there and watches the ghosts, hoping with all her heart, as she does at 11:05 every day, that this time she will see her parents.

Scott lives out of a little rowhouse a few streets from Jenny. But it's not here that Duncan leads her. Instead she finds herself standing on the top landing of a grubby tenement. There is a lock on the door in front of her, and she cannot remember the last time she saw one in the City.

Duncan knocks and waits sheepishly for a moment. Then takes out a key from his pocket — "Spare," he says — and lets them in.

The apartment inside is a lot less spartan than the one she's already seen, a place Duncan says Scott keeps as a casual crashing spot, but it's not the oddments he's picked up from across the City that draw her attention, not the total lack of Scott himself, but the walls. Scott's walls are covered — *covered* — in tally marks. They run from room to room all around the apartment, stopping with a couple of yards of bare wall in the lounge. There are numbers every 30. The last numbered batch is 5460.

"Days?" she says.

"He always told me he needed to know, even if there aren't any days and it's just sleeps. So he wouldn't lose count. So he wouldn't lose himself."

No one ever seems to get older in the City. You just feel older in your head.

"So where is he?"

"I dunno," Duncan says.

335

She tears her eyes from the mad chickenscratch tallies and looks at the things he's collected from across the City and the notes he's taken as he's done it. They form layers of history. Topmost on the stack is a charcoal drawing of a boy in smeary facepaint and a funny-looking top hat. Written next to it is 'Klein + Exchange'.

"This is a Maskelyne," she says.

Duncan pulls a face. Says, "Good luck with that, Jen."

"You've got to come with me."

His expression worsens, because she's right.

Two hours later and they're in the dusty stairwell of the subway station they call Blue Castle. "I don't know about your friend," the girl behind the concertina metal gate is saying. She has the same grime-and-chalk facepaint as the picture and a hat made from black-painted cardboard. "You're not Masks, so you can't come in. We don't let people in. Not creeps, non-Mask peeps."

The last sentence sees a hint of Maskelyne sing-song slip in. Jenny wonders if this girl is picked for work watching the door because she's not totally different to outsiders. Not yet, anyway. She's met a couple of other Masks in the City, both times with Scott, and they have their own way of talking. Like she's heard twins sometimes do, their own language. The Maskelynes spend all their time down in the station, even though they could stay anywhere in the City and it's not like there are any trains. All together, all slowly picking up their own weird way of speaking, echoing it back to one another. There are plenty of other gangs or tribes of kids in the City, sprung up out of a need to belong to *something*, but the Masks are more shut-in than most.

"He came to speak to you before. You let *him* in." It's a guess, but the girl doesn't need to know that. "And now something's happened to him. We just want to know what he talked to you about, what he was doing. *One* of you's got to know."

"Go go, bye bye. If Masks want to talk, they come out. You don't come into the Castle, rascal."

Jenny pulls out the charcoal drawing and shows it to the girl. "Did he come out?" she says. "This Mask? Did he come out and talk to our friend?"

336

The girl looks at the picture for a moment, silent. "Maker King, in, in," she says, and opens the gate.

The station is broad, three platforms spanning four tracks, all dead and criss-crossed by plank bridges and lines of motley flags and pictures lit by fluorescent tubes repainted in swirls of inky colour. Jenny can't count the number of Mask kids down here — and in the chaotic murk it's hard to say how she sees more than once — but there seem to be a lot. The upper levels of the station, up the unmoving escalators, are given over to various stages made from junk wood and cloth, and the court of the one they call the Maker King. It's him the girl shows them to. He's a kid maybe a bit younger than Jenny and Duncan, dressed in much the same garb as the rest of the Maskelynes except his hat is a proper one, albeit dented and scuffed. He looks his visitors over and has a quick conversation with the girl before beckoning them forward with a flourish.

"Come, come.," he trills. "I hear clear a picture Mary Quick's sure's Tom Trick. See he?"

"Sure," she says, and shows him the drawing. "A friend of ours had it. Scott. I think he must've talked to you guys."

"Tom Tom, long gone," he says. "Your boy brought us toys, things with string and wings, asking Tom, Tom. Where and when he was gone, gone. The how and who and why and I told, for Scott was bold and old and brought us Masks more than *gold*."

"What did he want to know about Tom? What happened to him, anyway?"

"Tom? Scott thought he'd gone — got out — but not, we say, not Tom. Scott says no and asks us how. Again, again, and we tell him about the train. Tom hit, struck, run by the train."

Jenny looks at Duncan. "But there aren't any trains," she says.

"Clear, not here." The King shakes his head, but now there's a look of genuine puzzlement on his face, as if she's said something really silly. "Deep, like sleep, drop down another line to find."

"Another line deeper down? How do you get to it?"

"We hear the trains, each midday, times on the chimes, but the way only Tom may know to go. A place, lost or hidden or ghost. Masks search, never learn. Now we stop. Not Scott." The Maker King smiles and waves. "Go, go, more questions no, no."

With that, they are ushered back to the gate. Jenny thinks about the note beside the drawing of Tom's face: 'Klein + Exchange'. A street address. Duncan's obviously figured the same thing because he says, "Are we going to look for a way down to the trains at that intersection tomorrow?"

"It sounds like that's what Scott was looking for, so yeah."

"What about the time, Jen? The King said they heard the train at midday."

Midday. No time to get from her spot by the park, waiting for her parents, and make it to wherever this place is, to find the way underground and make it down to the train line — if there even is one — before the train appears. She's never missed a morning by the park since she started looking for her mom and dad.

"Yeah," she says. "The time. The time."

It is 11:05. Jenny is following Duncan down a long, cold maintenance ladder. Rust bites at her hands and the air here smells of damp, but it's not that she's thinking about, not even the drop beneath her if she slips. She's thinking about the ghosts and her parents, and desperately worried that today of all days will be the one when they pass by.

"Careful here," Duncan says, but she's not, thinking of all the not-quite-there faces passing by in the street where she *should* be.

They've climbed in the dark for what feels like ages, down through the maze of manholes and stairwells beneath the junction of Klein and Exchange, doubling back whenever they hit a dead end, and they still haven't hit the tracks.

Eventually, they reach the bottom of the ladder. At the bottom, is a door. Plain, unmarked and unremarkable. Duncan looks at her and she turns the handle. Light spills through, stark blue-white, and they find themselves at one end of a subway station platform. It is clean, modern, and in much better condition than the ladder. The

338

signage on the walls is in a language she doesn't know, all squiggles and shapes. There is a clock, though. 11:58.

"Blimey," Duncan says, "look at this place. You think… I mean, it looks like it could be…"

She doesn't know and tries her best to stifle the hope rising within her. "It just means the Masks were right that there's a deeper line, that's all," she says. "Let's wait for the train."

"Scott could've caught it. He could be *out*."

"He could've been hit by it like they said Tom was. Let's just see." Thinking, *out*.

"I wonder where the station's exits are. I mean, it's *got* to have them. I wonder where they lead."

"I wonder. One minute to go." She finds herself fiddling with her hands, tying her fingers in knots, and forces herself to stop. There's another platform on the other side of the tracks. They're the only people here. Their voices are the only sound.

Then there's the noise of rushing air. A dim light in the tunnel to the right. Jenny holds her breath. Can't tear her eyes away. A building whirr of electric engine noise.

"Here it comes," Duncan says, but the light's wrong, she's thinking. It should be brighter already.

The sound builds and turns into a squeal as the train rushes past, but it's not *there*. As Jenny squints her eyes against the tears in them she can sort of see it. A subway train, sleek and smooth, but smoky, translucent, a swift-moving blur of fog-dreams of a world they can no longer touch.

And gone.

She watches the light recede, taking the brief hopes of a life outside the City with it, and sees the shape silhouetted just inside the far tunnel.

"What does that mean, Jen?" Duncan says. His voice sounds small. "What we just saw?"

"It means…" The words are hard. "The train's just like everything else. It's just a ghost. They're all just ghosts."

She stands and he follows her over to the mouth of the tunnel where the train disappeared. Scott is hanging there from a noose made of electrical cable pulled down from the ceiling. She doesn't look at his face. Doesn't *want* to look at his face. She can hear Duncan sobbing behind her.

On the far wall, written in chalk, is a message in Scott's handwriting. It says: 'There's no way out. I'm sorry. I'm so sorry.' On the floor a short way away she sees a dusty Maskelyne hat lying between the tracks. The cold grey of old bones around it. Gone, gone, Tom.

They stay there in silence for a while, then walk away.

It is 11:05. Jenny stands at the junction near the little row of empty cafés. The big clock on the tower across Evergreen Park tells her it is 11:05, and since neither she nor most of the other kids in the City have a watch, she has come to rely on it. As she does at 11:05 every day, in this place without true days, she stands there and watches the ghosts, hoping as she does at 11:05 every day, that this time she will see her parents just once more.

About the Author - Sean Cregan is the author of grimy near-SF thrillers THE LEVELS and THE RAZOR GATE, and as John Rickards also has a clutch of crime novels to his name(s). Find him at namelesshorror.com or @Nameless_Horror on Twitter.

Every Girl Should Be Married
by
Cath Bore

Living In The Now

When Jamie was born I sat by his cot every night, holding his hand as
he grizzled, dribbled and blew milky bubbles. His tiny fingers latched
onto my thumb until he sank deep into slumber, each digit loosening,
relaxing to flaccid until I pulled away. Letting go too early roused him,
his pink face glowing an indignant puce until I caved in and stayed. I
stopped fussing when he was six months old, the new baby heavy in
my womb and bearing down on my bladder. When we brought Joseph
home from the hospital Jamie's red eyes stared from his cot across the
room and cried, a lot.

One night Kyle picked him up and babied him, placing a cold
flannel on Jamie's hot forehead.

'He'll be fine,' I said.

'He will be now,' replied Kyle.

Kyle went to work the next morning. I packed lean ham and
salad sandwiches on wholemeal gluten free barms with low fat spread.
I included fruit, too. I knew Kyle lashed the lunch I made into the bin,
instead shoving a steak slice from the pasty shop down his gullet.
When he kissed me hello at night I tasted the grey meat on his breath.

After Kyle left the house, morphing from husband into
Detective Constable Breen, I stuffed a wriggling Joseph and sulky
Jamie into the double buggy. Jamie held out his limbs straight, stiff and
un-wielding, thrashing them about. I stretched the straps around his
protruding arms and legs and secured him tightly. He screwed up his
mouth in disgust.

I wheeled the pram out to the bus stop. Rain spat down. The
plastic rain hood on the pram was slippery and cold, slimy to the
touch. Pools of water collected on its surface, splattering into streams

341

of cold when the pram tipped, splashing onto my trainers and seeping through to my socks. As the pools filled I emptied them but the water ended up on me no matter what. I extended my arm to hail a bus trundling along the road. I peered through the thick layer of condensation covering the window. It had no buggy bay.

"What can I do?" mouthed the driver, shrugging his shoulders and not giving a shit.

Ten more minutes, and another bus showed itself. The bus doors tried to whoosh open. One got stuck, hissing. I yanked the rubber edge with both hands. It gave way. A tinny She Loves You rang in the air from the transistor radio the driver had lodged in his cab next to a tabloid newspaper, butty box and Everton Football Club flask.

The bus was packed. When the people at the front saw me they edged back, the gridlock loosening like particles shifting. Two tall young men wearing rugby shirts held everyone up. They were the type I went for, before I had Jamie. Not necessarily before Kyle though. I still felt a bit guilty about all that but he had me now, didn't he? Big blokes this pair, but not a scrap of body fat between them. With one blond the other dark, no matter your flavour, you were sorted on this bus.

'Coming into Liverpool tonight?' one asked the other in sharp home counties vowels. His mate opened up his mouth to reply, revealing perfect white teeth but clocked my pram and nudged the other to shift. Both beamed glorious surfer boy smiles at the passengers as they moved, kicking off a sigh of lust from the women and girls. I blushed at the Adonises myself.

Not bad. Not bad at all.

The blond one took in my sweatshirt, eyes flickering over my protruding stomach and uneven breasts heavy with milk, his sunshine smile clouding over. Acid tears burned my eyes. I blinked them away. The pair's conversation blathered on. Their voices scraped the air.

'We'll go to the Raz. Lots of nurses are in there!'

'Really? Ha!'

We get it. You're going into town, afterwards. On the pull. Aren't you the lucky ones? Like them blonde, do you? Slim with big tits? I shoved back my shoulders, sucked in my belly and stuck out my chest. An impatient cough came from behind me. I glanced around. A wannabe silver fox in a loud purple Regatta anorak reached out as if to shift my pram. I barred his way.

'Come on love, people are trying to get on here.' He rolled his eyes to his audience of housewives, pensioners and students.

Was that a smirk in his voice? I shook my head. Don't be soft, Helen. Have a word with yourself.

The man sighed, moisture from his breath itching at the back of my neck. I manoeuvred the pram slowly, each movement exaggerated to piss him off, into the part of the bus where old people, the disabled and those with kids were meant to go. On the seats sat two young women. At their feet were piles of bags. Primark. New Look. H&M. Both women had long un-styled hair; one curly, one straight. Clean but no shape to it, with long thick fringes hanging heavy over the eyes like a horse. Not a scrap of make up on either of them. What a pair of mingers.

'Bloody students,' I muttered loud enough for them to hear, but the women smiled at me with gentle mouths before looking away.

The driver's radio sang out Please Please Me. The women bobbed their heads to the tune. I swore inwardly, angling the pram in the bay and resting my aching back against the luggage rack. The bus started up, lurching forward, jerking the pram handle into my Caesarean scarred belly. Curly Hair readjusted her carrier bags.

'Stop pushin' the pram into my stomach!' I blurted out.

Curly stared at me blankly, her mouth parted but no words came out.

'Why did you push into my stomach?'

'I don't understand,' the woman said, in a thick eastern European accent.

'You're meant to move, you know!' I jabbed my finger at both women. Startled eyes blinked back, following my finger as it stabbed back and forth. My hands wondered whether to punch them

343

in the face or just leave it. A man, Italian I thought, threw me a look of understanding. He held on to a strap above his head while a chubby toddler clung to his trouser leg with fat dimpled fists. The child murmured to herself. Was she singing along to Please Please Me? The man was humming the tune. I noticed how handsome he was. He's a tall one. Nice.

My tummy flipped. I tossed back my hair, wishing I washed it that morning. I gave him the look. Joseph gurgled. I rearranged his blanket. 'Shush. Shush. Good boy.' Another sympathetic look was flashed from the Italian's direction.

The bus bell ordered the driver to pull up. The two women stood and elbowed to the front, belongings banging against legs, a paper Primark brown bag tearing against my pram wheel. A cheap polka dot bra flopped into the aisle. Curly Hair eyed the white and pink polyester wisp, dipped down, then thought better of it and left the bra on the dirty floor.

That's a fiver you've wasted there.

My stop loomed next. Giving the Italian a ghost of a smile I pushed past with the pram.

We hit the pavement. The rain stung my face and hands. Under the shelter of the rain hood Jamie cried. I pushed the buggy onwards, praying the motion of the wheels would rock him to sleep but he squeaked then squealed then screamed. He screamed again, hitting a high C.

'Quiet, Jamie,' I ordered.

Jamie ignored me. Normally in the confines of our two bed terrace he shut up but this morning he clocked a woman standing across the road by a post box, letter at its mouth but poised in the air, giving her an excuse to just stay there and gawp. My oldest child had an audience and knew it. Joseph gurgled away in wordless baby talk. My children morphed into a noisy orchestra, providing a tuneless frantic soundtrack to my journey.

I marched on regardless to Crosby beach. The rain dried up and sun came out, blasting down hot rays. I pulled forward the buggy's

344

hood, black canvas casting a cool shadow over the babies' faces. They quietened. I parked the buggy on the mud beach.

Iron men stood in sober rows, ignoring me and looking out to the flat sea. The shallow water mingled with sand into a muddy slush as I made my way to meet them. Dirty water splashed on my jeans and soaked right through, the chill stinging my skin. I came to a standstill. The sea water covered my trainers. After a minute my feet warmed, like I wore an extra pair of socks.

Peace. Quiet. It smelled like Southport. Not of fish and chips and sickly sweet candyfloss, but the malty perfume of soft salt water. The sun's rays kissed the water's surface in the distance. Tiny molecules of moisture evaporated upwards building a hazy band of mist, a slender opaque stripe under the blueness of the sky.

I closed my eyes, breathing in memories. It smelled of carefree, like when me and my mate Karen, aged about thirteen, snogged Jay and Liam from off the dodgems at the fair. They didn't go to school, not like we had to. We thought they were like pop stars, those boys in Converse trainers doing what they wanted whenever. Then I saw Jake pushing Lisa Bayliss from Year Ten up against the Portaloos, his hand way up her pleated navy skirt, Lisa's knees splayed wide apart. Jake and Liam would be on the dodgems forever I realised, necking and fingering girls in every town.

A wet spot hit my cheek. My eyes flew open. The sky darkened above me, a huge grey cloud mushrooming like an angry ghost. The sun struggled, the far edge of the cloud afforded hard edges by its rays before they softened into a dove's wing, then nothing. As the electric yellow pattern reflected on my retina faded to blue then a dull purple, my mobile sounded.

'Where are you?' Kyle's voice crackled down the line.

'Out.'

'I called the house but you weren't there.'

'Because we're out.'

'Oh. Right. I'm just having my lunch,' he said. The steak slice thickened his words, ones that told me intricate details about his morning. He'd been on his feet for three hours, taking witness statements. The paperwork was going to be a bugger.

Jamie began to cry. Plaintive and bleating like a sheep at first, then louder and stronger, into a hysterical crescendo. Joseph joined the chorus.

I returned to them head bowed, under fresh sheets of hard rain.

About the Author - Cath Bore was born in Chorley, Lancashire but escaped to Liverpool when she was nineteen. She has worked as a radio station presenter and manager, tutor to disadvantaged young people and those in the youth offending system, music writer, civil servant - and cleaner in an old people's home during her student days. Cath has an MA from Liverpool John Moores University in Creative Writing. She won Marie Claire Magazine's Inspire & Mentor in Jan 2012 and also writes for Hello! Magazine on-line covering women's body issues, The Liverpool Daily Post (shortlisted for the Online Media Awards 2012) covering politics, and appears on Liverpool's City Talk 105.9 and Warrington's Wire FM each week. Cath is represented by Caroline Michel of Peters Fraser and Dunlop for her crime novels, featuring Liverpudlian DS Constance Ward.

Bringing Up Baby
by
Stav Sherez

When you're pregnant, people want to hurt you.

They don't tell you this.

Not your tutors in the pre-natal clinic nor your friends at the coffee klatch who've already gone through this and should know better. It's not on the instructional videos and Dr Spock never spoke about it. Your mother didn't say a word to you and your sister thought better you find out when you get there.

But get pregnant and you'll see.

Watch how people, accidentally on purpose, knock into you or take extreme enjoyment in depriving you of your seat on that blistering August tube that's stuck in the tunnel for what seems like forever. Wait till you're showing and go out into town. You'll see what I mean. You'll understand why most pregnant women prefer to stay at home. Why the streets are a dangerous place. You're marked as obviously as a Negro in 1920's Alabama or an Hassidic Jew in mid-century Lodz.

You can't hide it, not after the first few months, so you might as well stay at home.

You'll save yourself a lot of grief and you might even save your baby.

Take my advice. Before it's too late. You want to have three smiling children or maybe four? Some large brood where at least one of them is bound to turn out all right and rich enough to look after you in your old age? Then stay at home. Let your husband do the walking.

The thing is: pregnant women never complain.

Pregnant women never say anything about it. You think this is crazy, right? You think when you get pregnant and, god forbid, this happens to you, you'll go to the nearest person and ask for help? Well, try it. Learn what it is to be ignored. To be seen as nothing but an appendage for that thing inside you.

This is the rest of your life.

Once you have a child your husband can never see you in the same way again. You're somewhere between lover and mother.

You should have taken that pill or remembered to put in your diaphragm. You really should have made him pull out. Or gone to the clinic. That's what they're there for. You think *that* would have been more humiliating than walking the streets with a bowling ball strapped to your waist? You think *that* would have been more painful than the way the dark-haired woman scraped the jagged end of her nail across your bulging naked midriff that hot summer day out in the park? Remember how it felt as it ripped your skin like brambles when you were a little girl and, looking down, first seeing nothing but the round globe of your stomach and then suddenly like a river sprung from the earth, a thin line of red that drips down and pools in your belly button.

But the woman was already long gone and all you could do was put your finger to your skin and feel the warmth of the blood and press against it and hope that would somehow stop it. And all around you people move out of their way, snarling and swearing, because you've committed that most heinous of city sins, you've stopped dead in the middle of a busy street and it doesn't matter that you're seven months pregnant and your back is killing you and the heat is terrible and you're bleeding from a cut inflicted by some passing stranger with dirty bitten nails and you look around you and you look up at the sky which is almost malevolent in its unrelenting blueness and all you can think about is that little scrape of you, the tatter of skin which that woman has taken away with her, snuggled under her nail, and if you believed in voodoo and witchcraft you would start to get freaked out but you don't believe in any of that, at least you didn't think so until last month when your husband came back from work and he'd been to the video shop and he'd rented *Rosemary's Baby* and you both smoked too much weed and you watched the film and you were convinced it was you in that apartment building and you knew exactly why she had to have her hair cut like that - you couldn't bear it but your husband made you watch. "As good as pre-natal classes," you remember him saying.

But you don't believe in that. You're rational, empirical, a scientist and a teacher. Or at least you were until this thing began to grow inside you. And it seems that the more it grows the less of you there is. And the nearer it comes to entering the world, the further you're slipping away from it.

Once you were a scientist. Once you were a teacher.

Now you're a pregnant woman that everyone's trying to avoid as they rush home to their own troubles and miseries and sadness and who in their right mind would also want yours?

How you got in this predicament doesn't matter. Or rather there's only one way you could have got in this predicament. You were stupid once and now you'll pay for it. You think condoms are there to prevent the spread of AIDS? You think sexually transmitted diseases are the worst things that can result from rolling around between sheets and kisses?

You are beginning to think that being pregnant is a sexually transmitted disease.

You still think you would say something. You would shout. Make a scene. Shame the culprit.

Try it. You think people want to hear your troubles? That what the world needs right now is one more person complaining?

You piss and moan for nine months to your husband and your friends and your family. You tell them about your back pain, about mornings puking in the sink like a cancer patient. You moan about having to buy new and shapeless clothes. The way you look. The way you now smell. The weight. The heat. The cravings.

You moan about the price of baby furnishings and how you'll have to get a new house, somewhere with a room for the baby and a garden and a dog and all the things you never had. You talk about sores appearing on your thighs and how your ankles have swollen from carrying all that weight. How your hair's always greasy and your culinary clock has gone haywire. How your favourite food tastes like cardboard and plastic. You complain about the waiting line at the clinic and how your husband seems to be getting home later and later these days. How despite your expanding size you've become almost invisible to him.

You leave your job because you can no longer walk around comfortably. They're all happy to see you go. They turn that joy into pre-emptory congratulations for you.

When you're pregnant no one wants to know you because there's a possibility that you might lose the baby.

So go ahead and complain. They'll just think you're trying to be the centre of attention. And what better way to be the centre of attention than walking around with a cannonball shoved up your blouse?

In the bookshop, prepare to have your ass felt by every passing man. Wait until women walk in front of you accidentally bumping your bump. Take note of elbows and handbags and hats. Watch their eyes as they say sorry. You're a target. You might as well have a bull's-eye painted on your dress. Your little girl – she's a miscarriage waiting to happen.

There's the smiling man who stands motionless as the elevator doors are closing on you. Or the guy on the tube who holds the door for you and then lets go just as you step through, knocking you against the glass and sending you to your knees. You think someone will offer you a hand? Well, listen carefully to the groans of the passengers as they curse you for delaying the train.

Go to a park. Take the weight off your feet and sit down. Doesn't matter where. Within five minutes someone will be sat adjacent to you with a freshly lit cigar blowing the smoke into your face. Cough and make some polite gestures of annoyance. Watch them being ignored. Watch the smoke get denser like bad TV fog.

The waiter at the restaurant who knocks over the leftovers from a particularly greasy duck a l'orange all over you. The cabbie who takes you at sixty miles an hour on a route that is comprised exclusively of streets humped with sleeping policeman. Note the way his eyes dart up to the rear-view mirror as you puke and the way he slams the brakes and makes you get out. Or the bus driver who, seeing you standing on the open end of the routemaster, decides he's Steve McQueen for a day as he barrels down the streets of Hampstead.

After a while you get sick of this. After a while you start thinking about desperate measures. You look at the calendar and work out if it's too late to get an abortion. You consult your mother about the latest possible moment and you search the web for herbal self-induction pills. You notice how many sites cater to the self-service market. It's a boom industry. You send off for these pills. You order the whole gamut, just in case you say, just in case.

Of course you don't end up needing them.

There are natural ways to lose a baby and there are unnatural ways.

There are also in-between ways.

You begin to notice the men. The special ones. The ones who only have eyes for pregnant women.

Most men will look at you. You know this is to check out the size of your breasts and though they're not huge they're certainly much bigger than they were a few months ago and it is a new thing for you to have to watch an endless procession of men's foreheads and bald spots as their eyes sight along your chest.

But the other ones. You get to know them.

They think you're easy prey.

The thing they do: they check your left hand.

If you're a single mother so much the better. They smile at you, a smile that promises they are the most responsible, loving, fatherly men on earth but in their teeth you can see things that are no longer white.

The ones who slip a hand in your crotch as you enter the tube elevator. They're just trying to see what it feels like. The ones who smile and chat to you. They're the ones to watch out for.

An easy rule: the nicer they are, the worse their desires.

They think you're a fuck waiting to happen.

They tell you you're beautiful. They know no one has told you this for a long time. They say that being a mother has bought out the best in you. That you look sexy and content. They compliment you on how the rest of your figure hasn't changed. They know all the new age riffs. They say every woman needs to experience motherhood if it makes them look like you. They're as charming as a summer sunrise under unfamiliar skies.

They think you're vulnerable. They know your husband probably hasn't looked at you for a couple of months. Not in that way. They know he hasn't touched you however much you've screamed at him and tried to force his hand. They know he certainly hasn't fucked you since it started showing. Men who impregnate women to have children are often the ones most disgusted by the process itself. As if this act they've committed has now taken shape, this sin, taken form, and turned the woman of your once dreams into something less than a woman and not quite but almost a mother.

This is how these men think. Believe me. Don't be fooled by them.

The foot rub they give you after a long day carrying your load. In their account books it's tallied up next to a hand-job. The shoulder massage: that's a blow job. The head rub: don't even ask.

These men treat you the way you believed your husband should treat you. You believed this when you were a little girl and these men know your dreams.

The restaurants, the way they lavish you with deference and space, the low music and sympathetic ear.

They just want to fuck you with another man's child in your womb.

They understand where this places them in the hierarchy of men and deeds. They see the generations and destiny of such things.

Whatever they buy you, whatever they say - don't even respond to their entreaties, just walk away. You're better off without them. Unless your husband really hasn't fucked you in seven months and you've suddenly realised the kind of man he is and will always be and it's too late now to split or do anything but have the damn baby and you think well, what the hell, I won't get out much after the little one comes.

And then one rainy day an umbrella pokes you hard, right in the belly button.

You feel a contraction and a sharp pain like a spike of ice curl around your stomach and you bend over in the wet street and the blood that runs down your legs is quickly diluted by the rain and runs in rivers through the cracks in the pavement. And you collapse and people walk around you, heads cocked down but uninterested really, and you spill all over the pavement and the rain washes away your little girl and your fingers scratch and rip at the concrete trying to save her, to scoop up a little bit of your girl and the pedestrians look at you like you're crazy, this fat woman on her knees in the wet street trying to grab the rain - who in their right mind would stop and help you? Besides it's rush hour and it's raining. And your fingernails break and tear and crack as you try to save any part of her and eventually the blood from your fingers and from your void mingle together and then mix with the rain before finally disappearing down the dark drain.

And you get over it. Because after all, what else can you do? This is just the way life is.

You either get over it or you don't.

The ward you're placed in, all the girls there have suffered the same thing. Everybody has a story to tell but it's the same story. They're mostly younger than you and you wonder whether that will make it easier or harder for them to get over this. The door two beds to your right, it says: *Recurrent Miscarriage Clinic* like it was some swanky gym or drinking club and this is the member's entrance.

You walk around the streets armed now. You hold a sharpened nail file and a pair of filed-down tweezers in your hands. When the woman in the supermarket queue steps on your left foot with her four-inch heel, you carefully slice her dress with your file and watch as she leaves the queue not yet aware that she has been cut. The man who slams his briefcase into your throbbing belly as you turn a corner, you thrust the tweezers in the region of his groin until you see his face turn white and he slumps like a pillow that's seen its day.

353

Your midriff is strapped with part of an old duvet you cut up. You moulded it and stuffed it inside a pillowcase which you then strapped to your skin with brown tape. It hurts but it's worth it.

You walk the streets a lot now. You haunt train stations and Underground platforms, cafes and bus stops and street corners – high incidence places – you've got to the point where you know when an attack is coming, the woman ostensibly looking in the shop window with her handbag about to be flung into your belly, the school-kid with the cigarette which will accidentally burn through your new maternity dress, the nurse with the foot stretched out at just the right moment.

You can see it in their eyes, smell it in their breath, sense it in their motion, and you are ready.

About the Author - Stav Sherez is the author of The Devil's Playground (2004, Penguin) which was shortlisted for the CWA John Creasey Dagger, The Black Monastery (Faber, 2009) and A Dark Redemption (Faber, 2012). He can be found at www.stavsherez.com or you can contact him on Twitter @stavsherez

The Life of Brian
by
Helen FitzGerald

Port Philip Bay is a giant claw poised to snap shut and stop you slipping out.

I'm standing in front of Pasquini's Cafe in Point Lonsdale, Australia, watching a container ship push against its better judgement towards the small opening that leads into the Bass Strait.

You can't get much further south than this: water, then just the end I reckon.

A few streets away, my Dad's sitting in his nifty new armchair, dying. The chair and the walker and the bed stick and the bed rail and the shower chair and the special toilet seat and the wheelchair and the alarm mat and the thrice-daily nurses and the private room for emergency visits to St John of God Hospital (complete with foot massages and jamming sessions with Peter the harp-player) are all free because of his WW2 Veteran's Gold Card. It was worth going to war.

Every day there's something new. Brain tumours are entertaining that way. Not slow, like other deaths; twisty-turny, pacy. Today I couldn't get him out of the chair, let alone into the car. We were going out for a coffee. "No worries," I said, "I'll nip out and get you a take-away instead."

"Thanks Nellie," he said, leaning back into his chair, exhausted from trying to stand.

"Are you okay?" I asked, pressing the button for the foot rest to come up.

"I'm great," he smiled, meaning it.

The two minute drive is good for a cry. I always save my tears for Fellows Road, sucking them back in before parking at the beach.

Pasquini's Cafe is mobbed. It's either the weekend or a school holiday. I have no idea which.

355

"One Brian," I say to Jane. I don't need to explain more than that. He's come here so often over the years that Jane's like a daughter to him, knows exactly what a Brian is: weak flat white, hotter than it should be. There are three people waiting to be served. "I'll come back and get it in five," I say.

I walk across the road and watch the ship nudge against nature. I can make out the shapes and sizes of the containers packed on top. Neat, no innards on display, just rectangles and squares in reds and yellows and greys. They're so beautiful and mysterious that my mind's transported to the yard in Port Melbourne where it was loaded and I find myself packing them.

I'm packing bits of life. In the red box goes an eighteen-year-old Airforce pilot with a cheeky grin. In the yellow, a 35-year-old widower with four brylcreemed boys and four ringletted girls. In the orange, the love of my mother's life. The green, my Dad, installing telephones into the fancy cubby house he built for me and Ria. Hundreds and hundreds of boxes. I'm not telling you any more about the contents of the boxes, except that in each and every one of them is the attitude he's carried no matter what: *Living is something to smile about.*

And when you're dying, you're living.

I've finished packing now.

And I'm standing opposite Pasquini's watching the front of the ship edge its way through the rip. The pincer tips of Port Nepean and Point Lonsdale look like they're trying to stop it. Reach out! Grab hold! We're so close! Ship, please don't go out there! Don't go out there!

I can only just make out the ship, a dot.

Bye, I say out loud, and it's gone.

The crowd at the cafe has grown. Must be holidays, I decide. Or is it lunchtime?

"One Brian," Jane says, handing me the cup. "How is he?"

I'm tempted to say: Awful, things couldn't be more awful. But over the last few weeks his attitude has finally started to sink in.

"He's great Janie," I say with a smile. I almost mean it.

356

About the Author – Helen FitzGerald is the author of six thrillers including The Devil's Staircase, The Donor and Cry (out 2013). She also writes Young Adult fiction (Deviant, out 2013). Her website is www.helenfitzgerald.net and you can follow her on twitter @fitzhelen

The producers would like to thank...

Paul D. Brazill –

Cheers to Luca Veste

Steven Miscandlon

All the writers involved and...

David Essex.

Luca Veste –

You, for purchasing and reading this anthology. You're making a difference via the charities being supported.

Paul D. Brazill for all his work.

Steven Miscandlon for the incredible cover.

All the writers who gave up their time and talent to contribute to this anthology.

Chris Ewan for stepping in last minute, and providing an excellent foreword.

Nick Quantrill for his unwavering support and for all his help in the process.

Helen FitzGerald who knows the score...about everything.

Howard Linskey, Adele Wearing, Linda Moore, and Elizabeth A. White for all their work in spreading the word.

Muller Light yoghurts and orange juice (I'm on a diet this time around).

David Bishop, Rebecca Murphy, and Caitlin Sagan for their help with my own story

And finally...

Emma, Abs, and Migs for being my world.

fin...